"A moving tale . . . Rebecca Blake is an astonishing character . . . with great respect and care, [Harper] delivers an emotional story of a young woman's journey to fulfillment."
—*Rave Reviews*

"Superb . . . a story to steal your heart away."
—Heather Graham

"A romantic, adventuresome tale."
—*The Anniston Star*

"Deeply moving and uplifting. I loved it."
—Susan Elizabeth Phillips, author of *Hot Shot*

"Appealing, winning, unusual."
—*Publishers Weekly*

"A lyrical and emotionally satisfying novel told by a deeply perceptive and gifted writer."
—Linda Barlow

"Brilliant . . . an incredible picture of a Kentucky mountain child adopted into a Shaker settlement—how she grows, lives, learns, and loves."
—*Heart to Heart*

Circle of Gold

Karen Harper

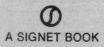

A SIGNET BOOK

SIGNET
Published by the Penguin Group
Penguin Books USA Inc., 375 Hudson Street,
New York, New York 10014, U.S.A.
Penguin Books Ltd, 27 Wrights Lane, London W8 5TZ, England
Penguin Books Australia Ltd, Ringwood, Victoria, Australia
Penguin Books Canada Ltd, 10 Alcorn Avenue,
Toronto, Ontario, Canada M4V 3B2
Penguin Books (N.Z.) Ltd, 182–190 Wairau Road,
Auckland 10, New Zealand

Penguin Books Ltd, Registered Offices:
Harmondsworth, Middlesex, England

Published by Signet, an imprint of New American Library,
a division of Penguin Books USA Inc. Previously published in a Dutton edition.

First Signet Printing, June, 1993
10 9 8 7 6 5 4 3 2 1

As always, to my husband,
DON

Part I

Becca, Wild Mountain Rose
(1823–1825)

The rose is fairest when 'tis budding new,
And hope is brightest when it dawns from fears;
The rose is sweetest washed with morning dew,
And love is loveliest when enbalmed with tears.

—Sir Walter Scott
The Lady of the Lake

Chapter One

April 23, 1823

"From the high up heavens to the low down earth, it's a right fine day!" The girl recited the familiar mountain blessing with a nod and a smile, just as Gran Ida always had.

A fat single braid of chestnut hair bouncing against her back, Rebecca Blake strode down the steep mountain toward the only meadow of Shelter Valley, Kentucky. The narrow gravel path clung to the stony skirts of Concord Peak down to the tiny town of Shelter on the South Fork Branch of the Kentucky River, but she would not be going to town today. She was off on a fifteen-mile ramble to make deliveries of her mother's medicinal herbs to mountain people scattered up the rocky ridges of Snow Knob across the valley. She had left her family's Crawl Crick cabin almost at dawn. Below her, the meadow draped its early wildflowers across the upland rise just above what her father called the confluence. There, numerous mountain rills, runs, and creeks churned together to make the Shelter River, which crashed like foaming cream into the coffee-colored South Fork far below.

The air was brisk and bracing this early, but for once Rebecca's hands were warm. She let her sack of herb packets and tonic bottles bounce against her bony hip so her hands could cup the hearth-baked potato her mother had given her. It was not a firm one but the kind with gray spots and yellow eyes, fetched up from the springtime dregs of the root cellar. Yet almost until the edge of the meadow, it kept the eleven-year-old's hands warm. She concentrated on the now tepid potato and ignored the cold gravel and dew-chilled grass against her bare feet.

From the narrow cleft between Concord Peak and Snow Knob, the giant finger of morning sun only pointed down the middle of the meadow, so she was yet far from being really warm. Her exertions today would have to take care of that. She had not worn her only cloak, for it would just get in the way climbing and fording creeks. Yet, chilled as she was to her young bones, the sight of the rainbow-colored realm below warmed her heart.

It was a foot-stopping scene, but soon she hurried on again. Below, she curled her bare toes into the thick, slick grass that edged the meadow. Tears prickled her eyelids as she surveyed the pretty package of her valley tied together by the silver ribbons of distant waterways. The massive purple wall of Concord Peak and the green-gray of smoother, shorter Snow Knob sheltered this valley, hemming in its hills and hollows. Far below, the tiny town of Shelter was barely visible through newly budded yellow-green foliage. Awestruck anew by this familiar beauty, she remembered to breathe. When she sucked in a gasp of inarticulate joy, the morning breeze bit deep into her lungs, surprising her with the knowledge that she was separate from the scene.

Rebecca Blake that spring of her life was a bud of a girl ready to sprout. She looked all lanky limbs and wiry frame. Long wrists protruded from what had once been her mother's gown. Leg-o'-mutton sleeves now hung limp on bony shoulders and thin arms. The once-stylish blue muslin dress had gone dove gray with time and wear. Its high waistline, formerly adorned by frills and ribbons, clung to her tiny waist.

Her mother had stitched in an old cambric handkerchief of her father's to cover her bare skin above the low-cut bodice. Rebecca had already shoved her floppy brown bonnet back to dangle by its tattered strings, even though the sun threatened to raise a new spring crop of freckles on her porcelain skin. She had a pert nose. But huge, moss-green, dark-fringed eyes, a shapely mouth, and sharp cheekbones hinted at future womanly beauty in her long, oval face. Quickly she broke the now cool potato open and devoured it, spitting out spots gone too soft. She ate even the crispy, ash-dusted skin. Then she tore across the rippling meadow, straight for that shaft of early-morning sun.

Pools of floating, knee-high meadow mists parted for her like curtains. She ran for a while into the flood of sun, cradling her pack so nothing would break. She lunged in limber leaps through patches of mustard plants. Blue-star blossoms of coltsfoot nodded their approval of her whirling steps, while daisies and dandelions danced in her wake as she passed.

But birds startled raucously, and the few cows owned by the Scott family in town looked up from munching to stare at her. Spent from her frenzy of freedom, Rebecca began to walk again, following the sun, even though it took her east instead of north. She stopped each time she came upon a new discovery. She smiled down at beds of purple and white violets, tucked in by blankets of dandelions. Slender-stemmed trilliums; emerald spearmint; tiny, bell-like May lilies; and woolly, new-born life everlasting vied for her attention. Gathering sprigs here and there, she began to sing one of her Gran Ida's mountain songs, her thin soprano soaring sweetly with the bird trills and humming breeze:

You are my flower that's blooming in the mountain
  so high.
You are my flower that's blooming there for me.
Some wear a smile and life is so worthwhile,
Forget the tears and don't forget to smile.
You are my flower that's blooming there for me.

She left the shaft of sun and headed toward Snow Knob reluctantly, but new treasures emerged to slow her steps. Her fingers flexed without stiffness for the first time in months as she picked herbs. Winter, though it bore beauty too, had seemed so long. Her feet frolicked to be free again without the press of the too-tight winter shoes that had been Gran Ida's.

At the cascade of so many memories of her grandmother, Rebecca halted, sunk ankle-deep in a feather-soft stand of dandelions. Gran Ida would have loved a day like this—if she hadn't been inside some mountain cabin helping birth a baby. And Mama, if she'd only glance up from her herb beds by Crawl Crick, would look at these dandelions and see more tonic and ointment to help folks who were ailing. Rebecca's seven-year-old brother, Jeremy, would see more salad greens, for Jeremy was always hungry. And Daddy—if he were here and not off keelboating for months again—would look at this and see dandelion wine and the good times they could have making and drinking it. And Becca, as her family called her—why, above all else, though she loved wild roses best of all the mountain flowers, she saw the butter-rich beauty of these dandelions among pretty patches of blue and white flowers setting them off against the thick, wavy grass.

Shouldering her pack, she began to climb again. Mama had told her true Kentuckians never wanted to seem in a hurry, but she was in a hurry now. She looked forward to passing time with each of the families she would visit and still having daylight to cut a wild rose planting the Widow Lang had promised her last time.

She crossed the icy plunge of water at Rocky Ford where it was shallowest. Still, holding her sack up, she soaked herself to her hips. She would dry soon enough, but her toes tingled. Last year's dried pine needles pricked her soles and mud mixed with the remains of slick autumn leaves made the steep slope slippery going. She skidded down on her backside once and fell and cut her knee. Still, there was nowhere else she'd rather be.

She hummed as she climbed the narrow, twisting path on the other side of the valley. She broke into a song Gran Ida had taught her of a fair maid named Barbara Allen and her lover, Jamie, who lived in a place called Scarlet Town. She'd like to see Scarlet Town someday, wherever it was. It sounded oh so pretty, like the streets would be lined with red rosebushes. It had to be a far sight more adventuresome than a place called Shelter. But with all Daddy's yarning about his travels, she'd like to see the far-off, foreign places too, like Cincinnati and Louisville! She especially liked how this song had two sweethearts who died for love of each other. And their buried bodies turned into a red rose and a green brier entwining over their graves. It sounded oh so very exciting.

She was out of breath from the song and the climb when she came to Claib Tucker's place. It was really two log cabins with a dogtrot between. He lived alone now. His first wife had lit out downriver because, it was whispered far and wide, she had just upped and decided she couldn't stand a man in her bed. His second wife had died from the milk sick no herbs could cure. It probably took some fancy city doctor for that, and Shelter had none. Then to top that off, his six children had all gone off one way or t'other. Claib's oldest boy, Ralston, lived with his family just up on the next ridge, where she had to visit today too. Folks knew Claib didn't have much use for Ralston, even if Claib did shoot game to keep meat on Ralston's table.

"Mr. Tucker! It's Becca Blake with your yarbs! You here'bouts?" she called into the little clearing with room for only one corn patch. No smoke curled from the chimney, so she might have to just leave things, though Mama and Jeremy would be disappointed. Claib Tucker was one of the finest shooters in Kentucky, next to old Dan'l Boone. With Daddy gone and Jeremy so young, they were all hankering for meat on the Blake table.

"Hey, girl!" the voice called from up in the trees just beyond the cabin. She heard the familiar yelps of the coon dogs before six of them spilled down ahead of Mr. Tucker. "How you keepin'? Just acomin' back from a speck of early hunting. You brung that cure I ast for last time?" he called to her, sweeping off his three-squirrel-tail cap. He leaned his rifle against a tree and hooked a bunch of newly shot squirrels up in the limbs so his dogs couldn't get to them.

"Yes, Mr. Tucker," she assured the lanky man as he loped closer. Claib Tucker was older than Daddy, but had been an influence on him, Mama said, probably because Mr. Tucker roamed far and wide hunting. Not that Daddy liked to hunt, but maybe he caught the itchy foot for wandering from his friend Claib. Mr. Tucker, Becca also heard tell—but not from Mama—got all riled without a woman here. He was supposed to have been handsome once, but she thought his face looked like a weathered fence post now. And his once thick head of raven hair was high off his forehead, getting silvery as hoarfrost, and thinning too.. That was what he wanted a special cure for.

"All right, 'splain this fer me now," he said as Becca handed him the dark green bottles stoppered with corncob tips while his dogs churned around their feet.

"First off, on your scalp you rub on a bit of this grapevine sap, the smaller bottle. Then, this here castor oil same way," she repeated Mama's instructions. "Rub it in to beat all. Then cover your head with hot, wet towels and set there for a spell real still like. Last, boil some of this sage tea and drink it down." She fished a paper packet of dried leaves from her sack for him. "And don't expect a miracle, Mama says, and save the bottles for me to pick up next time 'round."

"By thunder," he growled, kneeing one too-eager hound away, "Claib Tucker don't need no miracles to find hisself another wife, but a full head of hair jest might help if she's a young un. The miracle, my girl, will be the woman who comes to live here. That un's gonna be so clever she can flip me a hoecake inside on the hearth, then run wa-aaaa-y outside here to catch it when it comes aflyin' up the chimbley!"

His dark eyes twinkled and he bellowed louder when Becca laughed at his funning. Becca was going to tell him that Mama meant miracles about growing back hair and not about fetching in a pretty new wife, but since he was laughing, she let that pass. Best not to tell a man like Mr. Tucker he didn't catch on too fast sometimes.

"Too bad you un's so young," he teased her, " 'cause you sure got some of your pretty mama in you. You got any of your daddy Chase's highfalutin notions to see the world? That kind a thing's bad in a woman. Leastways, like to make 'em put on airs."

"Got me a notion to go on downriver and find Daddy and bring him back straight off," Becca declared with a decisive nod that made her braid bounce. Chestnut tendrils turned like wild vines around her serious face now that she'd run and been blown a bit. "That would make Mama happy. Oh," she added, "you all still want a bottle of these spring tansy bitters for what ails you, Mr. Tucker?"

"Sure, but the cure for what ails me's gonna come from growin' some a this head o' hair back and a new woman up here," he muttered more to himself than her as he put his cap back on. He gathered his treasures and disappeared into his cabin, more than twice the size of the Blake home over on Crawl Crick. His dogs moved with him like a wavy mud puddle at his feet, but they knew better than to go farther than their dogtrot. Becca noted he hadn't even closed the clapboard door while he'd been gone, but left a stick leaning there to tell strangers he was out. She smiled in anticipation when he came back out with two newly killed rabbits tied feet up with a vine. He swung the game over her back and handed her the end of the vine.

"Tell your mama, much 'bliged. Tell her soak the meat first in vinegar from punkin parins." He patted the girl awkwardly on her shoulder. "You know, I haint talked so much in days, but that's real good. Got to sharpen my courting skills again if I'm agoing wife-huntin'. Say, if'n you's headin' up to see my Ralston and Jemmy, tell 'em I'll be up to see 'em by and by.''

"I'm going right up with tonic for them and a few things for Mrs. Tucker. Be glad to tell them and bet they'll be real glad to see you,'' Becca assured him with a nod and a smile. The last time she'd been here, Ralston had been too. Mr. Tucker had called poor Ralston simple as an ax handle and said he was a real disappointment as a firstborn son. He said he couldn't abide those squally youngsters of Ralston and Jemima's either, so his sudden change of heart, though she didn't understand it, cheered Becca up. She couldn't bear for people, especially families, not to get on.

"You know," Mr. Tucker said, his eyes looking real moist right into hers, "you look somethin' like your daddy Chase when you smile. Crazy noodlehead to go arunnin' off keel-boating all the time when he has a right nice family to home.'' Mr. Tucker looked back toward his cabin and Becca saw his shoulders slump. He wiped at his eyes quickly with the back of his hand as if he were just rubbing them. Becca thought there were times when people needed to be alone, so she hurried away with another quick farewell shouted over her shoulder. She realized she could send the things up to Ralston's place with Mr. Tucker to save time. But Mama had given her strict instructions to be certain Jemima Tucker was faring well in her seventh pregnancy.

Becca set off uphill again at a good clip, though the going was much steeper. She did not want to let anyone down. Since Gran Ida had died and this area had no granny woman with the arts of midwifery, a woman's friends had to get her through her travail no matter how far off they lived. But high up on Snow Knob as Jemima Tucker was and with her nervous condition, the birthing herbs had to bring comfort to her head as well as her body. "Jumping Jemima," Becca always had called Mrs. Tucker, even the time she'd come up here with Gran Ida for the last baby's birth. The child was in the breech position and Gran Ida had to actually turn it inside Jemima before it could be born. Becca had been considered too young to do much more during a birth than boil water and tend the youngsters, but that time when things got desperate, she had held the lantern for Gran Ida and seen it all.

It was nearly an hour before Becca spotted the clearing for the second Tucker cabin, this one awash with yelping youngsters instead of hunting hounds.

"Becca, Becca! Got any lic'rice? Got 'lasses candy?" the chorus of squeals greeted her. She had no sweets to give, but had come prepared with second-best offerings, newly pulled from the meadow.

"No, sorry, none of that. But lookie here. I got you all fresh mint to chew and some dandelion greens for your mama to cook up too!"

At the ensuing hubbub, Jemima Tucker came out with a baby balanced against her hip and big stomach. She looked worn and old to Becca; after all, Mama said she was twenty-six. Becca didn't see Ralston anywhere about. Often he fussed in the garden or just took walks. "How-do, Becca," Jemima called to her. "Daddy Tucker dint send us those there rabbits, did he?"

Too late, Becca realized she should have hidden the rabbits no matter what Mama might say about messing up the inside of the sack. Jemima Tucker was always on the lookout for food for her noisy brood. "No, ma'am, they're pay for Mr. Tucker's daddy's yarbs, but he said he's coming up here by and by."

"Now, won't that be fine? Hope he does some huntin' on his way up. Haint seem him for weeks and can't go traipsin' down in my condition."

Becca followed her inside and sat gratefully at the narrow plank table. She pulled out and explained the feverfew and other herbs which would lessen the labor pains when they began. "Got all that?" Becca asked. "Make the feverfew tea hot, but drink it cold." She lined up the four bottles of tansy tonic and explained about doses for the little ones, two teaspoons to one jug of water. They chatted between the times Jemima yelled at her youngsters for quiet and flitted here and

11

there in the cabin. They exchanged news to share with others. "As if," Jemima confided to the wide-eyed girl, "I got me anyone but these wild injins and the squirrels to talk civil to."

Becca listened closely because this woman had a habit of jumping topics the way Becca jumped spring rills. "Drat, but if your Gran Ida hadn't counted ten balls on that birthin' cord when I was delivered of my first, so I got three more young uns to go after this seventh one! Even when her gout got bad, Ida Blake'd come on her mule to get me through my travails." Jemima ended her wandering recital with a mournful glance at her swollen belly.

"Maybe you be like to drop this next baby easier," Becca comforted and reached across to pat the woman's fist.

"You may be just a slip of a girl," Jemima told her, "but I wish you'd take up midwifin'. You got a good way 'bout you. I recall you stayed right calm when this one tried to come all twisted up inside me and I was screamin' so." She bounced the fussy baby on her hip again. "Glad you come that day, especially with that mama o' yours bein' like she is to just stay 'round home, I mean."

"Mama took up the yarbs from Gran Ida, but not the birthing," Becca explained, feeling she had to defend her mama from something Jemima had not quite said. " 'Just not chosen by Providence nor suited by temperament,' " she told Jemima, repeating the very words Gran Ida had used more than once to defend her beloved, sensitive daughter-in-law when everyone expected Mama would take over granny duties in these parts.

They shared a saucer of hot mint tea brewed from Becca's meadow herbs. Jemima paid her with a sack of walnuts she pulled from under a loose floorboard after she shooed the children out for the fourth time. The Blakes had very few nuts left, so Becca praised the barter highly. Suddenly Jemima clasped Becca's hand; the pale blue eyes so clearly cried out for her to stay longer, but Becca had to move on to be home by dark.

"Jest one more thing," Jemima told her when Becca stepped out into the sun, and pulled her back into the dirt-floor cabin. "Something for you and your Mama to share. It'll be all moldy if'n I save it for my oldest girl to 'preciate, and it matches your eyes. Here!"

Jemima Tucker pulled something from yet another hidden crevice in her cabin. It rolled open in her hand, green ribbon enough to tie back a thick hank of hair. Becca's eyes widened. "Oh, I couldn't. You wear it."

"No, not up here. Not with—everything. You take it. My oldest boy found it caught in a bush way down by South Fork. It's for a girl who wants to find a boy to love."

Embarrassed, Becca laughed. She never thought like that—not really. Not beyond mooning over Gran Ida's songs of sad love. Not beyond being so pleased when Mama taught her the Virginia reel so she'd be right ready when a beau or a frolic came her way someday. Not beyond thinking sometimes on how Mama and Daddy met so romantically and fell deep in love. But she took the gift.

"It's beautiful," she told Jemima. Though she was so much younger in years and experience than this woman, she suddenly felt they were friends, and it moved her to her toe tips. "It's green like the river in the summer when there's sun and not much rain."

The woman squeezed Becca's hand in both of hers. "It's green with all of life ahead like I was once—green like you."

By the time Becca hiked across the high ridge to the cabin of Ephraim and Prudence Johns and their ten children, it was early afternoon. Sometimes hungry wolves came down after the wild hogs up this high, so she had carried a long elm limb that slowed her down. She chewed mint leaves to settle her rumbling stomach and took a cold drink from Snow Crick where it plunged past toward the valley and river below. Redbuds and dogwoods embroidered the still barren cliffs and knobs up here, but soon maples, giant elms, and chestnuts would dye the mountains green. This spot was a fine lookout, but not magic like her own secret place above the Crawl Crick cabin.

Prudence Johns heard their old hound bark a warning and came out to meet Becca, wiping her hands on her brown linsey-woolsey skirt. "How you been keepin'?" she greeted Becca.

Prudence Johns must have been pretty once. But her blonde hair seemed washed out now, and her blue eyes had gone pale and watery. Little birds' feet perched here and there on a face the sun had tanned to leather. Her life was hard since her man Ephraim seemed to love drinking Old Monongahela whiskey from Scott's Distillery down in Shelter more than he loved his big family. But the youngsters were clean and mannerly, all with "A" first names as if the parents never got further in book learning: Alfred, Andrew, Abigail, Alice, Ardith, Alvy, Abraham, Absolom, Americus, and Abner, the last four still shirttail boys. Their mother was a whirlwind of work, darting here and there to care for her children and her cabin. Her sad eyes always glanced up toward the woods along the high ridge, so Becca thought that was where Ephraim and his latest jug of Monongahela must have gone. It wasn't seemly to ask. Maybe it was no wonder that Pru, as Gran Ida had always called the woman, had stomach complaints. Becca had once overheard Gran Ida tell Mama the woman's real pain was in her heart.

"Now I got a bit of baked possum here for you my Alfy shot and a sliver of tart from them fine Shelter Valley dried apples from last year." Pru settled Becca down to the welcome if meager helpings. Becca felt hollow and tried not to bolt her food. Most Kentucky cabins, however poor the family, had floor space and some food to offer a guest, but Becca and Mama understood that pot scrapings were the most they would get from Pru. And not to hurt the woman's pride, they never asked for more, not while Ephraim was so shiftless. After her meal, Becca thanked the woman heartily. They exchanged more news about who was sweethearting who, who was helling around in Shelter, and who was likeliest to have a spring frolic. Then Becca explained how to shave the calamus root called sweet flag she had brought Pru for a stomach-settling tea.

"Best thing is with sweet flag, any shavings you got left you can make you a sweetbag!" Becca told her with a smile.

"Why, whatever for?" Pru demanded as if Becca had suggested tossing several of her precious youngsters off the ridge. "I got no drawers of linen nor some hope chest! I haint got time for fancy city fripperies!"

"Just for pleasure, to lighten your load, like they say. You can just—"

"Why," the woman interrupted and hit both bony hands on her knees, "I said I got no time for such. 'Sides, haven't got a scrap of cloth or string to make a sweetbag neither!"

Becca regretted she had got the woman nettled. But then she saw the haunted sadness on Pru's face, a look she had glimpsed on Jemima Tucker's, and on Mama's more than once when she thought Becca wasn't looking. She sensed Pru was not angry at her for suggesting something nice, but because she regretted having no nice things for herself anymore. She hesitated only a moment before she reached into her sack and pulled out an extra paper packet and the precious green ribbon.

"Look, here's one nearly ready made," she told Pru, not flinching at the woman's frown. Becca took her knife and shaved a bit of sweet flag into the paper sack, then crimped its neck and tied the green ribbon around it. She wasn't ready to wear a ribbon anyway; she was not looking for a man, even if some mountain girls did wed at fourteen or so. She had years and years before that. Besides, Daddy might bring her something for her hair clear from New Orleans, and here she'd be sporting a ribbon already!

Tears puddled in the corners of Pru's eyes as Becca handed her the bag. The woman nodded, shook the bag, and sniffed at it. "I can't thankee enough and sure can't pay you," Pru began, her voice gone croaky as a frog's.

"It's thanks enough if you enjoy it," Becca assured her

and hefted her burdens to head down to the old Widow Lang's cabin, on the bluff above the wild roses that Becca coveted much more than she ever had a green ribbon.

Amrine Lang, mostly called the old Widow Lang, did not seem exactly old to Becca, but ageless. Sometimes when she looked right at Becca and smiled, she seemed young. When her gaze drifted away and she chattered to people who weren't really there, then she seemed very old. Her father had been one of the first white men to settle Shelter Valley, and got along with the Shawnees and Cherokees who used to hunt in the area. But he had died long ago. Her husband and two maiden sisters, Ernestine and Albertine, who once lived in this cabin, had died too. Becca remembered none of them. Still, it seemed their presence hung about the place like the odor of honeysuckle in the summer or the way winds whirling up from the valley always made the roofshakes rattle. Becca never told anyone, but her visits to the Widow Lang were her favorite. Up here, it seemed she could stand among wild pink roses and almost touch clouds blooming like white roses in the wide skies overhead. It made her feel one step from heaven.

The old Widow Lang, people said, had had no children in her bearing days and that was the tragedy of her life. But to Becca, Widow Lang did not seem a bit tragic, but special since she often talked to her two dead sisters as if they were still of this earth. And though others said she was cranky and always put them to work and her face was cobwebbed with wrinkles, Becca didn't mind. She had just learned not to speak until spoken to, and even then the widow didn't hear because she was almost deaf. Today, to get her attention, Becca had to beat her fist on the open door of the cabin and call out her name loudly.

Widow Lang seemed to float to the door, swaying ever so slightly. Her packed dirt floor looked as cleanly swept as ever. She wore pale gray as if to reflect the silver hair that drifted loose from its knot at her nape, partly obscuring her crinkly face.

"It's you, girl. About time! My cough is worse and worse! I told Albertine you'd come soon. Ernestine pegged a lock of my hair in the hole of a tree. Right at my head level too. It done no good. At my age, I say such precautions is just head stuffin'!"

Widow Lang's fingers flitted like sparrows as she gestured Becca in. Her skirt billowed in the breeze from the door. Becca spoke loudly. "Mama said this here goldenrod tea is something you haven't tried! Gold-en-rod tea! Maybe it will help your cough!"

"I've tried it all in my day. Set a spell? I'm agoing to plant my squash seeds right now. 'Plant taters in the dark of the moon, squash in the light of noon,' you know."

"But it's late afternoon!" Becca protested, forgoing to mention that such wisdom might just be more head stuffing. But she had to smile inside. The old woman lived mostly from her fine garden, but every time in season when Becca had come through, she had found an excuse to put the girl to work in it. She always pretended Becca could just sit and watch, but Becca knew her game. "Why don't you just set a spell, and I'll do it for you?" Becca volunteered with pointing and digging gestures.

She worked quickly as the sun sank lower, hilling up the well-worked soil with a cracked wooden trowel and dropping three squash seeds in each mound. Sitting in the western doorway, Widow Lang chatted on, sometimes addressing Becca, sometimes her long-departed sisters. Finally, as the sun sank toward the jagged crests across South Fork, Becca stood and clapped soil off her hands. Not once had the old woman coughed in all her dry-throated chattering. Becca followed her inside to get her things. Now, Becca thought, was the time to remind the widow that last time she had promised her a cutting of her roses early in the spring.

"Something to show you, girl," Widow Lang told her and bent stiffly over a humped traveling trunk carved from a hollowed tree stump. "Just in case Albertine and Ernestine forget it when I fly up yonder. It's here. Thought you should know. Tell the folks that come to take me."

Puzzled, Becca stared down at the beautifully worked quilt draped across the woman's thin arms. On a grass-green background, rings of blue and gold and white interlocked in a never-ending pattern. "My wedding quilt," Widow Lang said. "Tell them to bury me in it, understand?"

Two brown eyes in the wrinkled face bored into Becca's green ones. "Understand?" Widow Lang repeated.

Becca nodded. She suddenly understood so much. The woman's linking of the two momentous events, her marriage in the past with her death in the future. How she talked to her dear departed ones for company just the way Becca sometimes—she knew Mama did it too—pretended Gran Ida was still around. But what captured Becca's thoughts and stopped her tongue was the sudden realization that this quilt looked like the meadow all spread out below with those same interlocking hues of flowers and herbs amid greenest grass. The usefulness and loveliness of growing things were all interlocked by the great, skilled hand of an ageless God the way these embroidered patches had been stitched together by Widow Lang. It was the first moment Becca ever remembered feeling really grown-up and wise, even though she was still, as Jemima had said earlier today, green.

"I understand," she said, whispering this time, but the old lady nodded. While Becca watched, the quilt went back in the trunk and Widow Lang floated over to the tin flour box on her table. She lifted out three nut-brown, crisp-crusted corn dodgers, as always with the baker's handprint on each one. With the winter supply of cornmeal low, Mama had not fried any in weeks. Becca's nostrils flared with the rich aroma and her mouth watered.

"One for each of you," the woman said.

How ever, Becca wondered, did this strange woman who never left this place remember there were three of them at the Crawl Crick cabin? She'd always forgot before about Jeremy. Or did she think Daddy was home and that made three? No, probably she had forgotten that Gran Ida, who was once a friend of hers, had died last year.

"Now Albertine and Ernestine," the old woman went on, "are going to walk you to those wild roses on the ridge below you want a cutting of. Then they'll take you clear down to the medder. Each of you eat one of these corn dodgers on the way."

Now Becca smiled broadly, even as she nodded. Widow Lang had remembered about the roses! Mother would have to let her plant roses up in her private refuge high above Restful Knob if it was a gift from Widow Lang and they wouldn't be beholden! Becca packed the corn dodgers, knowing how excited Mama and Jeremy would be with her day's gleanings: rabbits for burgoo stew, walnuts to munch, and three delicious corn dodgers. Becca especially valued the corn dodgers for the mark of Widow Lang's hand. It was as special as her handiwork on that quilt for her death, the quilt that reminded Becca so much of life.

She thanked the old woman, waved good-bye, and started down the path. She almost felt she should thank Ernestine and Albertine for their company since she didn't feel alone—not after today. The mountain people she brought things to always gave her much more in return, and not things you could eat or see.

Quickly she selected a sturdy cutting of the wild mountain roses that sprawled in a dense thicket six feet high to bloom under Widow Lang's cabin once a year in a riot of pale to deep pinks. She took out her herb knife. She dug; she cut. Mama had told her this sort of bush was no good but to look at. And with the harsh winter that had killed much new growth, she said she couldn't give Becca a cutting of the precious apothecary roses from the herb bed at Crawl Crick.

Becca ignored the profusion of thorns in her hurry. Bristles threatened on every inch of the leggy canes, but not on their sturdy brown stems. The snags and pricks to her hands felt no worse than stepping on a bee or cutting a knee on a stone.

19

Burdened by the rabbits and her sack, she lifted the root ball, trailing six looping, reddish canes behind her. But for some reason she looked back and up. There, windblown on the fold of ridge above her head, stood Widow Lang, hand lifted as if to give a blessing. Her hair blew free like silver wings behind her shoulders and her head; her skirt and petticoat flapped as if she flew.

Becca shouted a good-bye and hurried down the path toward the valley. She forgot to bid farewell to Ernestine and Albertine when she saw shadows brooding from the deep hills and hollows. She dashed across the flower-quilted meadow toward home, cradling her very own first rosebush in her hands.

Chapter Two

The next morning, promising Mama she would not stay long, Becca carried her rosebush up toward the knobs of Concord Peak. The springtime rattle of the creek kept her company. She followed the twisting, narrowing path along the stand of white sycamores not far from the cabin. Just like her, they loved the streambed. Their white bodies grew stocky here. Their sturdy roots and curved arms made them look like dancing spirits, especially on moonlit nights when clouds were flying.

Crawl Crick, that sleepy stream of summer, was in a rush now to join the confluence and then the Shelter River and then South Fork to flow westward into the big Kentucky, which Becca had never seen. When she left the creek, she turned and squinted back through the arch of sycamore arms at the tumbling, frothing water. If only she could be a little piece of bark in it, she could float down the Kentucky to the Ohio and then the Mississippi to find Daddy down in New Orleans.

From the first big ridge, the Blake cabin looked like the house she had built once from sticks for her cornhusk doll.

21

On a grassy, slanted rise clustered the herb garden, the greens garden, the small corn patch they tried to protect from varmints, and the cabin itself. It wasn't much, Becca supposed, but Daddy still had a paper they had stuck in the family Bible that said their claim was from the sassafras clump to the sycamore snag to the large rock. Becca could see it all from here, with a long curve of smoke that looked like a heavenly finger pointing right down the chimney from the clouds.

As she started upward again, her steps felt lighter. Past the elderberry bushes, now only rabbit ears of green pushing up through last year's leaves. Past three barren corn patches she and Jeremy would hoe and plant soon. Each gray patch perched precariously on its steep, narrow slope, like a bird on a branch in the wind. A good summer gusher and the corn crop could just disappear over the side and have to be replanted if it wasn't too late. And then, sometimes, unless Daddy came home for a winter spell, the table fare got pretty thin at the cabin.

Becca paused by the knee-high rail fence surrounding the Blake graveyard up on the gentle, grassy slope called Restful Knob. Small, matching log gravehouses with sharply slanted roofs to shed snow protected the stones and graves of Ida Willett Blake, 1763–1822, and her husband, Jeremy Roscoe Blake, 1757–1818. Becca remembered the old carpenter and farmer who was her grandfather, for she had been six when he died. Like Gran Ida, he had come through Pound Gap in the Appalachian wall from Old Virginia with his family after the War for Independence was won. Here lay Gran Ida's brother Merit and Granddaddy's parents under their old, weather-worn gravehouses. Here too, under wind-smoothed stones as if they hadn't lived long enough to earn gravehouses, lay Gran Ida and Granddaddy Jeremy's four dead infants. Each stone pillow at the top of its grass coverlet said only, "Little Lamb."

Though Mama had said Becca wasn't old enough to understand, Gran Ida herself had explained how all of her babies but Daddy had been born strangled by their own birthing cords. Daddy's was around his neck too, but he was such a lusty, stubborn one, Gran Ida said, she managed to blow breath into his blue body. Mama had said it was an irony of life that Gran Ida was the midwife that brought babies for other women, but couldn't save her own. Becca knew then that an irony of life meant something really sad. She hoped she never met any ironies of life when she was grown-up.

Still, this place never made her sad the way it did Mama. Becca had so many happy memories that made happy feelings even this close to the Blake family graves. Besides, the view from here was fine, though it got better even farther up. Remembering that Mama wanted her back before noon, Becca decided to sing just one song for Gran Ida. Instead of Gran Ida's favorite holy song about crossing the River Jordan, she sang one Gran Ida liked and Mama hummed often lately when she thought no one was listening:

> Tonight I'm alone without you my dear.
> It seems I long for you each day.
> All I have to do is sit alone and cry.
> In our little cabin home on the hill.
> Oh, someone has taken you from me,
> And left me here all alone.
> Listen to the rain pat on our window pane,
> In our little cabin home on the hill.

The song went on forever with more verses, but Becca dared not sing them all today. But she added in a louder voice even than she used for Widow Lang to hear, "And I got me a wild rosebush from your old friend Amrine Lang to plant up yonder, Gran Ida!" She turned and went on.

Now the terrain got even wilder, with no path. She loved it up here more than anywhere around Shelter. Gran Ida had showed her the place on one rare day when she wasn't busy with her midwifing and her gout didn't pain her too much to leave her mule partway up and climb. Becca knew Daddy and Mama had been up here, but no one but Becca came anymore. It was her special place. She stopped and sighed. She wished she could make it perfect here someday with a cabin of her own all surrounded by roses and her own herb bed.

Although the entrance to her spot had room for a person to walk around the windy ridge before it opened up to a sheltered ledge, she usually chose to catch hold of a grapevine on the vine-latticed cliff face and swing in. But not today with her hands full of her rosebush. She walked in, noting that the tiny, rock-sprung rills that glazed the cliff were no longer shiny ice. This sandstone corridor to her private world was what she called her ice palace in the colder months when its polished, frozen walls glittered in the sun.

She ducked under the stone arbor entrance and smiled as her little patch of thin soil and scrawny grass greeted her. Even the shrill whine of wind sounded sweetly welcoming. Daddy called the knob below this ledge Shrieking Peak, but she had renamed it Whistling Peak. Since this was her place, she guessed she could name things what she wanted. Sometimes she sang along when the wind made tunes like some high-pitched fiddle played by one of God's angels.

She quickly knelt to dig a hole in the shallow, rocky soil with her knife. The curve of cliff would shelter it from the worst of northwest winds. The wash of rainwater down the rocks would make it grow, no matter what Mama said about the soil being scant up here. Why, in a few years she might even have to cut it back if it went all wild like the Widow Lang's roses.

She walked back and forth from the grassy ledge to the entrance to cup her hands to the cliff. She leaned over to gather handful after handful of melted snow to splash on the new nest for the roots. At least, she thought, Mama had let her plant it here, probably to keep her from asking the Scott family in town if she could have a slip of their roses, which Mama said were English sweetbriers. Lately, the more Daddy was gone, the more nettled Mama seemed about being beholden to anyone, especially the Scotts. But Becca didn't deliver lung syrups to the invalid Mrs. Scott very often. And she'd told Mama she never went farther than the back door in the walled-off Scott garden.

Becca crossed her ankles and lay on her back with her hands hooked behind her head and gazed up at snow-capped Concord Peak. Racing clouds always made the mountain look as if it were tumbling at her, as if her whole world could fall apart. Her insides cartwheeled even though she knew nothing but the sky was moving at all. And if the sun and mist were right when she was gazing up like this, she could see a rainbow. Best of all, and rarest too, if the moon was full and she could find her way up here in the dark, there was a moonbow, Daddy said. She'd never caught one yet because she couldn't be up here then.

The craggy face of Concord seemed always to change expressions like a person. Sunny, frowning, joyous, worried, anything at all. Sometimes it looked as purplish black in the rain as a wet Concord grape, but Gran Ida had told her the mountain was named to remind everyone in these parts to live in peace and concord. Then too, like the meadow pond, Concord's colors changed all the time, reflecting the sky. Bluish gray to palest purple, depending on the western light. Down Concord rushed wild waterways this time of year like Medder Run, Rill Run, and Crawl Crick. Mountain people always told where they lived by what creek they were near, and most had useful as well as yarn-telling names: Cutshin, Quicksand, Frozen, Lower Devil, Tight Hollow, and one Daddy told her of on the sly called Hell for Sartin'.

She sat up and scanned the varied vistas in all directions. She clasped her hands around her bent knees and tossed back her head, springing more curls free from her braid. She was certain she could see clear to Boonesville where Mama had been raised and Daddy had found her. Even though Becca thought sometimes she could just fly away from up here, she never wanted to leave this mountain or this valley the way Mama had left her home. Down below here in years to come, again and again, she would watch the colored seasons. This yellow green of the trees would turn to apple green and then the deep moss green of summer. Then it would burst to the flaming sugar-maple reds and rich water-maple yellows and the purple hues of blue ash. Scarlet sumac would surpass this white dogwood and pink redbud lace below. Then the leaves would drift to dry browns with another white winter come to bury it all. And then she would be a year older and maybe want a green ribbon in her hair and some man besides Daddy to come calling at the Crawl Crick cabin so they could go walking out the way he and Mama did once.

She jumped to her feet, the spell of the place broken. She had promised Mama she would come right back for the learning lesson! She slapped soil off the knees of her skirt and ran through the stone arch to grab a dangling tangle of grapevines. "Whee-ah!" she shrieked as she flew along the cliff face to land easily on her feet. Her cry resounded off the shiny walls of her palace, drowning out the whistle of wind.

She ran downhill whenever she could keep her feet. She ignored the bite of loose stones on her winter-tender soles, which soon would be hard as leather again. She wondered whether the learning lesson today would be from *Pilgrim's Progress* or the Bible, the only two books the family owned, not counting Mama's herbal book. And she wondered whether Mama would want her to hoe the herbs or help Jeremy with his ciphering afterward. But she never wondered for one moment if the wild rose cutting she got from Widow Lang would grow in her special place. Just like her, unless some ironies of life got in the way, she knew it would.

Becca's eyes and attention wandered about the cabin while Jeremy haltingly read from the Bible and Mama sat in her rocker and peered over his shoulder to prompt him. The boy's delight in life was to carve little animals from chunks of wood with the jackknife Daddy had brought him from Cincinnati, so he had asked today to read the part from the Good Book where Adam got to name the animals in the Garden of Eden. Becca's turn to read would come soon enough, but right now she was grateful for the block of sun sliding through the open cabin door to warm her feet.

Like most mountain cabins, this one had two doors, east and west, to take advantage of whatever sun there was. The cabin was wider than it was deep at about twenty-seven feet by twenty. Built years ago by Granddaddy Jeremy and Gran Ida's older brother, Merit, right next to an earlier lean-to, it was all thick roofshakes and rough logs gone gray. It had hardly been improved, as Daddy took no fancy to such work, but Becca thought it was a fine place to live.

After all, only about half of the floor was packed dirt and the rest was puncheon, old enough now that most of the big splinters were worn away. The stone and clay chimney and hearth were wide, though chinks made the fire sputter in the worst winter winds and rain that came whipping through holes she and Jeremy patched with mud and moss. The single grease-paper window rattled even under its board shutters in a gale, but they were so used to it, things sounded strange when it stopped.

Up under the steep slant of eaves, on the hearth side of the cabin, there was a sleeping loft big enough for four. She and Jeremy slept up there when Daddy was home. They climbed up by pegs sunk right in the wall. Corn-shuck mattresses were changed once a year to keep fleas and lice from sleeping there too. They had three patched blankets to share. Of course, the rope lattice bed that was Mama and Daddy's— it had been Gran and Granddaddy's once—was better yet. And Becca loved the soft, straw-stuffed tick in the trundle bed that slid under the big one. While Daddy was away in cold weather, Jeremy slept in the trundle and she with Mama in the big one. Still, she and Jeremy were so glad to have Daddy home that when he came back they moved up to the loft without a peep.

The cabin furnishings, she thought, were pretty too. The Indian harvest cradle that both rocked and swung stood empty now on the hearth until there would be another baby. The plank trestle table had four stools with woven rush seats, a bit sunk in. Between the bed and the rocker lay a soft oval rag rug in muted blues someone gave Gran Ida once for helping birth twins. Her old, squeaky comb-back rocker for ladies to dry their long hair in was Mama's favorite place now. She often carted it outside to sit in the sun when she worked her herbs. A three-shelf maple corner cupboard held the six pewter plates, four cups, and iron forks and horn spoons that had come clear from Virginia and maybe from England too. Becca usually pictured England as being just on the other side of Virginia beyond Pound Gap.

But prettiest of all in the Blake cabin were the ceiling adornments Becca was so proud of. Mama's drying herbs draped up there in loops and bunches to fill the cabin with mingled smells, better than some of the ones sneaking out of the cookpot. Sage and parsley, catnip, clover, ambrosia, lavender, fennel, tansy, marigold, and a hundred others. And then too, though the supply was low now, dried pumpkin rings and strings of dried shucky beans Becca had run a needle and thread through bobbed up there in cross-breezes. But best of all by midsummer would be the scent of bags of sweet apothecary rose petals drying to make medicines. Mama had promised to let her pick the petals again this year.

"All right then, Becca, you read a spell starting right here," Mama's sweet voice interrupted her musings. She lifted the heavy book onto Becca's knees and luckily, since Becca hadn't been listening, pointed to the spot with a smile.

Becca reveled in the warmth of Mama's presence as she began to read about God creating man in His own image, "male and female created He them." She loved Mama so much and tried to be like her and help her. Since Gran Ida had died, those feelings had become even stronger, as if she must protect the woman who had sheltered her all her life.

Ann Mercer Blake was thirty years old; she had been wed for twelve years. She was tall, shapely, and graceful with copper hair and auburn eyebrows that arched over eyes as blue as coltsfoot flowers. Her expressions were as tender and sensitive at the hint of anyone's troubles as her pale skin was to freckles in the slightest hint of sun. Her full mouth smiled easily, especially when she worked her beloved herb bed across from the west cabin door or taught Becca to dance on the brow of hill outside.

But sometimes, Becca had noticed lately, there was a shadow that swept down from Mama's brow and hid in the depths of her eyes. The oval face lengthened and the rich voice rang hollow, though if Becca asked if anything was amiss or tried to distract her, Mama usually put on a sunny smile, even if her eyes still looked cloudy. Lately, thinking on the things she knew of other mountain women's trials, Becca had begun to wonder about Mama. Was it something deeper than just Daddy's going keelboating? Would she still be that laughing, joking woman when Daddy came home next time? Mama scolded a bit more of late. The older Becca got, the more Mama seemed to want to keep her closer, even when they both knew she needed to be out making deliveries.

Becca's mind jumped back to her reading fast when Mama corrected her. "I swan, my child, that's rightly said *herb*, not *yarb*, no matter how folks about here talk. Read that again, please, Becca."

" 'The Lord God made the earth and the heavens, and every plant of the field before it was in the earth, and every *herb* of the field before it grew.' "

"Good. Just remember, folks about here say things different from Boonesville where I learned to read in a real good rote school Mrs. Winchester kept in her house."

"But we live here and not in your old haunts, Mama."

Haunts—that word stunned Ann for a moment. Haunted by thoughts of her past was just the way she felt sometimes. "But I want you and Jeremy to say things correct, even though you will live here all your life," she amended.

Ann Blake listened as her daughter read on, but Boonesville had snagged her thoughts. Why, it was so much more of a town than Shelter! In Boonesville, people wore shoes all year, not just in the winter and to Sunday meeting. Her six-room family farmhouse had been a palace next to this cabin, where she would have died of grief when Chase lit out that first time if it hadn't been for her mother-in-law. The girl was right to say they lived here now for good. Her old home at Boonesville seemed farther downriver each year. More than the distance of miles, there was the distance of the heart, the distance of people's lives flowing by that she'd never be part of again. But she dared not think of that. It would bring the dark, drowning memories back. She bit her lip to stop the threat of tears. She dared not think of all that.

" 'Therefore shall a man leave his father and his mother, and shall cleave unto his wife,' " Becca read on as if to intentionally loosen Ann's hold on herself again. " 'And they were both naked, the man and his wife and were not ashamed.' "

"Enough of a lesson for now," Ann insisted and quickly shooed both children outside to work the herb bed. She sensed that Becca wanted to stay behind to speak with her, so she told her she could carefully prune the bushy apothecary roses she so loved. Jeremy didn't fuss a bit about having his ciphering lesson postponed. He knew his daddy never paid a bit of heed to learning anything but what amused and pleased him. And, Good God help her, thought Ann Mercer Blake as the memories came crashing back, Chase Blake had always been so very, very good at getting what amused and pleased him!

If the Mercer family barn hadn't burned, maybe, Ann mused, she wouldn't have burned for Chase Blake either. Lightning sending the barn up in flames that year she met Chase was the only catastrophe of the Mercer family's ten years in Kentucky. She remembered how they'd come from Old Virginia by the Wilderness Road with a good nest egg her father had worked hard for, as he used to say. In that prosperous first decade on the frontier, her father and his two hired hands cleared more and more land to plant wheat and corn. Soon they were selling grain downriver as far as Beattyville. The

Mercer river-bottom land was lush, the house grew with the family, the livestock multiplied.

They lived one mile outside the little town of Boonesville, one of several named after Daniel Boone along the stretch of Kentucky waterways. Filled with friendly people, Boonesville was where the four Mercer daughters went to school and the whole family rode the big harvest wagon in to Sunday meeting. Ann, as the eldest with three other sisters, Sarah, Penelope, and Beth, was the family's shining example of industry and propriety in that autumn of 1811 when the Mercers and their neighbors gathered for a raising to rebuild the burned barn. A week after the task was done, everyone returned to have a frolic.

A bran barn dance, they called it, and giggled when they tried to get that twister off their tongue ten times in a row. They spread bran on the floor of the new barn, and shuffling dancers helped polish it with their feet. They combined it with a box supper to raise money for glass windows for the church in town. All the women, married or not, fixed their best box suppers and put them in baskets covered with crepe. Husbands bid boldly for their own wives' cooking. For the unwed women, it gave young men of courting age a chance to publicly declare their intentions—and to spend an hour or so unchaperoned with their lady loves.

When her basket went up for bids, eighteen-year-old Ann rose to stand by it as was the tradition. She looked nervously across the crowd to see if blond Abel Wheelright would start the bidding. They weren't promised exactly, but there was an understanding between their parents, since their cornfields abutted each other clear down to the river. It was in that moment Ann first beheld twenty-three-year-old Chase Blake with his devil-dark, curly, windblown hair and burning eyes. He was leaning against the wall, hands stuck under his armpits, cocksure with his white teeth flashing bright in his sun-bronze face. At that, Ann felt so warm that lightning might just as well have struck this barn to start a fire too!

Chase's gaze held hers as he dared to open the bidding at

two dollars when everyone knew the offers were to start at a dime and go up no more than that each time! Heads turned to study the stranger. He later explained he had been passing through on the way home upriver when the sound of fiddling drew him. He was a steersman on a keelboat, but if he'd been the painted war chief of some savage Indian tribe, his impact on Ann and her family and friends could not have been more stunning. He'd upset everyone, including poor Abel Wheelright, by the time he claimed her basket and her company for the sky-high sum of seventeen dollars he ended up donating when other bidders fell away. Her father looked livid, her sisters gawked, and Mama seemed as embarrassed as if he'd bought her eldest daughter on the slave block. But from that moment on, even in front of everyone in all of Kentucky, Ann Mercer would have followed Chase Blake to the ends of the earth in her petticoat.

"I take it there's dancing after," were the first words he ever spoke to her. His big brown hand held her laden basket so easily. His square jaw softened to a dazzling smile, and his thick black brows lifted over intense eyes. Ann loved to dance more than anything, but right now, she was certain she could not recall one step of one single dance.

"Yes," she managed, falling into step beside him across and then off the new barn floor. "Dancing after, reels 'til real late."

They both laughed awkwardly as if she'd said something funny. They shared the meal. He praised her sweet potato pie, beaten biscuits, and smoked ham. He talked, then she talked; finally, they both talked. She began to dream. He was just passing through, of course, and lived far upriver in a place she'd never heard of called Shelter Valley. Still, even the name sounded lovely.

Time drifted away from her, yet everything seemed distinct and precious. Each sensation came roaring to life like a brush bonfire: the firm press of his hand on hers or on the small of her back when they turned in the Virginia reel. The tang of crisp air drifting in from outside amid the body heat of the dancers; the windy scent of his hair; the way she went all shivery at the sound of his deep laugh. How the let-us-smile cider he had hidden in a jug outside was tart on her tongue. They danced the cotillion he said he'd learned in New Orleans—N'Olins, he pronounced it. Such a world traveler! He spoke of the beautiful view from his parents' home high on a hill. Every word from the vigorous, handsome Chase Blake's taut but tantalizing lips sounded to her eternally important or amusing. The blinding light of raw life seemed to shine from him.

She shut out her parents' frowns and slipped outside with him when he asked to see the layout of the farm. She, the girl who had been the pride of her parents, who, her father hoped, would set a good example to her sisters and wed a local boy to help run the family farm. She, who had not really been much interested in more than a bit of sweaty hand-holding and dry-mouthed kissing from Abel Wheelright. Now this woman she had suddenly become clung to a stranger from upriver she had not been properly introduced to as he embraced her amid the corn shocks. Why, he'd kissed her so hard she thought he might devour her.

As she lay tensely beside her sister Sarah in bed that night, she knew she wanted to be devoured by Chase Blake's mouth, his hands, his life. It was the strangest thing, as if she no longer had control of her mind, let alone her body. She had always been so docile and obedient to her parents, anxious to please them. Now she only wanted to please this dark stranger who had stepped into her life and moved her so deeply.

The next day, she lied to her parents to get out alone and met Chase down by the river.

· "I really shouldn't be here," she began. She felt the blush again that started at the tops of her breasts and prickled up her throat and face to heat the tips of her ears. Yet, for the first time in her life, she was aware she was a woman with power over a man.

"My beautiful Ann, you *should* be here. Here and anywhere with me. Never felt this way either, honest.'' He grasped her ivory hands in his big brown ones. ''It just happened so fast, I know, but there's no going back. We're meant to be. It's fate.''

''I don't really believe in fate. The plan of Providence, perhaps.''

''Sure, that's it. Providence telling me to follow that fiddle music like it was a rainbow and you were the gold at the end of it. You're special, Ann. We'll talk to your father. I'll stay a few days and then come back to ask for your hand. He'll have to let us be together! I know it sounds all crazy like some rip-roaring keelboater's hook and line, but it's not! I love you, Ann! I want you with me forever and ever, sharing the fun of life. It will all work itself out the way you want, you'll see!''

But nothing worked out quite the way she wanted after that, as if Chase's loving her was the last gift Providence— or fate—would allow. When she asked her father if Chase could come calling, he exploded.

''You, my girl,'' he bellowed and jabbed his finger almost in her face, ''are to apologize to your poor mother. And to Abel and the Wheelrights! Dancing with that man all evening and then stepping out with him—a keelboater, no less! I've talked to the Wheelrights, I tell you.'' He didn't let her get a word in. His ruddy coloring rose with his voice. ''And if Abel sees himself clear from the public drubbing you gave him and asks for your hand, you are to give it forthwith before your reputation is permanently soiled and the family's plans for you are—''

''No, I will not!'' she cried, jumping back from the reach of his long arms. ''I've been a good daughter! I *am* a good, loyal daughter! You just don't understand. You said you and Mama were a love match! Chase Blake is from a good family! His father farms and does carpentry! His mother is a midwife and everyone depends on her in their town and valley! And I am old enough to make decisions on my own about people now that I'm all growed up!''

It was the first time, and the last, she stood up to her father. Dragged out and confined to her room at age eighteen! They had loved her only as a child, not as the woman she was now. They were too selfish, too blind to feel for her. Her sister Sarah was her only friend. The next day, Sarah sneaked Ann a love letter in a fine hand. She assumed it to be Chase's until she found out weeks later he could not read or write, but knew only how to count money. The letter said he wanted to take her with him to his family, to marry her in town first so it was all done properly. He had even seen the preacher about it, and the man had been willing to speak for them to her father. But when the preacher had ridden out to broach the subject, her father had refused to listen. So, the letter concluded, if she loved Chase half as much as he did her, she must come and talk to him down on the river where his boat was hidden in the willow trees.

Again, it seemed her body and her mind were no longer her own. Could she really love a man she had met but three days ago beyond all caution? Could she defy her parents? Not wanting to involve her sister or the preacher further, she risked all to tiptoe out at night to see Chase down by the river. Surely, surely, if they went calmly together to her parents and said they wanted to be wed, they would understand. Didn't they see that their making her choose between them and Chase was killing her? Must she give up her past to have her future? She had no choice but to love where she loved!

When they faced her parents together in the front yard the next morning, her mother cried and her father refused to listen. He took a horsewhip after Chase and told her he would disown her next time she defied him. When she sobbed and Chase stalked off, Father must have thought he had broken them to his will. But that night, with a bundle of garments tied in a quilt, Ann stole out again. Out past the familiar flower and herb gardens she had helped Mama work, under the curtain-shrouded windows of her sleeping sisters, she walked with tears tracking jagged paths down her cheeks.

She joined Chase where he waited by the river in the stand of weeping willows.

Everything blurred faster, faster with the river current when he took the pole and shoved his little push boat away from the banks of the Mercer farm. Her heart thundered and her passion crackled like the fire she had helplessly watched destroying the barn. Surely when her folks realized the depths of her and Chase's devotion everything would be patched up. But now all she had known and loved fled far back into the dark. She watched Chase plunge his pole into the murky water, and felt emotions deeper than she'd ever fathomed.

He married her the next day at Conkling upriver. They spent their first night in a tiny storage room above the noisy common room of a tavern where Chase knew half the men, who sang loudly and drunkenly to them all night through the ceiling. Still, it was so wonderful when he touched her bare ivory flesh, when he kissed and loved her. And when he told her he had donated twenty dollars for the Boonesville church windows "as a memorial to the devoted and departed Mr. and Mrs. Chase Blake," she cried again.

"Honeylamb, don't carry on so. Smiles, no tears from here on out for us! I'll take care of you! Why, I made me seventy dollars on this haul to N'Olins for only eight months' work, and I'll do the same again, only more! And when I'm away, my mother will love to have your company."

She nodded wildly and swiped under her eyes with her long copper hair. She loved him so, it hardly sank in that he was telling her he'd be gone for months on end. All she knew was she felt stunned by all that had happened so fast. But not as stunned as when she saw the tiny, ramshackle cluster of buildings that was Shelter, Kentucky, and the crude Blake cabin up at Crawl Crick.

At least Chase stayed home those winter months. They bundled together in the loft upstairs amid Mother Ida's fragrant herbs, which made Ann so homesick. They tried to keep the floorboards from thumping when they loved and smothered their laughter against each other's naked shoulders.

And when they went out together, each day was filled with the beauty of the mountains they wandered far and wide and the way he loved her body so brazenly even out under God's great open skies.

Still, in the strangest moments, thoughts of home haunted her. Father had never kissed Mama when the girls were around; Chase kissed her all the time anywhere. She giggled when he patted or pinched her bottom; she lived for the sound of his voice at the cabin door when he went out roaming with his friends Claib and Ephraim.

When spring came crashing in like the streams off the mountains, she saw Chase's dark gaze swing more often toward the river. She began to panic. He would be going by her farm, her family, and she was staying here without him. But she feared that after everything she would not be welcome there. She had hurt them too deeply. She had broken the family circle. She could not bear the thought that she'd be here at Crawl Crick for years without her family and with Chase gone too. Chase's mother was away sometimes for days with her midwifery, and his father wasn't much for talk. She might have died if it hadn't been for her savior, her mother-in-law, Ida Blake.

"Now, Ann, my dear," the sturdy woman told her the first night Chase was gone to see about getting a ride downriver on a salt barge from Goose Crick. "Don't you look so woebegone. At your age, there's always a tomorrow, and there's more to this life than the love of a man." Mother Ida's strong arm hugged her trembling shoulders. "Time you started learning all about my medicinal yarbs, don't you think? They can cure a hurtin' body, jest like having a purpose in life can cure a hurtin' heart. And tonight, you jest ask Chase to take you on up Concord and show you the moonbow. Always talking about rainbows that might not exist, that boy, but the moonbow's real." And it was that same night—the last night Chase was home the first year—that the moonbow helped heal her homesick heart like one of Mother Ida's herbs.

* * *

Carrying a flaming pine knot, Chase took her hand and led her up the creek path and higher, past the ghostly tall white sycamores. Past the graveyard where his paternal grandparents and his Uncle Merit lay. That place always bothered Ann. What if one of her dear ones from home took sick and died and she never knew? Chase led her up into the crisp, clear black night lit by pinpoint stars winking at the swollen April moon.

As they approached the moon-glazed, water-washed cliff face below the highest peak of Concord, Chase wedged the pine knot between two rocks and pulled her on by moonlight.

"Oh, it gets steeper here and twisty too!" she said and clung even harder to his hand.

"You've got to have both a full moon and a breeze to see a moonbow, but you might get a bit wet watching," he said. She felt softer grass under her feet now. They had entered a rocky corridor with spring rills cascading down its face and gurgling through the boulders in the cleft at their feet. Under a windy ledge partly gripped by tangled grapevines, he turned her back to him and tugged her against his hard, angular body. His left arm around her tiny waist, he lifted the other to point upward. "There!" he announced, his voice triumphant. "Lean close in. See, when the wind blows spray out from the rock face. There!"

She saw and gasped. In the mist which hovered near the ageless cliff face, a snowy rainbow seemed to glow. The full moon between the peaks of Concord and Snow Knob across the valley looked like a large, luminous river pearl. And there, in the evanescent drops, hung a silver moonbow, a dangling white column of curved light dancing up and down the mist as Chase and Ann swayed or moved their heads.

"Is it real?" she whispered.

"Real for us. Real and beautiful, like you."

They stared together awestruck, but his hands soon moved up to cup her breasts, which always felt full to bursting at his merest touch. "I don't want the beauty to end, ever!" she cried as she stared mesmerized at the opalescent beauty captured in mist and air and felt his magic hands caressing her.

He laughed deep in his throat, that amused but possessive sound of a man who knows he holds sway over his woman. It sent her senses all ashiver. "It will never end, my darling. It won't!" he declared as he lifted her and carried her only as far as the flat little ledge and laid her down on the grass and his jacket. "Anytime we look for the beauty between us, we'll find it!"

His hands roved everywhere along her lean limbs before he bent closer over her. She feathered kisses on his jaw and nipped the sinews of his neck. She unbuttoned his shirt and tangled her fingers in his curly chest hair as he lifted her blue gown to make huge folds of it around her waist. Briskly now, she helped him remove her garments and then his; they shed everything. Now the nip of wind and fragile spray from the blowing rills refreshed her. They were both naked, the man and his wife, and were not ashamed. She skimmed her palms down his powerful back muscles, formed by days at the keelboat rudder post that would take him away from her. Desperate, she clutched at him as he pressed over her. Then he spread her legs to kneel between her moonstruck thighs.

Their mouths molded each to the other, familiar and yet ever new. She ruffled his dark, damp hair, which tickled her as he bent to love her. She responded, stroking him with sensitive fingertips, urging him on. When he could hold back from their union no longer, she thrust to meet him. Dazed by the impact of their bodies and their love, she stared at the top of Concord Peak swept by moon-gilt, racing clouds. Even if the earth and the heavens had tumbled on her then, she would have felt fulfilled.

He moved within her, and she matched him with interlocking circles. Faster, wilder until their intimate dance steps soared and swirled far above the peaks of passion.

They lingered, clinging to each other while their breathing slowed. Later, somberly, they dressed and shuffled hand in hand away and down the pebbled path.

The breeze had died, lessening the spray. The pine knot had guttered out. Ann tugged at him and turned to look back. At first, she thought the magic was gone with the moonbow. But the whole mountainside shone before a cloud clasped the moon and all went dim. Ann bit her lip to keep from sobbing at how quickly precious things passed. Silently she mourned the next loss looming in her life.

She did cry on Mother Ida's shoulder after Chase went chasing his own rainbows the next day. But she got busy learning the herbs. Until Chase returned, she would stay about the cabin tending herbs while Mother Ida ranged far and wide to see her people. Ann's respect and love for her mother-in-law grew apace with their friendship. And she forgave Chase for leaving her when she learned that he had given her a gift far greater than the memory of moonbow. By midsummer, she knew for certain she was breeding, and she knew which night she had conceived. With a child to love and protect and keep by her side after next December, surely she would not miss her family anymore!

Over the years, Chase stopped by the Mercer farm to tell Ann's folks about Rebecca's birth, and later Jeremy's. When Ann's mother heard their firstborn was named for her, she sent the Indian harvest cradle that had been Ann's and her sisters'. But Chase was never invited to stay at their farm, nor did they say they wanted to see Ann. So she gave up those hopes and tried to keep her mind closed in here at Shelter Valley. She hardened her heart toward the family life of her childhood, which seemed now as beautiful, yet as insubstantial as a moonbow.

Eventually Chase's parents passed away. Chase was gone much more, with his schemes to be a rich man. Becca was growing up and seemed to have some of her daddy's love of wandering. Now Ann desperately needed to keep Becca a child and by her side. She'd never let her daughter—she was certain sons were not the same—lose her family and leave the place of her birth to suffer as she did. No, not ever, even if a luring man like Becca's own daddy came into her life, who was so skilled at the pleasure that came before the pain—

"Mama, if Jeremy cut his foot with the hoe, do we use crushed knotgrass or dandelion leaves to stop the bleeding?" Becca's question pierced Ann's tangled musings. The past fled into the present. Becca, so calm, yet so concerned, stood on the threshold of the cabin door and on the threshold of womanhood. Ann jumped up so fast the Bible tumbled off her knees. The rocker squeaked behind her, bumping the backs of her legs before she hurried outside to help her children.

Chapter Three

The way Mama seemed so bothered by the Scotts was a puzzlement to Becca. Mostly folks liked the Scotts. The family of Angus and Corabell Scott was the only one in Shelter, Kentucky, Becca would call well-to-do. In a way, they kept the town going. Of the six permanent buildings, the Scotts owned three of them, their fine big stone house, the wooden gristmill, and Scott's Distillery and Brewery in one big stone and clapboard building. Most rural districts, like Shelter, had a distillery before they had a church. People came from as far upriver as Goose Crick for the gristmill and the distillery, bringing in news and some trade.

Across the small, grassy commons above the stone landing in the twist of the river, three other buildings balanced the town: the Stockton public house and tavern; the Wentworth house, where the rote school and Sunday meetings were held; and the Barney house—and Robert Barney worked for Mr. Scott. Then too the cow shed in the meadow and the small stone barn upriver were the Scotts'. Sometimes Becca thought Shelter might as well be renamed Scottsville, but the name Shelter stuck anyway.

On a hot day in mid-May, Mama couldn't postpone Becca's visiting the Scotts any longer. The Scotts had sent a message uphill with Claib Tucker that more lung syrups and teas were needful for Mrs. Scott. She was so poorly she was still confined to her bed. So, tight-mouthed, Mama prepared a sack laden with honeysuckle syrup and cowslip tea leaves and some basil to sprinkle in the sick woman's food.

"And after you drop these off, don't you stand just staring down the river either, Becca Blake. Your daddy won't be back for weeks yet, and you've got two more deliveries on the way back up here!"

"He'll be back soon, Mama. I can feel it in my bones!"

Mama looked away out the door and toward the sunny path to town and the river. "I hope so, my sweet. I swan, indeed I do!"

All the way down the mountain Becca wondered what it was about the Scotts that Mama, who mostly liked everyone, didn't like. The Scotts were prosperous and tight-knit and loving, as far as Becca heard. There was one son and five pretty sisters in the family and a farmhand who tended their cows and planted the few good fields around, which the Scotts owned down the river. Now, why would any of that make Mama so touchy?

The Scott son was named Adam and he came in the middle of his sisters in age. He was thirteen and was kept busy at his lessons and learning to help manage the distillery. He wasn't seen much. The girls seemed to be the pride of their father, who paraded them around town, some said, looking for proper beaus so he wouldn't have to ship them off to their uncle somewhere downriver to find someone suitable to marry. The girls were Mary and Aileen, pretty, red-haired twins of seventeen, Cora, fifteen and blonde; Desma and Letitia, one blonde, one red-haired, both ten but not twins. They were, though, born close together with the help of Gran Ida, who always praised the family to the skies; maybe that was what bothered Mama. Anyhow, people whispered that so many children so close together was what had worn out Mrs. Scott's health.

Since she had taken to her bed over a year ago, the family had been burdened, so Mrs. Scott's spinster sister had come last autumn all the way from Richmond in Virginia to care for them all. Becca hadn't seen this lady close up, but she had seen once that she had silvery hair and limped. Becca thought she must be frail and old. When Becca knocked on the back door in the big, stone-walled Scott garden with its sweetbrier rose tangles taller than a man, she expected the cook or one of the daughters. But today the spinster aunt stood there herself. Only her hair wasn't silver, but like palest spun sunbeams all swept up around a heart-shaped face. She was slender but for curvy hips and a full bosom. Short for a full-grown woman, she stood just a bit taller than Becca. Becca thought her sweet smile could no doubt light the heavens.

"How-do, my dear," the aunt said. "Mrs. Scott's cures from the apothecary on the mountain, I hope. Do come in."

Now Becca felt the sweat running down her back like a little mountain rill of its own. She shifted from one foot to the other. She almost felt as if Mama had come down off Concord to block her way in. She glanced over the woman's shoulder at the broad, busy hearth of the cheery, whitewashed stone kitchen. It was bigger than the whole Blake cabin and, even on this hot day, breathed out coolness. White curtains hung at shiny glass windows set ajar so Becca could see the sky and rosebushes reflected. The roses hadn't bloomed yet but with sweetbriers the leaves smelled as good as the flowers, mingling with the scent of fresh-baked, white-flour bread from inside.

It seemed to Becca this lady was a sweet-smelling flower garden in herself. She was not Becca's idea of a spinster aunt come to be a comfort to and drudge for a sick sister. She smelled like lilacs and was gowned in palest blue muslin with flower sprigs all over it and a lace collar and a dark blue bow around her small waist. She looked so cool on this hot day. Becca could barely see a resemblance between this lady and her stocky, brown-haired sister, Mrs. Scott, as she recalled her.

"I will need the cures explained and want to pay you. I'm Aunt Euphy Murray from Richmond. Don't hesitate a bit, just do come in." The woman touched her shoulder.

Becca stepped inside and Aunt Euphy closed the door behind her. Becca found her tongue. She gave her name and explained about the cures. Listening intently, Aunt Euphy perched straight-backed on a chair at the floury kneading table while the cook made pots clatter in the background. Becca soon learned that Miss Euphy Murray sat down whenever she could to rest her weak right leg. She sent the cook to fetch Becca a whole dollar for the herbs, then stood as Becca thanked her and made for the door.

"Oh, you know, Rebecca, I want to enlarge the cookery herb part of the garden this summer, and I wonder if you might advise me about some things," the melodious voice followed her. "With Mrs. Scott sick, things have gone to a bit of a tangle out there."

Becca turned back. "Oh, surely, pleased to. Much of what we grow up by Crawl Crick is for the pot as well as the cures."

"And I was wondering if you would be so kind as to take some of my China tea in exchange for this tea you've brought. I think it's good for the girls to have an opportunity to chat with those who live outside of town. Would you do me that honor, and I won't keep you long? I mean, to take afternoon tea with us if you don't think it's a bit too hot for that," she amended with another dazzling, coaxing smile when Becca didn't budge. "I've ordered a crate of lemons for lemonade from Cincinnati. I'm expecting it when the river calms, but it's tea for now. Do stay!"

Becca nodded before she realized she should not. Maybe because of Mama, maybe because she had other stops, maybe because she realized Aunt Euphy wore shoes and dressed fancy and she'd never done more than nod at the Scott girls before. All of them were so pretty. But how could she refuse Aunt Euphy anything? Besides, Becca was curious to see what a house with this fine a kitchen would look like.

Becca left her herb sack by the back door and, head high, followed Aunt Euphy's hesitant steps into the house. She soon came to see Aunt Euphy as a princess in a palace, as in one of Gran Ida's old songs. Some of the walls here had painted paper stuck right on them; carpets thick as meadow grass with woven designs hid a lot of the floors. Why, you'd think they were dirt instead of shiny oak! Becca curled her toes in a soft carpet as Aunt Euphy had her sit on a chair with green-as-grass velvet pillows built right into the seat and back. Velvet curtains that fell right to the floor guarded tall glass windows which flooded light into this room Aunt Euphy called a parlor. Cherry boughten furniture was everywhere, and over the shiny stone mantelpiece a looking glass big as a puddle had a carved wood frame of its own. When the five pretty, chattering Scott sisters were summoned by a bell at Aunt Euphy's elbow, Becca jumped to her feet for introductions.

They all were as polite as they could be and asked her about her rambles and different families here and there back in the hills. They stared at Becca, but she knew she was studying them too as if they had words written right across their faces. She noticed that when they started to murmur among themselves, Aunt Euphy reeled them back in with just a word or two. It was obvious to her they respected their smiling aunt, and Becca could see why.

"I'd love to be able to ramble up the valley," Aunt Euphy said with a sigh as she passed around a plate of nut bread pieces spread thick with butter and strawberry jam. Becca wished she could take some of this back home, but she took just one piece, like the others. She watched Aunt Euphy lift the lid of a pretty box of deep reddish wood with pearly carvings of butterflies and flowers set right in it. "But trage-dies of life do happen and we must learn to carry on, right, girls?" Aunt Euphy measured out spoonfuls of tea into a china kettle and added boiled water. She poured the steeped tea into small cups with handles. The cups looked thin as ice with light seeping through them and were painted with a gold rim. She dropped in a square of sugar white as snow and stirred each cup before she passed it around. No maple sugar lumps to be bit off a string here. Becca thought Aunt Euphy's hands were as graceful as floating leaves.

Becca's cup felt delicate and warm to her touch. She savored the sensation because it was so cool and still in the parlor, even with the girls gathered close together talking and the sun pouring in.

"You see, Rebecca," Aunt Euphy was saying, "I thought I had my life all planned once, and then I was kicked by a carriage horse. It broke my leg, which didn't set well. And so I can never run about or dance again and walking's bad enough. But I found my calling in caring for my parents until they departed this life. Now I'm here to tend my dear sister Corabell, but I have lots of loving help here from my nieces and dear Adam too."

Their talk buzzed just like the horsefly that got in. Letitia asked permission to swat it, and Becca was surprised to see they had a fancy fringed swatter just to kill insects. Becca added to the conversation when she could, explaining to them about other herbs Mama used to cure lung troubles and telling them she'd never tasted lemonade, but she knew crushed lemon balm in a glass of cool crick water was real good. When Desma got what Becca called the *hickets* and Aunt Euphy called the *hick-ups*, Becca told them to have her eat some dill seed and it worked. Becca was grateful no one seemed to mind her dirty, bare feet, which she kept tucked under the skirt of her worn blue gown. In Aunt Euphy's shining presence, she almost felt at home.

"Now, girls, up to kiss your mother before her afternoon nap and then back to school!" Aunt Euphy bustled them off. Each bade good-bye to Becca, who kept every one of their names straight. Full to bursting with all she had seen, she watched them troop up to an entire boarded-up second floor on solid wooden stairs all laid with bright blue carpet. And despite the warm day, every last Scott daughter had shoes on with heels that were neither dirty nor worn down.

"You never come to Mrs. Wentworth's school here, I believe," Aunt Euphy observed as she slowly escorted Becca through the hall that led back to the kitchen.

"No, ma'am. Mama teaches my brother Jeremy and me at home."

"And she never comes down to Shelter, I believe I heard."

"She keeps close to home."

"Well, whatever her reasons, you tell her I do too, so I regret I cannot visit her to see her herb gardens. But I do not like it one bit and envy you your freedom to walk about! I should like to see your Crawl Crick and this entire valley. Thank you for telling me a bit about both today."

She laid a light hand on Becca's shoulder again. Becca felt her admiration and affection shoot right up that graceful arm from her to this lovely woman. She had to make Mama understand how special this was. She had to make Mama realize the Scotts were good, not bad.

"You know," Becca blurted before she even planned to say it, "my grandmother got the gout real bad it pained her to walk, but she wanted to go out far and wide. She rode her mule Harlan and it did real well. 'Course, Harlan upped and died about when she did, as if he wanted to go with her on her heavenly journey, but—"

"A mule! Oh, dear, whatever would Angus Scott say about that little gift?" Aunt Euphy mused more to herself than Becca. Her face flushed warm for the first time today. When she saw Becca staring, she changed the subject. "Now, you remember that I can use at least several kegs of rosewater when your mama makes it next month," Euphy said as Becca picked up her sack. "Nothing sweeter than bed linens washed in rosewater and dried on those bushes out back in the breeze!"

They shared a smile as Becca opened the door. But it was pushed in so fast, she stepped backward into Aunt Euphy.

Tall and broad-chested, red-haired and red-faced, there stood the bearded Mr. Angus Scott, out of breath.

"For the love of heaven, Euphemia, have you seen the lad?"

"Adam?"

"Of course Adam! We're about to add yeast to the beer vat, and I told him he was to help!"

"I'm sure he's not in the house, Angus. If I'd thought he was, I'd have had him to tea."

"The lad does not need to take afternoon tea with his sisters! Wait until I lay hands on him!"

Becca sidled out behind the two adults, but not before she realized how easily Aunt Euphy's calm, sweet demeanor had helped soften Mr. Scott's wrath. Though his words were still angry, his face showed he was willing to stop looking for his son if he could look at Aunt Euphy instead.

Becca hurried around the tall green hedges of rosebushes and started toward the back stone gate. Two more stops before she could head home, and that tea-taking had set her back. She quickened her pace around the next turn and almost tripped over a boy's bent back. Big-shouldered with red-gold hair, he was obviously the missing Adam Scott. She froze inches from him. If he heard her, he did not look up. She thought at first he was hiding from his father, but he was dangling carrots down a molehole between his spread knees.

"Excuse me, but your father's looking for you."

He shot a narrowed, blue-eyed look up over his shoulder at her. "Sh!"

"And he's angry."

"As usual," he responded so quietly she almost didn't catch the words.

"Whatever are you doing?"

"Trying to save moles," he whispered as she leaned down to hear. "Father told our hired hand to stick spades down into their tunnels to trap them and then slice them to pieces." He gave the carrots a disgusted shake and raised his voice.

"But you might know they're stupid as well as blind. It's hard to help some poor creatures if they won't let you."

"You want them to stay out of the garden so they won't be killed?"

"Of course. You're Rebecca, the Blake girl, aren't you?" He shook soil off the carrots while she nodded. "The wounded rabbits get these then if the moles won't come up so I can trap them and put them elsewhere to save their furry little hides."

He rose to his full height. He was very tall for a boy just two years older than she. It had been years since she'd seen him close up. His face was broad and serious with deep-set, clear blue eyes edged with thick gold lashes. He had little hollows under his cheekbones and a firm, narrow mouth. His big hands and feet promised much more growth.

"Castor beans," she told him.

"What?"

"Castor bean plants will make moles move their tunnels away. Besides, your aunt says she likes to sit in the garden among the roses and you don't want her twisting an ankle in all this burrowing."

He looked at her differently now, as if she were more than just a stranger. "You're smarter than my sisters," he said.

"But I've just met them, and they're lovely."

"Smarter," he repeated and looked her over head to feet. He seemed to be very interested in her tangled hair and bare toes. "Would you like to see my animals?" he asked. "I have to feed the rabbits before my father finds me."

The thought of being there when that happened, with Mr. Scott knowing that Becca had heard he was searching for Adam, was not a happy possibility, but she agreed. Adam led her out to the back stone wall. He put one hand to it and cleared it in a sideways leap. She let him help her over, though she needed no boost. She kept up easily with his long, booted strides around a bramble thicket and into the deep woods behind his house. The shade thickened here, and it was cooler.

"Why keep them way out here?" she asked.

"Father doesn't believe in my tending wounded animals. He just believes in my learning brewing and distilling day and night."

He showed her seven slatted cages, each holding an animal with a broken bone or a ragged wound. She got down on her knees too and stroked a brown rabbit's petal-soft head through the slats as she fed him a carrot. "You've got the gift," she told Adam, her voice awed.

His head jerked around, a lock of gold-red hair springing loose on his broad forehead. Their eyes met in splotched sunlight filtering through shifting leaves overhead. "The gift?"

"Of healing. My Gran Ida had it too."

He nodded. "The midwife. It must be something wonderful to see a baby born. I've seen rabbits born and eggs hatch."

"That's special too. I saw a robin just last week throw a sky-blue eggshell out of a nest. That's the sign another bird is born for the Shelter Valley skies!"

Adam stared her full in the face. They each had a half-nibbled carrot in their hands. Their eyes held. It was the oddest feeling for Becca, kneeling there next to him. It was not just that she'd found a kindly person to admire, like Aunt Euphy, or a surprising new friend, like Jemima Tucker, or someone with a special touch, like the Widow Lang. This was something new, something strange. They stayed like that, three feet apart, silent while the breeze brushed their hair and rattled leaves overhead. Finally he spoke.

"If you have castor beans on the mountain, I'd like to buy some."

"We planted them. They'll be up real soon. I'll get you some to plant then."

He nodded. He pushed his carrot, then hers into the rabbit cages. "Last week, Claib Tucker told me I was plumb crazy to try to save a buckshot-wounded squirrel," Adam said.

"But my father's worse. Don't tell anyone where these cages are hidden."

"Oh, I wouldn't. And after Mama and I make rosewater and I bring some down to your aunt, I'll bring you some too. It heals cuts and scratches, so it might help your animals. Besides, it's good you keep them out here where the rain can't be so bad and they won't get hot in these cages."

Adam smiled, revealing big, even teeth. "I'll show you where I go when it's hot. Have you seen the icehouse?"

"The big one by the distillery?"

"No, the one for our house. The other one's too busy. Come on, I'll show you on our way back."

She followed him again, uncaring that time was fleeing, over the wall and to the far corner of the garden. "Mother used to oversee the garden before she took to her bed," he said with a shake of his head that showed his deep regret. Becca saw that he stooped low to walk even amid tall tangles of roses, and he kept his voice low. "Maybe Aunt Euphy will fix it all, like she has my father's temper. Honest," he told her with a slight smile and shrug when he saw her eyes widen, "it used to be worse before she came. In here."

He went down two stone steps into a hut built half underground. He tugged open a thick wooden door. A refreshing blast of coolness, like Becca's breeze up in her refuge, reached out and drew them in. The humped room was windowless; straw and sawdust covered a stone floor cluttered with crocks and wooden pails of milk and buttermilk and trays of cheese. "I usually close the door and enjoy the dark," he told her, "but I won't today. The walls are double and packed with sawdust too. Those lumps lining the wall under that straw are blocks of ice from the river cut last January. Doesn't it feel good in here?"

It did. Too good for words at first. She nodded her agreement. He closed the door partway and cut off two hunks of mellow-flavored cheese with his jackknife.

"This place reminds me of what I call my ice palace up on the mountain," she told him, staring, suddenly shy, at the shiny walls of slowly melting ice. "It's cool up there and when it's cold, the cliff face glazes over where it leads to my secret place."

She stopped, astounded she had told him, an outsider, such a secret. He looked at her so solemnly for a moment she was certain he would tell her she was silly or stupid or just plain lying. But he didn't.

"It sounds wonderful," he said. "A great place to hide my animals if—"

The door behind them banged open, flooding the dim, cool room with light and heat. "Adam!" Mr. Scott roared. "Out! I've spent a good half hour looking for you when the beer is ready! Both of you, get out! Curse it, time you learned what it means to be heir to all this, Adam! I swear, I'll take a whip to you again!"

Becca leaped out behind Adam as his father yanked him out. There was no whip, but Mr. Scott had a walking stick in his hand which he swung at Adam, smacking his shoulder as the boy jumped back into the rose thorns to escape. Round-eyed, Becca backed away, but she found her voice.

"Mr. Scott, he was just showing me the icehouse," she said, her voice trembling. "It's a real nice one, and I just—"

Suddenly Aunt Euphy appeared, red-faced and out of breath, moving as fast as she could with that dragging leg. "Angus, please, not here, not now. You'll wake Corabell in her room up there with all this noise, as I opened her window. We don't want her to think you and Adam aren't getting on, do we?"

Becca stared wide-eyed as the big man lowered the stick. He hauled Adam out of his prickly refuge in the roses and shoved him past his aunt. "Get over to that distillery right now, lad!" Adam went, not daring to look at Becca or his father, but he shot a quick glance at Aunt Euphy, who nodded.

"You go too now, Rebecca, and don't forget my rosewater in a few weeks," Aunt Euphy told Becca and patted her shoulder. Becca fled. She wouldn't forget any of today. Not ever.

In the real heat of mid-July, Becca reveled in working with herb bed roses. Up on the mountain, even in this sun-swept summer weather, Mama's apothecary rosebushes bloomed later than the wild American ones at Widow Lang's or the Scotts' English sweetbriers in the valley. But Mama's were worth waiting for. Their heady fragrance kissed the clear air with their one big blooming frolic of the year.

Large, dark, ruby-red roses with bright gold centers nodded their heavy heads on every stem, especially where Becca had pruned them the day Jeremy cut his foot with the hoe. The flowers both in bud and in bloom sprawled to the ground and burst anew from tight clumps of canes, as if each bush itself were a big, brazen flower.

This entire week, all three of them worked sunrise to sunset outside on the brow of hill overlooking the valley. They had built a tripod of limbs over a fire for the hanging kettle. Jeremy had gathered wood for days. Becca plucked basket after basket of blooms when the dew dried off; she never tired of this task. She discarded the tiny white bitter part of each petal and then floated the red satin ovals in half kegs of rainwater. These sat in the sun for several hours. Then they boiled the water and skimmed off the oily film and strained out the petals. The cooled water was rich with the sweet smell not of just roses, but of all the flowers of the world, wrapped in just one whiff.

"Mmm!" Becca murmured again as she stirred the latest batch and inhaled deeply. Meanwhile, sometimes while the three of them sang songs as loudly as they could, Mama carefully spooned the cooling liquid into the dark green bottles Jeremy cut corncob stoppers for. After Mama stuck these in the bottle necks, he carried them to the root cellar for safe storage. It was their biggest crop of herbs to be gathered at one time and sold for medicine, for fragrance, and, rarely, for food flavoring. In a way, it was a family celebration.

"I could swim in this rosewater, Mama!" Becca told her. Today, Mama's happy smile matched hers. Working her herbs to help people and profit her family, Mama was the happiest Becca had seen her in days. Now and then, they even stopped to dance a few cotillion steps while Jeremy clapped time, but he still refused to let them teach him how to dance.

"Daddy will learn me the men's part when he gets here," the boy said, his little face so serious. "Besides, he wouldn't want me making rosewater for ladies' sheets!"

"You know you like working with anything where you can use your precious knife," Becca teased him.

"It's passable, but I'd rather be carving my animals. Becca, I'm hankering to see Adam Scott's animals you told me about. Did he name them all like Adam in the Bible did?"

Becca knew she was caught when Mama squinted at her through the plume of fragrant kettle steam. Not only had Mama not wanted to hear about the Scott house and how close the sisters were to each other and their mother, and how Mr. Scott got mad and yelled, but she had obviously not wanted Becca telling any of it to Jeremy.

"Mama," Becca began the next time the boy carted some bottles to the root cellar, "do you think the Scotts are a bad influence on me? Really, all they have down there doesn't make me hanker for their house or even a sister."

"It's not really that, Becca," Mama began, and then Becca saw her freeze with her skimming spoon dangling in the air.

"Mama?"

"Sh! Didn't you hear that?"

Mama threw her spoon down on the grass and turned away to wipe her hands on her big stained apron. Then she started untying it and running for the path. She dropped her apron behind her and smoothed her hair as she ran, skidding on the gravel. And then Becca knew before she too heard the distant shout.

"Jeremy!" she screamed as she broke into a run behind Mama. "Daddy's home!"

Becca flew like the wind, but she stopped and let Mama run to Daddy's open arms first. Tears flooded Becca's eyes, making two Daddys whirling Mama around and around with her feet off the ground. Then Becca was in his strong embrace and Jeremy thudded into them and held hard to Daddy's waist. All four of them stood there like that, laughing, sobbing. Daddy looked so handsome, so fine with his face all sun-browned and his dark hair blown but curly too. He had little white birds' feet where he had squinted into the sun and wind on the river. It seemed everyone and everything wonderful came to them when Daddy was home.

"In such good keelboating weather, I never imagined," Mama choked out, her cheeks as shiny with tears as her eyes. "Never imagined you'd be back until snow fell."

"Came home to tell you all how good things have been!" Daddy said, as if they needed to be cheered up now. "Wait 'til you hear how we're goin' to be rich—rich as the Scotts, and we'll have a frolic up here to beat all!" he promised with a grand sweep of his hand.

Becca's eyes met Mama's wary gaze, but Mama looked back at Daddy quickly. "I've got a couple big sacks of gifts for you all down below," Daddy told them and walked them up the path toward the cabin, his arms hard around Mama's and Becca's shoulders while Jeremy clung to his leather vest. "Gonna own my own keelboat with just one other man. Finally got me a partner to make all our dreams come true, Ann."

Right in front of Becca and Jeremy, he pulled Mama toward him and gave her a long kiss with his big hand clutched in her copper hair. Becca beamed and Jeremy's face nearly cracked from his smile.

"A frolic up here?" Becca managed when Mama clung to Daddy's shirt open in a V to show his chest hair and just laid her head there a minute.

"He's just talking, Becca," Mama put in and lifted her head. "No floor big enough for dancing up here."

"We'll have it outside on the grass and ask everyone!" Daddy insisted. "I've got plenty of money for beer from the distillery and folks'll bring the food."

Mama looked dazed. She still held so hard to Daddy that their progress was slow up to where she'd thrown her apron down. Becca bent to retrieve it for her. Mama seemed to want to say something, but couldn't get it out.

"You'll have to teach Jeremy to dance first, Daddy," Becca said, her heart full to bursting with his arrival and his news. "He just had to wait to learn until you came home."

"That's my boy!" Daddy shouted and swept the laughing child up to ride on his shoulders just the way Becca used to do before she got too big. "We'll have fun now, I guess!"

Mama's happy face went still and pale. Becca bit her bottom lip. She knew they were both thinking about the long days Daddy had been away and would go off again.

"But Daddy," Jeremy said from his bouncing perch as if to speak for them all, "jest don't go leaving us again after the frolic and then it *will* be fun!"

Chapter Four

Every moment seemed like a frolic when Daddy was home. Mama laughed and sang and would go anywhere with Daddy. The whole family took picnics up in the hills. He'd brought them wondrous gifts from distant places, like a looking glass from Louisville, a little Indian drum from Memphis, lace collars from New Orleans, and garden seeds bought from a place upriver called Shakertown.

"Some real interesting folks live there who don't believe in marriage or man-woman loving neither," Becca, from her spot in the sleeping loft, overheard him tell Mama one night. "Never seen it, but they do dancing in their holy meetings real wild to shake out all their sins. Not sure what sins there'd be with no fornication, no gambling and all. They take in orphans and treat them like they was their own. They have a huge farm they all work together, and do they know how to put hearty food on a table!"

"Meaning I don't, Chase Blake?" Mama shot back at him, but she giggled.

"Meaning it's a good place for wandering keelboaters to lay by for vittles. Right now, I'm int'rested in all the things *you* dish up for me."

"I swan, Chase, blow out the candle if you're going to start that right now after all that this morning!"

Becca remembered Mama and Daddy had gone for a walk up the crick this morning. They took the longest time and then Mama's dress was all grass-stained on its back as well as its skirt as if she'd been doing more than just lying back looking up at the clouds.

"Mmm," she heard Daddy say, his voice muffled. "We gotta have our own little frolics leading up to that one next week, so—"

Someone snuffed out the wan candle below. The sleeping loft went blacker than black. Mama giggled again. Becca lay there tensely, wondering about man-woman loving. It must be special and exciting with talking and funning and teasing first. Not at all like the animals who seemed to nuzzle a bit, then get it over fast as greased lightning and walk away. It stood to reason that since Adam in the Bible named all the animals, man was far above the animals in loving too.

She stretched and yawned and decided to wear her new blue hair bow from Daddy for the frolic on Friday night. Daddy and Jeremy had been all over the Shelter area asking people to come up for sulfuring apples and a frolic after. The work bee had been Mama's idea. Not right, she said, to just celebrate until some real work was done. Daddy's keelboat plans, which Mama called his rainbow, hadn't taken any work but talking yet. Meanwhile Mama had kept Becca from going here and there with Daddy to ask folks to come. She said she needed Becca at home, but Jeremy later told Becca that Mama did not want Daddy introducing Becca to wandering keelboaters he knew who might put in to Shelter.

Becca flopped over and smiled smugly. She recalled how Mama had got her comeuppance for keeping her at home. Becca would leastways have warned Daddy how Mama felt about the Scotts if she'd gone down to Shelter with him instead of Jeremy. She could still see Mama's face set hard as baked bread crust when Jeremy burst into the cabin just ahead of Daddy, shouting, "Guess what, Mama! Everyone's coming to the frolic, even the Scotts!"

Becca had not seen Adam Scott since that day nearly two months ago when he'd showed her his animals and the icehouse, but she thought about him often. She thought about Aunt Euphy too, the five sisters, and poor Mrs. Scott in her sickbed upstairs hearing bird songs outside and seeing sun sweep by her windows just the way her family came in to see her but then were gone. She wondered how someone with Mr. Scott's temper got along with a sick wife all these years when Claib Tucker went so plumb crazy without a woman. Was it the same thing? Was the way Claib went to lengths to get a new woman the same thing spoiling Mr. Scott's temper?

Becca felt bad that Adam and his father didn't get along. She was glad she got on fine with hers. But it bothered her that the more she tried to be independent to help Mama, the more upset Mama got. More than anything, Becca wanted to be close to Mama, even to be her best friend, at least when Daddy wasn't here. She wondered how long Daddy would stay this time to make the sun shine in Mama's shadowy eyes. Lying in the sleeping loft, staring up into the darkness wafting out its sweet herb and rose petal smells, Becca wondered oh so many things.

The frolic was full of people and food. Becca counted more than forty far-flung neighbors, and Jeremy added up twenty different kinds of victuals. From Shelter, the Barneys and the Wentworths came early. Pru Johns, all smiles for once, and her Ephraim, who no doubt came for the drinking, brought their brood, wide-eyed and well-behaved, at least at first. The Tuckers—Jemima with her two-months', seventh child still suckling, and Claib, who seemed to be speaking to his simpleton boy Ralston for once—came early and planned to stay until the next day with all their children sleeping out under the stars. Mama kept telling Daddy to keep Claib away from gawking at the Scott girls if they came. Becca saw Claib eyeing Mr. Barney's maiden aunt, even though it didn't look to Becca as if Claib had grown one more hair on his head. She strained her eyes watching and listening down the path for the Scotts as the sulfuring began. If Aunt Euphy had to walk all the way, she worried, they'd never get here.

Though they weren't dancing yet, Sam Jenks played a gourd fiddle he'd strung with horsehair. Maybe, Daddy said, Sam's music would scare the skeeters away. A keelboater friend of Daddy's played the Irish bagpipes, which he pumped under his arm like a little bellows. Everyone pitched in to slice sacks of apples from the valley and pack them in earthen crocks smoked with sulfur. This preserved the apples for months, and when they were plumped up with water to make a cobbler or pie, they were almost as good as fresh, and without the eggy smell. But now the children ran about shrieking and holding their noses and pretending to fall down dead as their mothers saturated the apples with fumes from sulfur candles. The men found excuses to wander off and start in on some of the Blue Ruin whiskey Daddy had bought from Scott's Distillery. Still Becca did not spot the Scotts, and her excitement about seeing Adam and the others again began to waver—until the women called everyone to eat.

The men went first, of course. But when Becca passed down the plank table with Jeremy on one side of her and Jemima Tucker and her newborn on the other, there was plenty left. Claib Tucker had brought rabbit, squirrel, and possum, which Mama had cooked up in the spicy stew called burgoo. There was syrup in gourds for hoecake, beaten biscuits, and scrapple, and seven different apple dishes. Becca had provided honey and elderberries for the biscuits. And it was at the very moment when she first savored the sweet honey-berry taste that she looked up and saw the Scotts. Aunt Euphy was riding on a mule while Mr. Scott walked on one side and Adam on the other as if she'd topple off.

Becca ran to greet them and stood beside her parents. Everyone kept quiet for a spell, but the noise and activity were soon back to normal. Becca breathed more easily when Mama

61

was civil and smiling to the Scotts. But Becca knew she had not imagined the whole thing. She saw that squinty, frowning look back in Mama's eyes when the Scott sisters all sat close together on blankets to chatter and eat. From where she sat on a blanket by Mr. Scott, Aunt Euphy waved a lace-edged handkerchief at Becca and at the mosquitoes. Adam nodded and lifted one big hand before leaning against a sycamore along the creek to watch the goings on while he cleaned his heaped plate. Earlier today the Scotts had sent their hired hand up with their own plates, spoons, and blankets as well as kegs of beer and ale, which Ephraim Johns quickly helped unplug. Soon the real frolic began.

Pru Johns's oldest boy added his harmonica to the fiddle and the pipes. The late-afternoon breeze swelled with tunes as rippling as a mountain rill. Daddy himself called the dancing, beginning with "All hands, now circle left!" as adults and children big enough to know the steps scrambled to make cotillion squares. Becca was partnered by the oldest Johns boy, Alfy, but kept wishing it were Adam, who was just watching. As soon as she could, she decided, she'd free herself to go over and ask what Aunt Euphy thought of the rosewater, which Daddy and Jeremy had delivered with the castor bean plants when they invited the Scotts to the frolic.

When everyone took a rest to drink and talk, Becca could hear Daddy singing that old keelboater song, "Hail Columbia, happy land. If I ain't ruined, I'll be damned!" to the tune of "Yankee Doodle." She overheard Claib Tucker telling Clemmet, the Scotts' hired hand, "I'd never really court that McMillan gal down the next valley, Clemmie. Sure, she'll get in bed with you faster'n the river at spring gusher time, but who knows who's had her! 'Course if I was a half-horse, half-alligator keelboatman like my old friend Chase over there, she'd be achasin' me!" Both men laughed loudly, but Becca didn't let on she heard. She took a pewter cup of cool lemon balm tea over to Aunt Euphy. Adam, sitting beside his father and aunt now, rose to his feet, so polite that Becca blushed.

Aunt Euphy thanked her and tried the tea. "You are absolutely right, my dear," the smiling woman told her. "Just as good as lemonade. My crate of lemons came and you must come down and try that too."

"With Daddy home and all, we're pretty busy up here," Becca said when she saw the stern stare Mr. Scott shot both her way and Adam's.

But that look hardly cowed Adam. When the bouncing tune of "Skip to My Lou" began, he said, "Guess I'll try my hand—or big feet—at that, Aunt Euphy."

"Yes, you just run along and have fun!" she told him before Mr. Scott could protest.

"Well, come on then," Adam told the wide-eyed Becca. The breeze made her blue bow bob in her chestnut curls and lifted her new lace collar around the neck of her only good gown. He tugged her hand. "Let's go!"

For the next few dances, Becca felt she flew instead of skipped. Adam smiled each time he stepped wrong, but he soon caught on. Mama and Daddy were partnering each other, and Mama said to Daddy as they swept by under the arch of arms, "Remember that first night we danced—" Mama obviously wasn't listening to the words they all sang so loudly, Becca thought: "Gone again, what shall I do? Gone again, what shall I do? Gone again, what shall I do? Skip to my Lou, my dar-lin'." No, today Mama wasn't thinking about Daddy pulling up stakes again. Everything was wonderful today.

Through "Pop Goes the Weasel" and "Way Down in the Paw-Paw Patch," Becca was twirled and promenaded by Adam Scott. Other folks went by in great interlocking rings of arms, but she hardly saw them. Not that Adam was a beau, but this was so special a moment, a magic time. She wanted to remember it always. Friends here, Daddy home, Mama laughing, Jeremy trying a step or two, Adam so close. Now and again he danced with one of his suddenly shy sisters. Over on the blanket as the sun slipped behind the cross-river hills, Aunt Euphy clapped her hands and nodded to the music. Even Mr. Scott seemed to unbend a bit. If only Widow Lang were here to see all this and maybe watch her dear Ernestine and Albertine turn a toe, Becca thought with a laugh. She flushed, radiant, as Adam returned to take her hand for another dance.

As darkness descended, Daddy lit pine torches. The night breeze blew the mosquitoes away, but lightning bugs blinked their bright lights. People fed themselves again, then danced some more. And when Becca was done toting water from the creek to make more cold lemon balm tea, she saw in the wavering firelight that Adam stood by Aunt Euphy and Mr. Scott had disappeared. Becca watched as Adam helped Aunt Euphy to her feet. He was holding her hand and dancing around her while she just laughed and swayed a bit. Several of the Scott girls were joining the dance around their aunt, so Becca went over too.

"See, Rebecca, I'm dancing after all!" Aunt Euphy cried. "And my mule Nell you put me up to will give me the freedom of the valley!"

The Scott children got more boisterous, as though, Becca thought, some spring had snapped to turn them loose. Desma and Letitia grasped wrists and leaned back to swing themselves around, around. Adam laughed and picked Aunt Euphy up to whirl her too. Virginia reel music swirled and swelled.

"I'm dancing. I'm dancing!" Aunt Euphy shrilled as her upswept hair swung loose in a big blonde tail.

Becca laughed with sheer joy. She was so happy that Aunt Euphy was happy! She was part of these people, even the Scotts, part of this wonderful place where she lived and loved and—

"Adam, damn you! Are you demented?" Mr. Scott's shout sliced through the music. Desma and Letitia flopped to the grass, then scrambled up, silent. Becca's hands flew to her mouth. Adam had tried to stop spinning too abruptly and had toppled backward with Aunt Euphy sitting down hard across his knees. Both Becca and Mr. Scott lunged for Aunt Euphy to break her fall. With Mr. Scott's big hands on the woman's waist and shoulder, Becca stepped back. The music, the dancing went on amid the torches across the way, but here it felt so dark.

"I told you such tomfoolery up here was a mistake, Euphemia!" Mr. Scott muttered. He helped her up. "Too much change too fast! All of you children, get away. Adam, I shall deal with you later!"

Becca had no doubt Aunt Euphy would defend Adam later, but right now she looked dizzy. "Really, Angus, I'm fine. It was quite the most fun I've had in—"

"You look like some bedraggled, mountain-bred wild thing!" Mr. Scott clipped out. Adam stood and folded his arms across his chest as his father led his aunt away. It was then that Mr. Scott's words sank in and Becca darted off. Adam ran after her and pulled her around.

"He didn't mean you," Adam told her. "He's referring to my animals."

"It's all right."

"It isn't. We were all having fun. He ruined it as usual."

"He's just trying to see she didn't get hurt."

"He's been ranting about her mule. He'll probably forbid her to have that just like he tries to keep me from my animals."

"He didn't find them?"

"No." His eyes lifted over the top of Becca's head. It seemed to her in that moment that torchlight flared in each blue eye as if smothered fires raged within him. Then he added, "Looks like your mother's sent Aunt Euphy inside your cabin to lie down a bit. I still say it was good for her, and she wasn't hurt—not until *he* came along." His voice had gone so bitter, Becca feared for him. "Sorry, because it's a real nice frolic," Adam went on. "At least he let us come, whether it was for his precious business reasons or not."

"I see him over there kind of sulking, Adam. Maybe you should tell him you were all just funning."

"Funning isn't in his heart. My thanks for all the dancing,

Rebecca, and I think you and your mother do it the best of anyone here. You've got a real nice brother too who loves animals as much as we do, you and me." He nodded to her and stalked back to his original place by the sycamores along the creek, now glittery with lightning bugs.

Becca ran his words through her mind over and over. He liked her dancing. He liked her brother and the frolic. We share the love of animals, you and me, he had said. She smiled in the gentle darkness as she skirted two squares of dancers. The best of anyone here . . . you and me . . .

She watched Mama and Daddy dance together as if they'd been born to it. Mama so light on her feet; Daddy laughing and practically sweethearting her with everyone watching. Even with what had just happened, Becca had never been so content, so much a part of these dear people and this black satin sky that arched over them to merge the mountains and the valley and the river.

And then she remembered Aunt Euphy and went to take her some more lemon balm tea. The cabin where she had gone for a rest was pitch black; she was probably in Mama's rocker or even on the big bed. But Becca knew each step by feel against her bare feet. She stepped through the door and took two steps right until she felt the puncheon floor. She was glad now she had scrubbed it smooth with creek gravel to prepare for this special night. Her eyes became accustomed to the faint gray light that barely flitted in the cabin doors from the torches outside.

She opened her mouth to call to Aunt Euphy, who must be standing in the western door. But there, outlined against it, she could make out two people, not just one. One was short with tumbled hair, Aunt Euphy, and one was—

Becca froze. The cup trembled in her hand. The world seemed silent. "Euphemia, I can't stand not touching you anymore! And you will do as I say. That mule, this defiance! I'll not have it!"

"And you'll not have me, Angus!" Though whispered, Aunt Euphy's tones carried to Becca. "With Corabell lying there like that and the children in the house, we cannot just—''

The two forms, blacker than the hill behind them, merged into one. Becca stood transfixed. Cool water slopped down her wrist as she began to shake. If she ran, they'd see her. If she stayed, perhaps not.

She shuffled slowly farther in. She expected Aunt Euphy to shove the big man away, but she did not. Instead, she clung to his shirtfront, she looped her arms up around his big neck. They crushed hard together. Their profiles blurred as their lips met. Then their heads merged into one shadow; they were not kissing now, just holding, holding and breathing very hard. And then it happened.

Becca moved again and bumped the seat of Mama's rocker. It squeaked as it moved.

Mr. Scott leaned Aunt Euphy back against the wall. "Who is it?" he demanded. His black form grew as he came forward.

"Becca Blake, sir. I just stepped in to get—to get—"

"Get out, damn you, you meddling girl!"

"Angus, it's her cabin," came the strangled cry from behind him.

"She's nothing but trouble. Didn't you see Adam earlier—"

The horrid words pursued her.

Becca fled. She wanted to say first that she would tell no one, but she did not. She had tried to convince Mama that the Scotts were good. She had cared for Aunt Euphy so. Her heart thudded in her chest; she felt strangled. She thought of Mr. Scott chasing her with his walking stick, chasing her clear into the thorny roses of Mama's herb bed until they tore her apart.

She started up the path to her refuge, but turned back. She huddled behind a sycamore with its arms uplifted, its wooden feet curled into the creekbed. She pressed against the tree, her legs trembling and her breath coming ragged. Leaves overhead rattled as if she shook the whole tree. She sobbed and sobbed.

Devastation racked her. Somehow she had ruined everything. Could Mama have sensed something was wrong at the Scotts' house? Had she tried to warn Becca away, but thought she was too young to understand? Yet it had seemed as if Aunt Euphy and Mr. Scott were touching for the first time that way. She shivered with fears that were worse for being unnamed. It was as if her past, present, and future, so bright just this evening, lay dimmed and dirtied now. She felt yanked apart and away as the creek plunged down into darkness. She sank to the ground and put her feet in the water, clasping the trunk of the tree as if it were her only friend. She stared through shimmering tears into the black ripples and then back at the cabin. Somehow, music still played and people still laughed, but she felt alone as tears rolled down her face and fell on her new collar.

"Becca?"

She swiped at her cheeks. Mama's voice.

"Becca, you out here?"

Mama found her before she answered. Mama knelt beside her and turned her face up and squinted at her in the dark.

"Is this because Mr. Scott made Adam leave without the boy saying good-bye to you?"

Becca yearned to tell Mama the truth, to tell her all she'd seen. But for Aunt Euphy—Adam too and the girls—she just nodded. But what Mama said was enough to make her cry all over again.

"My dear, sweet girl, some families are like that—so tight-knit. They can hurt each other—outsiders too—real easy."

"That's why you didn't take to them?" Becca managed, her voice quivery.

"A great part of it."

Becca slumped into Mama's embrace and hugged her in return. Even more than being friends with the Scotts, she wanted to be a friend to Mama. Now they were sharing, weren't they? Now maybe that shadow of darkness that went deeper than just Daddy's wandering would leave Mama alone. She hugged Mama hard.

"Let's go on back now, sweet," Mama coaxed. "We got ourselves responsibilities tonight so all our guests have fun. Come on now."

"Mama, how did you know I needed you? Did you see me run off?"

"No, I was dancing with your Daddy. I just looked up to see you gone when the Scotts left and knew you needed me."

That helped Becca feel better. That was one thing friends did for sure, needed each other and then came running. They walked arm in arm back to the torchlit frolic. Mama's words of comfort were swimming in her head, but she kept hearing Adam's earlier words, the ones warning about his father: "Funning isn't in his heart." This night, with precious joy all mingled with the pain, she wasn't sure it was in hers anymore either.

The Blakes slept outside that night so Jemima and her brood could have the cabin and sleeping loft. Becca agonized over everything again, but finally tumbled into uneasy slumber. But she didn't dream of Adam or of his father's wrath, or of how she had no doubt lost her friendship with Aunt Euphy. She dreamed instead of the one person who had not been here, the Widow Lang.

Her meadow-colored quilt flapping behind her, Widow Lang flew overhead in the star-sprinkled heavens. The quilt became the whole saucer of sky; meadow and mountains merged to meet it. Widow Lang swooped down to dust Becca with rose petals scented sweetly, then soared up to the clouds that were in satin shades of pink and ruby red. Her silver hair flew out behind her like angel wings and she beckoned Becca on up into the heaven of her refuge on Concord Peak. The quilt made in the image of the meadow was moving to meet Becca with its sweet herbs wrapped all around her. Becca gathered herbs and flowers, wounded animals and people. And then it ended and Daddy was kneeling beside her, shaking her shoulder.

"Becca. Becca girl!"

Her face was wet. With dew or tears? Then everything flooded back. The frolic, Adam dancing, Angus Scott kissing Aunt Euphy so hard her mouth melted into his. Becca shook her head and rubbed her eyes as Daddy helped her sit up.

"What? What is it?"

"Claib Tucker just found the Old Widow Lang dead in the medder when he started home. It's almost like she was on her way here for the frolic, poor old thing, and after she told Pru Johns when they passed by she never left home. Now, Mama said she told you about some burying quilt. Becca. Becca?"

Feelings rolled through her as hard as Crawl Crick crashed down in the spring. Holding tight to Daddy, Becca shook and cried. "She was like my angel, my good angel," she stammered, her face pressed to Daddy's solid shoulder. An overwhelming sense of loss terrified her, worse than her pain last night. She had always felt so at one with the world and its people. But Widow Lang, Aunt Euphy—she knew as sure as she was waked up now that Mr. Scott would forbid Adam ever to speak to her again. And she was right. Daddy admitted he had heard Mr. Scott tell Adam that very thing when they started down the mountain last night.

The day after the frolic, the neighbors buried Widow Lang in her quilt up on Snow Knob among her father's, husband's, and sisters' gravehouses. It made Becca almost angry how close sad things came with the happy ones, as if they just meant to ruin them—maybe another sort of irony of life, as Mama would say. And Becca hated to see that beautiful quilt go into the ground, even if that was what it was useful for. She comforted herself by thinking she would always have the meadow to recall it by.

But the strangest thing was that Claib Tucker told everyone that when he found the widow, evidently headed for the frolic with her sack of corn dodgers to contribute, she had three shawls. The one wrapped around her shoulders and the two which dropped on either side of her as if she had held them out at stiff arm's length when she fell. Everyone just clucked in his throat and shook his head, but Becca knew what it meant. Ernestine and Albertine had been coming to the frolic with her, and they'd all flown off together.

Daddy was gone by mid-August. He said he had to get the keelboat built and line up its first cargo, and then he'd be back before the first snow flew. Becca and Jeremy had walked him all the way down to the river, where he caught a salt barge, but Mama stayed at the cabin working like a person possessed the minute Daddy cleared the sycamore stand. Herbs to get gathered before snow flew, she told Daddy, as she kissed him, looking desperate, one more time. It all tore Becca's heart. Besides, she heard in the village that Mr. Scott had sold Aunt Euphy's mule to a new settler in the next clump of mountains, and that meant two bad things to Becca. He was bossing Aunt Euphy just the way he did his youngsters. And the poor, sweet lady had lost her beloved freedom. Becca did not see any of the Scotts on the street the day Daddy left. Then Becca herself got busy up by the cabin and in the hills, just like Mama.

There was good news then, as Becca should have guessed since there had been so much bad. On a nippy October day when Becca was almost thinking of shoving Gran Ida's old shoes on her sun-browned feet, Mama told her she was going to have a baby.

"I been waiting years, nearly eight now since I had Jeremy!" she told Becca, her eyes shining even through their sadness. "Maybe you'll get you that sister you want this time, Becca."

"Oh, Mama, such right fine news! Wait 'til Daddy hears!" Becca leaned down over the rocker to hug Mama's shoulders hard. "When will it be?"

"Mid-April, I reckon, just when the first herbs are popping too."

They shared a little laugh, which Becca treasured. Mama was joking with her and sharing woman's things just the way she would with a grown-up friend. But Becca still knew Daddy should be the one here doing the hugging and the sharing.

In November one brisk late afternoon with snowflakes flying like tattered pieces of lace, there was a banging on the west door of the cabin. Becca leaped up from the table, spilling the dried shucky beans she'd been stringing. Jeremy jumped up from carving by the hearth. Mama moved a bit more slowly now, so she did not rise from her rocker near the fire where she'd been reading her herbal book. She just motioned Becca to the door. For one crazy moment, Becca prayed it could be Daddy come home early for Christmas and to hear the good news about the baby. As of today, his promise to be here before snow flew was broken, and Becca could tell Mama did not expect him.

She pulled open the door to a blast of cold air and a peppering of snow pellets. Adam Scott stood there, red-faced and panting, with two huge, bulging hemp sacks in his leather-gloved hands.

"Oh, Adam! Come in!"

She and Jeremy helped with his sacks. "Hello, Mrs. Blake," he greeted Mama, but he didn't smile. "Broken cages in one sack," he told Becca as if he'd shown her his cages just yesterday instead of six months ago. "The animals that didn't run off or get stomped are in this sack."

"Your father found the cages!"

Adam shrugged, his high brow crumpled in a frown. "It was bound to happen. I had to bring them closer to the house when the weather changed. Here, Jeremy, you like animals. I've got some money and I'm going to pay you—and Becca, if she'll help—to hide and care for these critters up here until spring when I can risk hiding them again. We've just got to get them through this winter!"

The Blakes gathered around Adam's second sack as he brought out his salvaged treasures, some with crude bandages or splints: a pigeon with a broken wing; a rabbit that had lost a hind foot in a trap; another that just hung there limply in Adam's hand with weeping eyes; a tiny mole with a huge cut on its little back.

"One that evidently didn't mind the castor beans," he told Becca, and she nodded.

"Jeremy and Becca will be glad to help you with your animals, Adam," Mama told him, "but not for money. Still and all, your daddy doesn't know you're up here, does he?"

"No, ma'am, he doesn't," Adam admitted and his firm young face took on more lines.

"And would forbid it, I suppose," Mama prompted.

Adam nodded. "They're still so busy pressing and straining cider, I thought I could chance it."

Becca held her breath. Would Mama make Adam leave? Would she take out her old feelings against the Scotts on him?

"Well, then, you mustn't stay too long so he misses you and you have to face his anger upon your return. But I think a bit of rosewater might help that little mole and we can dose that weak rabbit with diluted tonic."

"I'd be ever grateful for your help, Mrs. Blake, you being an herbal healer and all." His eyes went to the table where Becca's beans and Mama's herbal book lay, then returned to Becca.

"I can't thank all of you enough. And, I must admit, Aunt Euphy knows I'm here, and she sends her regards."

Becca finally looked away from his intense, clear blue gaze. She studied the poor, weak rabbit held so tenderly in Adam's big hands. How much about his father and his aunt did Adam know? And, even though their love was forbidden, had Aunt Euphy again given in to her need to hug and kiss Angus Scott right back the way Becca had seen them do in this cabin?

But the snowy day had turned so bright inside with Adam here! Jeremy showed him his animal carvings, and Adam was thrilled to see that Mama had a book on herbal cures. He looked all through it intently. "I love books," he confided to them over steaming mint tea after they had worked on the animals and got them settled in makeshift cages in the corner beyond the hearth. "But I guess there won't be need nor time for such when I take over the distilling and brewing business."

No one said anything at that. Mama's eyes met Becca's, though. Adam insisted they keep his leather gloves "in case the mole would try to bite," but Becca was touched by his cleverness at giving them a gift Mama would accept and not feel beholden. Afterward, Becca and Jeremy bundled up to walk him partway down.

When they parted, Adam shook both their hands, but held on to Becca's longer. Her hands were cold again, but warmed up in Adam's big grasp. Whyever had he needed those fine-smelling gloves with warm hands like that? she thought.

"I can't thank you two enough. I envy you," Adam choked out, and then the words tumbled from him, "living up here all free with a mother that's so helpful and no father to tell you what to do—"

"But we miss Daddy something awful!" Jeremy blurted out.

"Of course you do. I didn't mean otherwise," Adam amended and dropped Becca's hand, evidently surprised he still held it. "It's just, up here you can follow your dreams. It's like a shelter better than Shelter Valley where nothing bad—" he got out before his voice went croaky.

Becca wanted to comfort him. She felt stunned by the surprising need to stroke his hair, to hold him. But she just stood staring as he turned and hurried down the mountain.

"I'm going to carve those animals for him," Jeremy said. She didn't budge for a moment. She felt almost as helpless as the times Daddy disappeared down the river. But Adam was still her friend. Adam had come back no matter what his father said or would do if he caught him. And she didn't want Jeremy's chattering to break the splendid swell of sweet feelings in her.

"Becca, you going to stand there mooning after him all day?"

She turned and followed her brother back up the steep gravel path, with wind and snow pellets stinging her eyes like tears.

Chapter Five

Ann Blake lay in bed that night of March 26, 1824, and listened to the wind howl. She had been awake for hours, as if waiting for something. Loud enough to be a late blizzard, she thought, and just when they reckoned the weather must turn mild. But even in the shriek of wind, she clung to the memory of Chase's voice this last Christmas and the warmth he had poured out to them all like the blazing hearth where he had sat.

Chase had returned later than promised, but he had come, thank God, Ann comforted herself. They had a double celebration for the coming birth of their child and the recent birth of the keelboat *Annie*, awaiting good weather at Beattyville. The smoke-blackened rafters of the old cabin rang as he retold all his best river stories. He knew by name each snag, eddy, sandbar, and shallow clear down to New Orleans, knew to avoid the hidden dangers and disasters. Ann's little smile in the darkness faded to a frown. Sometimes she wished Chase knew his own family that well.

"You named every one, Daddy? Bet no one names 'em better'n you!" Jeremy's excited voice echoed in Ann's thoughts. The boy had listened bug-eyed to his daddy's rough-and-tumble tales. But Ann's eyes had often met Becca's. The girl knew that even her daddy's having a rip-roaring time here didn't mean he wasn't getting the itchy foot already. On and on he'd talked and charmed their hearts. Knowing the pain of parting would come again, Becca and Ann had hung on every word.

"The *Annie*'s a beauty, fifty foot long, made of stout oak timbers," Chase had boasted. "She's got a pair of wide sweeps and a long steering oar just made to fit my hands. Still needs a right fine pair of stag antlers to nail on the cabin. Just hoping old Claib bags one 'fore spring, 'cause I'll have to head back on downriver then."

But Chase had got the antlers early and got cabin fever earlier, Ann mourned silently. Two months ago, in the first thaw, he'd been gone. And after that, despite her love for her children and her herbs, each day awaiting the birth of her third child weighed as heavily on her heart as on her body. It seemed harder than carrying the other two; her outlook was darker. It frightened her, but she kept it buried deep.

"Land o' Goshen, girl, don't you fret so." Mother Ida's voice came like a firm caress into her memories. "You got a home in a right pretty place and you are loved, so count your blessings!" Ann knew it was true. Her blessings were bountiful. But she, the inspiration for the *Annie*'s name, wished with all her heart that Chase was as excited about the baby's birth as his boat's. He had not been home when the other two were born, but Mother Ida had been here with her steady ways and sure touch. Then too, the older Ann got the more the thoughts of her own childhood haunted her. Where there were hauntings, there was death first, wasn't there, she thought, and shuddered.

It had been thirteen years since she had been home. Her sisters would be wed with children of their own. Her parents might have died, and she had never asked their forgiveness for lighting out with Chase, never told them again how much she loved them and valued her childhood. Her heart began to thud in her chest; the baby shifted and kicked; sweat ran down between her full, tender breasts.

Suddenly, in the middle of black night and shrieking wind, she felt frenzied, lying in the big bed with Becca and not Chase. She'd never begged Chase to stay. She should have this time! She should have made him promise if anything happened to her, he'd stay to home and care for his children!

She lay there, propped up on two pillows, tense, desperately lonely. Not just for Chase but for Mother Ida and worse—still lonely for her family. For her sisters, Mama, even her father, who had a temper like that Mr. Scott. Her mind raced as fast as her heart. The Scott family reminded her so of her own, but for Adam. How wonderful if Adam could stay friends with Becca until they were marrying age. How wonderful if Becca would find a boy in these parts to wed and never be torn away like Ann had been. But Becca would probably be as forbidden to Adam as Chase had been to her. "A keelboater, no less!"—she could hear her father's voice right now. And Mama crying that day she and Chase tried to talk horse sense to them in the yard. Ha! Ann thought as the baby kicked her again. There was no such thing as horse sense when love came calling with all its passion and pain.

Tears streamed down her cheeks into her hair to mingle with her sweat. She cradled her big belly and thought she could feel the baby's panicked heartbeat too. Listening to Becca and Jeremy's easy breathing nearby, she tried to pray herself to sleep. When that didn't work, she tried to calm herself by recalling all the good times past, by imagining how happy they would all be when Chase came back in early April like he promised, in time for the baby to be born. It was due in several weeks, she was sure of it. Curses on the *Annie* that had seduced him to leave this time! Ann needed Chase more than the *Annie* ever did!

"Oh!" she cried aloud when the first pain twisted her, low in the back. It was more than the baby just kicking. Maybe if she carefully shifted positions, it would help. She had to lie here calmly. Her getting riled like this was making her think she had body pains when they were all in her head!

"Oh! Mmm!"

Becca sat bolt upright beside her, clutching the bedclothes. "Mama, a bad dream?"

"No. Just a—a little feeling, sweet. Humor your mama, will you, and peek out to see if it's still snowing with that wind?"

Ann clutched the covers to her as Becca got up and skirted Jeremy's trundle bed. The fire had fallen to scarlet coals and the cabin seemed all silvery. If the snow was not too deep, she'd send Becca down to Shelter at daybreak to fetch Mrs. Barney just in case. No good having this child coming and the woman who had promised to tend her caught down there by snow. At least the pains seemed better now. It's just they were so low in her back. She'd never had that before with the other two.

She heard Becca open the door to peek out. Icy air swirled in. Becca grunted as she closed it and shuffled back across the floor. The girl's white face glowed moonlike as she crawled back into bed and hunched over her mother's bulk.

"Mama, it's so light out there with all the snow," she whispered. "Real deep already, like a blizz—"

It was all Ann heard before another pain racked her. It seemed bright red, this pain, edged with jagged black. She screwed her face up tight to fight it off. Colors cascaded through her brain, her body. The pain ran off and dripped away in piercing rivulets of smaller hurts. Then came Becca's frightened voice all mingled with the wind.

"Mama, what is it? Not the baby already? I'll get dressed and get going to town now. Mrs. Barney—"

"No! No, you can't go now, not with that snow. Not even you, Becca, promise me!" Mama cried out and clenched Becca's wrist so hard she felt the girl flinch. But she could not let go. If this child was coming and they were trapped here, Becca would have to help. Together they would have to remember everything Mother Ida had told them about birthing babies. But she'd heard of false pains, yes, Pru Johns had those. That was it, false pains that would soon subside so they could all huddle here in the warmth together until Chase came back and spring came and then the baby.

"I won't leave you, Mama, don't worry. Jeremy. Jeremy, get up and build up that fire!" Becca's words were warm in her ears. It was almost like having Mother Ida here, almost, but Becca had just turned twelve and this baby—

Ann moaned again, though she hadn't meant to make another sound to alarm the children. When would these false pains stop?

"Too soon for this, too late for a snowstorm," Ann insisted. "It's all wrong, wrong." She realized she still held Becca's wrist. "I know it's false pains, Becca, but a fire would be good. Make it roar to shut out that horrid howling!"

She bit her lip so hard with the next pain she tasted blood. She hated blood, hated it even if she pricked her finger on a rose thorn. She reached for Becca but the girl moved away, pulling on her clothes, telling Jeremy to boil water and put some rosewater with it. Yes, Ann thought, rosewater would be so nice to bathe in for when Chase came home.

Before daylight seeped through the swirl of the still falling snow outside, Becca had prepared things as best she could. Jeremy was frightened, but she told him not to make a peep and just crawl up in the loft and plug his ears. A kettle of water was steaming on the hook over the hearth, and she had helped Mama sip some cooling feverfew tea. Still, Mama's back pains pounded against them all in here just the way the storm shook the cabin from outside.

Becca tried to keep her voice steady, her hands too, but, like Jeremy, she was frightened. Babies that came early were unpredictable, Gran Ida had said. Unpredictable and puny, with little lungs. Well then, Becca told herself as she mixed dried periwinkle in melted snow to ease Mama's cramps, if the baby was born with little lungs, they'd just have to help it breathe!

"Becca, remember how Gran Ida always walked a mother to bring the child?" Mama called out to her. "I don't think I can. I just don't remember—this pressure on my backbone before."

Becca took Mama's hand. Mama sat propped against pillows in the bed so that Becca could help her to the edge if the baby really started to come. Mama looked whiter than a bleached linen pillowcase. Becca knew Gran Ida always examined women between their legs when she first arrived to see how far along they were, but she had never done that and couldn't imagine doing it to Mama. Mama would just have to tell her when she was ready. They both kept praying these were just false pains and would stop. But they didn't.

By noon, when Ann tried to get off the bed to use the chamber pot Becca held for her, her bag of water broke. At that, Becca sent the frightened Jeremy upstairs again and mopped up, talking more calmly than she felt to Mama all the time.

"Oh, no, no, it's really coming, Becca. You'll have to help me. We'll do it together. I never liked this part and Gran Ida knew it. I don't like blood, Becca, it's not the pain—"

"I can help you, Mama. Together we will be just fine."

Becca bit her lip to stop her trembling. For the first time in her life, she felt anger at Daddy for not being here, full-blooming anger edging toward hate. But she shoved that aside and scraped her memories for things Gran Ida had said and done.

"All right now, there are what Gran Ida called the grinding or preparing pains that come first, Mama. That must be what you have. Now that we know this baby's determined to come today, you've got to get up and walk a bit, and drink more feverfew tea. Jeremy!" Becca shouted up toward the loft, "come on down and help Mama walk around the cabin for a spell!"

"Becca, he's just a boy, and this is women's work," Mama protested. It frightened Becca anew how white she looked, and yet she sweated so much she should have good color. But it touched Becca that Mama had evidently thought of her as a woman too, at least when times got tough and there was women's work to do.

After an hour of walking Mama, one on each side of her, they put her back to bed. The forcing or bearing pains began and Jeremy was sent to the loft again. It was getting dark outside now, even with the glare of the snow. Becca was amazed she did not feel tired; she knew Mama did. Becca forced herself to eat a bit of biscuit sopped in broth to keep up her strength. All Mama wanted now was water.

"Becca, you're going to have to take a peek now and tell me what you see. It just seems this youngster's not—dropping down quite like it should," Mama got out through jagged breaths.

"Sure, I can do that. I know how Gran Ida did it," Becca said before she realized she had lied to Mama. From here on, she had always been sent outside to tend the children or to boil more water if the fire was outside. Mama leaned back and hiked her nightgown up over her spread knees. Becca pulled the bedclothes down slowly, shaking the way a leaf would in that wind outside. Between Mama's legs, she saw Mama's reddish curly hair and a big opening for the baby to come through between Mama's white thighs.

"Can you see its head, its crown?" Mama asked, panting as if she'd run miles.

"No. Nothing there quite yet, Mama. Soon, I bet. Can you just bear down? That's what they say will bring it."

"Oh, Becca, Becca, come up here and hold my hand. Talk to me, sing to me. Make all this go away!" And Mama moaned again.

Mama's cries changed as her pain progressed. It went on and on so that Becca wanted to press her palms over her ears the way she knew Jeremy was doing up in the loft. This could not be happening, not like this. She wanted to run away and hide, out in the snow, try to make it down to Shelter, but she knew Mrs. Barney could not get up here through this snow anyway. And she could not leave Mama. She had to help this baby come, and soon!

"The cradle! The cradle!" Mama shouted just after it got dark outside and Becca lit the candles.

"It's over on the hearth, Mama," Becca comforted her as she leaned weak-kneed against the tall bed. "It's ready for the baby."

"My mother," Mama rasped, "she loved me. She wanted me to have it." She panted in that strange trapped-animal way between her thoughts. "I named you for her—and she knew how much she missed me. She didn't want me to—be separated from them all—like death."

Hair prickled on the back of Becca's neck. Her stomach turned over. "Sure she misses you, Mama. Now you just save your strength. Don't talk and carry on so."

"My father was so angry, angry at me, mostly at Chase," Mama kept on talking. "I'm angry too! He should be here!" Her voice rose to a shriek to match the wind outside. Becca realized Mama felt just the way she did. They both loved Daddy terribly, but he should be here for this. This was his doing—all of it!

Mama muttered on about her family, about being afraid they were dead, about dying herself. "Mama, stop it. You are not going to die. I won't let you."

"It's bad, Becca. I want to. I just want it to be over. It should be born, should be crowning. Look again. Sometimes Gran Ida manipulated it to start it, and I can't reach—"

Becca gasped at the intensity of Mama's next pain. She reared up; her hands thrashed and she cursed Daddy, not for this baby, not for leaving her, but for taking her from her family at Boonesville years ago! Becca stood stunned a minute and then she seized the candle and lifted the bedclothes to push Mama's legs apart again.

It came to her like a revelation. Maybe—just maybe the problem Jemima Tucker had with her last was happening here. Maybe the baby was not lying head down to be born after all this pain. And Gran Ida had reached in and turned the baby. Becca had held the candle for all that after Gran Ida had called her in from watching the Tucker brood.

"Jeremy," she shouted, "come on down here! You don't have to look, but I need your help!"

"I'm scared," echoed from the rafters.

"Mama's poorly and she needs us both!" Becca clipped out and lifted Mama's nightgown even higher to stare at the great expanse of white belly that hid the baby which must want to be born. The question was, what could Becca do to help? She couldn't just reach up inside like a granny woman would! Mama murmured something about Daddy paying too much money for her at some dance. Becca ignored that. She had to do more than just help Mama now. She had to be just as strong as Gran Ida and do something on her own.

She heard sniffling behind her. Jeremy stood there, a blanket wrapped around him, head to toes.

"Stand here and hold this candle like this. Then don't look."

"I won't!" he vowed, and she could see the shiny reflections of tear tracks on his face.

"And she's going to be all right, so don't be afraid. I'm not!" she lied again, but it felt like a good lie.

She peered at Mama's belly and thought she could see the bump that was the baby's head. Here, a foot or elbow, maybe a knee. Or was that bump the baby's bottom? If she couldn't tell, she would not know which way to knead Mama's belly to turn and push the baby right.

"I'm going to feel up inside, like Gran Ida said she did to turn Jemima Tucker's baby, Mama. I'm not meaning to hurt you." She repeated words she'd overheard from Gran Ida many times. "Please, Mama, try to hold still."

Becca could tell by the wavering candlelight that Jeremy was shaking as hard as she. She pushed her hand up inside Mama, trying to shut out that it was Mama here in pain and rambling on so plumb crazy about her past. Mama gasped in great breaths, but at least Becca's hand and arm were smaller than Gran Ida's. She tried to picture what part of the baby it could be she was feeling.

Yes! Something soft and slippery! An ankle or a wrist? A foot. It was a foot. Tiny toes, a heel. Carefully, trying to ignore Mama's deep groaning, she shoved at it, hoping the baby would turn itself. She pulled her hand out and wiped it off.

"Mama, maybe if you could sit up even more, like on the edge of the bed. Jeremy, climb up on the bed behind Mama and brace her back with yours. I'll help you. Give me the candle. You don't have to look. Here, don't be afraid, like this."

His hands hard over his eyes, the boy did as she said. He braced his feet against the cabin wall through the headboard slats. With a pillow between his back and Mama's, he held her almost upright. Becca dragged the table over and braced one of Mama's feet against it to be sure she stayed on the bed. Her other foot was propped against the footboard. She nearly snapped that and shoved the table away when she started pushing again. But Becca piled crocks on the table to make it heavier. She waited, sometimes forgetting to breathe while she tried to turn the baby more. Sometimes she pressed carefully on Mama's stomach, sometimes feeling up inside to make sure a leg or hand did not show itself first.

Finally, maybe near dawn, she saw the blackest bit of hair on a rounded head press against the birth opening.

"Mama, I can see it! It's coming now. Jeremy, you awake? Keep Mama's back real steady now!"

"I can't!" Mama cried. "I can't. No more!"

Becca astounded herself by shaking Mama's shoulder so hard she almost bounced her back off Jeremy's. "You have to! The baby's coming now!"

Mama's skin looked shiny gray like glazed pottery. Was she feverish or just exhausted? But Becca knew they had to get this baby out of her, the sooner the better so they would both be all right. As more of the head appeared, she prayed there would be no ironies of life like a birthing cord around the baby's neck.

"It's coming, Mama! It's coming!"

"Chase, is Chase coming now?" Mama said between gritted teeth, her voice hoarse from all her yelling.

"The baby, Mama. I said the baby's coming. Push! Push hard!"

"He had a push boat. We put out—from the Mercer farm. I never saw them again. I want—to see them—before I—die."

"Mama, please stop that talk. Push! Push!"

With a strange plopping sound the baby's head was born. Becca supported it, all wet and whitish, while one shoulder appeared, and then with another slopping sound, the other shoulder. It slid out into her hands. She had it now! A girl! A sister born right into her very own hands!

"A girl, Mama! A girl!"

Becca sank to the floor with the child on her lap. The little thing was so slippery. It didn't make a sound. It looked so much smaller than other newborns she had seen. Moving by instinct now, Becca cleared the milky stuff from the nostrils and mouth. It made no sound. Bluish, it did not breathe. Its warm flesh began to chill. Becca lifted it, head up, clasping it by the chest. It dangled limply. She lay it down across her knees and opened its tiny bud of a mouth and blew gently into it. Gran Ida said she had to blow life into Daddy when he was born to make him turn from blue to pink. Shaking all over, her eyes streaming tears, Becca puffed harder. She put her finger in its mouth again. She felt a tiny sucking movement. And then the baby opened its mouth and wailed weakly.

Becca washed it with warm rosewater and wrapped it in a piece of blanket before she even got Gran Ida's knife to cut the birthing cord. She tried to give the baby to Mama but Mama was swooning or sleeping. She laid the baby in the cradle on the warm hearth and hurried back to Mama to put a camphor bottle under her nose. Mama's eyes shot open.

"It's a girl, and she's fine, Mama. Jeremy and I have a sister."

"A sister," Mama said, but her eyes closed again. "I have three sisters, and I haven't seen their babies."

Jeremy watched the baby when she stopped crying to be sure she was still breathing. Becca tried to pull the rest of the birthing cord from Mama. To her surprise that and a lot more slid out, so Becca cleaned everything up. She bathed Mama quickly in a bath of tansy, mugwort, camomile, and hyssop and covered her up warmly. She bent down close to Mama's ear and said, "Mama, Mama. The baby's crying real faint like. I think she's hungry. Can you suckle her?"

Mama's eyes opened a bit. Finally her gaze focused on Becca. She nodded. Becca brought the baby over and put her in the crook of Mama's arm, but she had to help press the baby to her breast. She had to help Mama hold the baby there. But it didn't seem to want any milk since it was breathing through its mouth. Mama fell asleep. As daylight edged the door and slitted through the shutters and the grease-paper window, Becca, holding the baby to her, collapsed in Mama's rocking chair. It squeaked as she rocked the baby. Jeremy sat like a leaden lump on the hearth. Becca bowed her head. She shook as she sobbed silently until Jeremy came to hold her shoulders. The terror she had kept away for hours came back to swallow her up. The baby would not eat and wailed so thinly, she knew it was just the beginning of worse times.

The child no one had named died the next day when the sun went down. Mama had attempted to suckle it again and again, and they had tried sugar water on a twist of cotton teat, but it was working too hard to breathe to be able to eat. Those little lungs Gran Ida had warned about for early babies, Becca thought. Not once had the baby opened its eyes. She bit her lower lip to keep from screaming as she and Mama washed it in rosewater in a big bowl on Mama's knees on the bed, then wrapped it in a clean sheet. Becca laid it in the cradle and sadly moved it into the far corner of the room where it was coldest. The next day, they said some prayers and she and Jeremy trudged up through wind-whipped, knee-deep snow to Restful Knob to hack what grave they could in the cold soil. They would have a real funeral for the child when the weather turned and Daddy came home. But still, Becca sang one song while she and Jeremy piled gravel from the path on the shallow grave:

> *Death is an angel sent down from above,*
> *Sent for the buds and the flowers we love.*
> *Gathering flowers for the Master's bouquet,*
> *Beautiful flowers that will never decay.*
> *Gathered by angels and carried away,*
> *Forever to bloom in the Master's bouquet.*

They found Mama back in the cabin, embracing the family Bible to her breast where the baby should have been. She stared straight up at the ceiling. Becca thought she must be all out of tears, and she hadn't mentioned her family again. Becca felt odd, wavering and weaving on her feet. She wilted on the hearth and let the heat seep into her. Jeremy sank down next to her silently. He had let Becca wear Adam's leather gloves because she carried the baby. Now his hands looked purplish from toting the hatchet they'd used to dig into the ground, and she reached out to rub blood back into them.

"I dedicate my life to healing herbs and I couldn't help her," Mama said from across the room.

Becca almost blurted that it was another irony of life, but she held her tongue. She laid her hand on Jeremy's shoulders to stand, then went over to Mama to take her hand. "It was pure white and gleaming up there where we laid her, Mama. Maybe like heaven," Becca said.

Mama slid the Bible off her and tugged Becca down to hug her hard. "Becca, my darling girl!" she whispered very quietly in her ear. "You were so strong, so good. A great comfort. I could not have asked for a better, braver friend through it all. Don't ever leave me, Becca, daughter, sister, friend."

Mama's words got all garbled, but Becca held hard to her. After that, they were more to each other than they had been. Mama talked to her as if she *were* a sister or a friend. She told her all about how Daddy had won her heart and how she loved him so much despite all the pain of his leaving and her being away from her family.

Becca could understand. She could not imagine being taken from here, not even by a man she loved. She was going to stay in Shelter Valley forever, even if she did move up to her refuge and build at least a summer cabin someday. Mama explained to her how she couldn't bear to hear about the Scotts because they reminded her so of the family she had lost. "I envied them so that I almost hated them!" Mama admitted.

"I never thought of it like that," Becca said. "I thought envy was more like love."

"Well, it is, but a person's feelings can get so very mixed up!" Mama explained. "At least, we have each other. At least you understand now why I was downcast sometimes and it had nothing to do with you. You're the joy of my life, you and Jeremy—and Daddy."

Despite the grief of losing the baby, which Becca blamed herself for just a little since someone else might have known more what to do, Mama's words helped her. And she comforted Mama in her grief night after night, holding her hand, patting her shoulder, talking in a low voice to her in the bed where Daddy should have been. And when he returned a whole five months later, Becca almost thought it better that he had not come.

It seemed good at first to have him back. When he heard about the baby born and lost in the blizzard, he held Mama and spoke soothing words. He explained he had sent a letter and some money back in April with a friend, telling the family that there had been an accident and he was laid up with a wrenched back and neck down in Memphis. He said he'd kill the man he sent with the money if he ever saw him again. The money was the last he had. One of those newfangled steamboats had smashed the *Annie* to bits in the fog on her maiden voyage. His partner had drowned and Daddy had been ailing—"Longer than you, Ann, and without the comforts of family and home," he added. Mama had hugged him tight, but Becca felt sick when he said that. If he was without comforts of family and home, it was his doing. But soon things got even worse.

Daddy took to drinking with Ephraim Johns and wandering with Claib Tucker, who was still looking for a woman to wed as well as animals to shoot. Daddy was home but seldom. The circles under Mama's eyes that had come when the baby died grew bigger and darker. Flesh fell off her until she looked like a scarecrow. Daddy didn't even stay at home much the day they had the funeral. And one night when he came in late with his words all sloppy-sounding, Becca overheard her parents argue for the first time in her life—and maybe theirs too.

"... don't understand the ruination of my dreams, Ann!"

"... mine ruined long ago. Is the Mercer farm even there? Do you ever put in there to inquire when you float by hither and yon?"

"... don't want to see either of us ... Can't hold our heads up if I'd ever go to them for a new stake ... a man's pride ..."

"If you'd just been here, Chase, the baby might not have died! You're still chasing rainbows like Mother Ida said. She at least traveled to help others she loved and knew, not to desert them."

Becca curled up in a tiny ball under her blanket in the loft. She pressed her palms to her ears, but the next words hit her in the stomach like big fists of stone.

"... with only Becca here in that storm, Ann. And to have the boy go through all that, propping you up in bed!

What does Becca know about births? . . . both of you to blame . . . should have planned ahead, and not just had one child birthing another . . . ''

Daddy thought losing the baby was her fault and Mama's! It echoed Becca's own worst fears. If she had just done something different, turned the baby sooner, not been so afraid and stupid! But Mama's voice rose stronger than Daddy's now, slurred not by whiskey but by grief.

"She's not just a child, Chase. She's nearly thirteen and your friend Claib's daughters got wed at fourteen! Becca became a woman that night! It was God's will, not anyone's fault. At least I had Becca here with me in my hour of need!''

"Then hold to her, because I won't stay in a place where—''

More words. Mama's crying. A door slamming. Mama's calling his name over and over in a strangled way. Becca stifled her wild sobs with her blanket, but black despair drowned her, down and down and down.

Later that windy September, Adam Scott strode over the brow of their hill with a sack of animals just the way he had half a year ago. Becca, hilling up soil around the apothecary rose roots, put down her hoe and ran to meet him. As she got closer, she saw that Adam's eyes were black and blue and his nose swollen and smashed.

"Oh, Adam,'' she cried. "He found the cages again!''

"Not that,'' he said. He talked all stuffed up, as if he had a bad cold. "I told him I hated working in the distillery, and he said I despised my heritage. He's sending me away to Harrodsburg, Becca, with my oldest sisters, who are going to a school and to find husbands there. We'll be living with my Uncle James, and I'm glad. Aunt Euphy planned it. She told my father if he didn't send me with Mary and Aileen and give me a chance at a real school, she'd go with the girls and not come back. They argued something awful. But I guess you can see, he gave me what for before Aunt Euphy got to reasoning with him.''

But Becca's thoughts had snagged on the name Harrodsburg. Adam was being sent away to Harrodsburg. She had never heard of it. It sounded huge and foreign and as far away as England or Scarlet Town to her.

They walked up to the cabin together and Adam bequeathed his last wounded animals to Jeremy's and her care. "Mostly, though, I expect Jeremy to tend them because, like her Mama, Becca's calling is to help sick and wounded people," Adam said formally, as if he were preaching at Sunday meeting. "But Becca can keep a good lookout for hurt ones she sees on her rambles and bring them back here for help."

Becca nodded her agreement as Jeremy ran to get Adam a carved squirrel with a too-big tail for a farewell present. Tears prickled Becca's eyes, but she blinked them back. She was losing her friend Adam. He had visited them and his animals up here when he could get away. Her family cared for him deeply. His questions to Mama about healing herbs were endless—and, Mama said, showed he was nimble-minded. One time too, Adam had sneaked away to walk way up the valley with her on her rounds. But this! Daddy gone off and now Adam!

Becca felt panic rise in her as Adam said his good-byes and promised to write through Aunt Euphy. Mama kept Jeremy inside as Becca walked Adam out.

"You know," he told her, "I never did get to see your ice palace and that secret place in the clouds." He pointed up toward Concord Peak, shining proud purple in the golden September afternoon sun. It looked as if clouds clung to the cliffs up there today, trying to hide her refuge.

"I could show you now," she said, yearning to cling to this time they had left together. And she did.

They swung wild and free on her grapevines and she described again how, when it got cold, water glazed the face of Concord to create great columns of crystal ice. He followed her under the natural arch, awestruck at the view, onto her secret shelf where she could hide herself away from all but God's great heavens. She showed him the wild mountain rosebush Widow Lang had given her and told him how it looked when it sprawled, beautiful, in its summer pearly pink and red flowering.

"As beautiful as Becca, wild mountain rose," Adam whispered.

Even with Whistling Peak blowing its loudest tune below and wind whipping past her ears, Becca heard those dear words. "Aunt Euphy says you're like the river," he went on, his voice rough, as he pointed down toward the green ribbon of South Fork woven through the curly heads of trees below. "Deep and nourishing, she said, just running free through those hard cliffs of life, but pushing back at them to bite deeper in." He turned to face her. She longed to tend his hurt nose and eyes. "She means you're such a help to folks around here against great odds," he added and took her hand in his.

They stood astride the top of their world, touching hands, staring into each other's eyes, hers wide green and his clearest, narrowest blue. Becca felt as if she understood him then, as if she could see into his pain and longing because she had felt all of it too. She hurt inside so much for him. How could he bear to leave this place? But it was more than the looming loss that tore at her; it was the beauty of life all mixed with agony in this moment. The wind rippled their hair and tugged at their clothes as if they were flying. The whole rainbow expanse of valley arched below, cradled by these mountains.

"Let's promise when you come back—" she began.

"My father says for visits or when I learn what a fool I've been."

"You're never that. But when you come back, let's meet up here and still be friends, even if it's been a while, even if it's been the longest time."

He nodded and squeezed her hand. "We'll do our very best. We'll both be happy and help others too, you'll see!" he vowed in a rush. He hugged her hard, just once, quickly. Still, she savored the strong press of his arms around her thin shoulders right through her cape. She felt his chin rest on the top of her head and his knees touch hers for one tiny moment. It was sweet and filled her with strength.

Then he turned and ran, whooping, skidding down the path with her right behind him shouting too. He reached the vines first. But she was more used to this. Together they swung out over the edge and then back to earth. And their defiant cries echoed down the peaks and down the years.

Chapter Six

During Christmas, Daddy came back as if no harsh words had passed, as if no baby had died, no keelboat had gone to splinters. He and Mama seemed happy again, but Becca heard Mama's laugh grow shrill. She saw how Mama's eyes darted wildly toward Daddy and how she clutched his hand. Becca knew Daddy still went hellin' with Claib and Ephraim when the mountain paths were passable. That upset her, but she knew not to criticize her elders. Besides, lately she spent so much time when she wasn't worrying about Mama worrying about herself. In addition to her churning feelings, so many changes were going on inside her body, she almost couldn't keep up.

She was forming breasts like the swell of spring buds. Curly, brown-red hair was growing under her arms and where her legs joined. And her monthly flux started right after Daddy set out for Cincinnati in the February thaw. Now Becca felt even more a woman. When her belly cramping left, she and Mama celebrated her womanhood, sitting side by side on slump-seated stools at the hearth after Jeremy went to bed.

"And not yet old enough to be dosed with rue tea!" Mama teased Becca as they each ate a biscuit spread with applesauce. Mama explained how tall, thin mountain girls who didn't start the flux by age fifteen were dosed with rue tonic to bring it on. Some used mountain mint, but it was not as good as rue. "Rue tastes bitter, but then womanhood does too," Mama confided, as if she had to tell Becca *that* after the year they'd shared.

"I know rue's bitter enough to keep bugs off roses planted next to it," Becca told her, "but I didn't know about bringing the flux."

"Strange, isn't it?" Mama said and reached her arm around Becca's shoulders to hold her close. "The bitter things in life get all mixed up with the sweet." Becca nodded; she had learned that too. It was like roses, whose satin petals and sweet smell lured you to the thorns. A body just had to expect that sort of thing in life.

"Pain with babies coming," Mama went on, "cramps and bother each month with becoming a woman—"

"And the joy of loving folks and then getting hurt when they leave, one way or t'other," Becca added solemnly.

Mama turned to Becca. In the darting firelight, her smile trembled between sunny curves and sharp shadows. Tears shimmered in her eyes. She pressed her cheek to Becca's thick chestnut hair, all tumbled loose and looking almost red from the fire.

"But I want you to know," Mama whispered, "when it's the right man to love for sure, there are golden moments worth the hurt. Besides," she said with a shake of her head, "nothing a mere mortal woman can do to fight it when true love comes calling. Love is worth the pain of possible separations. Remember that, my dearest, no matter what befalls!"

Becca knew she should say something back, but the words caught in her throat. She kissed Mama's cheek. Together they watched the logs on the hearth shudder to crimson ashes.

That spring there was no time to sit and talk. The canker rash some called scarlet fever swept Shelter Valley, striking mostly children, though Ralston Tucker departed this life with two of his youngsters. Three of the Johns children died, and two adults in town, including the Scotts' hired hand, Clemmet. Mrs. Scott herself had died that winter, but from complications of lung disease and not the canker. Being so far downriver with news traveling so slowly, Adam and his sisters in Harrodsburg did not return for the funeral. But even in their dry, warm house, the canker did not spare the Scotts from a visitation. Pretty Cora, Adam's favorite sister, just two years older, died on her seventeenth birthday. But Mama and Becca were too busy fighting the disease to attend any funerals or burials.

Mama worried Becca would get the canker traveling hither and yon on her herbal deliveries. So for the first time, over Becca's protests, Mama conquered her need to stay at home and trudged out with the cold water root and marsh rosemary that helped battle the sickness. The symptoms were brilliant-hued skin eruptions, swollen tongue, ulcerated throat, and fever. With the help of the herbs, the canker did not kill everyone it struck. Sometimes Mama was gone for days at a time, helping others nurse their sick. When she came back, she always called to Becca, who dragged a tub of hot comfrey water outside the door, however cold the weather was. Mama would strip off her clothes and wash before she came in. But when June arrived and the disease began to fade from the valley, despite Mama's precautions it laid Jeremy low.

Mama and Becca worked to save him with a fever of frenzy to match his own. Mama blamed herself, but Becca talked her out of that. "You're not sick, so you didn't bring it back to Jeremy. I heard you once tell Daddy it was God's will the baby died and not my fault, Mama. You did what you had to do. You tried your best, just like me."

Mama nodded so hard tears flew off her cheeks as, together, they bent back over Jeremy. His face was bright pink but for a pale area around his mouth. His tongue slowly went from whitish to a red, raw look Mama called strawberry tongue.

"The milk sick's the other disease that coats the tongue so bad," she told Becca as they peered into the boy's mouth again. "I really think the Scott girl died from that since her tongue never turned red and she'd been drinking milk just like their field hand did. My herbs didn't help her one whit last week, and it did some others when I got there in time. But I didn't want to dispute Mr. Scott about it," Mama admitted with a shake of her head. "Milk sick is much more fatal than the canker. Poor Aunt Euphy took the girl's loss so hard she collapsed in Mr. Scott's arms and he had to carry her to her bed."

A lightning-quick look passed between Mama and Becca, but Becca read nothing amiss on Mama's face. She only hoped, whatever tragedies were happening at the Scott house, Aunt Euphy was not one of them.

Jeremy recovered slowly, but things did not get better. In mid-June, Mama took to her bed. She was nauseated but thirsty. Despite her growing weakness, she muttered on and on.

"Becca, I won't mind if it's me instead of Jeremy, like barter, my life for his! The angel of death's come back for me again this year, but in a different way, like it's my time and I cheated death before. Oh, my hands are so cold, but I'm burning up inside!"

Becca felt frozen in dread. It was the nightmare of the baby's birth again, with Mama raving and Daddy not here to help. Mama's tongue was coated white, just like Jeremy's in the beginning. And her rambling about the angel of death! Mama had been an angel of mercy, Becca agonized, and look what she got in return. Mama had sacrificed herself to make Becca's rounds for her and had nursed so many others. It just wasn't fair! Becca bathed Mama's face and dosed her with the last of the scant supply of cold water root and marsh rosemary. Again and again, she told herself that Jeremy had lived through this canker and Mama would too!

Becca was so exhausted she felt boneless. But she kept

putting one foot ahead of the other; she kept tending Jeremy up in the loft and Mama in her bed. She even cared for the wounded animals that Adam had left behind. She dreaded getting the disease herself, for then who would care for them? Some shunned those with the canker, though that was not the way of mountain people. But Jeremy could not nurse two of them.

At night Becca was too frightened and too tired to rest. She slept in snatches during the day, sitting on the foot of Mama's bed or nodding while she stirred herbal teas and poultices. She had to switch to elderberries to fight Mama's nausea and slippery elm salve when other supplies were gone. She used dandelion wine for a stomach-settling tonic and to slake Mama's raging thirst. She had never prescribed herbs before for such a serious disease, but relied on Mama. Now, as with the birth, when Becca had pretended Gran Ida stood at her side, she imagined Mama was well enough to tell her what to do. She waited and waited for her to get better.

But Mama's tongue did not turn from white to red. Suddenly Becca heard Mama's voice in her memory, but it did not say what she wanted to hear. "I really think the Scott girl died from the milk sick since her tongue never turned red. Milk sick is much more fatal than the canker." With a shudder, Becca remembered that Claib Tucker's second wife died from the milk sick, which no herbs could cure.

In that moment of horrid revelation, she crushed the precious dried elderberry flowers and bark in her hands so they drifted like dust to cover her bare feet. She stared down, her mind fighting the thought that Mama might not live this time. Milk sick and not the canker? Mama going to die after living through that dreadful time the baby came and died? Mama going to die without seeing her family again, just as she feared? Mama, her body turned to dust like this? Becca kicked the dust off her feet. No, she would not let that happen!

She carried the big Bible up to Jeremy in the loft and told him to hold to it and pray for Mama. She prayed too, while she dosed and washed Mama with every herb and tonic she knew to build her strength. But Mama got weaker, and her breath smelled like turpentine. The hours and days blurred Becca's determination into terror. Jeremy came and went from Mama's bedside, giving Becca things to drink, things to put in her mouth she must have eaten. She woke once, slumped across the foot of the bed, to see the boy bathing Mama's ashen face.

"I been praying for her like you said, Becca," Jeremy assured her, his eyes huge in his sunken face. "And I been praying Daddy would come home in time and you'd get some sleep."

Becca jerked to her feet. "I got some sleep, Jeremy. Thank you kindly." She took the rag from the boy and dipped it in rosewater, the only thing she had quantities of after her rage to try every cure Mama had. If only she could run down through the meadow and knew what new herbs to gather there that Widow Lang had blessed when she became an angel and flew away with her sisters. If only—if only—

"Becca! Did you hear that?" Jeremy's voice cut through her frenzied musings some time later. It was almost dark outside.

"Hear what? Maybe it's old Claib with more meat for us like Daddy asked him," she said and turned toward the boy as he opened the cabin door and stepped out. But even before Jeremy's shout, Becca knew. Daddy's voice down the hill! For once, Daddy had come home in time!

Daddy's presence brought Mama back from the edge of the grave. He sat by her bed and held her hand. Sometimes he cradled her reed-thin body to him, rocking her gently, though Mama protested he should not get too close. They talked between the times Mama slept and Daddy lay beside her.

Becca thrilled that Daddy was the best herb of all. Their hard praying had been answered, or maybe she had done something right in her nursing. This time, Daddy would not think having only Becca here to help was a mistake or anyone's fault the way he did when the baby died! Besides, with Daddy back, Mama knew what she had to live for.

"Sure," Becca heard Daddy promise Mama, "once you get stronger, we'll go to Boonesville. Yes, yes, Ann, I swear to you if anything happens to you—which it won't—I'll see Becca and Jeremy are well taken care of, I swear it!"

Late the second day Daddy was home, Mama said she felt better. Outside, silent so as not to wake her, Becca and Jeremy rejoiced. They held hands and whirled around in the June evening mist, just the way the Scott twins had twirled the night of the frolic while Adam danced with Aunt Euphy. Then Daddy came to the door and gestured Becca in.

"Mama wants a word with you," was all he said and went out to talk to Jeremy.

Becca perched carefully on the side of Mama's bed. "My darling girl," Mama said so quietly Becca had to lean down to hear. "Nothing will break you, Rebecca Blake. Your Gran Ida said that once, and I have—seen it's true." Her tongue was still swollen. Her words sounded so strange.

"Mama, you need more sleep. We can talk later."

"Listen to me," Mama said, her voice like the wind up on Restful Knob. Becca held Mama's hand. "Be strong now, because I have to ask your help again. I'm going to have to leave you, my sweet, and—"

"No! No, you're fine now!" Becca shrieked before she got hold of herself to quiet her voice. It was too much. She had made it through all the rest, but she could not bear this death talk again. "Mama, you are right fine! You said you feel better. Your tongue isn't fuzzy white now! Daddy is home, and you are going to live!"

"Sh, Becca, take my other hand too. That's it. We've been more like sisters lately, Becca, haven't we? Now, I want you to promise me you will help Daddy and watch over Jeremy for me. I want you to know you have been the best friend ever to me."

Mama's words seemed so shaky now. Becca stared down, aghast, wide-eyed, at Mama's face, at Mama's eyes dribbling tears, at Mama's mouth as it moved to say these things. How could she be so calm if she was dying? Why, she wanted to see her family back at Boonesville. She wanted to plant her herbs and make rosewater from the roses this summer, and—

"Becca. Promise me?" Mama pleaded, her voice so shivery that Becca shuddered.

Their gazes locked. Becca nodded.

"Be strong, Becca, my sweet girl, sweet rose. Chase—" she said and looked past Becca toward the door.

Daddy stood there now. He came over, looking stooped and afraid. Becca got up for him to sit. Jeremy came in quietly behind Daddy, and Mama smiled at him wanly. She closed her eyes to rest while Becca put her hand on Daddy's shoulder and, still as wooden carvings, the three of them stayed there watching Mama sleep. Soon, without opening her eyes, she said in a whispery silver voice, "Chase, it's so lovely here. So lovely to be home at the farm with Mama waiting."

Daddy sobbed once and hung his head. Becca gripped his shoulder. Jeremy sniffled. No, Becca thought. Mama would wake up now. Or else Becca was just having a terrible dream. But Daddy got up and fetched the looking glass to hold under Mama's nose. Nothing. Not the slightest fog of breath, not the barest breeze of life. Jeremy sat like a stone on the floor; Daddy slumped over the bed a long time. Becca left them to stumble outside to grieve in private.

She clung to a big tree trunk down by the creek and gulped huge gasps of air. Mama would not find her here to comfort her this time, to enfold her in a warm embrace. Overhead, the white arms of the ghostly sycamores swayed toward the sliver of racing moon. Slowly Becca slid to her knees, then huddled on the ground, so shocked, so frightened, so alone. She felt utterly bereft of emotions, dry even of tears. But hours later, in black night, fury wracked her; she beat her fists raw against the tree. Piercing pain, then leaden loss assailed her, all swirling together in interlocking circles like the pattern in Widow Lang's burial quilt.

*   *   *

Two days after they buried Mama, Daddy, Ephraim Johns, and Claib Tucker spent the day up on Restful Knob building her a gravehouse. Becca kept busy by planting herbs and trimming the apothecary rose canes. She felt stiff and hollow. She had finally sobbed so hard it even pained her to move her eyes. But she had promised Mama she would watch Jeremy and help Daddy, so she had to go on. She would have to work even harder, she told herself, to take Mama's place here and deliver the herbs to the neighbors too. She looked up when the men returned and Claib and Ephraim walked on down the mountain. Daddy leaned in the doorway watching her, so she wiped her hands off on Mama's big apron and went over.

"Becca girl, this is no place for you and Jeremy when I go off next time."

New fear bit at Rebecca's belly. "We'll be fine, Daddy, just fine, though I wish you'd decide to stay."

"You sound like your Mama already, Becca, but it won't work. Vowed to her I'd take good care of you. Know just the place to do that."

"What do you mean? You don't mean with Claib Tucker, Daddy!"

" 'Course I don't, but guess he'd be a better provider than I been. Becca, how'd you like to live in a place called Pleasant Hill that is heaven on earth, finer than Shelter ever—"

"What? Leave here?" she shrilled. "I could never leave Shelter! It's heaven enough for me. No, Daddy, not in a hundred years could—"

"Quiet, now," he said and came closer. He took the pruning knife from her hands and dropped it to the ground to hold her. She clung to him, though she smelled whiskey on his breath. Drinking, she thought, while building Mama's gravehouse.

"Becca, I made up my mind. Soon as the spring river goes down, I'm taking you and Jeremy with me to the Shakers. You'll love it there, you'll see."

She pulled from his embrace, precious as it was. "The Shakers? But—but I heard you tell Mama once they didn't let men and women together, and I have to take care of Jeremy."

"Sure, sure, you could there. They form big families, with lots of folks to love and care for. Men and women live right in the same houses, bigger'n the Scott house. Promised you a house fine as the Scotts' someday, didn't I?"

"But I don't fancy any of that, Daddy. I just want *our* family to be together, Jeremy, you, and me!"

"Now, listen, I said. There's good food and honest work and a rote school in Shakertown. They love children there. They'll take a lot better care of you than I could if I'm not here. I can't take up carpentry like my Daddy, Becca, 'cause keelboating's the only livelihood I know. No way you two can just stay here on your own," he plunged on with a loud sniff. "And Shakertown's closer to where I'll be. I'll visit you much as I can, and have peace of mind to know you and Jeremy'll be fed and cared for and taught proper, like I promised your mama."

At that, Becca's next protest died in her throat. She bit her lower lip hard and did not snatch her hand away when Daddy covered it with his.

"Can't explain all this to the boy," Daddy muttered, his gaze gone far past her now, "but I 'spect you to understand and back me up. 'Sides," he muttered and turned away with the shoulder-slumped walk he'd had since Mama died, "made up my mind."

Becca still missed Mama miserably. She worked like a whirl-wind to get through each day without her. And as the month of April reached toward May, Becca tried desperately to change Daddy's mind. But he was roaming with Ephraim and Claib again and scolded her once that she was making him feel just as guilt-struck as her Mama used to. Becca tried to accept Daddy's will after that. Mama would want her to care for him and not weaken the ties that bound the family.

She kept the cabin in order as if it were to be their permanent home. She made Jeremy read and cipher every day, just as Mama had. She kept burgoo in the pot and biscuits in the crock for when Daddy or his friends came in. She didn't like the way Claib Tucker looked at her sometimes, and she was grateful Daddy was always about when Claib was there.

She tried to ignore the way Daddy swayed Jeremy to his side with promises of showing him the river and of their having so much more time together on the way to Shakertown. At least there would be that, Becca tried to console herself. But she did not believe Daddy would stay around much longer at Shakertown than he had here at Shelter, even though he was giving the impression that he would. It just wasn't his nature.

By the end of June, she saw that the last snow-melt had stopped crashing down into South Fork. The river was quieting, but her heart was not. She did not respond when Daddy talked of all the push boats and salt barges that came this far upriver now. Just when Mama's apothecary rosebuds were ready to burst, Daddy said on his way out the door, "Tomorrow we'll be off downriver, Becca."

She looked up, dumbstruck by the reality of it. There was only the empty doorway, flooded with eastern sun, to talk back to. She turned her head jerkily around the dim cabin, so dear and yet suddenly so binding, since she had not said good-bye to the valley. What if something happened to her and, like Mama, she never got back to the people and places she loved so fiercely they were part of her?

She took a biscuit and her bonnet and called out to Jeremy that she would be back later. She ran downhill toward the meadow the way she had that day that seemed forever ago, when she got the rosebush from Widow Lang. Her bare feet even savored the prickle of gravel on the path. Her toes caressed the spring meadow grass with its circles of whites and blues and golds laid out like a quilt. She tore down through the morning mist, calling to the Scotts' cows before it struck her that they might have caused the sickness that took the hired hand Clemmet and Cora Scott and then Mama.

But today bird songs laced the air. She must not cry or grieve today. She must be thankful for this place and gather all its beauty into her heart forever. She picked a few colts-foot and daisies and stuck them in her hair. Then she went back to running until she could hardly breathe even in the mild, misty meadow breezes.

She climbed the path toward Widow Lang's cabin, passing the early blaze of rosebushes. This was the second year the widow wasn't here to see them. This year and years to come, these bushes and Becca's up on the peak would go from warm to pale pink to dark red hips and then to their yellow and orange autumn hues and finally the arching red winter canes, all without the folks who loved them. But, somehow, these wild mountain roses kept growing strong, the way Mama wanted Becca to.

The Widow Lang's long-tended garden stretched out big and barren before the cabin. Awed at the emptiness of it all, Becca pushed open the broken door. Neighbors had taken what was usable, as was the way; Mama had been given the old tin flour box from which the widow had once produced those three corn dodgers for Becca, Ernestine, and Albertine. A shutter banged against the wall in the breeze. The hearth stood cold and dark. Becca was relieved to see the widow's spirit was not here, but she had known it would not be. Widow Lang had become an angel and had flown away with her sisters into heaven.

That thought gave Becca's feet wings again. She ran down-hill and across the meadow and climbed Concord, stopping at the cabin only to see that Jeremy had eaten and was fine. She climbed the familiar Crawl Crick path past the sycamore snag that marked the boundary of Blake property. Up at Rest-ful Knob graveyard, she stared at the stones and gravehouses. Mama's looked bright and new compared to the gray weath-ered boards of the others. Becca felt too weepy to sing a song this time, so she just ran on. Just as the Widow Lang's soul was not in her coffin or her cabin, Mama's and Gran Ida's and the other souls of her departed family were not here but in another place—and partly caught forever inside her head and heart too.

Up at her refuge, Becca swung in on the vines and shouted just the way she had with Adam that special day she brought him here. She knew she'd find her roses still in tight buds. She would not see them blossom this year. But she would make a cutting from them the way she had once from their parent plant. She would take them with her to Pleasant Hill. That place's name did not fool her. This spot where she stood was pleasanter than any place on earth!

Tears blurring her eyes now at the finality of it all, Becca Blake walked for a last time onto her secret shelf. Then her mouth dropped open, and she halted in mid-stride. Daddy sat there close to the edge, one arm over his lifted knee, looking right at her.

"Oh, Daddy! I didn't know—"

"Saw and heard you coming, Becca. Mama told me you loved it up here." He cleared his throat. "Not been here in years, but I love it too."

Becca knelt and sat back on her heels beside him. They both looked off into the interlocking circles of horizons, awkwardly silent as they watched the rolling road of the river far below.

"Becca girl, you're not the only one who misses her something awful."

"I know. But when you sit up here, don't you regret leaving and can't we just try it here until next—"

"No! It wouldn't work, not for me, not for you. I know what's best, Becca. It's best not to look back."

"Even if you feel you belong here? Even if you feel you started here and can't let go?"

Daddy's head snapped around and his dark eyes bored into Becca's almost cruelly for a moment before his whole face softened. "You know, girl, going to tell you something I shouldn't, but guess you're old enough. This spot is where your Mama and I—where we made you the night there was a moonbow."

"You mean—made me—made a baby?"

Daddy stood suddenly. "Hard to believe for me too. Time changes things. Time will dull your sharp pain at leaving, Becca. Sunrise tomorrow," he said. He touched the top of her windblown head and walked slowly under the arch and away without looking back.

Emotions roared through her. Panic, anger, fear. For one second she thought she hated Daddy, but then she knew she loved him. That mixture of feelings she and Mama had talked of, that was it. Becca felt so sweetly touched by his being here, by his sharing with her, by his trying to comfort her. Yes, she thought and felt older once again as she had in other lightning flashes of discovery. Yes, she could see how Mama could love him so deeply she gave up years of her past in just a few days and left all she knew to follow him. Quickly Becca cut a rose planting and gazed around once more with tears in her eyes. Cradling the root ball, she followed Daddy down off Concord Peak. After all, there was a lot to do, and her family needed her, just the way she did them.

The next morning at sunrise, each toting a blanket tied to a stick and stuffed with a book, clothes, and food—Becca carrying her rosebush in a small herb crock—the Blakes set off downhill away from the cabin. Becca tried not to look back, but at the last turn of the crick, she did. She tried to gather it all into her mind so it would still be there every time she closed her eyes, perfect and warm and happy, waiting someday for her return. But Daddy had said not to look back, and after that she didn't. With not more than a wave when she spotted Aunt Euphy in an upstairs window of the Scott house, she just marched on behind Daddy and Jeremy, who was excited to be going on the river with Daddy. She was excited too, but each step, each breath pained her as she settled herself on the back of the salt barge from Goose Crick and saw the curve of river that was Shelter drift away. And then the narrow valley disappeared. And eventually through the trees, the top of purple and gold Concord Peak vanished, where her precious places stood alone now.

"Hurray, Daddy, we're on the river!" Jeremy cried. "Please tell me the name of every rock and snag and eddy all the way!"

"Don't think Becca feels like hearing it, my boy."

"Sure she does, don't you, Becca?"

"Sure. And I hope Daddy will point out to us which town is Boonesville so maybe we can stop and tell Mama's kin she passed on," Becca said, clasping her hands around her bent knees.

Daddy's face went thundercloud dark, and she knew she had overstepped after trying to be so brave and helpful yesterday. "Not our boat to put in where we want, Becca," he said. "If that's not a night stop, you'll just have to see Boonesville from the river 'til another time."

Becca was almost upset enough to ask Daddy if Mama's kin would take them in. That way, she figured, she would not have so far to go when she came of age and took Jeremy right back to Shelter to live on what she could make from herbs and rosewater. All sorts of desperate thoughts pounded through her head. But she remembered Mama's deathbed words and said, "Another time then, Daddy. Is Pleasant Hill far past Boonesville?"

"Good long ways, clear up by Harrodsburg."

"Harrodsburg? Jeremy, that's where Adam and his sisters live now!"

Jeremy nodded, his eyes aglow before he looked down into the brown river current. "But I'd hate to have to tell Adam we had to let his animals tend to themselves. Who will help them now?"

Staring away at the steep riverbanks so Daddy and Jeremy wouldn't see, Becca started to cry. Adam had said Aunt Euphy thought Becca was like the river pushing at these banks to cut deeper into life. But she did not feel that way now. She felt more like a bit of branch swept away by the current with nothing to hold onto. Who *would* help Adam's animals and all those sick and broke-boned folks who had depended first on Gran Ida and then on Mama and the herbs Becca delivered? Even as curious as she had been about the big world beyond the mountains, how could she ever survive without the oh so pretty places and precious people of Shelter?

But she dried her tears on her sleeve as Daddy called out, "White Oak to starboard!" just as if this was his keelboat. He told his tales each time he pointed out a place like Indian, Buffalo, Paw Paw, and Ford. Meanwhile, the South Fork heaved its big wet shoulder against hills overhung with rocky ledges. Some places along the way reminded her of Shelter so much the view stabbed her with homesickness again. She strained her eyes when they passed Boonesville the second day and Daddy pointed out the Mercer farm where he'd found Mama.

"Is that person there any kin to us?" Becca asked, pointing at a man bent behind a plow. "How about that girl there on the bank? How-do, are you Mercer kin?" Becca bellowed. The straw-hatted girl shook her head and pointed up at the distant house before the barge drifted on too far for them to hear her words.

Becca listened intently as Daddy told her and Jeremy some of the story of courting Mama, without realizing Becca had heard all of it from Mama, and not polished over for children's ears either. Becca tried to memorize the Mercer place, with its green fields and big black barn and more distant white house, fine as any palace Scarlet Town or Harrodsburg or Cincinnati could ever offer. She'd be back someday, she vowed, and tell the Mercers about Mama and meet her kin!

The next morning they passed Beattyville, where the South Fork joined with Middle Fork and North Fork to make the mighty Kentucky River. The fourth day they passed the spot where the Red River, which Daddy called the last of the big mountain streams, swelled the Kentucky for its broad swing through the bluegrass.

"Is bluegrass really blue, Daddy?" Jeremy asked.

"Only when it flowers, my boy. It's shiny green like emeralds!" Daddy promised, as if he'd ever laid eyes on such gems. "Bluegrass folks call this land God's footstool."

"Well, I swan!" Jeremy declared, but Becca held her tongue. Nothing could compare with her mountains. Why, even back at Beattyville before they saw the bluegrass, the blue limestone ledges were a far cry from the purple majesty of Concord.

But slowly Becca began to change her mind about the bluegrass coming up short next to her mountains. Maybe it was different, that was all. Rolling acres of fertile grassland enough to make a thousand mountain corn patches stretched before their eyes between steep embankments that reminded her, just a bit, of her ice palace cliffs at home. The soil was a thick, waxy mahogany loam instead of thin, reddish clay. Sometimes they glimpsed entire fields of new-sown tobacco, hemp, and wheat. The prairie grass, as Daddy called it, was broken only by huge oaks or stands of cherry, walnut, or locust. Grass grew even under the trees. She glimpsed pillared farmhouses and white-browed mansions instead of squat, gray log cabins.

"Right big farms here." Becca allowed herself that much of an approving comment, but she sniffed when she said it and looked narrow-eyed down her nose at Daddy.

"Why, sure," he told her with a charming smile. "Plant a nail in this soil and get crowbars. Put in a punkin seed and the full-growed vines snatch your feet 'fore you can run from the field."

"Really, Daddy?" Jeremy asked, but Becca only punched Daddy's arm. It frightened her how hard she'd really like to hit him.

The farther they went downstream, the more boats they saw of all sizes and kinds, piled with varied cargo. Daddy named them all and sometimes shouted a "how-do" to men he knew. On the fifth day the salt barge tied up at what Daddy called Shaker's Landing, where the Dix River poured into the Kentucky. Daddy swung Becca down to the bank. As the familiar Goose Crick salt barge set off again toward Cincinnati with shouts and waves from the friendly crew, her heart began to thud right in her throat. She started to shake. She might be a grown girl with at least one foot firm in womanhood, but she would have given the rest of her life to have Mama by her side right now.

"Just a little walk uphill," Daddy said, "and then we're there. Not a real climb like back where we come from. And maybe we'll meet us one of those fine big Shaker dump wagons on the road to ride. And if we do, both of you get into your Sunday meeting shoes quicker'n greased lightning! Won't have them rich Bluegrass Shakers looking down at us, even if they are so kindly!"

Jeremy jumped up and down with excitement. For one moment Becca felt so mean-spirited she could have shoved her brother into the river. How could he forget Mama and Shelter so soon, to be looking forward to this? Slowly she shouldered her pack and held her rosebush crock tight between her small breasts. The three of them began the walk up the wagon road to Pleasant Hill.

Part II

Sister Rebecca, Fragrant Shaker Rose

(1825–1837)

But earthlier happy is the rose distilled,
Than that which withering on the virgin thorn
Grows, lives and dies in single blessedness.
　　　　　—William Shakespeare
　　　　　　A Midsummer Night's Dream

Chapter Seven

"Sure is a pretty place. Pleasant, like its name, right, Becca?" Daddy said over his shoulder without daring to look back at her again. "Won't be long, you'll feel right to home here."

Becca knew he had seen her stiffen her backbone and slow her stride as they approached the boundaries of Pleasant Hill and its Shakertown. And when he made her and Jeremy put on shoes in the midst of summer, just to greet the Shakers when it wasn't even Sunday meeting time, her bottom lip set hard. Pleasant maybe for others, but the place bothered Becca, maybe partly because Daddy and Jeremy seemed so excited about it.

Here, on the uplands above the river cliffs, the horizon looked too far, too flat to Becca, even with its gentle knolls and rolling green hills. Teams of blue-clad men with their shiny horses tended fertile fields of grain and corn. Lush gardens in ordered rows and straight-lined orchards both astounded and annoyed Becca. Painted frame, limestone, and brick buildings popped up everywhere she looked beyond a finely laid fence that seemed to stretch forever. But for the

Scotts' walled garden, she'd hardly seen any fences. Were they to keep people and things in or out? Stones like these were made to be strewn by God's hand down the mountainside or used as natural bridges across a cold, rattling crick.

She followed Daddy and her capering brother up cleanly hewn stairs cut right into and across the broad stone fence. On the top step, she paused, starved for any high, rocky vantage to view the sweep of the scene. From here she saw village men in identical, broad-brimmed hats bent over metal hoes in garden after garden full of plants she could not even name. Women with deep straw poke bonnets, clad in somber hues with kerchiefs across their chests and white aprons around their sturdy middles, bustled here and there in pairs or groups, as occupied as buzzing bees in a hive.

"Sure something to see, eh, Becca?" Daddy flashed Becca his warmest smile. He looked both hurt and hopeful. He lifted his hand to her elbow to help her down the fence steps. She almost shook him off. His touch made tears prickle behind her eyes. Mama had said to help Daddy, but on her deathbed Mama had also made Daddy promise to take good care of his children. And in bringing them here so far from home and planning to light out again, he had broken that vow, as far as Becca was concerned. Yet she warred with herself to keep calm, to love him in spite of his betrayal. Curse it, just like this place, her feelings were too big, too bounteous, too busy for a mountain girl to handle. Yet, head held high as a queen in one of Gran Ida's old songs, she set her shod feet inside Shakertown.

They walked a smooth, curving road toward buildings clustered around a fine reddish brick mansion. "What's that building? What's that one?" Jeremy's voice bit deep into Becca's resolve as he pointed things out, chattering like a squirrel. "What's that one there, Daddy, that humped building?"

"Reckon it's an icehouse for one of these big Shaker families, my boy."

An icehouse, Becca's thoughts echoed. Adam had showed

her his family's icehouse that day she had first shared his animals, his fears, his dreams. Adam was now lost to her in Harrodsburg, but if she had to run away from here and needed to borrow money to get home, maybe she could find him there. And it was then she lifted her eyes past Daddy's broad back just ahead of her.

There, a way off beside the brick building, awaited a garden of pink and red roses in full, fervent flower.

"Oh, so many roses!"

"Thought you'd dropped your tongue in the river," Daddy tried to tease her before his voice went solemn again. "Told you there'd be plenty here to tend, Becca. Herb garden just beyond that brick place too."

Even that did not lighten her load or her feet as they approached the half-log, half-frame house at the very corner of the village proper. Becca's eyes widened. Sweeping the front steps with a neat, flat broom was a woman with the darkest skin she had ever seen. She was beautiful with large, chiseled features that demanded Becca's gaze. Her huge, tea-dark eyes, broad nose, and full, shapely mouth fascinated Becca. She was humming a strange tune to herself, and because of the swish, swish of her broom and her bonneted head bent to her task, they came up close to her before she saw or heard them.

"Oh, my!" she said, those two words so melodious it seemed she sang them. "You all, just wait one minute, an' I'll fetch the elders."

She disappeared inside with a swirl of gray skirt. Becca saw that under the deep brim of her bonnet she wore a white lawn cap but her slate-black hair, twisty as a morning glory vine, peeked out too. Soon two older Shaker ladies came out and invited them in. Both were dressed much the same, but Becca thought their similarities stopped there. The one who introduced herself as Sister Alice Triplett, Elderess of the East Family, was spare and strong. Things about her seemed harsh despite her friendly nature as she invited them all to sit at a table inside. Her nose and chin were pointed; her narrow, pale gray eyes seemed filed at each end. Her hands looked a bit like claws. The other woman, named Sister Faith Goodrich, another elderess, was short and plump as a pigeon, with blue eyes and rosy cheeks. She seemed as soft as Sister Alice seemed sharp.

The dark-skinned Shaker, named Sister Sally, soon came in with a crockery pitcher of cool lemonade and almond cake for the three of them. Everything tasted delicious, but Becca only sipped and sampled. She had no intention of gulping and gobbling before these watchful women as Daddy and Jeremy did. Her stomach felt as if it were tied in kneelboat rope knots, tugging and tightening.

"The elders are out right now, so we will explain things to you, Mr. Blake," Sister Alice was telling Daddy. "You understand then you must legally rescind all parental rights." Daddy jerked out a nod and shifted in his chair.

"And you understand the Society of Believers must be protected from people who later change their minds?"

"Just so's they can make up their own minds later about staying," Daddy said.

"Of course. Each member has that right of free choice before they sign the Covenant as an adult."

"I'd want to visit them on occasion."

The two women's gazes locked, then returned to Daddy. Becca gripped her hands hard together. Jeremy might not grasp what was happening here, but she did. Daddy was giving them away to these strangers miles from home!

"While they are in the Children's Order, it would be seemly enough," Sister Faith said, her voice so gentle. "The boy is young, so he would be there for several years until age sixteen, if you think visitations are suitable, Mr. Blake. But at age fourteen the girls join the sisters in a family dwelling house, and your daughter here," Sister Faith assessed Becca's sullen stare anew, "is what age now?"

When Becca didn't answer, Daddy floundered, "Let's see now, Becca was born in 1812, in the month of—in the winter—and the boy's a few years younger, ah—"

Becca leveled a stare at Daddy that made him drop his eyes. He did not remember the months, let alone the dates of her or Jeremy's birth! "I was born December thirtieth, 1812, and my brother Jeremy on May the eighth, 1816."

"Then your daughter, Mr. Blake," Sister Faith said with her blue eyes obviously trying to soften Becca's stare, "in just six months will come to live in one of our three big Shaker families. After that, it is hoped she will flourish in the society, and choose to break off ties with the world— though occasional family visits for business concerns may be requested through the Trustees."

"Becca here," Daddy said, his voice sounding as trembly as Becca felt, "is real skilled at herbs, tending apothecary roses, and delivering curative medicines to folks far and wide. Taught by her grandmother and her mother Ann."

The two sisters exchanged quick looks again as if Daddy had said something momentous. "Her care for herbs and roses will be a welcome contribution, but it won't be seemly or needful for her to deliver them," Sister Alice said, looking down her pointed nose at Daddy. "And now, Mr. Blake, if you would just kindly step over to this desk a moment, I'll explain these papers . . ."

Becca perched on her chair, as still as one of Jeremy's carvings. Sister Alice had *better* explain, she thought bitterly, for Daddy could not read, and wrote only numbers and his name. She wanted to jump up and scream and run. Daddy actually thought she would become one of these folks! She frowned down at her clenched hands on her knees. Her fingers, woven together, had gone white as sausages.

The adults were joined by two men called elders who glanced over at the children and apparently nodded their approval. "Great blessings from Mother Ann," Becca overheard the men say in bits of broken conversation. Yes, she thought, my angelic Mama's blessings ruined by my devil of a Daddy.

Daddy signed some papers, the quill pen scratching loudly amid the buzz of voices. Becca did not believe he would be back, not even when he kissed them both good-bye with shiny eyes, "just 'til I come this far upriver next time." Jeremy cried for Daddy not to go and held to his waist. When Daddy unwound the boy's arms, Becca took her brother's little hand and held it tight.

Suddenly, while Jeremy sobbed, her eyes went dry as her heart. She barely felt it when Daddy kissed her good-bye on the cheek and said some jumbled words she did not heed. Strangely, after a few steps away, he came back to hug her stiff body and ruffle Jeremy's hair. The tears now puddled in Daddy's eyes did not break down Becca's resentment, even hatred, which had gone as hard as a Shaker stone fence.

Shortly after Daddy departed, Sister Sally was asked to walk them a half mile down the road to what was called the Children's Order on the North Family Lot. At least she and Jeremy would be together, Becca thought as she took her brother's hand again.

"Could I plant this rosebush from—from home with the others out there?" she asked Sister Faith. "I see it's a different kind, but it's real hardy."

"It doesn't look like a damask, and that and apothecaries are all we are allowed to grow here for usefulness' sake," Sister Alice answered for Sister Faith.

"Perhaps you should plant it along the boundaries beyond the North Lot where you can tend it easier," Sister Faith said and patted her arm. The portly woman was no taller than Becca, but she seemed to hover over her. "Now, I sense you are very unhappy, dear girl. I know the world's strivings are dreadful to bear. But that's one of the beauties of the Shaker life. Here, there is calmness of spirit, peace through self-discipline, you'll see. Sister Sally, kindly take Brother Jeremy and Sister Rebecca along with you now, won't you?"

Sister Rebecca. Her new name rattled through Rebecca's cold core with each step along the Shaker road. She carried only her rosebush now. Their goods, including the family Bible, *Pilgrim's Progress*, and Mama's beloved herbal book, had been donated to the Shakers. Sister Sally pointed out various things they passed, but Becca—Sister Rebecca—felt so empty it terrified her. She looked back once behind her, the way Daddy had gone off over that stone fence. Though she tried to hold the feelings back, fear and fury came crashing in to fill all the hollows inside her.

Rebecca never knew that they'd been poor until she saw Pleasant Hill. Even the way the Scotts lived had not made her feel needy, until now. Here everyone wore shoes all year, made by village cobblers who replaced Gran Ida's old ones their third day in the Children's Order. The tidy, trim buildings, even the older log ones, were kept in perfect repair, sullying her memories of the ramshackle cabins of Shelter Valley. Floors were polished, everything swept and dusted, for "there is no dirt in heaven," as Sister Betsy White, the strict girls' caretaker, was fond of saying. Rebecca did not mind the constant cleaning, but she preferred the tasks outside.

She thought she felt almost calm the day Sister Sally came to take her for a walk in the village. Jeremy was out on an excursion with the other boys to watch the plowing of new fields. Rebecca had been appalled to find that she and Jeremy must live in separate cabins in the Children's Order, but at least she was allowed to see and speak with him.

"How can grown men and women live together in the same house as a family and be—you know, kept separate?" Rebecca asked Sister Sally as they headed toward the village proper.

"You just haint been in the family dwellings yet," Sally told her. "You can see men an' women got their own sep'rate doors, but inside they also got their own staircases, their own retiring rooms, an' their own side of the dining hall. It works fine, just fine. I got wed jumping over the broom once to a big buck of a man with a hard temper, an' I tell you, this suits me better. But the Believers hold union meetings at night sometimes where a few of us women set in facing rows of chairs an' chat with a few of the men, everything nice an' equal.

"The Believers are striving," she went on, "not only to be celibate, but perfect, not even speaking nor thinking carnal desires. It's worth the price, I say. I'd do anything to please my Shaker brothers and sisters and make 'em proud of me!"

Under her split-rye straw bonnet Rebecca rolled her eyes at such blind loyalty. But she had to admit she liked Sister Sally better than the other sisters. Sister Sally never scolded and was not so primly proper.

Now she watched Sister Sally stretch her strides almost as if something was suddenly chasing them. Then in a proud voice the woman said, "The Shakers done bought my freedom from my master up Lexington way and set me free, that's what they done! I'm equal to all of 'em just like other Shakers who was once slaves. An' want more'n anything to prove I'm worthy to be a kitchen deaconess someday! The way here is love and kindliness an' it won me right over! I'm honored to 'put my hands to work and my heart to God,' just like the Shaker song says."

Rebecca felt awed at that outpouring. But she had not come here from slavery but from freedom, so this was a worse place by comparison, not a better one! Still, she could not resist one question, however much she didn't want to be won over by anyone here the way Sister Sally had been.

"What song talks about putting hands to work?" she asked.

"Lots of 'em. We do singing and dancing to lift the spirit up to see angels, least some of the folks what see visions do." Sister Sally lowered her bell-clear voice a bit. "There's angels here at Shakertown, all right. Both the kind what buys a slave girl to save her an' the kind what comes down from our dear Mother Ann in heaven during laboring at the dance," she said with a nod.

"There's angels where I come from too." Rebecca bragged a bit, not wanting Shakertown to outdo Shelter in Sister Sally's eyes. "I used to just think it was the dear old lady named Widow Lang, but now I know my own Mother Ann was one of them!''

Sally shook her head at that, but didn't argue the way Rebecca knew Sister Alice or the girls' schoolteacher, Sister Hortency, would have. In True Religion class Rebecca had learned that the Shaker beliefs had been set down by an Englishwoman named Ann Lee who saw heavenly visions and claimed to be sent from God just as Jesus Christ was. Only Mother Ann was to establish a perfect heaven on earth to help folks earn heaven after they died.

In her youth, Mother Ann had been forced to work hard in the mills of Manchester, England. Her family had made her wed a rough blacksmith, and her babies had all died. She had decided then that carnal relations were the ultimate sin that separated man from God, starting with Adam and Eve. She had come to America and suffered much cruelty when she preached her beliefs before she could found the first Shaker village. Mother Ann Lee had died, but her work went on in nineteen Shaker communities here and in the East.

Rebecca felt sorry for the Shakers' Mother Ann for dying young the way hers had, but the Shakers' always quoting their Mother Ann made Rebecca miss Mama worse and curse Daddy more. The awful anger just stayed bottled up inside her. She recalled the incident last week when she'd been sent away for such feelings.

"Now this, girls," their teacher, the bright-eyed, smiling Sister Hortency Hoosier had begun one of their rare geography classes, "is going to be a lesson on the globe. Not, of course," she added with a tap of her finger on its shiny brown belly, "that you will be traveling. But no one shall say we Believers do not know there is a huge world out there we must avoid and that it is filled with folks who need to know our ways."

Rebecca duly raised her right hand and was recognized to stand and speak. "Then why is it," she asked, "the Believers don't go out to teach others the best Shaker ways? Why, even my grandmother's songs of old England told of people sad and dying"—she was careful not to say they died longing for love—"so surely everyone has the same needs and could benefit."

Sister Hortency's smile faded and her full lips tut-tutted. "Sister Rebecca, I am afraid you do not know the world's people, and that is just as well. However, since you mentioned England, please step up front and point it out for the others. Now, here, you see, young sisters, is our Shakertown near Lexington," she told them, beaming, while Rebecca walked forward.

Standing before the class, Rebecca leaned down to squint at the globe. She tried to see the dot called Lexington under the tip of Sister Hortency's index finger. She couldn't tell if Shakertown was there either, but of course, on a Shaker globe, it must be. She could barely make out the fine-as-a-hair line that was the Kentucky river squirting out from under the teacher's quarter-moon of trimmed, clean fingernail.

"May I just find Shelter first, where I was born and raised up?" Rebecca asked.

"*Reared* is the more proper way to express that thought, Sister Rebecca, but I am afraid you will not find Shelter," the teacher told her with a shake of her white-capped head.

Unbelieving, Rebecca bent even closer to follow the river east. Why, she couldn't even see where the forks came together, let alone the names of any river towns! How dared these Shakers have a ball that was supposed to be the world and leave out Shelter! All she could see there were letters spelling out "Appalachians" over a bunch of black bumps that didn't look anything like her purple and gold mountains.

"Now, here, sisters, is England, where Mother Ann came from," Sister Hortency was saying, turning the globe to point way over a big blue puddle of water. Rebecca gasped. That meant England wasn't even near Pound Gap or attached to Virginia!

"But," she stammered, flushing beet-red, "where is New Orleans then? Isn't it there either? My daddy probably went to New Orleans, but it can't be far as he used to come home to visit us from there!''

"Now, Sister Rebecca, it is needful that you lower your voice. New Orleans is of no consequence because you are living here now, and worldly family relations are no longer coming back to—"

Rebecca did not hear the rest. She was furious. At Daddy . . . at this woman . . . at all these pious, proper, proud Shakers! The fact she knew not to criticize her elders seemed suddenly stupid. Shelter wasn't even on the map! Her precious past seemed paltry and pitiful. Before she knew she would move, she grabbed the globe so fast by its stand that it spun around, making her dizzy. She smacked it to a stop with her other hand and peered down its curve to the south. At the bottom of the black thread of the Mississippi River, there was New Orleans!

"See, there it is, and it's of consequence to me!" Rebecca announced. "And I have a friend named Adam who lives at Harrodsburg too, so it's got to be here near where you had your finger!"

More than tut-tutting now, Sister Hortency took the globe back from Rebecca and set it on the desk. "That is too small to be there either. It is only seven miles away, but sisters never go there unattended, and certainly, never Shaker children!"

"At home, since I was ten, I went all over!" Rebecca declared. "I'm not bragging on it, just saying I did it and nothing bad happened, only good things, visiting folks to take them herbs. I sure do know the world's people, some real fine folks too! But the real Shaker world is just inside the Shaker fences! All that's really mine here is one rosebush from home. Even if there are thousands of acres and sixteen gardens here, it's not the same, not like I'm a part of it, not—"

With a firm grasp on her arm, Sister Hortency escorted Rebecca up the aisle and out the back door of the schoolroom while pairs of eyes went wider and mouths hung open. The teacher quietly closed the door behind them, then loosened her hold.

"I simply cannot allow unseemly outbursts in my classroom, Sister Rebecca, however agile-minded a student you are. You are part of a greater whole here. Individual pasts are best forgotten and futures merged as one at Pleasant Hill. I am heartily regretful if your father is lost to the world and you cannot find your birthplace on a globe. But, believe me, you will find that this place and people will become your loving family and your future if you let them. Now, I must ask you to ponder these things in the silence of the sisters' retiring room. And when you return to the classroom tomorrow, I expect you will wish to apologize for your—your worldly behavior."

Because she felt Mama would want it, Rebecca had apologized, though the whole time her stomach had felt as though she'd eaten green apples. Worse, today she found she was wrong about Sister Sally not scolding.

"Sister Rebecca," Sally's voice interrupted her brooding, as her hand stayed Rebecca's arm, "you all got to learn to stay on the square walks an' not go cutting 'cross on the grass. Just like in Shaker workshops and kitchens, 'there's a place for everything an' everything in its place,' 'cluding people."

Rebecca stepped guiltily back onto the neat flagstone path that ran the length of the village, connecting the three main clusters of buildings. At home, there were no man-made paths but where trees hemmed in the way to form a natural passage. At home, such grass would be a thick carpet of wonder to run right through, and barefooted too. But here the village layout was planned and orderly. Each family had its own group of structures. Stone or brick dwelling houses sat on sturdy limestone foundations called Kentucky marble. Workshops painted cream or yellow with immaculate trim were backed by sturdy barns and service shops in key colors of red, brown, or lead.

"Don't you all want to see that herb garden you been

askin' 'bout?'' Sister Sally prompted. Rebecca stopped frowning and nodded as they started down the path again.

Sally introduced Rebecca to Sister Jerusha and Sister Tiney, who were weeding among the perfectly parallel and neatly labeled lines of basil, lemon balm, mint, and rue at one corner of the herb garden. Sister Alice came out of the big brick house called the East Family Dwelling to join them, her hawk-eyed face hidden by her bonnet.

Sister Alice was evidently here to oversee these workers, or maybe to oversee Rebecca herself. She'd called Rebecca into the Trustees' Office for a bit of extra learning each afternoon, since Rebecca would be of Shaker age soon. Sister Faith had been there too but Sister Alice did most of the questioning and talking. She even asked Rebecca not to refer to Mama as Mother Ann, as Rebecca had taken to doing when she saw how it disturbed them. After all, Sister Alice said, brothers and sisters might think she was quoting the beloved founder of Shakerdom when she only meant her own mountain mama. A bitter taste came up like bile in Rebecca's throat again as Sister Alice bent close to hear the conversation.

"Now, I hear you know herbal gardening, young Sister Rebecca," Sister Jerusha said, straightening from her stooped position. "Can you tell me what rue is useful for?" she questioned, pointing at the rigid row of yellow-flowered plants.

Suddenly the memory of Mama leaning close to Becca before the blazing hearth rose up whole in her mind. How could she ever let such warm memories go with the rest of the world? That deserter Daddy had said to never look back, but the old Becca just couldn't keep from it!

"Why, besides keeping bugs off roses, rue is right fine to dose young girls with," Rebecca drawled, her voice heavy with a mountain twang not her own. "That is, if their monthly flux doesn't start on its own so they can bear babies from bedding with their husbands." She ignored Sister Sally's gasp at such blatantly spoken carnal matters and the jerk

127

of Sister Alice's head that sent sunlight shooting up under her bonnet. She wanted to shock, to hurt them all—to hurt herself in their eyes, since she had lost everything dear, maybe through her own fault.

"Of course," she plunged on before they could stop her, "my mother Ann said some use mint to start the flux, but rue is better. And if you really want to know what I think, I think your Mother Ann just hated being married and that's why she thought all this up about men and women staying separate! I know a man named Claib Tucker and his first wife lit out because she couldn't abide a man in bed! But my parents had a happy marriage!" she cried before those words too turned to rue on her tongue. "I'm really sorry your Mother Ann's babies died when they were born but my Gran Ida lost four that way and my mother Ann one and they both kept right on loving the man they were wed to without deserting him and—"

"Sister Rebecca!" Sister Alice hissed. "Mother Ann only teaches us such holy strictures because they are the fulfillment of God's word. The Shakers stay celibate only so we may escape the sins of the world and love all mankind chastely and universally. If you would kindly look around here, you would find love and peace, not this serpent of dissension that festers within your bosom! Sister Sally, kindly walk Sister Rebecca back to the Children's Order, and we shall all pray for forgiveness and for an understanding in our misguided sister, Rebecca Blake!"

Rebecca marched away willingly at Sister Sally's side. Now that she had really exploded, she felt deflated but not a bit regretful until she saw Sally looked sad.

"What will happen now?" Rebecca asked when the North Family Lot came into sight and they had not spoken a word.

"Just like they said, they'll pray for you. If'n you all was really one of us now, you'd have a mighty lot of confessing to do 'fore everyone tonight!"

"I'm sorry I nettled you."

Their eyes met from the shadows of their bonnets. Sally

nodded. "That's a start to confession. You all should put the past away. I did."

"But you said your past was unhappy. Mine was happy, mostly. I can't help how I feel here, all lonely and trapped!"

Sister Sally's strong brown hands rested on Rebecca's white fists. "Then pray God send a miracle to change your hard heart toward these fine folk, Sister Rebecca. Pray real hard an' work real hard, an' you'll see it'll all come out a blessing."

Rebecca sighed. Time after time, it just seemed the old Becca came roaring out. And she didn't know how she was ever going to get that independent mountain girl inside her to behave the Shaker way.

After that, Sister Rebecca prayed hard and worked hard at her duties and in school in the Children's Order. But still the cold coil of hurt inside would not unwind and let her go. Why, Mama had told her to watch over Jeremy and now even Jeremy didn't want her to! She saw him slowly drift away from her as he made new friends and apparently shifted his allegiance from Daddy to Brother Rufus Culp, the boys' caretaker. This evening, Jeremy played beanbag games with his friends. He didn't even look her way when she walked behind the buildings toward the privy, but then wandered farther out toward the back fence.

The road to the city of Lexington ran past here, but as dusk fell, it looked deserted. She should not have wandered off alone this far, but again, she felt she had every right to overstep so-called proper bounds. She rambled a bit farther along the fence to the spot where she'd been allowed to plant her rosebush. Still in shock from being cut and moved, it had not put forth one bud.

Glancing behind her once again, she hiked up her brown skirt and boosted herself to sit on the sharp slant of stone-stacked Shaker fence. She swung her long legs over to the other side. Gingerly, hoping not to soil her skirt, she dropped over into the meadow. Flowers muted by the low slant of sun bowed their heads in greeting. And then she saw a girl staring at her from across the curve of fence, and she jumped.

"Oh! I didn't see you! Who are you?"

"I didn't mean to give you a start. I'm Christina Benton, the new orphan girl. I guess I was supposed to wait for a sister to walk me down here from the Trustees' House. But no one came, and I didn't want it to get dark. I saw you walking and knew by your bonnet you're a Shaker, just like I'm going to be when they get me the garb tomorrow. The farm family who was keeping me just can't no more. Say, are you an orphan too?"

As they both leaned in, hands so close on opposite sides of the fence, Rebecca studied the girl. She had brown hair, brown eyes, and brownish skin from the sun, but they were all different, warm and lively browns. Rebecca liked her freckles, similar to her own, only there were lots more of them. She had a perky nose and a bow-shaped mouth in a round, friendly face. She was shorter than Rebecca, but probably about her age. She had so much thick hair Rebecca wasn't sure it could be tamed by a knot and a pin under the prim white cap, which hardly contained her own rambunctious ringlets. And Christina's body was curvy as these hills; Rebecca didn't think a Shaker shoulder cape crossed and pinned over her breasts could hide them either. All in all, Christina Benton was not pretty, but special somehow. Her smile adorned her face. She talked quickly, and her conversation was punctuated with movements of her strong, blunt-fingered hands. The old Becca, huddled for dear life inside the new Sister Rebecca, liked her instantly.

"No, I'm only a half orphan," Rebecca told her. "My mother passed on, but my father—he has to travel so he left us here."

"But you remember him then, and your mother too?"

Rebecca nodded solemnly. "My brother—my blood brother, Jeremy—lives here too," she added and pointed toward the log houses across the fence.

"Oh, how wonderful! You're so blessed! I'd give anything

to have such memories, but I didn't know my family at all nor nothing of them. Left in a manger of a barn, I was, can you believe that? But Sister Faith told me the Shakers are going to be my family now. And you will be my sister, won't you? I always wanted a sister!''

The agony of loss—all her losses—swelled in Rebecca. She might not be able to find Shelter on a map, but she could always find it, precious and pretty, inside her head and heart. She had known and loved her people, and she would not let these Shakers take that away from her. Like Sister Sally, how could this girl be so happy here?

But there was one thing she could not let pass. ''I always wanted a sister, too,'' she choked out.

''What's your name, then?''

''Sister Rebecca Blake, or just Rebecca when we're alone. But listen, if these Shakers think we're special friends, they won't like it. So we mustn't let all their rules come between us, because they try to keep real family members apart.''

They shook hands across the fence, smiling at each other in the fading light. Rebecca climbed the fence again. They both giggled for no reason but having found each other.

''There's ever so much they'll try to teach you,'' Rebecca told her. ''But let's remember we are secret friends—like real sisters—better than Shaker ones.''

Christina nodded as they made their way toward the dwellings. And, luckily, Rebecca remembered to retie her bonnet on her head before she led her new friend into the house to meet Sister Betsy.

Chapter Eight

With Christina as a sister and a friend, Rebecca's life among the Shakers went from bitter to bittersweet, but she still missed home and yearned for those she had lost. It pained her daily to see Jeremy slip further away from her care. And as for Daddy, she often gazed off in the direction from which he would come to visit—if he came. Just as she feared, he did not appear. Maybe, her inner voice cried, he really did blame her for the loss of her little sister, even of Mama! Because of her failures, he could not bear to look at her, despite how he had admitted once he made mistakes. Rebecca's eyes narrowed; her lips thinned. She turned away from the river road, wanting to love Daddy but cursing him for leaving his children just the way he had his wife.

The first six months at Pleasant Hill she would have been stiff and shriveled up inside if she had not had Christina. Together they built their own secret world of rebellion within the stern strictures of Shakerdom.

They were to keep silent at meals. So the two of them created a sign language of their own. Their dinner plates became clocks; knives slanted just so on them were hour hands.

"Can you get away from helping in the dye workshop at two?" Rebecca's knife would inquire of Christina's careful sideways squint, two sisters away along the bench.

"Ding!" clanged Christina's knife when she accidentally dropped it too hard against the crockery. Sister Betsy cleared her throat and shot a hard look at the offender. Notwithstanding, Christina's knife now said, "No, but I could get away at one."

Rebecca took a long drink of lemonade, meaning "Shall we meet by the river?"

Christina drank too, but only one quick swallow. "Best make it by the creek," that indicated, and the afternoon's escapade was settled. Smug, they stifled their giggles with mouthfuls of apple cobbler. After all, they weren't breaking the rule that meals here were to be a purposeful and shared spiritual experience.

Shared, yes, Rebecca fumed silently, but not at all like the old days when her family shared the day's events and their very lives at the table—in warm, out-loud conversation—no matter how little food they had compared to this Shaker bounty! As for the spiritual here under the watchful eye of Sister Betsy, life with Christina was a spiritual adventure of its own.

For one thing, Christina was deathly afraid of the dark. No prescribed prayers or pious devotions could woo her from it. But when she knew Rebecca was in the next narrow bed and she could reach out her hand to touch her when she went to sleep or woke in the night, she survived the darkened room the rules demanded. All were to sleep straight in their beds without moving, but Rebecca learned to expect a shaky hand to flutter over to clasp hers or touch her shoulder.

Then too, in a place that venerated cleanliness and order, Christina was disaster. She was forever getting herself dirty or splattering her skin with dye so that she seemed to have been stricken with some dread disease.

But Christina made Rebecca laugh and feel needed. They shared their thoughts and made up private songs. They knew each other so well a single look or word could send them into gales of laughter. They had vowed to stop that because they feared that poor, beleaguered Sister Betsy, who could hardly send them to their room together to chastise them, might separate them. For sins great and small, they had done penance on their knees. And there had been public confessions before the Children's Order, while Rebecca winked at Jeremy and got him to snickering and then had to begin confessing all over again. But soon they would be joining the East Family under the watchful eyes of elderesses Sister Faith and Sister Alice, and who knew what would happen then?

On January 20, 1826, after they had both turned fourteen, Sister Rebecca and Sister Christina went with great trepidation to live in the big brick East Family Dwelling House. Rebecca's insides twisted when she had to bid farewell to Jeremy, who seemed only a little sad to see her leave. With the other boys, he lined up to wave good-bye. Despite the no-touching-the-boys rule, Rebecca went back right in front of everyone to hug him and promise she would make application to see him when she could.

"I'll not really leave you, Jeremy, not ever!" she vowed as Brother Rufus stepped quickly forward to tug the boy back amid his brethren.

Her fervent vow echoed in her head as they started for the village. She and Christina had secretly sworn they would never leave each other. Sometimes, Rebecca thought, that was the only reason she did not do something so dreadful that they would put her out of Shakertown. It was why she did not take Jeremy and flee to Shelter and hope Aunt Euphy would see fit to feed them until she could get the herbs going again. Her promise to Christina had even been a blood vow.

"See, just a little prick on our fingertips with this jackknife and then we mingle drops of blood like this," Christina had said. "I heard it's what Indians do!"

"We're hardly Indians, my friend."

"We're in rebellion, raiders of the Shaker frontier!" Christina insisted with a low laugh, referring to their midnight marauding plunder of the kitchen. That was the night they were sent to bed without their supper for wearing scarlet aprons Christina had dyed on the sly.

"Blood oaths aside," Rebecca had said as she seized both her friend's hands, "we will *never* desert each other. I think the only good thing about living here is striving for a sort of permanent perfection. You and I will never be perfect like the Shakers want, but we will be permanent perfect friends! Now, in the adult family," she had added, hoping Christina took her subtle warning to heart, "I suppose we might have to obey more of the rules."

"That won't be hard, as I reckon we as good as broke all the ones here already!" Christina had said with a broad grin.

Today, even their steps matched each other as they headed for Shaker adulthood, Rebecca thought, and that comforted her somewhat. Each of them carried her possessions: a spare frock, undergarments, and the new pair of cloth shoes for Meeting House dancing. Sister Sally, who had been sent to fetch them, led them away from their brief Shaker childhood.

"An' you'll both be in the same retiring room with Sister Tiney, Sister Jerusha, Sister Mary, Sister Jane, Sister Anna, an' me!" Sally told them as they arrived before the dwelling. "That corner room, third floor, right up there!"

Their breath wreathed their heads like white halos as they tilted their chins up. In windows gleaming in the cold, late-morning sun reflected bare branches catching clouds. Imagine, Rebecca thought, living in a house bigger than Adam Scott's! But she would give all this up—except Christina—to be home at the tiny Crawl Crick cabin again.

Soon Brother Benjamin Dunlavy brought the new Brother Travis Truax. Brother Travis was a sturdy-looking, red-haired young man. Christina whispered that he was as shy as he was strong. She had seen him plowing in the fields and had heard he was an orphan too. Brother Benjamin, frowning at her whispering, intoned, "Shall we kindly go in, sisters?" Travis Truax bobbed his broad-brimmed felt hat as his blue eyes shifted from Rebecca to Christina. Rebecca squeezed Christina's arm as they entered through the women's door on the left. Brother Travis followed Brother Benjamin through the other door. And a rousing welcome ensued which almost touched Rebecca's heart.

The eighty-some East Family members waited to greet them. The brethren lined the hall to the right and stood two deep on the men's staircase; the sisters balanced them on the other side. Family members stepped forward to take the burdens from the three of them, and everyone broke into a melodic song:

> *Oh, my sweet Shaker home,*
> *Oh, my sweet Shaker home.*
> *'Tis my joy, 'tis my eternal song.*
> *Here in straight paths I'm led,*
> *And in purity fed,*
> *Oh, there's nothing like my sweet Shaker home.*

"Nothing like my sweet *Shelter* home," Rebecca muttered.

Handshakes and kisses flowed from the women and girls. The family elders and elderesses, deacons and deaconesses shook their hands. Christina beamed, but Rebecca only nodded. She still felt cold inside, even when the Shakers were so warm and generous to her. She had once felt more welcome than this, even if Christina had not: the simple "how you keepin'?" of mountain folk had been the only song she needed.

But Sister Faith had counseled that she must be grateful for this family, her fellow laborers. If only she could stop warring with herself by letting the world outside go. Here, she knew there would be no burdens to bear alone when someone fell sick or was in need. And though she'd never replace the love and friendship she and Mama had shared, with Christina and Sally and Sister Faith smiling at her, and even with Sister Alice watching so closely, she knew she must somehow try to be content.

After a rib-sticking winter meal of squash muffins, scrapple, succotash, eggs goldenrod, corned beef and cabbage, and sugar cream pie, Sister Sally took Rebecca and Christina around the big building. Besides some retiring rooms, the first floor included a parlor, a dining hall, and the huge kitchen which all sisters took a turn in. Sally was most proud of that, and Rebecca knew Christina would relish working there. There were three floors with a total of fifteen retiring rooms, each inhabited by as many as eight family members. Within the sturdy foundation stood massive storage cellars filled with a bounty of preserves and dried fruit, barrels of pickled meats, and hanging herbs. Under the huge eaves were floor-to-ceiling rows of deep, built-in storage drawers, all lit by ceiling windows. The whole building was spacious and bright, but she'd still rather have her small, dim, dirt-floor home.

Then Sally took them to their retiring room. It alone seemed the size of a mountain cabin. The ash floors shone. The walls were cleanest white paint with a head-high pegboard painted Shaker blue with perfectly matched, lathe-turned pegs at regular intervals. There one could properly hang clothes, candle holders, the single small looking glass, or furniture when the sisters swept and dusted. In these winter months, big blue cloths hung from pegs to warm the walls.

Furniture was spare, something Rebecca had always been used to. But Shaker furniture was lean-lined, durable but delicate. This room had eight identical low rope-mattress beds covered with matching handworked comforters, checkered white and blue. No old quilts on trundle beds here. The Shaker comforters looked perfectly angular and in line, unlike the tumbled wonder of a mountain quilt pattern. The single rocking chair—she knew without touching it that it would not squeak as Mama's had—was painted a cantaloupe color, with a braided tape seat that looked like a tidy checkerboard. There was a curly cherry washstand with a single pitcher and basin. Out a bit from the far wall stood a black stove with a pipe long as a tree limb radiating heat evenly to the whole room as an open hearth never had.

"Everything's so pretty!" Christina exclaimed to Rebecca and Sally. "I had my pallet in the pantry at the farm!"

Rebecca set her jaw hard. She was about to say it was people, not things that should make a difference in life. But it was Sister Alice, suddenly standing in the door behind them, who answered.

"But remember, Sister Christina, among the Believers, beauty is as beauty does." Her sharp eyes studied Rebecca's face so hard she blushed. "Kindly accompany me to my office, sisters. I've much to discuss with you about your entering the duty rotation and beginning lessons in the sacred dance. I believe you will find purpose here with no time to be frivolously frittered away." Her eyes met Rebecca's again before she led them downstairs.

The first two years as adult Believers were a bumpy road for Rebecca and Christina. They were kept very busy, though at least they were often together, working and learning. Occasional pranks or problems got them into trouble, but they had little free or private time to make mischief. Rebecca finally learned to keep her tongue curbed, as Sister Sally had suggested long ago. Despite all her inner turmoil, Rebecca found purpose at Shakertown, doing the things she had long loved. She sang and helped others. Tasks were rotated, so she cleaned, she cooked, she tended the spring North Lot garden. But most of all she lent her gifts to the herbs and roses in the village.

Grudgingly, Rebecca came to admit that work here was a sort of blessing. To the Shakers, the fields, the kitchens, and the workshops were as sacred as the religious meetings. Gran Ida, Mama, and Becca had always felt their labors rose above mere necessity or pastime. They too had believed that work was not as much for one's own needs as for those of others. Work was done partly in gratitude to God for life itself.

Like this gentle land, Shaker produce and crafts made these folks rich and, yes, fertile in their own ways. The Shaker mind was always busy inventing things to make life better: the clothespin, hangers, the circular saw, an apple peeler and corer, a horse-drawn mowing machine, the dump cart. Last year, the brothers had erected a horse-driven pump to lift spring water to a waterhouse so that at the turn of a key, a sister could have running water from lead pipes in the kitchens or to water the herb beds or gardens.

When they found time for a bit of leisure in what the Shakers called "releasement," Rebecca and Christina usually managed to be together. On July fourth, the summer they were both sixteen, they went to pick wild herbs along the road to the river. It had rained hard all morning, and they were glad to get out for a while. Later there would be a special dinner and service celebrating the nation's independence from England. After all, Mother Ann—the Shakers' Mother Ann—had declared her independence from her horrid life in England to come to America to found the Society of Believers.

Well, if they wanted her to be like their Mother Ann, Rebecca told herself, she should just declare her independence from her horrid life here, take Christina and Jeremy and found her own society in Shelter! But she knew she no longer resented the Shakers—or Daddy—as bitterly as she once had. Maybe, as he had told her that last day up on Concord, "Time will dull your sharp pain." It had in a way, but the poisons from the original wounds still festered deep inside her. All the restrictions, the rules and regulations, still chafed and made her want to rebel. Daddy had pretty much done what he wanted with his life, chasing his rainbows and teasing and joking even if he hurt others. So how dared he leave her and poor Jeremy someplace where their every move and thought was ruled by someone else!

"Independence Day, ha!" Christina said with a grin as if

she'd read Rebecca's mind. "They should give us one from work around here. Even on releasement, we're fetching something or other."

"At least it's fun to gather herbs. I'll show you."

They skirted huge puddles and climbed the steps cut in the Shaker fence where Rebecca had first entered the village more than three years ago.

"Oh, look, sister!" Christina cried and grabbed her arm. "A great big mirror down there, instead of that little one we're allowed in the room. Say, you can see all of us in it!"

Rebecca peered down into the huge, tea-dark puddle on the other side of the fence. Poised on the top step together, they could see their reflections, though at such an angle that they were looking up their skirts. Neither of them had ever seen a full-length mirror, and they were both momentarily mesmerized. They studied first themselves and then each other, despite the caverns around their faces made by the poke bonnets. Then they began to preen and pose, giggling all the while.

"Didn't you ever wonder if you're pretty?" Christina asked.

"The Believers aren't to wonder that. Sister Alice would say beauty lies inside a person striving for perfection."

"Oh bosh, if you're quoting Sister Alice now, what will become of us?" Christina said and made a sharp face with pinched-up eyes at Rebecca. Rebecca made one back; they both snorted a laugh.

"You know," Rebecca confided with a sigh, "a friend at Shelter told me I was beautiful once, like a wild mountain rose."

"I think you're beautiful too, with your fine green eyes and chestnut hair. Was it Adam?" Christina demanded.

"Yes, Adam," she replied, feeling a stab of homesickness.

"A boy once told me I was pretty too—I don't care if we're not to think carnal thoughts! But when old lady Green caught us together, she said I was an ugly little bitch, a temptation to her boy!"

Rebecca put her arm around the shorter, shapelier girl. They looked directly at each other. "But that isn't true," Rebecca assured her. "The woman had no right to say that! She was probably just riled because her boy knew you were pretty!"

Christina had told Rebecca the story of how the son and heir at the farm where they took her in had tried to bed her, but she'd said no. Still, she'd been caught with him chasing her and blamed for it all. Rebecca felt even worse that her friend was blamed for something not her fault.

"We'd best go on," Rebecca said. "And don't fret about the past, because I think you're pretty both outside and in!"

"But there's something I want to tell you, like confession. But I just want to tell *you* and not all of them."

Rebecca's arm dropped. To recall their blood oath, they hooked little fingers before they shared a secret.

"I lied, Rebecca, about Harmon Green not touching me that way. He did—twice."

"Oh, sister! He made you?"

"Not exactly. I liked him. I thought if he loved me, he could convince his folks I could be his wife and live at the farm forever. And, I liked doing it, the carnal act. It felt good in some ways. Really, he wasn't rough or anything, and he could kiss real good!"

Rebecca felt her face flush. She wanted to understand more about how the carnal act felt, but she knew such talk, even thinking, was forbidden. "Oh, Christina," she floundered, at a loss for comforting words for once. "It's sure a good thing you didn't go to breeding from it. But now, it's past. It's not—"

"It's not something I can forget, sister, any more than you can forget Adam or Shelter neither. Oh, I'm not stuck on Harmon Green, but I have thoughts about being pretty and about a man to love me and a family of my own. Don't you too?"

Rebecca dropped Christina's hand. Flustered by her own burst of hankering for all those things, Rebecca felt her eyes glaze over, and she hesitated. "Yes, I—yes I do!" she burst out.

"Then, sister, don't think less of me, please, I couldn't bear it! And there's one more thing I got to tell you—why I guess I'm so scairt of the dark. When old lady Green found Harmon kissing me with my skirts up, she screamed bad things at him and me. Then Mr. Green dragged me out of the house and locked me in the smokehouse. It was so horrid dark in there with smoke and all those dead, smelly, hanging animal parts. Like hell must be, I kept thinking. They left me there 'til they decided I should go to the Shakers. But her words stayed inside me about me being an ugly no 'count and all of that.''

"You're no such thing! You're dear and special and pretty. Now just smile again, see—'' Rebecca told her and pushed her shoulder just a bit so they could peer down into their puddle mirror again. But when they both shifted on the steps and leaned out to look, Christina lost her balance. Rather than fall headlong, she wheeled her arms and jumped at the last minute, landing on hands and knees in the puddle. Great gobs of dark water and mud sprayed up, splashing Rebecca, too.

"Oh, bosh!" Christina said as she got up to display her brown apron and muddy skin. She held up palms mucky with goo, then started to laugh. Rebecca hurried down the steps. She laughed and hugged Christina, despite the double disaster it made of their once-pristine frocks.

"My fault—'' Rebecca managed through her giggles.

"No, mine. 'There is no dirt in heaven,' so we're not there yet!" Christina choked out between guffaws. She made the mistake of trying to swipe at her wet cheeks with a slippery hand, marking them as with Indian war paint.

They decorated both their faces, peering down into the puddle. Trying to stifle hoots and hollers, they held their aching sides. The secrets from Christina's darkest depths were said now, and they were closer for it. But Rebecca had not yet shared her own dreadful secret, that Daddy might have gone off because he blamed her for losing those she held most dear, that, just maybe, he thought he'd punish her by taking all the other dear ones she had left including himself. She wanted to tell Christina, to have her say it was not true. But she was so afraid to tell it. Tears of grief began to mingle with the tears of laughter, smearing the mud on her face. She had to tell Christina now, but they were so giggly, so hysterical that—

"Young sisters, I cannot believe my eyes!" a deep voice rang out from the steps above them. Both girls gasped and looked up. Brother Phineas, a deacon from their family, gawked down at them. Behind him stood two other brothers, one appropriately shocked, the other, Brother Travis, trying to hide a grin at the sight of them. "I see you two have declared your own Independence Day!" Brother Phineas railed. "Shameful, lost little sheep!"

Rebecca hurt too much inside to explain or talk back. Their outing and hope of tonight's enjoyment lay in ruins. Worse, so did the one brave moment when she might have told Christina her shameful secret. And, as much as she wanted to hate and run from these people, she realized there was something that touched on love as well as outrage in Brother Phineas's Shaker scolding. Nor did she feel defiantly glad that Sisters Faith and Alice would be deeply disappointed in her again. Yet, dirty heads held high, hand in muddy hand, the two of them trooped back to the East Family Dwelling behind Brother Phineas to take their punishment.

On the first sabbath in May the year they turned twenty-one, Sister Rebecca Blake and Sister Christina Benton signed the Covenant to become full citizens of Shakerdom. Rebecca had signed mostly because of her friend and that old blood vow that they would never leave each other. Besides, Daddy had not come back. He either had forgotten them or hated them— or had died. Sometimes, Rebecca thought, God forgive her, his death would have been easier to accept than his not wanting to see them. With Jeremy living happily in the Center

Family now, there was no one for her to live with or care for outside Pleasant Hill.

She had never accepted all the Shaker teachings, but she admitted she had accepted the people themselves. They were clever, dedicated, and loving in their Shaker fashion. Despite her problems here, she had developed a deep affection for her Shaker sisters, even the elderesses. It was hardly like having Gran Ida back again and yet, Rebecca had to admit, they were helpful in their own ways. Still, she struggled with herself about abiding by their rules; far too often she dared to debate freedoms and fulfillments with Sister Alice. Sometimes the woman seemed to be her watchdog, one who would like to bark her right up a tree until she surrendered her past, her privacy, and her personality.

But it pleased Rebecca deeply that signing the Covenant as well as her hard work had won her the assignment to make rosewater as well as tend herbs. "You have asked to oversee the rosewater for years, but it's such an important task I could hardly recommend someone for it who hadn't made the commitment to the Covenant," Sister Alice had told her. Anyway Rebecca had signed, and how pleased *her* mother Ann no doubt was, peering down from heaven while the others looked for messages from *their* Mother Ann.

Then too, Rebecca loved the dancing here, but not because she felt she was shaking off the sins of the flesh. Dancing was a part of her. She cherished its freedom and passion, as if any doubts or pains could find release in it. Her garb for the service was not only so beautiful it seemed angelic, but since all the sisters were dressed alike, it made her feel closer to them. Today they had donned their summer white cotton dresses with blue petticoats, white and blue aprons, cloth shoes, and linen caps. The men in ordered ranks ahead wore blue coats over black waistcoats and pale blue cotton trousers. From the Center Family Dwelling the big village bell clanged to summon them to devotions and the dance.

The big white clapboard Meeting House stood at the very heart of the village. It did not look impressive from the outside, but it took Rebecca's breath away within. It was large enough to accommodate the entire village membership of more than three hundred, dancing all at once. The room had no visible supports to hinder seeing, hearing, or, most importantly, the holy dancing.

The women took their seats in rows of benches along the western wall, while the men removed their coats and sat facing them across the vast floor. Rebecca sensed Christina was nervous about something, probably about remembering the intricate steps and group maneuvers. Her skills were cleaning or cooking and she had neither the lightness of foot nor the concentration Rebecca did. But Rebecca had to force herself to listen to the respected village elder, Benjamin Dunlavy, as he spoke. More than once, she subtly elbowed Christina when her friend's eyes seemed to glaze over as she stared across the room toward the brethren. She knew Christina was not the type to have a heavenly vision.

"Shakers are the freest souls on earth because all bonds are self-imposed," Brother Benjamin was saying. "Remember, when the lures and hooks of the world snatch at your flesh, the Shakers live above all that. For freedom, we submit to the greater good. For elevation of spirit, we embrace discipline. Let us as we worship in the laboring of dance, look for those signs and gifts from above to lead our path, to search our hearts for ways to quiet the dissension among some of our members."

Rebecca started. Could he be referring to her or Christina? They had not been in trouble for a while, though she was tempted to stand and debate or defy many of the sermons like the one today. The Shaker idea of freedom and elevation of spirit was not hers. Sometimes she knew she should not stay here, but she would never let Christina down. And if she left, Jeremy might never forgive her.

And so she sat still until the announcement, "Let us now join in the dance of our releasement, our joy of salvation from the carnal desires and sins of the world!"

Everyone rose in unison for the dancing. A glimpse of

white shoulder kerchief caught Rebecca's eye from the small observation window, high on the wall. There, she knew, Sister Faith and Sister Alice peered out, as did elders from the other side, to oversee the dance. No, today she would not even consider that those stubborn old Shakers might be here to keep an eye on her.

In unison the sisters lifted the benches away and faced the ranks of men in perfect order. Though each step was dictated, dancing like this was the freest Rebecca had felt since striding the mountains. It was as it had been when she was young, feeling part of the world before she knew that life held pain and loss. It was as it had been when she and Mama danced together on the brow of the hill overlooking the great meadow of Shelter Valley, with Concord Peak smiling down its blessings.

"Blessings, blessings from above." The song-chant rose to the rafters and echoed in hundreds of hearts. First they went through the basic shuffles and marches, declaring their receiving of blessings and dispensing them to others. Next the worshipers formed the pattern for the Union Dance called the Endless Chain. Then came Rebecca's favorite, the Ring Dance, with the double circle of women dancers stepping clockwise, while the outer rings of brothers turned and whirled in endless joy and celebration. And then it happened.

"Shake off the flesh, shake, shake!" came from some of the brethren. "Shaker high, shake, shake!"

The shaking spread like wildfire. At first in place, then breaking ranks, individuals began to whirl around. Some vaulted toward the ceiling, arms upstretched in a full-blown "Shaker high." Rebecca and Christina took hands and twirled each other. Rebecca became Becca again, at the frolic with fireflies and fiddle music all around. Mama danced with Daddy, though no man and woman must touch here. "Dancing is just an excuse for carnal touching in the world," Sister Alice had said. But how wonderful it had been, how special that night with Adam. And how exciting that she and Christina had spoken fervently of such things more than once—

"Shake, shake, whirl, whirl!" The chants seemed to echo inside Rebecca from the ceiling, from heaven itself. Widow Lang swooped and swirled, her hair flying out behind her like angel wings. No, that was Rebecca's own hair come loose in a chestnut streamer as she vaulted, she ran, she soared down her mountain in a frenzy of joy and release. Her gown blew out like a blue coltsfoot bloom as she turned, she turned, she turned. All her fears flew from her. She was free again, rushing through meadow mist up to her refuge.

Exhausted, Rebecca collapsed in Christina's arms. They leaned together, panting hard. Some sisters sobbed, some sang, some swooned. Rebecca felt the very foundations of the building and the world rebound with her bold joy.

"Did you mark what I told you, Sister Faith? She always dances in the old way of Mother Ann!" Sister Alice insisted as the two women closed the small, drawer-sized window from which they had observed the dancing below. "Wild, free, her long hair snapping, like the early Shakers did when visions racked them. Sister Rebecca seems to soar."

Sister Faith held tightly to the banister as they went down the narrow back stairs. "But she's always had a free spirit, that one. Remember when she blasphemed Mother Ann in the herb garden right after she came here? And since then her—ah, indiscretions—have been legion."

"Yes, but don't you see, she had the serpent of worldly dissension in her when she came. She's been doing spiritual battle to cast it out. She's now such a giving, hardworking member despite her pointed questions—and her attachment to Sister Christina. I believe she might be the one through whom Mother Ann will send us a sign to increase our ranks, to bind the faithful closer to heaven. I have seen signs in her already."

They both blinked in the bright sun when they left the Meeting House and trudged back toward the East Family Dwelling House. "Such as?" Sister Faith prompted.

"Remember, she had her own beloved mother Ann when

she came to us. Could that not be a sign? And Sister Sally told me once the girl said she had seen and communed with angels before she ever came here. I tell you, Sister Faith, we must continue to watch Sister Rebecca but give her a bit more freedom too. If we let her expand her horizons, she may open herself more to the inspiration. She may be the one to initiate a whole new day here! I tell you, I would have wanted her cast out years ago, but I saw such promise in her. She reminds me of myself.''

"Hm, well," Sister Faith whispered at the women's door of the dwelling house, "I dare say, Sister Rebecca has no time for inspiration. She's always with Sister Christina unless duty separates them for a spell.''

They spoke not another word until they were in their office off the back parlor with the door closed. "Exactly," Sister Alice hissed. "So, I think we should not assign them together as much. Perhaps Sister Christina's fledgling attitudes hold Sister Rebecca back.''

"Well, that's settled for now," Sister Faith said as she wilted in her rocker. "I must admit, at least, that Sister Rebecca has worked herself out of such a shameful beginning that there must be better days ahead for her.''

Better days became months and seasons. Rebecca's responsibilities grew. She oversaw the plantings and placement of herbs and their uses in the infirmary. She helped with harvesting and drying them. Best of all she loved the summer days when the sisters made rosewater in a real copper still. Then her life was doubly sweet with memories of times and people past and service to those in her present and future. She mourned that there was little contact between her and Jeremy now, except for special days like his birthday or the anniversary of his being cured of the canker rash, when she made formal application to speak with him in the presence of the Center Family elders. But she swelled with pride when she stored rose hips in the oval boxes her brother had helped to make or used a flat broom produced in the workshop where

Jeremy's duty rotations took him. Why, those brooms were sold clear up and down the rivers by Shaker peddlers for $1.80 a dozen, so just think of all the useful blessings bestowed on the world!

Ever busy, Rebecca now buried deeper inside the fear that Daddy had blamed her for losing the baby and Mama. Though she had never told her fear to Christina, their solid friendship had helped to heal the hurt. She did not see her friend as much as she wanted anymore, but they had both matured and their bond ran deep as the Kentucky River. And through this private friendship and her public sisterly relationships, she had learned that Shakerism was, indeed, a spiritual adventure.

After all, the Shakers felt about their lives much as she had about hers at Shelter, but they knew how to put the feelings into words and deeds. They believed in some great interlocking beauty of things deeper than the visible. So, while they were sweeping out the hearth, they sang about sweeping dirt from the heart of mankind. The straight path they walked from the workshop to the springhouse was the straight path of their life amid the world's temptations.

"Kind of amazing how everything means something deeper," as Christina once put it. Rebecca agreed. Life among the Shakers was like living with hundreds of Widow Langs. But recalling the night of the frolic when the widow died, Rebecca realized too late that she should have remembered something else: even when life seemed sweet, catastrophe could creep around the corner.

Chapter Nine

Rebecca was pleased to be assigned in the afternoons to tend sheep, a task she liked because it was outside and gave her private time, though it usually kept her from seeing Christina. But, surprisingly, not today.

"Rebecca! I was hoping you were out here looking for the strays!" Christina shouted from the top of the knoll. She waved wildly and started down toward Rebecca.

Christina had been on washhouse duty this week. It seemed their assignments never matched anymore, but then Christina made a shambles of herb beds and always got blood from rose thorns on her aprons. She did not have the patience to tend sheep. Actually, Rebecca recalled, though their friendship was supple enough to bend under separations, Christina had not protested their different assignments as she had. Rebecca was thrilled to see her, but she became worried when she saw that Christina looked dismayed.

Carrying her shepherd's crook, Rebecca ran uphill to meet her. She grasped Christina's heaving shoulders. She must have run the whole way out.

"What is it? Someone's hurt, and they need to know which herbs—"

"No. No, not that again. I want to tell you something very special and very serious."

"You have been elevated to overseeing the kitch—"

"No, not any of that!" She grasped Rebecca's free hand. "It's about me, but one other too."

Suddenly Rebecca's legs felt weak as the blowing grass. She let Christina tug her downhill to the stone fence near where her old rosebush had finally spread and flourished. They both leaned against it as if they knew, without speaking, that they would need the support of the fence.

"Tell me then," Rebecca encouraged her. "Anything I can do to help, I will!" Yet her heart ached with foreboding already. Her friend might have special and serious news to share but it was evidently secret and forbidden too.

Christina plucked at her lower lip and looked down to draw a line in the grass with the toe of her shoe, back and forth, back and forth. "It's just if I disappear someday," she said, "I want you to understand and not think you can fetch me back like you do these sheep." She looked up with shiny eyes. "And I don't want you ever to forget all we shared, because you've been the most important person ever to me— before now, before Travis."

Rebecca gasped. Travis Truax! Her insides cartwheeled. And she had been so blind to it, maybe blind to anything that would shatter her sheltered life here. She should have tended Christina's restless soul better while she was struggling with her own. However secret Christina had kept this, she should have known!

"Oh, Christina," Rebecca began, pulling both her friend's balled-up fists into her own trembling hands, "you and Travis. How much have you been with him—how far along . . ." She wanted to support Christina. But the old terror of abandonment bit at her. She had partly stayed here for Christina. They could not mean to run off—to go away!

"We're in love. Oh, sister, it's just what you and I always dreamed of! Travis and I are going to be together, no matter what!"

"Yes, of course! You're very sure it's what you want?"

"Never been surer no matter what they say and do! Only, I can't bear that we will leave you, and want to know if you will go with us."

"How—how could I? He'll marry you, of course. The two of you will be—everything to each other. You must be! And stay together, don't let him take a job where he goes away alone! Oh, Christina, I can't believe I didn't know! I thought we were—so—close forever."

"We are, dearest friend! Things change, but I don't want to lose you. I am letting you down."

"No, I understand. You must do what makes you happy— what is *right* for you. I just didn't see this coming. If you'd told me . . ."

"I tried real hard to keep you from knowing. I promised Travis no one would know we were meeting on the sly, but I did it for your good too."

"Yes, I see, in case the elderesses asked me. And you've decided to leave, both of you?" Rebecca knew she was talking in circles; she felt drained, shocked.

"Tonight."

"Tonight!"

"We've got no choice if we're to be together."

Rebecca nodded jerkily. Her vision blurred with unshed tears, making two Christinas standing before her. She could not believe this had happened. And with Travis Truax, the paragon of young Shaker manhood! Travis and Christina—it meant their ruin here and expulsion into the world. It meant she would be separated from one she loved again! But through this grief of parting, happiness glowed from her friend's face, and that was worth loss and risk too.

"Dear sister," Rebecca managed in a ragged voice, "my mama told me once when you know it's the right man, it's worth any risk! You just weren't meant for the Shaker calling. And maybe somehow, someday I can visit you, if you don't go off too far."

"Somewhere near Harrodsburg, if Travis can find work

there again. Rebecca, I'll never forget you, even if it's a while before I see you.''

Shaken with silent sobs, they leaned together, arms tight around each other's necks. Then Rebecca stepped back and stared into her friend's face as if to memorize it.

''Believe me,'' Christina said, ''I don't mean to get you in a spot where you can be blamed as though you helped us. Not after all you do here, all you mean to them. But I wanted to say that if I ever have a daughter, I'm going to name her after you, my dearest, dearest friend in the whole wide world!''

Grasping hands hard, they stared into each other's eyes. Christina pulled gently away, and Rebecca let her go.

''I'll never forget you, you'll see,'' Christina choked out and took two big steps back. ''You're my real sister and not just my Shaker one.''

''Our friendship will always be with me. Somehow, find a way to tell me where you are, how you are,'' Rebecca called after her, until she realized she should lower her voice. With a gasping sob, Christina nodded and ran the way she had come. At the top of the hill, she turned back to wave. The breeze tugged at her skirts as if to hold her here.

Her clasped hands pressed to her trembling lips, Rebecca turned away, not to see Christina disappear over the rim of the hill. And then, like a lost, abandoned sheep—like the hurt and frightened child she had enclosed within the grown Rebecca—she collapsed to her knees on the grass. Her shoulder against the hard stone wall, she sobbed as the devastation of desertion staggered her again.

As soon as she could, Rebecca stumbled to the stream and washed her face. Her mind was in turmoil; her stomach knotted more tightly than it had when she first came here. Christina would be damned for leaving. But, strangely, Rebecca wanted not only to protect Christina, but to shield the Shakers too. Already she bemoaned the pain they would feel when they knew they had failed with another soul—two of them—going to the world they so detested. Unlike the time when

Daddy had left her and Jeremy, she realized she would share this agony with many more people.

That night, in the darkness she so feared, Christina silently rose from her bed. Rebecca lay awake, stiff on the next bed. They must not speak and wake the others. She knew there would be no hand looking for reassurance in the dark this time. She hardly breathed, her heart thudding as Christina scrambled into her clothes. Rebecca felt flushed; perspiration drenched her.

But her friend clasped her hand one last time. They both trembled as their grip loosened and their hands slipped apart. She should have gone with them, Rebecca tormented herself—but she knew that could not be. She would be a lost soul with the lovers. And—she could not have said this years ago—she was needed here. But the sharp slicing pain of it, the opening of old wounds Christina had once helped to heal!

In her stocking feet, carrying her shoes, Christina tiptoed to the door. She inched it open on its well-oiled hinges and went out. A hall floorboard creaked, then no other sound but Sister Jerusha's snoring. Tears ran from Rebecca's eyes into her hair and soaked her pillow.

The next morning everyone knew that Christina Benton and Travis Truax had given in to their carnal natures and gone to seek the flesh together. They were soundly condemned for it, in sermons, in journals, in whispered conversations over the daily striving for perfection. Through her double grief in seeing her East Family torn asunder, Rebecca listened to the rebukes heaped on the runaways' heads. She was grateful that Travis in his note had said that they had had no accomplice. That, no doubt, was all that saved her from censure too.

Rebellion roiled in her again. As she had not for years, she blamed the Shakers for their callous, narrow view of people's souls. Could they not admit that others had needs beyond theirs? Did worldly family love and the desire to wed have to be degraded as if they were filthy sins? Could they not just let people be different without damning them? She only hoped, though they had set out in the darkness, that Christina and Travis had found the light of these new days beautiful together. And she hoped for herself that she could manage to find the sweet amid the bitter at Pleasant Hill— this time without a dear friend's help.

But she battled a new, disturbing bitterness against Christina. Had not Christina vowed never to leave? She had broken Covenant rules to meet Travis in secret! But then, Rebecca admitted, she had taught Christina from the first to break those rules and sneak away for private, forbidden time together. Rebecca understood her friend's reaching for happiness with Travis, but sometimes, in darkest night, she doubted that love and trust, those precious foundation stones of her youth, existed. For one way or the other, everyone she had ever loved and trusted had left her.

"From the high up heavens to the low down earth, I have shared many pleasant times with you at Pleasant Hill." Rebecca's voice rang out loudly in the parlor where the family had assembled to hear nightly confessions. She felt stronger for starting with Gran Ida's old mountain blessing. She locked her knees where she stood in the circle of staring eyes. "But tonight is not pleasant for me, because I have offended you. And it is sad for me to think that, though I have made many confessions before, I shared most of them with another sister. She departed from us nearly two years ago. I confess to you I still miss her sorely."

At her indirect mention of Christina, people shifted, some sighed, eyes darted. Sister Alice, standing close, mouthed to her, "Confession for the dancing! The dancing!" Rebecca's voice shook but she went on with the speech she had agonized over ever since Sister Faith had told her that Sister Jerusha had reported her for dancing in the meadow by the North Family Lot. Shaker dancing was a spiritual union with God to be done publicly on the Sabbath, an honor paid for by sacrifice during the week. It was not to be indulged in for private pleasure, and she had done that. But she intended to say much more today.

"These last two years, thanks to my own personal battle," Rebecca went on, "though I say this not to defend myself, I have not been summoned to confess a serious sin. But that is not because I have not been a rebel within my own heart."

More murmurings before a hush descended. She sensed she held them spellbound. "Sister Jerusha saw me dancing in private today, and so I ask your forgiveness for that. And for my continued resentment of some ways of the Believers."

Out of the corner of her eye she saw Sister Alice shake her head, but she plunged on, "Since such offends my dear brothers and sisters, I shall try to forgo such selfish, purposeless dancing and resentment. Now, I would confess another thing."

Sister Alice's eyes bulged and she whispered to Sister Faith. Rebecca saw other eyes narrow, mouths set in firm lines. Heads lifted ever so slightly in the nearly imperceptible stir in the room. She sighed deep inside. It was such a lovely April night, and she would much rather have been out. Such evenings reminded her lately of the world beyond the Shaker fences, the world her friend had boldly faced with all its trials and triumphs. It was about Christina she would speak, despite the remnants of her own pain at feeling so alone—and yet so cared for—here.

"I must tell you that, through passersby on the road who called out to me while I was herding sheep, I have received a letter from the departed Mr. and Mrs. Travis Truax. Though they broke the rules here, I know in the life they have chosen you would surely forgive them and wish them well."

She knew nothing of the kind, of course. Confessing this and hoping it would soften hearts was a great risk. She bit her lower lip, lifted her chin, and leveled her gaze at the elderesses to assess the depths of defiance to which she had plunged. She had been hoping that the great prosperity of the village—the members now numbered five hundred, and times were good—would bring forgiveness for Christina and for her.

These twenty months the two had been gone, she had tried hard to heal Shaker hearts as well as her own. She saw now that her earlier bond with Christina and her bitter attitude had kept her from knowing others. Lately she had poured her love and life into other sisters. If someone needed of a listening ear, a companion, she stood ready. She loved working with the young girls, especially teaching them about herbs. Although she still did not agree with all the Shaker ways, she had finally achieved a deep and abiding admiration for these people. They too suffered, they too mourned, only sometimes not for the same things she did. She had vowed to herself that she would never hurt her big family the way Christina and Travis had done. Now she paused just long enough to realize she dared go on.

"In the letter, they say they have wed and gone to housekeeping as hired help near Harrodsburg, where Travis is using his fine Shaker-taught skills to work for a farmer. They send their best wishes to us all. They had a child but it died and are soon to have another, so—"

"God has cursed their lives!" Brother Phineas muttered.

Rebecca turned to face him. "But others have lost children too, and God is only good. I cannot believe He curses babies. Mother Ann lost all her babies. Did God curse her future?"

"Enough!" Sister Alice rapped out. "Your confession of wayward dancing and sinful resentments has been heard, Sister Rebecca. And it is good you realize such illicit correspondence from those flesh-seekers who have gone to the world must be shared as a sin. Sister Tiney, I believe you have a confession." Quickly she shooed Sister Tiney toward the center of the circle and pulled Rebecca to her side.

Rebecca stood between the elderesses as various confessions droned on for things she considered small and private. But this was the Shaker way and it did cleanse one's conscience and sometimes smooth over rough spots between the Believers. Yes, after all this time and loss, she had gained some things too. She could see the Shakers' side of things now and care for them yet. She knew the elderesses had been pleased lately—until tonight. And she must upset them soon again by asking to visit Christina. Since she could tell her friend was worried about her next child's birth, she should be allowed to go to them to help for a while. Poor Christina now knew the heartbreak of losing a baby, just as Mama and Becca lost that little mite at the Crawl Crick cabin so long ago.

Her musings were interrupted by Brother Stephen's announcement that English visitors would be living in the Trustees' House for a month to benefit from Shaker ways. They were Lord Ramsey Sherborne and his companion William Barnstable. Worldly visitors in Shaker communities were quite common. The Shakers hoped for new converts; the visitors hoped to acquire Shaker goods and inventions, which the Shakers were always willing to share. But having English visitors was something special to Rebecca. Ever since she had seen on the schoolroom globe how far away England was, she had wondered about it. But she went back to woolgathering as other announcements were made.

The fresh-earth smell of spring outside the windows lured her. There were such strong stirrings in her blood, like the old Becca hankering to be free. Her sheltered life rode hard upon her heart. She wanted to run down to the river and swim upstream to Boonesville to visit the Mercers and tell them about Mama. She wanted to see every place on the real globe! She wanted union with all the lovely things she'd never seen.

And yet she would not because she cherished the people here and would not hurt them for the world the way others had hurt her. Still, if they did not let her go to tend Christina in her travail, she would just run away for a visit, and let them fetch her back in disgrace as they had other bolters. Such upheaval tumbled through her—to stay, to go, to submit, to rebel, to save face or face them all down—

"Sister!" Sister Faith hissed at her. Everyone was filing from the room while she just stood there. "It's over. Up to your retiring room, I said."

"Yes, Sister Faith," Rebecca replied and hurried upstairs after the others. But in her room, she was glad the windows stood ajar so she could hear night sounds and smell the rose-rich breeze.

"What do you think?" Sister Faith asked Sister Alice in their office after confessions.

"I think she dared to lecture us about forgiveness when she was to be asking for it," Sister Alice said with a sniff. "But her need to dance is increasing. That's the way the message or sign will come, while she dances."

"But she's been here ten years," Sister Faith protested and knocked her stiff cap awry as she hooked her spectacles over her ears. "And most of that time she's been a rebel, if a talented, productive one!"

"You yourself said she's matured since that flibbertigibbet friend of hers ran off with her paramour. More freedom yoked with more responsibility and Sister Rebecca will bloom with our precious message from heaven. When times are so good for the village, hearts grow soft to the world. We need a spiritual reawakening to harden hearts toward the world. And I still believe a message can come through one who has never yet had—or admitted to—a vision. Think how powerful her testimony will be! Even when she breaks the rules, she draws others to her!"

"You, you mean, Sister Alice?"

"You saw how her force of personality held them in the palm of her hand! And yes, since it is confession time all around, somehow, as I have said, she reminds me of myself. It took me nearly twenty years to be ready and worthy to serve as elderess here. Twenty years to get over the world's losses and betrayals. I saw that that father of hers and Brother Jeremy's was a no-account the day he came in here all shifty eyes and worldly charm. I'd seen it before in someone I knew, and I wanted to rescue her from years of suffering while her worldly memory faded. She may have a lesson or two yet in the winnowing of her heart, but she'll come completely around to our way. You'll see."

"I will indeed," Sister Faith replied and picked up her pen. Quickly she bent to write Sister Rebecca's so-called confession in her journal before her own fading memory made her quite forget what the clever girl had said.

The morning that was to change Rebecca's Shaker life forever began as all summer days did at Pleasant Hill. The bell awoke her as dawn first silvered the horizon. In unison, the seven sisters in her room knelt for prayer—right knee down first— then rose to pin their hair, wash, and dress. Each sister stripped her own bed and neatly aligned the bedclothes for airing. Then they silently separated to clean the entire dwelling and prepare breakfast. They had now been awake an hour and a half and, at the bell, assembled in the parlor with the brothers, who had done barn chores.

In proper ranks, brothers and sisters filed in to breakfast through separate doorways and gave silent thanks. This morning's food included boiled potatoes, fried sausage, wheat bread, applesauce, and camomile tea. Platters and bowls were set every four places so no one had to reach or ask for things. Everyone "Shakered the plate," leaving it cleaned with any refuse piled at the top and pewter knife and fork neatly crossed. Rising—right foot first—on a signal, they all departed in seemly order for their daily tasks until they would be reunited at eleven-fifty for dinner and at six for supper.

Rebecca fetched her pruning knife and gathering basket. Her damask roses were at the height of their single-blooming glory. Intense fragrance wafted through the rich foliage. Each satin-petaled flower was ripe for cutting.

Joyously she buried herself among the rose canes, which were weighed to the ground with their bounty. The rue she had planted between the bushes to keep off insects had done its work well. She picked perfect petals and tore out each white sour spot while Sister Mary carried loaded baskets to the distilling shed and layered them in vats with salt. Rebecca felt a warm glow suffuse her skin from sun and effort. She worked quickly and surely with no gloves, despite the bristly hips and big thorns that made trimmed damask bushes such a good hedge.

She looked forward to beginning double distillation tomorrow. The only thing that saddened her in this entire process was the Shaker stricture against taking a single flower with a stem so that it might, even for a moment, become personal adornment. Like dancing for one's own pleasure, that was not done. Roses were purely useful here, not beautiful.

But in her heart, Rebecca knew better. Boldly she cut a full-bodied rose, short stem included, and stuck it in the criss-cross of her kerchief over her breasts. She could smell its heady bouquet wafting up with the warmth of her body. Willing to risk public confession if someone caught her, she stuck another flower in her hair so that it barely showed beneath her bonnet brim. The caress of the satin petals against her cheek both soothed and aroused her. Well, if Sister Mary looked nettled, she'd just take the flowers out and pluck them too, she told herself and bent to gather petals ranging from pink to scarlet.

Suddenly Gran Ida's long unsung song about Scarlet Town came to her. Such a lovely, haunting melody and tale, one to fit a day like this, sweet with love of life and memories. She and Mama had sung that song when they'd made rosewater on the brow of Concord Mountain. The next time Sister Mary walked away with a laden basket of blooms, Rebecca began to hum the melody. But she found herself singing the last verses, in which Barbara Allen finds out too late that the lad Jamie, who died when she spurned him, really loved her. The poor girl realizes that she too must die for love:

> *Oh, mother, mother, make my bed,*
> *Oh make it long and narrow,*
> *Young Jamie died for love of me,*
> *And I must die tomorrow . . .*

> *And there they tied a true lovers' knot . . .*
> *The red rose and green brier.*

"So beautiful—everything," said a deep male voice behind her.

She straightened and turned. A dark-haired stranger stood there, top hat in hand. It must be one of the English visitors. The clip to his few words was itself like a song. His broad smile with straight white teeth bathed her with blinding sunshine, muting the real sun. His gray eyes were warmer on her skin than the heat of the day.

"I—didn't hear you."

"I must admit I kept rather still, as I did not want to break the spell."

"Of the song?"

"And the singer."

"Oh. It wasn't a Shaker song. I should not have—"

"But you did, and it was charming indeed. I say, are there any true lovers' knots among your roses?" He pretended to peer deep into the foliage behind her, then grinned at her again. "I know that old song from my boyhood in Dorset, you see."

"Where is Dorset? I thought perhaps you were an English visitor."

"Dorset is the shire—the county—where I live in England. I am Ramsey Sherborne, at your service, sister. When I heard your voice and saw you—amidst the roses, I mean—I felt compelled to make your acquaintance."

His voice, his words, his very presence intensified the familiar fragrance of the roses. She could almost swoon in this private valley of arching canes which they shared. She was astounded by what he had said. He had thought her singing cast a spell. He knew the song from his childhood too. He had wanted to meet her. As they stared at each other in the merest breath of time, her pulse began to pound; when bees buzzed, she was certain it was her brain, with her thoughts flitting, flitting.

"Sisters aren't to speak with men, even brethren, alone, you know."

"Yes, but I am staying with permission for several weeks

in the Trustees' House just on the other side of this East Dwelling," he said with a sweeping gesture, as if that solved everything. "I've been speaking with many Shakers—sisters too—about how their skills might be made useful to the poor people in Dorset. I am looking for ideas and things to take back to boost the rural folk there out of poverty. Politics is the ultimate answer, of course, but one must admire your Shaker solutions to it all. Besides," he added and lowered his voice even more, "I see you are armed should I overstep proper bounds."

His eyes dropped to the pruning knife in her hands before darting back to her face. He lifted his eyebrows, then lowered them again. Despite herself, she laughed. No man had teased her since Daddy. Even that little joke seemed to fill an aching void she had not known still existed. And she had not felt like breaking into unseemly, loud laughter since Christina, but somehow, with this stranger, she did now.

Quick as lightning, she studied him. He was a good bit taller than she. His clothes were the finest she had ever seen, from the tips of the polished dark boots showing beneath his narrow-cut dark blue trousers to his white tie spreading like a butterfly under his winged collar. He rotated the brown, tall-crowned top hat in his square hands and the onyx and gold ring on his right hand glinted in the sun. Wind-tousled raven hair framed his high forehead.

But none of that quite captured the essence of the man. Most important, she noted, his face radiated feelings. She had lived so long among the controlled, sedate Shakers she had almost forgotten that a person could explode with emotion from his eyes and face and voice. Even the way his nostrils flared when he mentioned the poor folk he'd like to help at home made her curl her toes in her shoes—at least something about him did. Realizing she was staring, she reluctantly dropped her gaze. Her skin prickled and tingled under her shapeless garments as if he could see right through them.

"Yes, if it's allowed, I'd be happy to tell you anything

about roses or distilling rosewater that might help your Dorset poor folk. And do you miss them?'' she asked and forced herself to look away, bending again to her plucking and tearing.

"Very deeply."

She understood. She longed to look back into that restless face, but she did not. "And your family?"

"My parents and old grandfather are all of that. But yes, as charmingly exotic as your country is, I miss them all very much indeed."

"I too—my family and the folk where I was born, I mean." She straightened to face him eye to eye again. His expressions changed like clouds on a windy day, and she did not want to miss a single one.

"You are the first Shaker I have met who admitted to a past before finding this heaven on earth here," he told her with a twist at the corner of his mouth.

She caught the ironic cast of his words. She recognized a bit of herself in that sentiment, but rushed to the Shakers' defense. "The Believers are my family now, and I owe them a great deal. But I have long known that everywhere in life there are briers among roses."

"Such suffering makes you wise beyond your years. But that does not mean we have to accept things as they are handed us," he said, his tone so stern now he might be an elder lecturing in the Meeting House. "I say people can fight back to make things better. Those of us who are privileged to do so should take any knife we can get our hands on and help cut back the blasted briers. Don't you agree?"

She gripped her pruning knife so hard in her right hand her fingers cramped. She had not been asked her opinion for years, though she had heartily expressed enough forbidden ones. She wasn't quite sure of all that his passionate question entailed. But something swelled within, making her feel she was her own person again, not just a part of an ordered, massive body of believers.

"Yes. Yes, I agree!"

He nodded in approval, a lock of black hair springing loose on his forehead. She felt a surge of fervent feeling leap from him to her, then back again. Yet for one more moment, neither of them moved a muscle. Rebecca thought they seemed suspended. She could smell the heady leather and outdoor tang of him and see the slight rise and fall of his chest and broad shoulders when he breathed. She remembered to draw a breath again. She shook deep inside, but her heart beat strong and steady.

"Now, about your rosewater," he said. "For one thing, I can attest that it is good for healing. I cut my ankle clambering over a fence on a stroll last night, and I heard your name in the men's infirmary where they cared for me. Sister Rebecca, is it not?"

"Yes, Sister Rebecca Blake. Forgive me for not telling you."

"I rather think I would forgive you anything."

She wondered if that was a tease, but he looked very serious. His eyebrows rode low over his heavily fringed eyes, not high as they had when he funned her before.

He picked up their conversation when she had lost the thread of it. " 'Sister Rebecca makes all this fine rosewater,' the brother told me in the infirmary, so I thank you for helping my cut ankle heal."

"Oh, thank you," she said, then could have slapped herself for sounding silly. Yet she hoped Sister Mary would take a good long time coming back. She wished she could savor this forbidden conversation with a worldly man and not feel guilty or suffer confession for it. When he spoke, his firm, narrow mouth softened under his strong nose, which looked a bit crooked, the only real deviation on a perfectly balanced, handsome face. Again, realizing that she was studying him too intently, she forced herself to turn away to pluck petals. If she didn't hurry, she would not have enough for Sister Mary when she returned.

"Explain making rosewater to me, will you?" he asked. "I have found the Shakers to be so generous with advice."

He stepped even closer, his big boots making the grass rustle. She wanted him to be close. She wanted to keep him here, and that both frightened and thrilled her.

"You see," he added, "my mother oversees gardens behind our family home, but I think the servants only cook up rosewater for washing and not medicine or flavoring." He put his hat on his head at last. He produced a small black leather journal and a metal pen from a silk pocket inside his coat.

While he unscrewed the lid of the pen, she tried to picture what his mother would be like. And England far across the ocean. And English gardens. Having servants. English rural folk and Dorset poverty. Politics being the ultimate answer to anything. And how he knew she had suffered. She wanted to ask him each of those questions and a hundred more.

But at that very moment, Sister Mary came back with her basket and went beetle-eyed to see the man standing so close to a Shaker sister. "Oh," she squeaked.

"Sister Mary, this is Mr.—I mean Lord Ramsey Sherborne from Dorset in England. He wants us to tell him all about how we make Shaker double-distilled rosewater."

"How do you do, Sister Mary," he put in and tipped his hat to her before resettling it on his head. "Just Ramsey Sherborne will do. Titles are blessedly nothing here at Pleasant Hill. I apologized to you ladies if I am in the way—"

"Not at all. We can talk while we work, can't we, Sister Mary?" Rebecca said. *Ladies*. He thought of them as ladies. Suddenly she wished she could deck herself in roses for this man. She would like to burst into song and dance. She struggled to get hold of her best Shaker self. She surely looked plain to a man like this. She was a moony mountain girl who had finally dedicated herself to the strict Shaker life. She knew she was doing the forbidden even to try to keep him here, to stare into those gray eyes that seemed lit from within. She would never be allowed to talk to him again. She was joyous; she was grief-stricken. She was drowning in the confusing feelings bubbling up from a deep well of emotions she had not known existed.

"Oh, Sister Rebecca, you've a rose caught in your kerchief," Sister Mary interrupted her impassioned musings. "And in your hair—"

"I was saving them because they were special," Rebecca blurted to avoid being scolded in front of Ramsey Sherborne. Even his name flowed like a mountain stream. She yanked the forbidden rose from her kerchief and ignored the thrust of thorn that caught her breast. She turned away to pluck the one from her bonnet too.

"Now, about the way we make rosewater here," she began before Sister Mary could get another word in. And then she told Ramsey Sherborne more about rosewater than he would ever need to know about anything.

"Are you certain you are feeling quite well this evening?" Will Barnstable, Ramsey's friend and traveling companion, asked him. Will clipped off the end of his cheroot, lit it, and inhaled deeply. "I dare say one can't complain about this splendid food, so it isn't that." As was their custom after meals, they strolled outside the Trustees' House. "You haven't said one word all evening, Ramsey. Are you worrying about how the Sherpuddle villagers are getting on without you?"

"Does one have to be pondering something specific at all times?" Ramsey retorted. But he regretted that he had snapped, and hit Will lightly on the shoulder before he bent to lean his elbows on the top of the Shaker fence. He gazed out over the hills toward the river. Then he turned to stare off toward the now empty rose garden beyond the East Family Dwelling.

No doubt *she* was there inside the dwelling, he thought, behind one of those candlelit windows. Sister Rebecca's green, green eyes, both giving and yet strangely needy, haunted him. Nor could he forget her bell-clear voice or her face, partly hidden by that deep bonnet. He had wanted to pull it off to see her hair spill loose. He desired to study her fine features, to read the soul she had offered him in her abrupt admissions before she had pulled back like a turtle into her Shaker shell.

She seemed a rebel, like him, though in a softer way. She had obviously adorned herself with forbidden flowers. He had caught her singing what the Shakers would brand a worldly, carnal song. A true lovers' knot indeed! And yet that was what he had felt in his chest since he had seen her—a strange tugging of sensations, a coiling of emotion. And in the short time he had been with her, there had been an astounding tightening in his loins such as he had not felt for years, at least not just for an intriguing face in shadow and a body in a shapeless gown.

Since then, he had circumspectly inquired about her. He had learned that Sister Rebecca had been at Pleasant Hill for ten years and was twenty-four to his twenty-seven. She was evidently beloved and respected here despite some sort of black sheep's past. The old man's eyes in the infirmary had lit with pride when he had said her name. Those two prim-as-maiden-aunts elderesses he had interviewed about rotating duties obviously admired her.

Yet, somehow, she did not quite fit. Too much vitality, a sort of hunger for life that was missing among most of these gentle folk. Energy and emotion seemed to pour from her. The impact of stumbling on an enchantress in Shakertown had both devastated and regenerated him to his very core. Damn it all, he castigated himself, what was wrong with him to be brooding over a celibate Shakeress!

"Maybe I've been a blasted fool to come here," Ramsey admitted to Will. "These people are so placid when I need to find a source of power. Power to pull the Dorset farm laborers out of the mire those damned Whigs led by Prime Minister Melbourne have shoved and stamped them into. And when the old king dies to leave young Victoria as queen, Melbourne will work her like a puppet. Things can only get worse."

Will turned to stare at him while cigar smoke drifted between them. Ramsey knew it bothered Will when he spoke against the government that way. He had promised both his father and Will he would not promote violence. Anyway, protests of any sort only seemed to backfire in hidebound England. "Well, old chap, do you think we have made a mistake to come here?" Ramsey asked.

Will shrugged. The silver in his curly brown hair gleamed, caught by the red setting sun. His profile looked as if it were etched by flames and enveloped by smoke. "I'm just surprised you were thinking politics again, you mad iconoclast!" he said and elbowed Ramsey. "I'd have guessed you were thinking about that little Shakeress I saw you chatting with today." Will's full mouth curved in a grin that was almost a grimace. "I promised your fond father I'd keep an eye on you, you know. Just because you were too risky a devil for several of the nobility's daughters doesn't mean you won't find one whose family is willing to take you on, if you'd just settle down so Lord Melbourne calms down."

Ramsey pushed away from the fence and walked briskly back toward the Trustees' House, where he and Will shared a room. Will, who was shorter, hurried to catch up. "My fault for starting it, but let's forget the likes of Melbourne during our stay here," Ramsey threw back over his shoulder. "Within these fences all is gentleness and cleverness. Utopia. Eden. Heaven on earth."

He knew his voice stung. Sometimes that bitterness welled up in him as he sought good in mankind but too often found bad. Even here at so-called Pleasant Hill, it rankled him that the shining good of Shakerdom was tarnished by the lack of personal freedom and endless petty rules against human nature. Confessions at the drop of a hat. Separation from other people and the world. Celibacy, no less! Somehow, meeting Rebecca Blake had both soothed him and infuriated him. When he was with her, for the first time ever, his crusade to discover ways to help the Dorset poor seemed secondary. He wanted to discover her. But if he sought her out again, it would be a danger to her and would betray his fine hosts.

He bade Will good-night and left him to his cheroot, going into the Trustees' House and climbing the stairs. He valued Will's friendship, but sometimes the man seemed so intense that everything Ramsey said came under scrutiny. The only one he desired to have hanging on his every word here was the green-eyed Shaker rose, the Eve of this Eden.

As he removed his boots with the bootjack, he wondered what she would look like in a green gown to match her eyes. A silk gown, blowing and clinging to her body to go with that rich chestnut hair he had seen so severely pulled back from the face glowing even in the shade of the Shaker bonnet. If only he could dream of her instead of the desperation of his dreams!

Chapter Ten

The next day, in the small shed attached to the East Family sisters' herbal workshop, Rebecca worked quickly to distill the rosewater. She had hurried right back after breakfast and dinner. Crocks of the precious nectar cooling in the workshop next door were her reward as the afternoon stretched on and the shed became warmer. The so-called cold still hissing over its low fire added heat to the room. She wiped sweat from her face with her apron and had long ago removed her bonnet. Now and then, she pressed her kerchief and bodice to the valley between her breasts to blot the trickle of perspiration there.

Her tried and true recipe for each batch was one peck of salted petals mixed with one quart of the fresh springwater Sister Anna had hauled from the kitchen. Once the first distillation extracted the oil, the remaining water was siphoned off, then run through again to make the fragrant double distillation. Sister Sally had brought her a plate of rose petal sweetmeats from the kitchen, but for an hour now she had been alone. Still, she could hear the buzz of the sisters' voices through the wall. Despite the heat, she was totally content to be working here, but for one thing. The single doorway and tiny window that let in light and air did not face the Trustees' Dwelling, so she could not keep an eye out for Ramsey Sherborne.

"Ouch!" she cried as her attention wandered again and she brushed her knuckles against the hot belly of the gleaming still. She scolded herself silently. Ever since talking to the Englishman yesterday, her mind had been elsewhere but on her tasks. She had thrashed about all night and hardly slept. And, despite her best self-discipline, she had found herself gazing wistfully out any window that looked in the direction of the Trustees' House. But she hadn't caught the merest glimpse of him and had heard he was being taken out to the ryefields by the farm deacons today.

She sighed and forced her concentration back to her work. After each batch was done, she knocked on the wall to summon the sisters, who took the rosewater from her. In the workshop, they completed its bottling, labeling, and distribution to kitchens, infirmaries, and peddlers for sale to the world's people. Along with the famous Shaker seeds and brooms, her rosewater was in great demand.

"I hope I am not intruding, Sister Rebecca."

She gasped and splashed hot rosewater on her wrist. "Oh!"

"Here, let me help. I'm so sorry I startled you!"

As if she had conjured the man from her daydreams, Ramsey Sherborne stood so close to her she could smell meadow breeze and horses on him. He looked a bit disheveled and hot himself, his brown skin glistening with a sheen. In the corners of his eyes, he even had little white birds' feet like the ones Daddy used to have from squinting into the sun.

He took the jar from her and set it on the table beside the still. "I hope you didn't burn yourself. I *am* sorry."

They stood two feet apart in the shady shed. Her wrist began to ache to match her burned knuckle, but neither came close to the sweet scalding of emotion that churned inside her. He had sought her out! He was here and concerned about her.

"Here," he said, "let me go fetch some ointment from the infirmary for that."

"Really, no need. I'm used to it, and it wasn't your fault. I'll just rub a bit of the cooled rosewater on it and won't feel a thing."

This near, she had to tilt her head back to look up at him. Though the shed was small, she was certain he would dwarf any room. He, like the brethren in warm weather, wore no coat. But, unlike the proper brethren, he had unbuttoned his waistcoat and loosened his bow tie to flaunt a bit of skin at the base of his throat. He was bareheaded too. Rolled-up shirtsleeves displayed strong, hair-flecked forearms. To flee the funny feeling that she could pitch right into those arms, she stepped back against the counter and lifted her wrist to put at least that between them.

"See, it's fine," she lied and yanked it down again.

But he moved closer to peer at it, and his fingers lightly grasped her arm.

She froze, then pulled back.

"Forgive me again. I am forever forgetting the rules here," he said. "Not only no looking or talking, but certainly no touching. Do you favor all the Shaker strictures then?"

"Not really, but lately I try my human best to abide by them."

"But that is just it, you see. We are all human. Yet Shakers expect perfection!"

She almost smiled at that protest, for he seemed all the perfection she had ever expected in a man. To her relief, he stepped back against the wall where people walking by could not see him. She knew she did not want him to go, rules or not. And it was quite likely, since she had her supply of water and the other sisters were busy, that she could seize a few moments alone with him again. She *knew* it was wrong, but she did not *feel* it was wrong. Still, if they were caught it would mean she would not be left alone again, or worse, that he would be reprimanded or asked to leave. But this one fleeting moment of butterfly beauty held delicately in her hand suddenly seemed worth any risk.

"So," she asked, her voice a bit shaky, "don't you believe in rules, even in the world, in England and your Dorset?"

He leaned back against the wall in a casual way a Shaker brother never would. Despite his big shoulders, he had a lanky, graceful way about him. When he crossed his arms over his chest, his hands and fingernails showed he had actually been at work in the fields. Somehow, that moved her deeply too.

"I believe," he said, "in rules which benefit the progress of all mankind, not just the men in power who make the rules."

"Then you are not a maker of rules at home?"

"I want to be. I am trying to be. I will be. But when I am, the blasted rules will profit the downtrodden, the little man!"

His hands clenched to fists. Realizing she was staring, she went back to pouring rosewater into the still. She lit and placed a second squat beeswax candle under the still to make it boil faster.

"I find all that fascinating—your England too," she told him as she worked. "My family, I hear tell, both the Mercers and the Blakes, came from England to Virginia and then Kentucky. I suppose they would never have left England at all were they not once the downtrodden, the little man."

"I would like to hear about your family," he told her. Her insides quaked. Could he mean it? She had been encouraged all these years to forget her family. A high-bred English lord wanted to hear about the Mercers and the Blakes? She could not resist a quick peek around to see his face, but her glance was a mistake. His eyes were hot on her; a jolt of desire coursed through her, yet icy chills raced up and down her backbone.

"We'd best stick to Shaker business," she said as she hastily capped the still. "But I'll tell you when we made rosewater at home in the old days, Mama and I only had corncob stoppers and not those fine corks there beside you." She indicated the box of them on the window ledge next to the plate of sweetmeats. "I cut those to just the right size to keep the bottles closed but let them breathe a bit too."

"You *are* a Shaker striver for perfection, if you've shaped each one of these," he marveled, lifting and rolling one cork between his big fingers.

She felt so attuned to him, she too felt the soft press and resiliency of the dry, cracked cork. She could almost feel the skin of his hand, smooth yet strong. She sniffed in a big breath in surprise at feeling so linked with longing to this stranger.

"And what are these lovely-looking things?" he asked, peering at the sweetmeats.

She came closer before she realized she should not have. "Rose petal sweets made from some of those blooms you saw me picking yesterday," she told him with a proud smile.

At this close range, she had no choice but to pop one in her mouth and then retreat. The candied petal burst to rose, honey, and lemon flavor on her tongue, though she had trouble swallowing it with his eyes on her. Now he was staring at her hair, covered only by the stiff white linen cap perched over her topknot. She realized she had missed many little things in Shakertown that now seemed to be utterly important. Like chatting and eating with a man. Or having the way you fixed your hair appreciated or even receiving a personal compliment. The sadness of girlhood years lost amid Shaker strictures racked her. And in a flash of revelation, she not only forgave but totally understood Christina's passion to leave with Travis no matter what solemn vows had been made.

"Please help yourself to a sweetmeat," she said. "And then, so others don't disapprove, perhaps you'd best be going."

"I would love one. However, I am afraid I've still got soil

175

and ink on my hands. But if you would be so kind as to feed me one, I could be on my way.''

As if drawn to a magnet, she took one step closer. Their eyes locked in the soft silver light while the still seethed and sweet scents embraced them. She must refuse, she told herself. She had to say no. Forbidden—this was all strictly forbidden. But her gaze moved to the firm curves of his lips, which had spoken of wanting to hear about her family. Of wanting to share her rose petals. Of wanting justice for downtrodden people.

Those lips smiled as if to lure her on. She felt as if the plank floor of the shed had dropped away. She was flying as she had not in years, not even in the dance.

Not looking away from him, she took a step closer. She put her hand down and cradled a pink sweetmeat in two fingers. Neither of them breathed as her hand lifted, her arm bent, her fingers approached his lips. He opened them. The tip of his tongue appeared. She popped the sweetmeat in, barely brushing her index finger against his smooth, sleek lower lip. As if she had been burned again, she jumped back. She put both hands behind her skirts, brushing her sugary fingers together. She had the almost overwhelming desire to put them in her mouth.

''Delicious,'' he declared. ''If the Dorset poor did not need just plain wholesome food to fill their bellies, it is the first thing I would give them. Then they would understand the marvels I have seen here.''

She nodded, mesmerized. She still felt that slight touch of his lip and the caress of his intense gaze down into her belly and even lower. Her breasts felt heavy but her legs very light.

''You know,'' he went on while he licked sugar from his lips, ''I think I could help you by carving these corks.''

''Oh, thank you, but they're done. Next week the rosewater will be too far for the year, and I'll be back to herding sheep in the afternoons.''

''Really? I have seen where those fine merino herds graze beyond the ryefields.''

"I search for strays. Farther out than that. Sometimes beyond the North Lot buildings."

"I see."

They kept staring at each other. She could not believe she'd blurted all that out. She'd as good as invited him to the fields to find her. Even in this heat, her face warmed more. What was wrong with her? Had things between Christina and Travis begun like this? But this was not the same. This man was so different, so far above her in the world's ways.

"Ramsey, there you are!" the other Englishman said as he blocked the door. "Deacon James is going to show you the interior of the horse power pump for the waterhouse, remem—Oh, how do you do, sister?" he greeted Rebecca when his eyes adjusted to the dimness. He doffed his hat to her. His eyes went from Ramsey to her, then back again. Ramsey properly introduced them.

"We had best be off then," Ramsey said.

"Thank you kindly for your admiration of the rosewater," Rebecca said. Both men bowed and left.

"Are you mad, man?" she overheard Will Barnstable's words.

That was it, she thought, as she sagged against the counter. She was mad, demented. She was committing enough Shaker sins to demand centuries of confessions. And after all the heartbreak she had been through, she knew she was setting herself up for more disappointment and abandonment. She was daring to care deeply about someone she must surely lose.

She leaned her palms on the counter and gazed at herself in the still. The reflection was recognizable and yet it looked like a new and different Sister Rebecca: her face had a soft, golden glow that seemed to waver with the steaming rosewater within the still. Her green eyes looked huge and hungry. And today, the entire universe had tasted and smelled sweeter than she had ever known, even in those early days in Shelter Valley.

* * *

Rebecca only glimpsed Ramsey Sherborne from afar the next few days, as if she had dreamed their talks, their closeness. She agonized over things she had done and not done, said and not said in his presence. She could not keep her mind on Sunday service, but danced more passionately than ever during the Shaker high. But she knew Ramsey Sherborne and not Mother Ann was the true inspiration.

By Monday, when she began to walk the outer boundaries for strays, she had taken to both missing him and scolding herself for missing him. She was as silly and confused as a wandering sheep, she told herself. Since she had first laid eyes on him, she felt as if she had fallen into crevices, tumbled into gullies, and scratched herself on brambles. He would not come today, she tormented herself. He had forgotten her. She scanned the rolling green horizon for the hundredth time. He would not dare to seek her out here; besides, he did not want to. He was done learning about rosewater, so he was done with her.

With her shepherd's staff, she hooked and rescued a young ewe and sent it back toward the main flock as the sun sank lower with her foolish hopes. She wilted onto a rock by a gurgling stream that made its crooked way to Shawnee Run and then the Dix River and finally the Kentucky. It was no Crawl Crick, but it brought back yearnings for home. Ramsey Sherborne longed to help the poor and downtrodden where he had been born; she knew then with utter clarity that she wanted to return to Shelter to help folks there too. And yet she now accepted her life among these strong but gentle Shakers, with each step of each day as carefully laid out as these rocks some staid brother had aligned perfectly across the brook. Childhood rebellions aside, even as badly as she wanted to help Christina birth her baby and help the people back at Shelter, she would not hurt her family here by permanently living in either place.

"Too blasted many rules!" she muttered, then grinned when she realized she had echoed Ramsey Sherborne's sentiments and his favorite curse word. She flopped down on the bank to yank her shoes and stockings off. It was forbidden, but the day was hot again. She was quite far out from the village, and it was obvious he was not coming. Besides, the old Becca wanted her feet free and wet.

She waded in. It refreshed her body and her spirit. Crystal cool and crisp, the water swirled around her ankles. She hiked her hems up a bit so there would be no telltale wetness at supper. She tried to console herself for the loss of Ramsey Sherborne, but then, he had never really been hers, not even for a moment. She splashed and kicked. She did a step of the old Virginia reel and had a little frolic of her own. And then she whirled to make tiny waves and saw Ramsey sitting on the crest of hill above, just watching. She jerked to a stop, her skirts swirling down to stick against her wet legs.

"I was afraid to startle you this time," he called to her. "I like the way you chase stray sheep too."

Blinding white joy flooded her. She returned his impudent grin. He rose and strode down to join her. She did not think to seize her shoes and stockings. She did not protest as he pulled off his boots, rolled up his trouser legs, and joined her in the water. She did not realize that she was babbling like the brook when she began to tell him all about her town of Shelter and the people there. She even explained Mama's and her baby sister's deaths, but not how Daddy had blamed her. For the first time since Christina had gone, she unburdened herself about her early bitterness here among the Shakers and told how deeply she had come to admire them. She told how she lost her friend Christina. She did not care when the sun sank lower, for he was telling her how farm laborers in Dorset had been thrown off their lands by unjust rules called the English enclosure acts.

"Now farm laborers are forced to work for set low fees for huge landowners. They nearly starve. They live in hovels. And when they try to organize in groups called unions to demand a fairer wage from people who have taken their land and pride, they are persecuted anew by local and national laws. They have been pounded down by political powers into the very soil of the land by which they once flourished.''

"They need to find new heart to fight back," Rebecca told him.

"They need new laws," he insisted.

"But if they have lost heart, they must find that first. That's one thing others can't quite give you. A loving friend can help, but it has to come from inside you."

Ramsey turned to her on their side-by-side rocks where they were drying their feet in the breeze. She knew full well he had been eyeing her ankles, but he looked serious now.

"I am astounded how astutely and simply you put that. But now, to us. Since we can seize so little time together, I must tell you something, Rebecca Blake. I would like to be your loving friend. And I would like to hope such mutual feelings—such longings—come from inside you too."

Her mouth hung open. His confession had taken her unaware. Anyway, he would be here such a short time, not even three weeks more. Then he would go back to his world and leave her stunned and bereft for having cared for and lost him. Yet she recalled that she was better and stronger for having cared for and lost other dear ones.

"Yes," she told him, her voice soft as the breeze. "I would be honored to be your loving friend, if we can manage it."

"We *will* manage it!" he vowed.

He took her hand and she did not startle or pull back this time. But she bounded up when she heard another shepherd's distant shout, as if summoning her back to the real Shaker world.

Ramsey found her in different places and times every day that week and the next. Rebecca lived for those stolen moments. Dorset was wild, he said—like her. She could not imagine anyone calling a Shakeress wild, but she soon proved she was. She thought less and less of Shaker sin and more and more of Ramsey Sherborne. And he had said she was beautiful too. "Only the fairest can pull hair straight back

180

like that and yet look stunning," he had told her. At that, she felt more stunned than stunning. She even stared so long, so dreamily in the retiring-room mirror that Sister Anna scolded her. When she was not called to confess, she went back to dreaming of Ramsey.

Unknown to Rebecca, though, Sister Anna had reported this break in rules to the elderesses.

"You say, Sister Anna, she seemed to just be staring in the mirror?" Sister Faith inquired.

"Why, yes, for the longest time. Like in a trance or a vision. She's done it looking out windows lately too, I seen her. Looks just like one of the Inspireds when they get a heavenly message."

Sister Faith and Sister Alice exchanged excited glances as they escorted Sister Anna from their office. "I told you our patience would pay," Sister Alice exulted and clasped her hands heavenward. "She's getting closer, ever closer!"

"I just hope she's not hankering for that worldly friend of hers again," Sister Faith put in with a shake of her head. "You know, thinking of asking to go to Harrodsburg to visit her and"—she shuddered, hardly able to get the words out— "actually assist in the birth of her child."

"Oh dear. Just to be sure it's not that, I'll put a little bug in her ear, maybe get some of the other sisters to also. You know, true tales about how hard the world is for a woman."

"A good idea. She's made strides, such big strides," Sister Faith said as she sat down to list the next week's duties. With a whimsical conviction that Sister Rebecca's inner longings would be freed by working with her beloved herbs instead of sheep now that the roses were almost gone, Sister Faith changed the next week's duty roster. She wrote: "Second week, July, 1836, Sis. Reb. Bl. to pick herbs in cliff pasture inst. of chasing lost sheep."

Ramsey Sherborne's big strides shrank as the black mood enveloped him. He had thoroughly searched for Rebecca among the distant pastures where sheep roamed, but she wasn't there. Another sister had been the only one he'd seen. He was panicked that today would pass and he would not see her. What if she were assigned to household duties where he would never get near her in the five days he had left? His need for her beat like the pulse of his blood. It was all he could do to woo her gently and not just seize her in his arms to convince her she must be his. So far, but for holding her hand, he had not so much as touched her. He had to free her from this place to have her for his own—*if* he ever saw her again! Head down, breathing hard, he scuffed up the stairs to his room.

"Back so early for once?" Will observed, looking up from his letter writing when Ramsey strode in gloomily and tossed his hat on the bed. "Not such pretty diversions as usual?"

Ramsey sank on his bed. He decided to ignore Will's baiting. Once Will really knew Rebecca, he'd think the world of her too. Damn, but those old elderesses had evidently assigned her elsewhere this week. He only hoped and prayed no one had caught on to their secret meetings.

"It's probably a better day to walk a bit more toward the river," Will said with an obviously dramatic glance toward the front window.

"Meaning?" Ramsey demanded, his attention perking up.

"I saw a certain Shakeress walk that way with that big herb basket of hers."

Ramsey rose. If he ran after her right now, Will would know more than he had chosen to share yet. He would just have to understand. "Perhaps I will stroll that way then. And Will, as ever, I'm grateful for your friendship," he threw over his shoulder as he headed for the door.

Rebecca knew she'd find lobelia in the tall-grass pasture overlooking the river, but she unexpectedly found the rarer herb called life everlasting too. She began to pick that first. At least that cheered her up. She knew Ramsey would never find her here, and each day without him was a catastrophe.

There was a Shaker rule that only one herb could be harvested on a gathering trip, but she had no patience for that today. It did not make sense not to pick both herbs and just duck into the herb workshop to set them to drying so that no one knew.

Just being among the woolly stems and yellow flowers of life everlasting and the pale blue lobelia soothed her tormented heart a bit. The colors reminded her of the meadow at Shelter and of Widow Lang's beautiful quilt. But the continual ache, the urgency and emptiness the moment she was parted from Ramsey, still grew like a weed within her. And those rampant feelings terrified her: the old Becca's rebelliousness arose again, the bitter yearning for things she would never have.

"Re-bec-ca!"

She straightened and turned in the direction of that distant, familiar voice. He had found her here! However was he certain it was she under this bonnet and common Shakeress garb? But he was here, waving and calling her name as he strode across the fringe of the meadow toward her.

Holding her flat, loaded basket tight with one hand and her bonnet with the other, she began to run. When they got closer, he held out his arms and, without even thinking, she flew right into them. Her basket upended, baptizing them with life everlasting. His arms gripped her shoulders hard. They laughed from pure joy. Hands on her waist, he lifted and spun her and then sat them both down in the thick grass and herbs, taller than their heads now. They were hidden here should anyone come along who was not a bird or angel.

The whole chirping, whirring world stood still and silent. He tipped her bonnet back; it dangled by its strings before she pulled it off and tossed it away. His face loomed so close. Then he was kissing her.

His lips against hers, his hands on her chin and the back of her head surprised her only for a moment. Pursing her lips, she opened them slightly the way he did his. She learned to slant her head to deepen the kiss. No one could ever deny

Rebecca Blake was a quick student. She kissed him back as if it were the most necessary and natural thing in the world. Nothing mattered, nothing existed besides this man. Sweetly, gently, his tongue intruded. She caressed it with the tip of hers. He seemed to taste her but to allow her to savor all the sensations he showered on her. She opened her eyes once, but his were closed. Still, the mere brush of her eyelashes against his warm cheek, up then down, seemed the most intimate of motions.

She could not stop her hands from touching him. His chin and cheek felt a bit raspy with beard stubble; his shoulders were firm under the crisp stretch of his linen waistcoat; his hard hip and thigh seemed molded to her softer ones.

"My darling," he breathed between kisses. Then he tugged them down flat into the fragrant grass.

Kissing and caresses magnified and multiplied. So fervent, so forbidden, so fine. His big hands roamed her supple back, squeezed her waist, then gently grasped her heaving rib cage right through her loose gown and kerchief. When she pulled herself closer to his big, hard body with her arms linked around his strong-sinewed neck, his hands moved higher. Carefully he molded his palms to the fullness of her breasts; then a thumb under her kerchief flicked back and forth across her nipple with only chemise and cotton gown between. That shot fiery sparks all through her, and she moaned under his demanding kiss. And then he lowered his tousled raven head to kiss her breast.

She was instantly dizzy, but nothing had ever felt better. "Oh, my!" she managed.

"I want you, I want you," he breathed hot against her. He nuzzled her neck, then pulled her up into his arms. The heavy bounty of her hair pulled loose to spill a chestnut curtain between them to be tangled in their fingers.

She laughed softly as he laid her on her back again to smooth the wild hair from her face. She gazed dazedly up at him. His touch turned tender again, but she sensed he wanted to loosen his control like her hair. It surprised her that she did too. She wanted to be mastered and yet master him too. She wanted to writhe against him and cling to him and beg him to take her and show her all there could be between them of longing and loving.

She tensed her stomach and thigh muscles and felt a strange flowering of herself within, luring her even further on. But she seized control enough to tell him, "I want you too, but I'm not sure of all that means."

He moved his head between her and the sun so she would not squint. "I could show you."

"Mm. You already have. But what does 'I want you' mean to you, Ramsey?" she asked, her breath still so swift she felt she had no control over it any more than she did her languid limbs.

"It means I want you in my life, even after I leave here next week. It means I desire you—all of you, this fabulous face and body you Shakers want to deny can come alive like this. It means I want to share my life with you and show you the world, beginning with Harrodsburg, where I will go to visit when I leave here—"

"Harrodsburg! I could visit my friend Christina there. But . . ." She felt as if she'd been doused with cold water. She sat up and he helped her. He kept one hand pressed to the small of her back and one cupped over her knee.

"Then, dare I hope that you and your friend who left here for love of a man have a great deal in common? Rebecca, dare I hope?"

While his hands and eyes felt hotter than the sun on her, she began to gather and repin her hair. "You see," she said, stalling for time to regain her sanity, "Travis and Christina hurt the family terribly when they left and were consigned to perdition for it. I could never do that to my family, hurt them so. I've battled with myself to find acceptance here. And, I don't believe in—in betrayals."

"Surely you don't think—"

"I think if I ran off, it would be agony for those who have been so good to me here. They trust me and love me in their own Shaker ways. They hope for great things from me. I—really, we can talk later, for I had best go back.''

''But I hope for great things from you, too! Who could not when they know you? Rebecca, will you meet me here again tomorrow? Will you think about·my offer to take you with me? We can be married in Dorset. I cannot imagine facing anything without you, even the cause I came here to serve at any cost or sacrifice.''

She gaped at him through his impassioned speech. His strength and determination wrapped her more strongly than his arms had. *Married?* In Dorset? She could not believe he had said such marvelous and terrifying things, nor that she had heard them and wanted to believe them. Lord Ramsey Sherborne and Sister Rebecca Blake were most certainly not from the same world! Even if she were free of Shakertown and lived with him in his precious Dorset or her dear Shelter, they would not be from the same world. Could their love bridge it? Could she trust him not to betray her once they were away from here?

''Rebecca, are you all right? If I thought we would not get this opportunity again, I would carry you down to the river right now. We would flag a boat and run away together—forever! Are you listening to all I've said?''

''I—yes, all. So much.'' She shook her head as if to clear it. ''I have to gather these herbs and head back. If I can, I will see you hereabouts tomorrow.''

She pinned her cap back and retied her bonnet. They both scrambled to retrieve the now wilting stalks of her herbs. She felt dizzy when she stood. She must start back ahead of him in case anyone was on the river path. She stood unsteadily; this could not be happening and yet, somehow, it seemed the culmination of her very existence. But it was utterly impossible. An irony of life, Mama would have called it, dear Mama who had run off down the river with her own forbidden love.

''Tomorrow, my darling!'' he said, looking up at her. His brow was furrowed, his face earnest.

"I will have to think about the things you said. I will have to decide."

"Rebecca, wait!" He rose to his knees in the grass like the fondest suitor. "I will not have you immured here like some nun! You belong out there," he said and swept the meadow with his arm. "With me!"

She took several steps away despite the way his passion pulled her back. Unshed tears blurred the meadow to an arch of rainbow under her feet. She had overstepped. She had let this happen. She loved him more than life itself. She wanted to run back to him and beg him to carry her off as he had said he would. But that was no way for an independent mountain girl and Shaker sister to behave. She looked back at him and lifted her free hand in farewell. Then she said the words that would seal her love of this man for eons to come whether she damned herself to go with him or damned herself to send him away alone.

"I love you, Ramsey Sherborne. I always will!"

Chapter Eleven

How could so much love cause so much pain? Rebecca wondered. She waged that silent war within herself each day now that she knew she loved Ramsey, yet still loved her Shaker family too. Each moment, each choice posed an impossible dilemma. This morning, she oversaw other sisters sorting herbs in the East Family Sisters' Workshop. She pretended all was well. But all was not well and might never be again. Whichever way she turned, a path of pain and parting beckoned.

"You must have picked the cliffside meadow clean of this life everlasting herb," Sister Mercy remarked as Rebecca walked around the big table where a dozen sisters worked shoulder to shoulder. Others bustled back and forth to the stacked drying racks, or weighed herbs to fill boxes and jars on the neatly numbered shelves. Once such a purposeful pursuit would have pleased Rebecca, but neither her mind nor her heart was in it today. Her thoughts and emotions were with Ramsey and the wonderful and horrible decision she must make.

Forgetting she held a stalk of nettle, she clasped her hands together. The nettle pricked her palm with tiny splinters. But it was Sister Mercy's coughing that brought her back from her own problems.

"Here, sister," she told Mercy, "just chew a few of these flowers of the herb to soothe your throat. No need to send you to the sisters' infirmary when we have the cure right here. But if you feel the need to cough again, best not to be working over these herbs now."

"Sister Rebecca," Mercy responded with a grateful smile as she popped a faded yellow blossom into her mouth, "what would we ever do without you?"

Rebecca could only nod. Companionable talk buzzed in her ears as she walked on. What, indeed, she thought, would these sisters or the elders of her entire Shaker family, which meant so much to her, do if she ran away to the world with Ramsey Sherborne? The Shakers needed and respected her. The elderesses, especially, expected so much from her. She would shock and disillusion many: the retiring room sisters who were her friends; her own brother, Jeremy, who still looked up to her; children she taught about roses and herbs; her East Family—the entire village.

She had vowed once she would never hurt the Shakers, never deceive them as Christina and Travis had. But in meeting secretly with Ramsey these weeks, she had forsaken those vows as well as her Shaker ones. She had broken the most stringent rules of Shakerdom and had not confessed her sins. She had run headlong toward her own destruction just as she had run, arms outstretched, toward Ramsey that day he came to find her in the cliffside meadow.

Then too, the Shakers greatly admired Ramsey. They were pleased he had journeyed so far to understand their ways, and were honored he was taking so many of their products and ideas home with him. He had insisted on tendering overly generous prices for Shaker goods. From the unexpected profit—a heaven-sent sign of future bounty, Sister Faith said—the trustees planned to purchase more meadowland, which they would soon turn into productive fields. Then too,

Ramsey had bent his back and dirtied his hands to learn their ways and repay their hospitality; he had worked side by side with the brethren.

In the window light, Rebecca bowed her head to pick the nettle prickers from her palm, but she felt no pain at that. She could not fathom ever feeling bodily pain again after such great agony inside. She jumped when someone touched her shoulder.

"I think it helped my sore throat already, Sister Rebecca," Sister Mercy told her. "You're ever so clever, and here I thought that herb was just for bruises."

Rebecca answered her, hoping she made sense, and moved on to encourage and instruct others. Right now she felt anything but clever. Without Ramsey she would feel a broken heart and bruised soul—what herb could ease her torment? It was all she could do to keep from sinking to the ground and wailing out her panic and her pain.

Ramsey Sherborne loved her and wanted to take her back to England to make her his wife. She loved him beyond all reason, and yet, surely, she could not go with him. She had once lost her beloved Shelter home and family—how could she face losing this Shaker home and family too?

Tears threatened to spill. Desperately she blinked them back and glanced out the window toward the Trustees' House. Ramsey was no doubt over there packing his things. Soon he would depart for Harrodsburg, but he had said he would meet her in their meadow early this afternoon. And he wanted and deserved her answer!

Perhaps it would be best if she just stayed here and didn't go to the meadow at all. Cowardly, yes, but at least it would spare them both. A farewell to him would mean the end of her sanity. Yet if she went with him, she would lose the last shred of the Shaker self she had striven so hard to stitch together from those pieces of the deserted, broken Becca. If she never gazed into those gray eyes so lit from within again, nor heard his luring tales about his downtrodden Sherpuddle village people or his mother's roses behind the Sherborne manor house, nor felt his hands hot on her bare skin, nor his lips on her throat—

She leaned against the window ledge and bit her lip so hard she tasted blood. She loved him; she needed him. Without him, she would become as dead and dry as these herbs, though no doubt she would function like them over the years to help others here. But could she bear to be the husk of what could have bloomed within? She wanted to see and help others in the world, including someday the folks she had left behind at Shelter. They could establish an endowment and set up a school there, Ramsey had said. When she was his wife, he vowed, they could do so much together she could never do here. And she wanted her own family; she wanted to love her own children the way Mama had, and for Ramsey to do things better than Daddy! She wanted a son like Jeremy or Adam Scott, a son to protect and rear and love, a daughter like herself or Christina or Adam's sisters!

She felt turned inside out with longing for what might never be. But her love for Ramsey was real; she held to that. She sucked a drop of blood where she'd bit her lip, and forced herself back to work. Strange, how she felt separate from these dear Shaker sisters now, though she stood among them. After Ramsey left, would this anguish fade the way the agony of Daddy's leaving her and Jeremy had finally muted? Would she be able to stay so busy at Pleasant Hill that she could fill her heart with sedate, warm Shaker love in place of this soaring, passionate love for Ramsey? When she thought of him across the ocean without her, it would be eternal torment to think he had another woman at his side. At each proper Shaker confession, she would scream out how she had loved him so deeply. If she must send him away without her, perhaps it would be best if she could simply die.

"I said, what about my dye, Sister Rebecca? Are some of these marigold blooms to be set aside for my yellow dye?" the elderly Sister Elizabeth was asking. She had come in from the weaving workshop and Rebecca hadn't even noticed until the old woman touched her arm.

"Oh, yes, surely. Take what you need, please, and we'll dry the rest separately for medicine, Sister Elizabeth."

The woman peered closer. "Are you sure you are not feeling poorly, sister? You looked peaked a moment ago, but now you're all flushed."

"Bending over picking herbs too long, that's all. I'm just fine," she assured the sister, who took her basket over to the table to select flowers for dyeing woolen blankets.

This could not go on, Rebecca realized, this head in the clouds, this loving loyalty to two opposing forces. She went outside to the old well and gulped a ladle of water. It trickled down her chin; coolness wafted from the well. The wind was picking up, rattling maple leaves overhead; distant thunder thudded over the hills.

She wiped her mouth and gazed off again toward where Ramsey had lived this last month. With all her woman's heart she wanted to run to him and tell him yes, *yes* to all he desired. At the mere thought of him, she felt herself flower inside with sweet dew as when he had held her and kissed her. She felt that too familiar, forbidden fluttering of butterflies in her belly. Just yesterday, again in the meadow, she had almost given herself completely to him, despite the looming devastation of all she held dear here.

"I adore you!" he had whispered hot against her temples as he bathed her with kisses. His hands, which sometimes seemed to be everywhere on her, held and caressed. Like a madwoman, she had arched her back to present her throat to his tender, then tormenting lips. She had spread her legs and then clamped his intruding knee between hers when he rolled them over in the grass.

"I love you oh so much!" she whispered, clinging closer.

"Then say yes to everything we can share together!" His face, open, passionate, hovered just over hers. "You will go with me to Harrodsburg, then to New York and home! You will never regret it! We will be everything to each other, my darling, everything!"

She had longed to give him everything then, no matter

what befell when he was gone. That suspended moment of total surrender had seemed wrapped in splendor. Birds had lilted overhead; sweet grass and nodding flowers had cradled them; puffy clouds had wandered the blue sky like sheep. But then she had said the words that had held her back from that last step, from letting him inside her body as he already dwelled within her heart and soul.

"Ramsey, it will hurt my family so!"

"What about us?" he demanded and gave her a little shake. "We will create a new family! Can you make do without me? I know now I cannot live without you at my side. It is a blasted living grave for you here in this so-called Society of Believers! They do not believe in a real commitment to the sort of love we can share! No one on earth, including you, has the right to deny us this!"

"I will have to decide. I will tell you tomorrow! I made a vow to stay here, you see, and—"

"I do not see! That was before me, before us! Tell me you think our touching is really wrong. Tell me what we do to each other and our dreams and the way we feel is sin—" He broke off his challenge and began to love her again.

She responded so fervently that he tumbled them in the grass, this time with her on top, straddling him as if she rode a horse. Her hair cascaded loose; her shoulders were freed from her Shaker gown; her skirts, caught by his thighs, bared her legs. But for his trousers between them, which did so little to hide his blatant desire for her, they were almost one. She knew so little of the love act, but she felt united with him already. She trusted him completely and wanted him more than that. She felt in that flashing moment that she could conquer the world with him, conquer him, conquer her own raging doubts—

She shook her head to clear away the memory. Her knees weak, she wilted against the stone well. Somehow, yesterday, she and Ramsey had stopped short of the consummation of what they most desired. But today—if she went out there to meet him and knew it was time to go with him or bid him

193

farewell forever—she would want him that way again. Then she would have him always with the other precious things in her past, stoppered in a dark green bottle of memory for all her lonely, dedicated Shaker days ahead.

"Sister Rebecca."

She turned to face Sister Anna, who had come close before Rebecca saw her. Sister Anna stood staring up at Rebecca as if she could peer within her shuttered soul.

"Yes, Sister Anna? What is it?"

"You weren't having a vision just now, were you?"

Rebecca sighed and her shoulders slumped. "Not exactly."

"Well, Sister Alice saw you standing out here and says, kindly come see her when you've a moment to spare from the workshop."

Rebecca's heart beat even faster. Had she been found out? Surely Ramsey's patience had not snapped; he had not dared to go directly to the elders! He had sworn to her it was to be her decision.

"Fine," she told Anna. "Please tell her I will be over presently."

To Rebecca's surprise, Sister Alice neither asked if she was having special visions nor berated her because someone had discovered her trysts with Ramsey. Nor was she asked to make confession because she'd been staring off into empty air for weeks. Rather, it was Sister Alice herself who made confession. Rebecca sat bolt upright in Sister Faith's rocking chair, her fingers interlocked, trying not to look shocked as Sister Alice's story unfolded.

"I was eighteen then, you see. He was such a handsome man, Sister Rebecca, and I believed every word the liar said," Sister Alice went on as she paced slowly back and forth before the window. "He was so charming that butter would not melt in his mouth."

Rebecca stared down at her knees. If Sister Alice knew

about her and Ramsey, surely she would not choose this way to warn her!

"I thought I was betrothed to him. He had his worldly way with me, then left town without another word. Of course, I was ruined in my family's eyes. My father was a lay Methodist preacher—well, you can imagine how ashamed they were! So I cast them off and came here, a sanctuary of the body and heart. The Shakers cared for me and reared my son for me. He is Brother Drury, a deacon in the West Family, and so has become just another of the brethren I love kindly like the rest. I've seen him at Sabbath meetings and that's all."

Rebecca gulped audibly. She knew her eyes went wide as saucers when she looked up again. A man had led the young Alice Triplett astray. But Rebecca trusted Ramsey! She could read the sincerity on his face, the love in those burning eyes. It did not matter that he could make a fervent speech to convince anyone of anything. That was not a bit like Sister Alice's man, on whose tongue butter would not melt. Ramsey meant it when he said he'd wed her! Ramsey would never have his "worldly way" with her and then desert her! Nor was Ramsey like Daddy with his smooth ways, who could fun her and Jeremy all the way down the river where he intended to abandon them forever. Ramsey wasn't like any of those other men!

But her thoughts jumped to other things too. Sister Alice had borne a child. And worse, evidently with no regret because the child's father had deserted her, she had given that child away to be reared by others. And Sister Alice had dared to look down at Daddy that day he left them here! Sister Alice had cast off her family because they were ashamed of her, when Rebecca still grieved the loss of her family.

"Here at Shakertown," Sister Alice went on as though she'd said nothing amiss, "just as Sister Sally always says, women are equal to the men. Out there, they take you and use you in their carnal ways. Why, Sister Jerusha left a husband and six children out there to come here, and I can't fault her for it.''

Rebecca could fault her for it, but, stunned by the intimacies Sister Alice had shared, she held her tongue. ''Backbreaking, lonely labor and a child every two years,'' the elderess was saying, ''that's all Sister Jerusha or any woman has to look forward to unless she finds a heavenly haven like Shakertown.''

Rebecca knew better than to argue or bring up Christina's happiness at being wed to her Travis. Besides, what the elderess said was partly true; Rebecca thought of Pru Johns and Jemima Tucker and even poor Mrs. Scott, bearing all their babies so close together. As she was dismissed, she felt even more confused than she had been before. She wandered back into the workshop and then filed out in order with the others when the dinner bell rang. For once, the silence at the meal was a blessing. In a misery of longing, she reasoned through everything again. She was almost certain the distant thunder was her own brain heaving and rumbling.

She thought of Mama loving Daddy, though they so often parted. She remembered how she and Mama had talked about how a woman's lot in life was mingled joy and pain. How wrong she had been to think she had ever understood that before now! But Mama had said too when it was the right man, it was worth all the risk, all the pain. When Christina had left for life with Travis, Rebecca had told her that. Did she dare to risk all she had built for herself here for the unknown? Despite Sister Alice's words of warning, she was suddenly certain she knew Ramsey Sherborne.

That afternoon in the workshop among the sisters, she vowed she would never become a dry-spirited woman like Sister Alice or Sister Jerusha. That would be her fate without her beloved Ramsey no matter how much she helped others here. It would be agony to leave Jeremy and betray her Shaker family, but she could not live a lie all these coming years, alone, here, without Ramsey.

* * *

Despite the storm rolling closer across the hills, she seized her flat herb basket and headed toward the cliffside meadow. When she was out of sight of the village, she scanned the boiling gray horizon behind her, then began to run. As in her fondest memory of him, she saw Ramsey far off, waiting for her, then running toward her. They flew together and soared up into the clouds and down into the grass.

"You are going with me, I can tell!" he exulted.

"I want to, I love you."

"That's all we will ever need, my darling! I'll face them with you if you want or send you on ahead with Will and stay to tell them myself."

She put three trembling fingertips over his lips. "It can't be like that, like I'm just running away. I have to face them and explain."

"But if they should attempt to keep you . . ."

"They won't when they know. It will hurt them, and I can hardly bear that. But with you awaiting me in Harrodsburg, I can do it."

He clasped her chin and cheeks in his big hands. "You swear you will come to me? I will return for you, if you do not!"

"I swear. And I want to seal it now, here where I first said I love you, though I think I knew it from the first day I saw you among my—their Shaker roses."

"Seal it?" he asked. "Here and now?" His eyes widened, and she was certain he almost blushed.

"Yes. Seal our love with a vow, and then later—when everything is private and perfect, the rest. I must tell you, I think and wonder about—all that, so much."

"I too, my Rebecca. So much, I too." His eyes devoured her as she got to her knees and took his hand. He sat up, then knelt beside her. As it had before, everything seemed to grow still.

She darted a quick glance around the meadow to be sure they were alone, but even the storm held itself at bay. The meadow sheltered them beneath the arching roof of sky, gray as Ramsey's eyes.

"I vow to be your wife, to love you always," she said simply.

He looked as if he would cry. He swallowed hard. "I, my darling, will marry you and treasure you as lover and wife and helpmeet forever."

Their eyes met before he pulled her into his powerful embrace. They held hard to each other, ignoring the approaching thunder. She sucked in a breath as they seemed to become one body. "Oh, Ramsey, my dearest—"

They savored together the shattering of the old world and building of the new. Despite their different pasts, she had found her future. In trusting him, she rediscovered the sense of joyful, childlike oneness with the world she thought she had left behind forever, years ago at Shelter and then again when Daddy walked away for good. If only she could take Jeremy with them, but she knew he would not go. He was Shaker to the core and seldom seemed glad to see her anymore, as if her worldly clinging embarrassed him.

Now, desperate with desire, Rebecca and Ramsey kissed and caressed as they tumbled to the grass. Delicate raindrops cooled their bodies.

"We can't ignore the storm," she murmured, propping herself up, breathless, on one elbow.

He pulled her down again to kiss her neck and nuzzle her earlobe. "I've hardly ignored it. I've been swept up in it for weeks."

She smiled tautly, warmed by his teasing before her insides twisted even tighter. The old fear of hurting and deserting her family leaned hard on her again.

"I'd best head home—back, I mean," she said and sat up to smooth her wrinkled skirts down. "They'll know when they see me that I will never be the same again."

He hugged her hard. "Nor I. I feel complete and calm for the first time in so long."

"Mm," she managed, "you never act calm when we get that close."

His lips barely curved in a smile. "I mean complete and calm about our future, once I get you away from here. I will wait for you just outside the village."

"No, someone could see you there," she insisted as she repinned her hair and replaced her cap and bonnet. "It's only seven miles to Harrodsburg, and I will come to you tomorrow. I will tell them first thing in the morning and either get a ride or walk to town. I'll ask for directions. I know where to find you. And then our real life together can begin."

"Rebecca, I know you were independent before you came to Shakertown and you've managed somehow to keep your backbone here, but do you still plan to be that way?"

"It's the way I am."

"I know, and I want no other."

The rain came heavier now. It blurred the horizon; the sky trembled, yet they lingered. They peeked above the tall grass, then stood, clinging together.

"I am leaving here right away on horses Will has hired, rain or not," he told her. "If you are not at Graham Springs by midafternoon tomorrow, I will be coming back for you!"

"I want you to trust me, Ramsey. This choice is mine. I have to explain it to them. I just hope and pray I can make them understand—to soften a bit. But there's no need for you to suffer through it too."

She knew it would be like that awful scene when Christina and Travis left, only worse. But maybe it would make a difference that she wasn't just fleeing. Could that not work in her favor?

But when she turned away from Ramsey, her determination and strength evaporated again. She wanted to hold fast to him. She yearned to look into his eyes and memorize that dear face as if she had to remember it for years and not just a few hours.

"Tomorrow then," Ramsey insisted.

"Yes," she agreed. She glanced at him through the downpour; his face seemed to stream tears from heaven. "Tomorrow and then forever!"

Rain-sodden wind whipped them as they pressed tightly together again. Then she pulled away and ran across the meadow that had given her sweet herbs—and a new life.

She was thoroughly soaked when she went through the sisters' back door to the kitchen. Bedraggled and shaking, she held her dripping bonnet in her hand. Sister Sally looked up from stirring a huge copper kettle and her eyes widened. "Land, look at you! You all can't even walk upstairs with those clothes clinging close like that," she scolded. She grabbed a big towel and wrapped it around Rebecca's sodden shoulders. Rebecca cherished her concern now more than ever. But as she hurried to go upstairs to change, Sister Faith popped her head out of the elderesses' office door.

"Oh, dear sister, we were so worried! Praise Mother Ann you're back! But you look downright feverish! She's back, Sister Alice, so you can stop your fretting! Come in here by our stove, Sister Rebecca, and I'll send for your things! Now, tell us what happened that you stayed out so long you didn't even note the storm," she insisted, her eyes aglow. "You've been so uncaring about earthly things lately, we just know you've something special to share with us!"

At that, Rebecca could have laughed and sobbed at once. Inside the office, Sister Alice rose from her rocking chair as Sister Faith bundled Rebecca through the door. These dear old women expected her to report a wondrous vision or at least to walk the narrow Shaker path forever. And she had only shock and pain to give them. Suddenly, despite what she had told Ramsey about tomorrow, despite the howl of rain outside and night coming on, she knew she could not deceive them for one more moment. It would not be fair to sleep under their roof tonight otherwise.

But for one last time, Rebecca held to the warmth and security of her Shaker past, just as she clung to the warm blue and white checkered blanket Sister Faith wrapped around her shoulders over Sally's towel. She tucked away deep inside her the sharing and the purposeful bustle that had been Shakertown and her East Family. As she was about to shatter everything here, she treasured more than ever the kindly concern, the dedication, the beautiful Pleasant Hill. But she had been born too free to flourish here forever. She loved worldly folk and wanted a good man and a family. She savored the beauty in the world too much ever to be, like these dear women, a Shaker deep-bred in the bone.

"I must tell you something that will hurt you both. I would confess something to both of you before I go."

The two women exchanged lightning-quick glances. "About our hoping for a holy vision from you," Sister Alice put in before Rebecca could say more. "We won't press you for it, but if you would only open yourself to Mother's inspiration and confess your sins—"

"I'm sure you will think I have many to confess. But my only vision—my inspiration—is that I have met a man I want to spend my life with so I will be leav—"

Sister Alice's shrill cry jolted Rebecca. Gripping her forearms tighter, Rebecca held the blanket to her. Her teeth chattered as she dripped a puddle of water on the floor. Sister Alice's face, usually so controlled, turned livid and her features contorted as she shrieked, "What? What?"

Sister Faith sat down hard in her chair, shocked to silence.

"I bared my soul to you to warn you!" Sister Alice shouted. "But I only meant you weren't to go out there to visit that carnal friend of yours. A man? Who is he? What brother?"

Rebecca jumped back against the stove, then away when her sopping skirts hissed. Sister Faith, her cheeks sleek with tears, got up to seize Sister Alice's clenched hands. Rebecca grieved it had come to this already; pain pierced her.

Her explanation came out jumpy and broken. "I will be moving to England soon. Dorset. After Harrodsburg. I'll be— gone. I won't be a reminder—to anyone, even peddlers in town." She got hold of herself then. "I wish the family and especially the two of you to know how much I have respected and loved you all—''

"Love?" Sister Alice cried. "Carnal love is evidently all you know! When I saw that father of yours that first day I should have known what you would be like!"

"That isn't fair. I'm not like my father any more than you were like yours, Sister Alice!"

Sister Alice gasped. "How—how dare you be a serpent of dissension among us all these years—a wolf in sheep's clothing! I suppose you met with *him* out there, when we let you tend sheep to have time for the visions, but you haven't a holy Shaker thought in your wayward body!"

"I am only a woman in love, sister. A woman who finds the world a lovely place and always has. I regret—"

"Get out! Leave now! We will tell them what you've done, but I'll not have you spread that poison to the entire family! We'll not abide another of your so-called Shaker confessions, where you dare to preach your doctrine of forgiveness and union with the world!"

Rebecca's hope of softening their hearts shattered, but she could not bear to leave this way. She could not abide losing this family and years of her life as if they had never existed. She had contributed here as well as receiving much. But there was no stopping Sister Alice.

"Sister Faith, please go up to this sis—this woman's retiring room and fetch down dry garments. Since the Englishmen we all foolishly trusted are off the grounds today, she can stay in the Trustees' House tonight and be gone at first light." When Sister Faith hurried out, Sister Alice sank into her chair, but she sat bolt upright in it, her hands gripping the maple armknobs. "Which of the Englishmen?" she inquired icily.

"Ramsey Sherborne. We're to be wed."

"You stupid, stupid, deluded girl. You think a high-born man like that wants more from a mountain girl than a quick tumble? Your body is just another trinket to him. He'll desert you tomorrow after he has you, if he hasn't already. Has he?''

"I know Shakers don't believe in such, sister, but that is my private affair."

"Affair, indeed! He's had you then, that two-faced jackal, Ramsey Sherborne!"

"The brethren liked him. You do not know him."

"I know he took our Shaker goods and now he's taken you!"

"I love him."

"Bah!"

"But if I live in the world, I can help others there, show them some of the best things of the Shaker way."

"You've ruined everything," Sister Alice muttered and began to cry. "All my dreams for you."

Rebecca knelt at the side of her chair, though she did not dare to touch her hand. Even after all this, even the unjust accusations, she longed to comfort Sister Alice. "I promise I will take the best of Shakerdom to those it will help, sister."

"You've sullied it. Get out. Just get out!" Sister Alice wailed and lifted her clawlike, mottled hands to cover her face.

When Sister Faith returned with a bundle of clothes, Rebecca got to her feet. "I am sorry it had to hurt you both," she said. "You've been very kind to me. But this is the right thing for me to do, and the best thing for all of you too. I couldn't stay here now, but I'll be back to visit someday. Perhaps then—''

"Get out of this family's house and get out of the village at dawn!" Sister Alice insisted from behind her hands. "I never want to see the likes of you again!"

"I'd like to see my brother Jeremy to explain," Rebecca said in a low voice to Sister Faith.

The ever kindly face, now set hard and cold as stone, lifted to hers. Sister Faith had already wiped her tears and cried no more. "You have no brethren here, Rebecca Blake. Speak to no one and be gone by dawn, as Sister Alice says."

The full impact of the looming separation hit Rebecca then. Like a fist to the stomach, it sapped her strength and made her steps to the door unsteady. It was the nightmare of leaving Shelter all over again. This time no one was giving her away but herself. But this time Ramsey was waiting.

"Good-bye, then," she said. "And though you will all curse me, I will bless you for all you've given me."

Sister Alice's hands did not move from her face. Rebecca was surprised to realize that she already regretted never being able to look into those challenging, watchful eyes again. Sister Faith tugged her out into the hall and marched her out of the warm, dry dwelling, redolent with the smells of supper, through the sisters' side door into the chill rain. Rebecca yearned for a farewell hug or kindly word from this woman who had been dear for years, but she steeled herself for what was coming.

"Tell them to put you up where guests stay over there," Sister Faith ordered Rebecca when she stood in the dark, driving rain. "I just hope you haven't been a carnal visitor in those guest rooms over there already—" She choked back a sob, half lifted a hand as though she longed to bid a better farewell, then ducked inside and slammed the door. That sound reverberated to the depth of Rebecca's soul.

Clutching her dry clothes to her chest, she stood there, stunned. So quickly begun; so quickly ended. Learning, laughter, leadership, and yes, love. But it could not be love if it ended so suddenly, so bitterly. And those warnings about Ramsey toying with her and deserting her—surely not.

She stumbled across the straight-laid paving blocks to the Trustees' House. There she met with more accusations, more condemnation when she told them she was leaving. In the little room where they put her, she changed her clothes. She sat on the edge of the bed all night while lightning flared and thunder crashed. Staring at the rain-smeared window, she remembered and regretted. Perhaps she should have left earlier, any one of those many other times when she had rebelled or had doubts. But then she would not have been here to find Ramsey.

Torment made the time tick slowly. She waited for the dawn of day to begin her new life. She could not wait to feel Ramsey's welcoming, comforting arms around her. But she was nervous too, about the things she would face, about the man-woman loving she wanted so desperately with him. Still, when she went outside the next morning, she could hardly bear to set out down the main village road toward Harrodsburg.

Already everyone knew. Shakers shunned her as they passed on their before-breakfast duties. Sister Jerusha, standing with a broom on the front steps of the East Family Dwelling House, not only turned her back, but swept rain-soaked leaves her way, as if to say, "Good riddance!" Rebecca's feet felt like lead as she walked by her roses across the fence. The rain had polished each dark green leaf and red hip for her departure. She had at least come here with a rosebush from Shelter, but she could take none of these away. If only there would be roses in England, their tending not just the task of servants! How much did she really know of her future home or of Ramsey's world? Suddenly she was terrified.

Tidy rows of herbs nodded at her from her tenderly cared-for garden. The comfrey and ambrosia should be picked today, one herb at a time, of course, as was proper and seemly. She should be overseeing their sorting and drying in the workshop again. She dared to squint back at the East Family Dwelling House; the windows of her retiring room glinted back at her. She wondered if one of the sisters sweeping or dusting within looked out to see her go.

Broken pieces of a song resounded in her head: "Oh, my sweet Shaker home . . . my sweet Shaker home . . . my joy . . . my eternal song."

She sobbed aloud once, then lifted her chin. "Here in straight paths I'm led . . ." She strode past the Center Family buildings, wishing she could see Jeremy but afraid to. She knew he was Shaker to the core as she had never been; he would condemn her too. "And in purity fed . . ." Past the Meeting House and the West Family Dwelling House. Soon even these families would know of her worldly, carnal sins. "Oh, there's nothing like my sweet Shaker home . . ." Down past the graveyard where sisters and brethren she had known and loved lay beneath the wet grass and simple stones. They were no more dead to her now than all the others.

She turned again past the pond. Daddy used to say never to look back, but it was her nature to do so. Shakertown at Pleasant Hill stood there on its brow of bluegrass hill. It was bigger than it had been the first day she had beheld it from the other end of the village. Now, with Ramsey, she had another life to go to, one where people needed her too. She just knew it!

"I love you all and always will," she said as if each strict Shaker soul would hear and heed.

Then, swinging her arms and stretching her stride, for the first time in ten years she marched out into the vast, waiting world.

Chapter Twelve

Rebecca thought Harrodsburg, Kentucky, a huge city. It must be as large and crowded as Ramsey's London! Harrodsburg had ten intersecting streets crowded with buildings and brick walkways lined with hitching posts. Wagons, carriages, and even a stagecoach rattled by, astounding Rebecca with their clatter. Stores displayed arrays of fancy goods in their windows. On one corner, a boy sold a newspaper called *The Central Watchtower*, yelling out worldly events like "Turnpike to be built connecting Lexington and Harrodsburg! Steamboat explodes on the Ohio River!"

Some brightly dressed folks just stood around chatting as if they had no tasks to do. A few pointed at her; no doubt they had not seen a Shaker woman in town before, at least not one alone. She walked on. Children ran by in a disorderly clump, laughing loudly and rolling a hoop with a stick. Men and women strolled together, touching shoulders, linking arms. Folks didn't even stay on the walkways, but wandered off if it pleased them.

Dusty, hot, and exhausted in the August afternoon, Rebecca leaned against a brick building in the shade and just stared.

Her stomach rumbled, but she ignored it. She felt so confused. Everything seemed wonderful, yet forbidden. She trembled with mingled grief at her exile from the Shakers and her excitement at entering this new promised land with Ramsey. She asked a woman for directions to Graham Springs and trudged on toward the southern edge of town.

She felt twisted in knots by the time the vast green grounds of the mineral springs came into view. Ramsey had told her people came here from all over the south—Natchez, Vicksburg, Nashville, and New Orleans—to take the waters and escape the hot summer with its dangerous diseases. But she had not imagined this fine a scene. Instead of a Shaker stone fence to climb, two bronze lions guarded the gates, roaring a silent welcome to the sleek horses with their riders and shiny carriages parading in and out.

Within the fence were clusters of trim buildings and lovely trees. In the very center of her view stood the tallest, widest building she had ever seen. Four stories high with white pillars reaching to its flat roof, it must be the Graham Springs Hotel Ramsey had described. But if a place he stayed in just for a spell looked like that, what must his home in England be like?

Rebecca leaned against a tree trunk and gaped. She could not believe she had come here. She would never in a hundred years fit in. So many strange people to meet and chat with and learn their names. She started to shake all over. She was yet a Shaker indeed, she thought, trying to give herself courage with humor, but that didn't work. She was as frightened as she had been that day Daddy gave her and Jeremy away.

She pressed her clasped hands to her chest as if to still her thudding heart. She gawked at the way these people fixed their hair and dressed, grander than she'd ever seen except maybe for Adam Scott's Aunt Euphy years ago. The women wore tight-fitting bodices that showed their upper bodies and bell-shaped, swaying skirts that hid their lower parts. They had pretty feathered hats instead of the deep Shaker bonnets. What if, when Ramsey saw her here, he realized he could not take her home to England where they maybe dressed even finer than this? What if she was too different? What if—

And then she saw Ramsey. He rode out through the gates between the two roaring lions. She stepped out from under the tree. She waved to catch his eye, but her arm wilted above her head. She tried to call his name, but no sound came. Then she remembered their cherished talks, their vows, their love.

"Ramsey! Lord Sherborne!"

His head jerked around. Grinning, he rode right for her across the grass. She ran toward him, tears wetting her dusty cheeks. He reined in and jumped down. She held tight to his strength.

"I was going to start back along the road for you!" he told her, peering inside her bonnet. "I could not bear the waiting. Come on, I will take you in before we both lose control and really give everyone something to talk about."

She had never ridden on a horse before, but he held her tight before him on the big, bouncing beast. They rode right in between the lions to a grassy yard behind the massive hotel.

"I have leased a room for you on the top floor," he explained as he lifted her down. "And I have taken the liberty of purchasing you some things. I have let on that my country cousin from upriver is coming for a visit. In this way."

Boldly she draped her wrist in the crook of his elbow as she'd seen the women do here. He smiled down at her. She let him lead her up polished wooden stairs around turn after turn of hallways with more doors than a Shaker dwelling ever had. On the top floor, they stopped at a door numbered 414. He produced a key and they went in. He closed the door while she removed both her bonnet and her linen cap. He pulled her close.

"Oh, my dearest Ramsey," she said. And in this strange world and town and room, with him, she was at home.

The grandeur of Graham Springs could not match the grandeur of their love. That night he stayed with her, holding her in the biggest, highest bed she'd ever seen, one with a brocade canopy built right over it like an inside roof. They whispered low, though they were finally alone now. He kissed and caressed her. She felt so swept away by passion and her need for him that she would have welcomed a consummation of their love. But he was wonderful and dear. He saw how exhausted and distraught she was still, how she balanced on the edge of tears.

So, in the moon-silvered, warm August night, he assured her of his love and passion—but let her sleep in his arms. She could tell that it was torment for him. She had thought he had a deep reserve of stoicism and self-sacrifice, and she was right.

"It's all right, my darling, now that I know you're mine and always will be," he vowed when she awoke. "Beginning tomorrow we'll take it slowly, savoring every bit. I want us to get to know each other in calm circumstances, to give you time to adjust."

They talked on and on. She admired how much he respected his parents, though he admitted he had let his father down at times. So, she told herself, they did have a lot in common, though they came from different worlds. She was deeply moved by his desire that they wed publicly in England so his parents and friends would see how proud of her he was. Ramsey was convinced she would be dearly beloved by his people, so she tried to put aside her doubts. Ramsey was a wonder, she thought as she drifted off to sleep again in his arms.

When daylight came, they gazed out at the acres of gardens, boardwalks, and wide gravel promenades. He pointed out to her the roof of the huge ballroom, the ten-pin alley, the gazebos in the gardens, and promised they would take them all in today. Will came up with a tray of breakfast. Rebecca blushed when he teased them about his being their servant. She wondered what he thought of her Shaker morals now, when Ramsey had been in her room all night. But once he was out the door, leaving them alone again, it hardly mattered.

Again they talked and planned, then lay like slugabeds in each other's arms. At midmorning he left her, explaining that a maid Will had hired would soon be up to help her dress.

It was a good thing. When Rebecca looked more closely at the rainbow-hued bounty of clothing Ramsey had bought her, she realized she could hardly have gotten herself into any of them. So many strange pieces, with names the maid Polly recited, like a corset, chemisette, and false bottom bustle—and all of that was just underpinnings. Up the back of the gown marched a row of buttons that needed a hook to close. The gown was grass green with little flower sprigs printed right on it. Its sleeves were big as bushes at the elbows, then tapered so tight to the wrist she'd never be able to so much as pick an herb. When she was finally dressed, her big skirts bobbed and bumped the furniture when she moved. Her leather shoes had tiny heels that made her wobble a bit.

Polly used an iron that hissed and smelled to put her hair in even tighter ringlets than her natural curls. No more linen caps and big bonnets. This pert, jauntily tilted bonnet trimmed with feathers and ribbons seemed tiny on her head, but the buttercup-yellow satin parasol would shade her face.

She studied this new Rebecca in the biggest mirror she'd ever seen, one that was in a wood frame and tilted up and down. Well, she thought with a toss of her head, she finally had her green ribbons like the ones Jemima Tucker had tried to give her years ago—and a beau too! She hardly knew what to do with the small silk string handbag hanging on her wrist. It wasn't even big enough to hold a pruning knife. It just got in the way when she clung tightly to Ramsey's arm as they promenaded out.

Everyone seemed to know Ramsey from the time he had spent here before his month in Shakertown. He had even been asked to give a lecture next week about rural problems in England. But today he did not stop to converse. He only tipped his hat and said some of the people's names as he and Rebecca walked on. Rebecca learned to nod or incline her head. Evidently in the world, people didn't know everyone's name or business. Here no one shouted, "How you keepin'?" or even intoned "Make yourself kindly welcome." But what really annoyed her was that black-skinned slaves scampered here and there, fetching wicker picnic baskets or dishes of ice cream or holding parasols for their owners. That set these fancy folks far behind the Shakers who treated black-skinned people like equals, as far as she was concerned. Ramsey had said all the blacks here were slaves, and that he thought that was just as wrong as she did.

"There is one other thing here I wanted to show you before dinner," he told her. "You said your high window view reminded you of your Kentucky River home. Wait until you see this." He leaned toward her and pointed to a shaded grove down by the lake. "The owner and host here, Dr. Christopher Columbus Graham, journeyed to the forks of the Kentucky River to bring out exotic mountain greenery. I rather thought you might recognize some of it."

She did indeed. It was not exotic to her, but familiar and dear. Purplish-leafed blue ash and scalybark hickory. Tulip trees and pawpaws and even a clump of blackberry bushes like those that had grown near home. The redbud and dogwood were not in blossom now, but past them, along the lake, she glimpsed a tall white sycamore just like the ones that clung to the creek bank by the Blake cabin. Ignoring the others strolling the area, she lifted her bothersome skirt and began to run. The flock of ducks edging the lake scattered and quacked, then flew.

Homesickness hit her, for Shelter, for Shakertown, for her Blake family and her East Family. Tears prickled behind her eyes and her nostrils flared while she tried to hold them back. Ramsey hurried beside her, steadying her elbow when her heels stuck in the grass.

"Just like the trees at Crawl Crick!" she cried. She hugged the thick trunk the way she used to, even though it made her skirts bob and knocked her hat askew. Then she hugged Ramsey hard.

"Thank you for showing me this, so I'd feel at home here!" But as she surveyed the lovely scene, her excitement began to deflate. Others were staring at her. She heard one pretty lady sitting on a blanket laugh behind her gloved hand and saw a gentleman point her way.

"I'm sorry," she said and stepped back from Ramsey. "I've drawn attention to myself."

"You always do. And I mean that as the sincerest compliment. I would not want you any other way."

Too late, she recalled that she was supposed to be his country cousin. But cousins could hug, she thought. She had never been more touched by someone's concern and love for her. Still, she guessed she'd have to try harder to fit in here for Ramsey's sake.

The next evening, Ramsey and Will took her to theatricals and then dancing in the ballroom. It was the fanciest frolic she'd ever seen. She wore yet another gown Ramsey had bought for her. It was a beautiful dawn-pink color of a yard-good called organdy, stiff with bows. You could see right through to her satin underdress, but that was obviously the style here among the southern belles twirling like flowers on the dance floor with their gentlemen beaux, called young bloods. Covering Rebecca's arms and hands were long kid gloves, which she detested; women here actually ate and danced wearing them. They were snow white with pearl wrist buttons and so easy to splash with punch or food. People seemed to eat so much from the buffet tables, yet left so much food behind too; no one here knew to Shaker his plate!

"How can you abide a place like this when you told me your Sherpuddle folk hardly have enough to fill their bellies?" she asked Ramsey, but his explanation was interrupted by the approach of yet another curious couple, this one with a long-necked daughter in tow.

It seemed to Rebecca every southern couple had a daughter

whom they flaunted as if this were some sort of marriage market instead of a place to take mineral waters. And the fact that Ramsey was an English lord evidently made him look a great catch for their bait and hooks. It was obvious to her even during polite introductions that this particular, plump southern mama wished Ramsey's ''country cousin'' would just drop through the polished floor. Eventually, this trio too drifted off, with another squinty-eyed perusal of Rebecca.

''Do you think they know I'm not really your country cousin?'' Rebecca whispered as the orchestra struck up another sweeping tune which Ramsey had told her was a waltz.

''I really don't care, unless it bothers you,'' he said. ''In a little over a week, we will be on our way east, and no one will snub Ramsey Sherborne's wife at home.''

Rebecca saw Will's mouth tighten. Her heart fell. Will evidently did not think things would be that easy for them. Ramsey's clipped comment worried her a bit. Perhaps he felt guilty over what she'd said about the food, but she could not help it. This mingling with rich, luxury-loving people when his rural laborers were hungry and the Shakers worked so hard for everything—

''You all glad to be back in civilization again, Lord Sherborne?'' a portly man asked Ramsey. More than most of these people, this man dragged his words out long and slow. ''Pretty sparse on entertainment out there among those simpleton Shakers, I don't doubt,'' he added and sniggered.

That made Rebecca's blood boil. When the man merely held out his hand, his slave, attired in a green and gold coat, snapped open a silver-filigree cigar case. The boy adeptly clipped both ends of the cigar for his master, handed it to him, then lit it with a suphur match while all the man did was breathe smoke in and out.

''Actually, Mr. Putnam,'' Ramsey responded, his voice on edge, ''at Shakertown, the people seem to know what to value and what is mere pompous show.''

''Do they now? Cigar, Lord Sherborne? You, sir?'' he asked Will, who alone accepted the cigar and the light. ''I was wondering if you'd honor my eldest daughter, Dorothy, with a dance, Lord Sherborne.''

"My regrets, sir, but I was about to take Miss Rebecca for a turn on the floor," he said and steered her away by her elbow.

Rebecca should have balked—she'd never even heard of a dance called a waltz before this week. But she'd been longing to be in Ramsey's arms, even publicly. He had been slowly courting her, teaching her physical delights in private without quite losing control. Yet she hoped he'd lose it, and love her and never stop. But as badly as she wanted to be his bride, she too wanted it all done in proper English fashion. Daddy had wed Mama before he'd showed her humble Shelter and the Crawl Crick cabin. Rebecca had told Ramsey how shocked Mama had been, and he said he wanted her to see what she was taking on when they wed. Rebecca also realized that Ramsey must think his parents would be pleased he had not simply sprung a wife on them. She only hoped there weren't too many people like that Mr. Putnam back in Dorset to contend with.

"I said, darling, shall we have a go at it?" he asked.

It looked so strange to her Shaker-trained eyes: men and women whirling together, touching, gazing raptly into each other's faces on the dance floor. Yet it seemed wonderful and not wrong at all. Perhaps that was the way Ramsey saw all of this fancy living.

"I take it you do not let these rich and powerful people get the best of you," she said as they turned to face each other in a distant corner of the crowded room.

"I cultivate them for the common good. You will see."

"Courting the rich to help the poor, you mean?"

"More or less."

"Does it work?"

"At home it has not yet, not as I want it to. But it will!"

"Doesn't it hurt your pride to cultivate them, Ramsey?"

"Yes, but that's a small price to pay."

His determination moved her to her very toes. But she

wasn't sure she could move those toes correctly now at all. If only they would play "Skip to My Lou" or decent frolic music, she'd show them all a thing or two!

But she put on a brave smile and told him, "Lord Ramsey, I'm blasted honored you selected your country cousin over that Mr. Putnam's poor daughter. But I am regretful to say I don't know the waltz."

He laughed. She saw the lines on his forehead disappear so he looked so much younger and happier. "A mere waltz will not stop you from conquering the world, Miss Rebecca. You move like a dream. You will pick it up at once. Here, one, two, three, just follow me as I turn you."

His right hand took her left one. She wished she could rip off her gloves and his to better feel the touch of their hands. She always needed his touch. But his left hand rested properly in the small of her back to guide her; she placed her other hand trustingly on his broad shoulder as they began to move. She faltered once, but it was because of the heeled silk shoes and not that she couldn't follow his firm lead.

Then they were turning, gliding, even dipping together around the room curtained in blue velvet. Candle flames blurred by; other dancing couples appeared, then faded as they passed. For one moment, Rebecca thought there should be a little window high on the wall so elders and elderesses could peer down to watch and judge. There should be spirit gifts given here where there were only worldly ones. Someone should shout, "Shaker high! Shaker high!" and the whole room should explode with fervent cavortings. But she soared high in Ramsey's love. Luminous-eyed, with a smile trembling on her lips, she gazed up at him, dizzy in love.

"There evidently are certain things," she said, "of your world I shall dearly love."

"As I indeed love you, my darling. How easily and beautifully you adapt to things. Smooth sailing for us—just like this—from here on," he assured her.

But she was not so sure. She had kept herself from speaking out tonight so that she did not offend Mr. Putnam, but she was certain she would never adapt to nor accept some things she saw among Ramsey's associates in this elegant world. Here people gossiped behind their hands instead of spitting things straight out, whether about a tragic steamboat explosion in Ohio or, she was afraid, Lord Sherborne's strange country cousin. That and a great deal needed to be changed. And she was still positive that such change came from changing hearts, as she had changed hers with help from Christina and then Ramsey. Change did not come from courting the rich nor from political power. And when the time was right, she'd find a way to show him that was true.

The dance ended with chatter and glove-muted applause. They walked outside onto the cool half-moon-shaped patio and stared up at the stars. "When you are meeting with those folks tomorrow who want to make donations to the Dorset poor, would you mind if I went to visit my old friend Christina and her husband?" she asked Ramsey. "It is a wonderful gift that you located them."

His smile flashed white in the dim light. "By all means, visit her tomorrow. I am certain Will won't mind escorting you out there. And I want to meet them too, as soon as I can."

"They hardly live like this, according to what Will found out."

"I know. And I did hear your protest earlier about my mixing with the rich to help the poor. But I promise you, Rebecca," he vowed and took her hand, "if I could mix with the poor to help the poor, I would."

She nodded. She could try to adapt to Ramsey's world for his sake. But more doubts arose that their ways would ever blend as smoothly as they had waltzed tonight.

Rebecca was still fretting the next day as Will drove her out of town in a hired phaeton to visit Christina and Travis. "I know it will take compromises from both Ramsey and me, but I'm certain we can make a go if it in England," she told Will.

" 'Make a go of it'? You're beginning to talk more like him despite your eastern Kentucky accent, at least."

"I realize it might take more than talking like him to be accepted there."

"Actually, Rebecca," Will observed with a quick, slanted look her way, "some of your great appeal to Ramsey is your uniqueness, so, if asked, I would advise you not to change much. Just be yourself. If he had wanted an English heiress to wed, he could have found one."

She appreciated the kindly advice, but the word *heiress* bothered her. She had come to Ramsey with nothing but the clothes on her back. But if the Sherbornes were rich enough to have a big house, why would they need a dowry from an heiress? Money did not matter to her, and she had thought it didn't matter to Ramsey. Back home, if a girl took a goat or a patchwork quilt with her when she wed, that was considered enough, so she hadn't even thought she might be too poor to wed Ramsey—only too different. But she certainly was not going to question Will Barnstable about the Sherbornes' financial situation or what heiresses he referred to. She trusted Ramsey to be honest with her, and she'd just ask him. Besides, sometimes, however friendly the way Will put things, she sensed either high amusement or deep disapproval beneath his words, and that unsettled her. Still, he was Ramsey's friend, so she meant to get along with him too.

"I appreciate your bringing me out here," she told Will to break the awkward silence. "I'm sure a farm laborer's cabin is not the sort of place you usually go calling on at home."

"If it is a friend of yours from the past, I'm most interested, so say no more," Will said with a nod and a smile. "From my directions, I assume that is the place." He pointed to a small, low-roofed log cabin across a stretch of waving wheatfields and a split-rail fence.

Rebecca's heart began to pound. She prayed Christina and Travis were home. Wait until Christina heard all about what had happened! Wait until Rebecca told her she would probably still be here when their child came and she could help Christina in her travail.

Before the cabin, Will reined in the phaeton and came around to help Rebecca down. She was learning fast; she had almost just hiked up her skirt and jumped down on her own. She was glad she had insisted on wearing her Shaker gown, even though she had belted the waist and put her new lace shawl over her shoulders. She wore her heavy hair coiled up under her new tilt-brimmed straw bonnet. She had wanted to look more like her old self to her friend and not one of those fancy Graham Springs women.

The way it would back in the mountains, the front door stood open. "Christina? Travis?" she called.

The small, two-room interior seemed deserted when she peeked in. It was sparsely furnished with a broad hearth that gave Rebecca a pang for her old Crawl Crick cabin. "Christina?"

"There's a woman coming around in back," Will called to her.

Rebecca ran around the corner of the cabin. Slowly, unsteadily, a pregnant woman in an apron and maroon cotton gown came barefoot along the back path from the field. Her bonnet flapped by its strings. Her brown head was down to watch where she walked. She looked wan, dusty, and burdened. She cradled a cluster of cabbages in her arms. Rebecca yelled, then ran toward her.

"Christina, Christina! It's me, Rebecca!"

Christina looked up and squealed. Cabbages flew and bounced and rolled. Despite Christina's bulk, they embraced. Rebecca grinned and brushed dirt off her friend's chin. How she envied her those bare feet and that cabin set amid all this country beauty! But they were back together now and there was so much to tell.

While Will insisted on sitting in a chair just outside the door with his mug of cider, the two old friends talked and talked. Travis had been sent clear to Cincinnati to bring back a new plow by Mr. McClintock, their landlord and owner of this big bluegrass farm. He had been gone ten days, so Christina was certain he would be back by the time her child was due, in about a fortnight. Though the cabin seemed small after Shakertown, they were doing fine, she said, and saving all they could to buy a place of their own. Then Rebecca told her about Ramsey and their plans.

"Better than any of those love stories in your grandma's old songs," Christina said. "I've never been happier for anybody—not even myself!"

Later, Rebecca talked her friend into letting her help chop cabbage, despite Christina's claims that no proper lady should work with her hands. "I guess I'll never be a proper lady then," Rebecca teased her back, but her laugh rang hollow. Later, with Christina, she might share her doubts about England.

"Real sorry we both had to hurt the folks that took us in, but guess we're more blood sisters than ever now," Christina said. "I bet they're cursing both of us and our worldly, carnal men we love more than life itself."

Rebecca could only nod. The Shakers were hardly anywhere near perfect, the way they strived to be, but she was still sorry she had had to betray and hurt them.

"I worried real bad the Believers put a curse on me when we lost the first child," Christina admitted and rested her hands protectively across her bulging belly. "Makes me worry a bit about birthing this one now, and I can't thank you enough for saying you'll be here with me. Didn't much like the midwife the McClintocks sent over last time, but could hardly look a gift horse in the mouth, Travis said. Now, I'll be glad to tell them not to send her back when my time comes."

"You mustn't feel guilty about your and Travis leaving the Shakers," Rebecca assured her. "And your losing the first baby was not because of some curse! If the Shakers thought that, they'd have to say the same for Mother Ann losing all of hers!"

Christina's pale, drawn face brightened a bit. She reached over to squeeze Rebecca's hand. "You always did know how to comfort and heal, Rebecca. You know, you and Travis are the only two who could ever make me not be so scairt of the dark. I'm so glad we're best friends still, 'specially after I let you down."

"Life's like that, I'm learning the hard way," Rebecca told her. "Only the thing is, to keep caring for folks, even if you lose them . . ."

With promises to see each other again soon, they walked outside and parted. Christina waved until the phaeton's dust swallowed her. Rebecca could not wait until Ramsey came with her to visit and Travis returned. She hoped Ramsey would not mind if they left for England a week later so she could be here with Christina for the baby's birth.

And, bouncing along next to Will, she had made a decision. Just to be certain that nothing went wrong for Christina this time, she was going to use some of the money Ramsey gave her to hire a doctor in town. She refused to face again the task of delivering a baby on her own with no help. Though so many of the painful parts of her childhood had faded in her memory, she would never quite put to rest the time she had lost her own little sister. Christina was the closest thing she had to a sister now, and she meant to see that nothing went wrong with her baby's birth.

That made her feel much better as they headed back to the elegance of Graham Springs. She hated to admit it, but, except for being with Ramsey, she still felt more at home in Christina's little two-room cabin.

The first week of September was as hot as July, but many guests were leaving Graham Springs to return to their plantation homes. That night, the moon rose full and pink as a ripe peach as Ramsey and Rebecca sat in a dark garden gazebo. They fed each other ice cream and exchanged kisses that were both chilly and hot. They ignored the glasses of sulfurish water one of the stewards brought them. They had been making plans to go to England as soon as Christina's husband returned and their child was born. Ramsey had met Christina and thrilled her with his "kingly manners," as Christina put it. Though he did not want Christina to know it yet, Ramsey had set aside a generous amount for a christening gift for the child. In the little more than a week they had been living at the springs, Rebecca mused, so much had happened.

In the ballroom one afternoon, Ramsey had given his speech on helping the Dorset poor who were cruelly treated by the Whig government of England. Rebecca had sat enthralled at his ideas and plans; others had, evidently, been scandalized by his "liberal, iconoclastic" stand. "For a man with money, he sets a wretched precedent," Rebecca overheard one man say. "In this civilized world, it is damned obvious that some classes were born to serve others!" And so, instead of lionizing Lord Ramsey, the stylish people at Graham Springs ostracized him—as politely as possible. That taught Rebecca two things: Ramsey would bend his beliefs for no man no matter what the cost, and she admired him more than ever. Besides, now she had him almost to herself.

Still, she thought he left her too early at night after such passionate embraces, just to be certain he was not seen coming out of her room late. She was eager for the whole act of loving, which they had agreed they would like to save for after their marriage. But they had admitted neither of them could hold off much longer. And, after all, even if she went to breeding, they could be wed right then so the baby wouldn't come too early. But Ramsey said he wanted to make a statement back in England that they had wed publicly and proudly because they wanted to and not because they had to.

"Mm," she said as she took another spoonful of ice cream. "This vanilla flavor is delicious, but I'm going to make you some with rosewater first chance I get in England. A Shaker recipe."

He laughed and dumped first one glass of the odoriferous mineral water in the azalea bushes and then the other. "I'd think this vanilla was good too if I didn't keep smelling this

222

blasted egg water our clever Doctor Graham has built his fortune on here—''

"Ramsey? Are you out here?" Will's voice cut in from the distant darkness.

"Here, Will!" They saw the red glow of his cheroot before they smelled the smoke. Will's booted feet sounded hollow on the wooden floor of the gazebo.

"A letter just came for you by special messenger from town, old chap. Evidently from your mother," he added and extended a square of vellum to Ramsey.

"Let's go up to the hotel to read it."

The three of them hurried across the thick grass. On the lighted portico, Ramsey read the letter and blanched. He leaned his shoulder against a pillar. "Father's had some sort of stroke. He's very ill. And this letter was posted more than six weeks ago. We've got to leave tomorrow, Will."

"I'll fetch a valet and get us packed," his friend said and strode off.

"Ramsey, what about me?"

"You too, of course. Christina will have to understand. Surely her husband will return soon, and you have arranged for the doctor to tend her."

"Yes, of course. My place is with you!" Rebecca said. "But I'll have to write her to explain."

"And I will get someone right up to help you pack while I make arrangements for a carriage to the steamboat landing."

They hurried into the main entry hall. Rebecca waited for Ramsey to speak to the clerk about their sudden departure. Several people including Mr. Putnam and his daughter Dorothy were clustered around the daily Harrodsburg newspaper posted on a pillar. But this edition, Rebecca could tell from here, was banded with black.

"Blown to bits so it took this long to be certain which passengers were dead and which just horribly burned," she overheard. "Damned steamships, and we've got to take one of the newfangled things clear back to N'Olins!"

Rebecca shuddered. Daddy had hated steamships too.

When people drifted off, she rose from the silk settee and stood looking at the newspaper. FOUR MERCER COUNTY FATAL-ITIES FINALLY IDENTIFIED, the black-boxed headline read. She hoped none of the Shaker peddlers had been aboard, for they often took wares down the river that way. No, this steamship had been coming back from Cincinnati, she read. And then she saw in the list of the dead, "Travis Truax, known only to be from Harrodsburg area."

She screamed. Ramsey ran to her. Horrified, she pointed at the words.

"I can't leave her now, Ramsey! I need to be with her. She'll be so afraid without him, afraid she's being punished when the baby comes."

He crushed her to him, his chin and throat cradling the top of her head. "I cannot believe all this," he muttered. "Almost heaven on earth and then all this. Yes, you will have to go to her, help her through everything. I will leave you money and directions about coming to England. I will get someone here to suggest a lady's maid to accompany you."

"Oh, Ramsey, we can't be apart!"

"Do you see another way?"

They stared deep into each other's eyes. "Not and remain the people we want to be."

"But I do see one other thing we must do before we are parted," he said. "We can be married tonight. I'm tired of waiting and playing the saint. Besides smoothing things over with my parents, I wanted you to know that I did not wed you just to—possess you or that I wasn't proud enough of you to take you home to wed."

"Oh, my love, I didn't!"

He pulled her close again. "My parents will just have to understand. They will adore you once they get to know you."

"But you wanted everything to be done just right at home!"

"Nothing's done just right at home," he muttered. "I should have known that, though you almost turned me into an idealist. Anyway, this newspaper article says Travis Truax's address is unknown, and I doubt Christina sees the newspaper out there. Tomorrow, I will board the coach east with Will and you will go out to help your friend survive this tragedy. Then as soon as she is settled, you will follow me to England. But when we part, we will be man and wife and have had at least one precious night together that way."

Man and wife, together, that way, the words kept resounding in her head. She could not believe the tumble of plans, the churning of her emotions. But in the depths of chaos, her love for this man stood firm and strong.

"Yes," she said. "Yes!"

Besides her hurried promises in a stormy Shaker meadow, that "yes" was the closest she ever came to formally accepting Lord Ramsey Sherborne's proposal of marriage. The hasty reading of the holy words by the Graham Springs chaplain in the lantern-lit gazebo with Will and two other witnesses looking on that September 4, 1836, was the closest she came to the formal English wedding they had planned. Wearing her dawn-pink organdy gown, she clasped a bouquet of flowers in her quaking hands. The mood stayed deeply solemn, despite the brief champagne toast afterward. Yet, even facing their looming separation, their hearts were one, and she had never, never been so certain she was doing what was good and right.

In her room Ramsey and the new Lady Sherborne spent the shortest night of their lives. Grief for those they loved and the coming dawn made their seven-hour honeymoon painfully poignant as they merged their bodies and their lives. There was no teasing and funning she knew would come before the later loving over the years. No instruction was offered or needed now, as he had tutored her tenderly before. Desperation and desire swept them, whirling them together.

If life ended right this moment, she knew she would feel fulfilled. He was so strong, yet so gentle. He looked transported. They kissed so long she could not breathe. All doubts and fears subsided. He pressed close to the beating of her heart, her pulse, her very core.

Their eyes met and held as he pressed to her. She sucked in a breath as they became one. "Oh, Ramsey, my love—" was all she managed before he began to move with her in a powerful, rocking rhythm that put all other dances she had ever known to shame.

"I will love you until the day I die!" She heard his words hot in her ear before she soared a second time. She had not dreamed such heights were possible, not even among her majestic mountains.

Why was it, she asked him later drowsily, that important, life-changing things had to happen so fast? They clung to every moment, refusing to sleep even when exhaustion and emotion swamped them.

"I will not feel whole again until I see you in London or Sherpuddle!" he said. "Write me ahead if you can, and I will meet the ship. After her baby comes, nothing must delay you!"

"It won't! You've been generous with money for my trip and the baby. Oh, Ramsey, I grieve so deeply for her and feel so guilty when I have you and the rest of our lives to look forward to."

"Remember, even apart, we share everything now, my darling, the wealth, the loneliness, the pain, but all the joy too."

"But I will miss you so much that—"

His kiss stilled her lips and seared her soul. In desperate desire, they blended to lose their separate identities again. She rose to meet his passion, moving in circles of love. Her arms entwined his neck, her legs embraced his, she gave and took. And in their quiet moments, she prayed that the harsh shocks of life were past and that the love they shared would somehow make the world lovely again.

He helped her dress when dawn came. He insisted they say good-bye in this room with the lofty view where they had spent these precious days together. "I will have a carriage waiting downstairs for you to go to Christina, but are you certain you want to live out there with her?"

"Yes. Believe me, it's best. In a way, being in that cabin with her will be like going home before I leave the past behind. But I'll check for letters from you here before I set out to follow you. Nothing will go wrong, my dearest. Nothing ever again."

They held each other so tightly they could not breathe. She had vowed she would not cry, but she did anyway. Still, she smiled at him too, through her tears, as he strode to the door. He was, she knew, despite this pain of separation, worth any price, or risk, or sacrifice.

"I told you in our meadow, Ramsey Sherborne, that I love you and always will," she said when his hand touched the doorknob. "As soon as I can, I will tell you that again on the dock in London, in Sherpuddle, in our own bed."

He nodded. His gray eyes shimmered with tears. He tried to speak and could not, the golden-tongued spokesman for the Dorset downtrodden. He nodded again, blew her a kiss, and was gone.

She stood staring at the door. She ran to the window and watched him become only shoulders and a top hat below. Just before he disappeared into the carriage behind Will, he looked up. She leaned out and waved.

"I love you, Rebecca Blake Sherborne!" he shouted at the top of his voice and waved back broadly.

She laughed through her tears. What would any of the elegant elite getting up early think of Ramsey's country cousin now? The mountain girl and her fancy Lord Sherborne were as fine together as Mama and Daddy had been once. After all, how many times had Mama stood on the brow of the hill and waved farewell to Daddy as he headed down toward the river? But unlike Daddy, Ramsey had not abandoned her, and he never would.

She shook her head to clear it as the carriage rumbled down the driveway and disappeared through the gate. She had to get to Christina. She had to help her through this terrible shock. Christina had to learn to part with her beloved in a far, far different way from the way Rebecca had just parted from hers.

By the time the girl Polly knocked on the door to help her pack, Rebecca was waiting with everything ready. Someone she loved needed her. And this time, the only healing herb she had to offer was herself.

Chapter Thirteen

It was barely nine in the morning when Rebecca reached Christina's. Her door was closed; perhaps she was still abed. That would be just like the old Christina, Rebecca thought, as the carriage driver unloaded her trunk and satchel and departed. She hoped her friend had slept well last night, for she faced a long stretch of sleepless nights now. Her fist shaking, Rebecca knocked on the door, then waited and knocked again.

"Christina! It's Rebecca and I've come to stay awhile!"

Sleepy and frowsy, Christina opened the door and smiled at her. "Not had a spat with your fine lord, have you?" she asked. "Travis and me never argue but we don't make up before we go to bed. Come in and—oh, you mean it about staying for a spell. You brought your things!"

"Yes, never mind them now." Rebecca longed to blurt out that she was wed, that she had come to comfort Christina, but there was no way to do this but the awful truth. "Sit, my dear. Now remember above all, you're to take good care of this baby you carry. Travis would want—would have wanted—Oh, Christina, a tragedy. A boiler exploded on

Travis's steamboat and many were hurt and killed. Travis is—''

"No!" Christina said, shoving Rebecca's hands from her shoulders. "You could not know it was Travis's boat! And if it is, he can't be bad hurt. He's strong! He'll be back soon, maybe today."

"It took them a long time to be certain, but the town newspaper has printed the list of the dead. Christina, I am so, so sorry, but Travis is—''

"No! No!"

Christina clapped her hands over her ears. She bent low in spite of her bulk. She beat her fists on the table and then swiped it clear of pewter plates, which clattered on the floor. Rebecca bent to hold her, urging her to remember the child. Finally Christina calmed enough to look at the newspaper clipping.

"And I won't even get his body back," she interrupted as Rebecca read it haltingly to her. Her tears dropped on the newsprint as she leaned in close to Rebecca. "A mass—mass grave? But he has to be here when the child comes, he has to be here to get that new plow and so we can buy our farm, and to hold me at night—hold me—''

Rebecca knew she was not the one Christina needed, but she held her tightly. Not since she and Mama had lost the child had she shared such piercing pain. Eventually she helped Christina to bed and settled down to tend her and the cabin. But when Christina would eat nothing, even for the child's sake, Rebecca began to fear she would not keep up her strength. As darkness descended, Rebecca made herself a pallet at the foot of her friend's bed from long meadow grass covered with a blanket. She could not bear to lie down with Christina where Travis should be. She burned a lantern all night and got up many times when Christina cried out. Rebecca stood there, wavering with helpless concern, holding Christina's hand as she had years ago at Pleasant Hill. But this time, it was the darkness of grief which haunted her friend. And all that turned to fear when Christina began to suffer labor pains just before dawn the next day.

"His death brought this on," Christina raved to Rebecca, her weeping eyes darting everywhere. "Don't let his death bring another death!" She clung to Rebecca's arm. "I'll lose the child too. I'll have nothing then, nothing but a cursed life!"

"Stop that talk. You are going to bear this child just fine. Travis would want you to be brave. I am going to walk out to the main road now and send the first Harrodsburg-bound traveler I see for Dr. White. He's been practicing in town for years. I won't leave you then. You and this child will be all right, Christina!"

Her friend's eyes focused on her at last. "How can I ever thank you, sister? Everyone's left me, my parents, Travis—"

"But none of them chose to leave you, and *I* will be right back!"

Rebecca ran for the road and got a rider to promise to summon Dr. White. On her way back, cutting through the field, she came upon a golden puddle of black-eyed Susans. She quickly pulled some and took them back where Christina could see them. But Christina was in the grinding pains already, the grinding pains of childbirth and loss and fear. Rebecca boiled water as Gran Ida had taught her long ago and tried to keep Christina calm. But when the morning dragged on with no doctor, she began to fear the worst could happen again.

It was early afternoon when Rebecca heard a horse outside. She ran for the door, then stood there shocked and still. The man who dismounted with his black bag was not old Dr. White. The man was the tall, grown-up Adam Scott.

He gasped too and stared at her. "Rebecca Blake?"

"Yes! Yes. Adam!"

At first she could not believe it was really he. How sweet were those needy and loving feelings for him she had treasured, locked away inside her, all these years. But this vibrant, compelling man exploded her muted memories. Her thoughts grew jumbled at the sight of him. What different turns their lives had taken! The confusion of old feelings surged through her: the depth of her grief and passion that night at the frolic and the day they said good-bye at her refuge on Concord. How Mama had hoped she and Adam would wed someday, but how his father looked down on her and made Adam suffer for his stubbornness about that too. How much Adam had meant to her once, and, strangely, still did. For he was now real again—and very much needed, for Christina if no longer for herself.

He hurried to her, his long legs taking big strides. He took her hand. When he swept off his top hat, his clear blue eyes and gold-red hair glittered in the sun. His nose was still crooked where his father had broken it that last day she had seen him. They both realized they were gawking and dropped their hands and their eyes.

She stared at his leather satchel. "So you're a doctor."

"Yes, Dr. White's new partner. I do most of his traveling for him now. Rebecca, I can't believe—but this woman in labor is . . . ?"

"Christina Truax, my dearest friend. Do come in! Oh, Adam, I should have known you'd become a doctor! I'm so glad you're here!"

For hours there was no more time for the two of them than that. Adam's big hands were as sure and gentle as when he had tended rabbits with broken bones or birds with shattered wings years ago. And after all, Rebecca thought, Christina was broken and shattered now too.

Rebecca worked willingly at his side, doing as he said, pressing drink and food on him in his rare pauses. She was still shocked by his sudden appearance. Christina labored long, but there was little to show for it yet. Rebecca explained to Adam about the first child she had lost and the recent shock of Travis's death. Adam simply nodded, but tears made his eyes shine. And now, each time he comforted Christina through the worst pains, he told her, "You're a fine brave lady, Mrs. Truax!"

"Poor thing," he whispered to Rebecca as he dipped his silver instruments into hot water while she held the pan. "Together, we'll get her through this, Becca."

She stood trembling at the table as he turned away to bend back over his patient. No one had called her Becca for so long. Adam. Adam, the love—yes, love—of her youth had come back all grown up and a doctor, and she was so proud of him. And together they must help Christina and her child.

Beads of sweat stood out on Adam's head. Christina gripped the spokes of the bed's headboard now and gasped for breath and strength between spasms. Rebecca wiped the sweat from her friend's face, then dabbed at Adam's too. "Thank you," was all he said, but he did not look her way again. Finally the top of the baby's head appeared, but seemed to stop there with no other progress.

After dark, as they worked by lantern light, Adam took Rebecca's elbow and led her across the room. "Her birth canal is too small. Perhaps that's what happened last time. I have to enlarge the opening. You dab the blood." He looked solemn as he tilted his big square chin down at her. "You're not afraid of blood like your mother was?"

"No. I can do it."

He nodded and turned to his task. Rebecca felt surprised and touched that he recalled what she had told him about Mama. Without Jeremy, Adam was the closest she had to a brother now. He had to be a brother now, for when this was all over she must tell this man from her past the news about her future with Ramsey.

Christina and Travis Truax's daughter was born shortly before midnight, but not without a good deal of blood loss and Adam's using what he called forceps to help bring the child. The little pink mite cried lustily and flailed her fists as if most annoyed at being pressed in a tight place too long or being forced to make such an unceremonious entrance into lantern light.

"You have a beautiful daughter, Mrs. Truax," Adam announced to Christina when Rebecca had washed and bundled the child. "What will you name her?"

Christina looked drawn and pale. But Adam's heartiness evidently gave her strength enough to answer. "Her name," she told them both in a hoarse voice, "is Rebecca, for the dearest friend the world—and Shakertown—could ever give."

At dawn, when the mother and baby slept at last, Rebecca and Adam sat on the wooden settle before the low-burning fire, sipping cider and eating hotcakes with honey. At last they exchanged the first news of people and events since they had seen each other twelve years ago.

He told her how Aunt Euphy had married his father and how they had seemed happy. "You know she always calmed him like no one else. But he died of heart trouble two years ago, and she still misses him. As soon as I get enough to buy a place of my own here, I'm going to have her come keep house for me. I won't use the money she keeps offering, not after she spent so much to send me to medical college in Lexington."

He told her things about others she had not seen for years. Claib Tucker had finally found his woman by wedding his dead son's wife, Jemima, and taking good care of the youngsters who were both his grandchildren and his stepchildren. Adam's sisters were all married, some with children, he told her, but he had been too busy to wed. But when she told him about her past—and that she had wed just three days ago—his eager manner became muted and his thick-fringed lashes dropped to shutter his eyes.

"An English lord," he said. "Rebecca, I always knew you were special. I just hope you'll be happy in your new life.

If that's your choice, I hope you'll be as fulfilled by it as I am with being able to help folks with my doctoring.''

"Ramsey and I are going to help folks too," she said and explained about the Dorset poor to him. "And someday, I'm going back to Shelter and do something good there. Adam, have you ever thought they could use a doctor there?''

"Sure," he admitted and tipped his head against the wooden back of the settle. "But this area has been my home—my refuge from my father—all these years since I've seen you. Not everyone has such happy memories of Shelter like you, Becca. Lady Sherborne, I mean.''

She thought for one minute he meant to tease her, but his voice was serious and his face solemn. "So," he added and cleared his throat, "I guess we won't ever meet up there again at your secret refuge on the mountain.''

"I guess not.''

"But we've each made our dreams come true and that's what we vowed there," he said and yawned. He stretched out his legs and propped his big booted feet on the andiron as though the two of them were the oldest and most comfortable of companions.

"You—do you think I will have a hard time adjusting to life in England?" she asked.

"I think you can do anything you put your mind to. I've got to be heading back," he said, as if that subject were closed. "And you've got a long, long way to go to England soon.''

They were silent after that. Rebecca darted a glance at him to see if he had fallen asleep. His eyes were half closed. It seemed so easy to pick up with him right where they'd left off, despite those other feelings leaping between them which they both tried to ignore. He would be heading back, he said, and she had a long, long way to go to England. So true, she thought, heading back in her memories to Shelter with Gran Ida and Mama, Daddy, and Jeremy. And all the others, Claib Tucker, Jemima, and Pru Johns living there across Widow Lang's quilted meadow. And dearest Adam, grown now into a handsome man she loved—could have loved, once, before Ramsey. So far to go to England, so far to go to fit into her beloved Ramsey's world . . .

Some time later she jerked awake. She and Adam both slept, slumped against each other, shoulders touching, heads huddled as if they were whispering. Sun blazed through the single window. She eased Adam's head over to the edge of the settle and got up to look in on Christina and the baby. She had evidently fed the child again; they lay sleeping, the child in the crook of her mother's arm. When she came back in to tell Adam, he was up, holding his bag.

"If those stitches I put in her don't heal right or there are any complications, send for me," he told her. "I'd best be off."

She nodded. Their eyes met and held. For one moment she saw something flicker in the depths of his, then flare, then fade. He turned away. "God be with you, Becca." He closed the door firmly.

She ran to open it, to wave good-bye. He was already mounted. "Thank you for everything! I think—you are a wonderful doctor, Adam!"

His eyes in the shade of his hat swept her. She could not see them this time, but she felt them.

"If you ever need another American friend when you live over there," he said, "just think of—Aunt Euphy and me."

He turned the horse. She waved and waved, but he did not look back.

"What did Mr. McClintock say?" Rebecca asked Christina a few days later as her friend came back, carrying little Becky, from a conversation with her landlord in the front yard.

"He said the new farm worker's family will be here soon to take over the cabin," she told Rebecca. "But I'm not worried. I told you Travis was a hard worker and we've been saving for our own place. Here, hold your little namesake, will you?"

Rebecca bounced the infant while she watched Christina pull up the rag rug and pry up a short floorboard with a knife. "Hard luck, but if you have money, you can always move to town," Rebecca assured her. "That and the money Ramsey left for you will tide you over until I can send you more from England. And there are women who take in mending at Graham Springs and you've never minded that like I have. What's the matter?"

"It's—it's gone! Nearly two hundred dollars in a metal box we kept here. Gone! No one else knew but Travis and me!"

"Perhaps Travis just moved it before he left. Think carefully!"

"It's gone! He had talked about looking for a farm for us on the way out to Ohio, and said he'd surprise me, but I thought he meant with a little gift he'd bring back. He—oh, dear heavens, Rebecca, it's gone and he must have taken it with him. It's gone up in flames, just like him!"

The baby wailed; Christina wailed. They ransacked the cabin. Rebecca found herself comforting Christina in the agony of yet another loss. "How could he?" Christina raved, suddenly furious at poor dead Travis. "Our whole future gone! He left me and then took that too. Why did he leave me? I love him, loved him so!"

"He loved you too, my friend. He was only doing what he thought was best, what would make you happy. And here is your future, yours and Travis's too!" Rebecca insisted and handed her the baby.

But panic was written clearly on Christina's face. "Rebecca, after the fifty-dollar christening gift from you and Ramsey is gone, I might have to ask the Shakers to take me back just so the baby has good food and a place to live. But then she'd never be mine anymore and the Shakers would all hate me so for leaving!"

"No, you are not going back to the Shakers!" Her thoughts leaped: she had never seen Daddy after going to the Shakers; Sister Jerusha had left her six children to go there; Sister

Alice had given up her son, Brother Drury. But she knew she could hardly take this new baby and her grieving mother with her across the ocean to spring them on the ever-generous Ramsey. Besides, she didn't have the money. The money, that was it!

"Christina, did you say the fifty dollars from Ramsey and me? My dear, you must have still been confused then. It is *two hundred* and fifty. That will surely let you live in someone's house in town until you can get things settled. Besides, by then I'll be in England and be able to send you more. I'll not have my namesake reared where she won't see her mother or her Auntie Rebecca too, when she comes visiting!"

Giving Christina most of the money Ramsey had left her for her passage to England was one of the most impulsive things Rebecca had ever done. But she knew she would do it again. Within the week, she and Christina situated in two rented rooms in a widow's house in Harrodsburg. She had promises from the Graham Springs Hotel that Christina could take in their linens for mending. She had received a loving letter from Ramsey, posted from New York City, and she sent him one in London explaining she would be a bit delayed because of resettling her friend.

Not to worry him, she did not tell him that she had very little money left, including not one cent to spare for a lady's maid. If she had stayed here with Christina and had written him to send more money, by her calculations it would take at least twelve weeks, and she intended to be in England by then. Besides, she had promised him on their wedding night that nothing would delay her after she saw to Christina. And—since he was no doubt used to heiresses, as Will had mentioned once, she did not want his parents to know she was so poor that she had to write and beg for money after he'd been generous already.

Quickly she put her plan into action, one she had pondered a long while—really, ever since the day Daddy had taken her down the river past Boonesville toward Pleasant Hill.

She had yearned to visit her mother's people, the Mercers. And since they were well-to-do farmers and she was kin, she would ask them for a small loan. That, added to the forty dollars she had left, could get her to New York by boat and coach and then by ship to England. Ramsey trusted her; he would just have to understand that she was coming as fast as she could.

On October 9, she bought a deck seat on a keelboat heading up the Kentucky. Such memories that ride evoked! The boat passed the Shaker landing and the other spots Daddy had once pointed out. They put her and her baggage down on the very stretch of bank beyond Boonesville where she had called out to a girl fishing. She hid her trunk in a clutch of willows and carried her satchel up toward the white farmhouse she hoped was still the Mercer place. A stern-looking woman who vaguely resembled Mama but for her silver hair and frowning face answered her knock on the front door.

"Ann's girl?" she cried at Rebecca's explanation. "Ann's girl after all these years?" She dropped the saucer she was drying and it broke on the floor. "I'm your Aunt Sarah. Beth Ann! A girl is here who says she's Ann's girl!" she cried and ran into the well-appointed parlor, leaving the nervous Rebecca standing in the half-opened door.

Her two aunts were kind enough, but they seemed much more nervous even than Rebecca. Over tea and cakes, they asked her a hundred questions, sniffing or exchanging pointed looks each time Daddy's name came up. Finally Aunt Sarah blurted out part of what they were evidently thinking. "How could Ann dare to name you for Mama after she hurt her so by leaving and never coming back?"

"My mama loved her mama dearly. In her dying breath she wanted to be with her, here at the farm. I know you said she's an old lady and quite ill, but can't I pay my grandmother a visit? I'm used to working with ailing folks, and I wouldn't tire her a bit."

"Well, I suppose," Aunt Beth said. "Briefly. She's bed-bound and an invalid. So don't you fill her head full of those claims about being married to an English lord. Just like your daddy, full of grandiose schemes!" she blurted.

"My recent marriage to Lord Sherborne is no scheme and not some fantasy as you seem to suggest," Rebecca began, then realized she'd best rein in her anger if she wanted to be allowed to see her grandmother. And why should these women believe her story when she had not so much as a wedding ring or full purse to her name to prove it? She had actually come here to beg, though she hadn't breathed a word about that yet. And they were partly right about Daddy, she thought, and blushed under their intense scrutiny.

She found herself tiptoeing when Aunt Sarah led her into the dim room upstairs where a tiny woman lay under sheets in a big bed. Aunt Sarah drew open the drapes a bit, woke her mother and explained who Rebecca was, then perched on a chair across the room.

"Who?" the scratchy voice said. "Oh, Ann's girl. Ann's girl. The one named after me?"

Rebecca finally could not hold the tears back. She had forced herself to stay strong and stoic during Christina's trials, even when she was so touched that the new baby was named for her. She knew what that meant, the bonds between women it stood for. Her voice caught in her throat. Suddenly she had come not to ask for money or to talk of her past, or even to tell about Mama, but just to share love with this old woman, this beloved stranger who was family.

"Yes, Ann's girl, Rebecca," she choked out and could say no more.

They both trembled as they clasped hands. Her grandmother's skin seemed to be wrapped tight around her oval skull and high cheekbones. Her sharp eyes were pale green. The hair peeking from her nightcap was pure white but curly like Rebecca's own. The cool, papery fingers closed tightly around her hand.

"She's dead, isn't she?" the woman she already thought of as Grandma Mercer asked. "I felt it when she died. So dear to me, dearest when we were apart. Here, my sweet girl, don't cry. I'll give you this ring I have always meant for her—"

"Now, Mama," came sternly from Aunt Sarah as she bobbed up and hurried over. "That's your wedding ring. You keep that. You're not ready to pass on to your reward yet."

"I surely am. But my reward for living this long is here. My Ann's daughter has come back to see me. Can't be helped, dear Sarah. The parent loves the children who stay home, but the prodigal one—the lost sheep, that's the one you grieve for. Here, here, my dearest girl, Rebecca," she said and struggled to take her thin gold ring from her swollen finger, "keep this in remembrance of me and your mama too."

Rebecca was afraid to glance up at Aunt Sarah's stormcloud face as the old woman got her ring off and held it out to her. Rebecca could tell Sarah wanted to snatch it and order her out. But Rebecca took it and slipped it onto her finger. It fit perfectly. She knew then that if she had to swim all the way to England, she would never sell that ring. There would have to be another way.

She spent the night in the house her mother had loved and left. Conversation was stilted over dinner; her aunts and their husbands and four of her cousins asked about the Shakers but obviously did not give one bit of credence to her story about Ramsey. Rebecca realized that Abel Wheelright, Aunt Sarah's husband, was the man Mama had once thought she'd marry, but she didn't let on she knew all that. She understood the hurt and anger of desertions eating away at someone's heart.

So she left, head high, without asking for a penny, after another brief, loving interview with her grandmother the next morning. Somehow, maybe partly out of Blake pride she had got from her father, she just could not ask for Mercer money. And it saddened her that she would never spend more time with the grandmother she had known so briefly.

She sat on the riverbank to wait for a keelboat or salt barge to drift by. She had just under thirty dollars now, but she was far richer for having stopped here. Ramsey would understand when she explained to him. And, as if Mama had been watching out for her from heaven, she had a wedding ring. It glinted gaily in the morning sun. After meeting her grandmother and feeling the love that could have turned to bitterness so long ago, she was prouder than ever that Mercer blood flowed in her veins like this deep river, along with the Blake blood that crashed through her as swift and eager as any mountain stream.

She spent ten of her last dollars for a steamboat ticket to Cincinnati, where Ramsey had told her to take a coach east. She mistrusted steamboats, but she would do anything to get to Ramsey. She was excited to be part of this worldly life. She loved to stand out on the noisy, throbbing deck to see people go by both off and on the boat. The big side paddle wheels churned the river the way her brain churned her thoughts.

Aboard were settlers, trappers, peddlers—though no Shaker ones—artists, government agents, and Sioux Indians, who had just been to see President Jackson in Washington. In the bustling "Queen City of the West," as people dubbed Cincinnati when they weren't calling it "Porkapolis," she sold two of her gowns for food and funds to rent a room, so that she could keep her last twenty dollars. Then she went out looking for work to earn enough money at least to reach New York. She was convinced that getting money here was still going to be much faster than waiting weeks for Ramsey to get a letter and send her the funds. She had vowed to get there as fast as she could.

Until her feet had become so swollen from walking that night, she had been confident. Now she ached everywhere, and her head hurt. Darkness was falling, but she could not face her lonely dingy room tonight unless she knew she had work.

She paused on Pearl Street to squint at a copy of the day's

Cincinnati Advertiser posted on a wall. She shuddered involuntarily; the last time she'd read a newspaper, she had learned of Travis's death. There were no employment offers here she could take. Offers for labor in lard works, breweries, pork packing houses, and a farm implement factory—all for men, of course. Fear began to bite at her. What if she did have to write Ramsey for more money and stay here twelve weeks without him, waiting for it to arrive? How would she survive while she waited? She sniffed back a sob. This was not the way things were supposed to be. He was home with his ill father, who needed him. Blast it, *she* needed him!

She saw a few jobs for seamstresses and laundresses, but they paid a pittance. Still, it might be the only way. She had to decide tonight. As she started back to her shoddy rooming house, she felt so homesick for Ramsey, even for the busy security of Shakertown. Then, at the corner of Front Street, she heard distant music. It drew her. This street meandered along the river and was crammed with hotels, taverns, chandleries, and rooming houses for noisy deckhands and keelboaters loitering outside. But the song she heard was the old tune "Skip to My Lou" from her childhood. She had never really believed in the Shaker passion for signs from heaven, but when an old man called out to her, "Don't go down there, girlie, 'cause it's Scarlet Town!" she walked on.

Her heart beat very fast. She felt drawn by the music, the man's description of the place, her curiosity to see if people were having some sort of frolic down there. And then she saw the words painted on the swinging sign and knew she was meant to step inside: SHELTER, SPIRITS, FOOD, it said, QUINN'S HOTEL AND TAVERN.

Inside, Rebecca edged along the back wall. The big tavern room was dimly lit but for a raised platform up front where four women danced to loud pianoforte and banjo music. The guests were noisy too, with glasses clinking and men talking and playing cards for coins. Some clapped and shouted out to the dancing girls right in the middle of the music! A haze of tobacco smoke hung heavy in the air. She bumped into a spittoon, then skirted it. She heard more than one language spoken; she knew many Irish and Germans had come here to live.

She gaped at the four women dancing wildly on the stage. No Shaker high was ever quite like that. They wore low-cut dresses all alike in bright ruffled red and kicked their legs to show black laced boots and bare knees.

She noticed that several men were elbowing each other and staring at her. "Lose your man, honey?" one of them shouted.

"I'd like to see the owner of this establishment, please," she told them.

"The lucky bastard," another one said and scraped back his chair to fetch him. A bald, fat man ambled out from behind the bar, looking her over as he came. He had a folded tablecloth tied around his large middle for an apron.

"Well, now. What's a lady like you doin' here?" he asked as he took in her green gown, hem to neckline.

"I'm looking for work, but I don't dance quite like that. I could sing, however. I know a lot of old songs about love."

"Bet you do. Run away from home, did you?"

"No, but I am trying to earn money to rejoin my husband."

"No married women work here."

"Please. I have experience."

His bushy eyebrows seemed to shoot halfway up his white bowl of a head. "That right? What kind?" he asked and leaned closer so she could smell whiskey on his breath. She supposed she should have left right then, but she was desperate. Besides, she just knew her Daddy had once inhabited places like this, and Daddy had been, more or less, a family man.

"Experience singing for years, actually in several places, like the Kentucky mountains, even at Shakertown near Lexington," she blurted when she sensed he was going to turn her away.

"With the Shakers? A pretty thing like you? Well, that

might be a good calling card. I could get you a dress and you can try it out tomorrow.''

"I'd like to wear my own dress, please. And I've danced for years too, but I would only feel it proper to lead country dances, not ever ones like that,'' she said and pointed at the stage where the nimble four pranced to hoots and hollers.

"That right?'' he asked. Her heart fell. She could not believe her mountain pluck to march in here and dare this. She just knew he was going to laugh in her face and pitch her out.

"You come on back tomorrow afternoon then, 'bout two, and we'll just see how it goes.''

"Oh, I can't thank you enough! You won't be sorry, Mr.—''

"John Quinn,'' he told her with a big smile. "And maybe we'll just bill you real mysterious as the 'Lady from Kentucky.' ''

She agreed, though that nickname worried her. It was not that anyone in this place would ever guess she was a real lady, but that she wondered if she could keep this work she needed so badly and still act like a lady.

Until the Christmas holidays, "Lady,'' as they all came to call her, performed at Quinn's Hotel and Tavern in "Porkapolis.'' Men seemed to quiet a bit when she took to the stage. But if things got wild, she would silence them with one of Gran Ida's old, sad songs like "Scarlet Town,'' or if they needed to let off steam, she would lead them in a romping mountain tune. More than once the crowd shoved the tables and chairs back against the walls and, just as Daddy used to, she took them through a Virginia reel. Men she wouldn't turn her back on danced with each other or the four nimble dancers and bellowed along, usually out of tune. The foreigners sang out in their own tongues.

The audiences swelled. The pay was not as much as she had hoped, but she sometimes received what they called tips, and Mr. Quinn, beneath his rough exterior, had a heart of gold. He kept the men at bay who waited for her at the back door, and he often walked her all the way home. He let her eat meals at the hotel to save more money. He actually believed her story, which she blurted out to him once when she was feeling she'd never see England and had let Ramsey down dreadfully.

"Better not tell that fine lord of yours you been trusting a man like John Quinn to walk you home," he told her once.

"He'd be honored to know you," she assured him.

She had posted a second letter to Ramsey when she took this work, telling him what had happened. Although he was probably in Dorset, she had sent this second letter to his London address, as he had said it would be delivered more quickly and safely that way. She had been certain she would receive a reply, perhaps even money, but she heard nothing. She began to worry that she had described her situation too honestly. Could he be angry with her? But she was certain Ramsey would trust her. She had assured him the Quinn Hotel was her only alternative to recoup her funds quickly. Then on Christmas day, John Quinn gave "Lady" the ultimate proof of their strange friendship. He presented her with the rest of the money she needed to get to New York and buy a cabin class ticket on a transatlantic sailing vessel. She vowed to pay him back and gave him a big hug.

"I'll never forget you, my friend. Someday when Ramsey and I return, we'll stop and thank you together." John Quinn blushed and beamed. And it was then Rebecca realized that the Shakers were wrong about the world being such an awful place. Granted, there were sinners in it—everyone did things wrong and some worse than others. But there were folks like her Grandma Mercer and John Quinn in it too.

New York City shocked Rebecca's sensibilities. By then she'd ridden clear across the Alleghenies on the Great National Pike and north to the city by stagecoach. She'd been snowed in at Columbus and Zanesville in Ohio. She'd met many different people. But she had not been prepared for New York City.

It seemed to be inundated with unwashed immigrants, who were ignored by well-washed folks in clean carriages. Evidently some banks had failed and factories had closed. The Shakers never would have allowed it. People were calling it "the Panic of 1837." As one newspaper put it, "UNEMPLOYMENT STALKS OUR LAND! TIMES TO WORSEN!" When she saw homeless people begging on the streets and could not resist giving them coins, she remembered her discussion with Ramsey, when they'd agreed that charity never helped people to pull themselves up by their bootstraps. By the time she waded through those with their hands out and arrived at the ship office she almost panicked—she had barely enough money to buy what they called steerage passage to London.

Still, she rejoiced when the ship set sail across the big blue pond that was the ocean she had first learned of on a Shaker globe. Once they were at sea, she adapted to the rhythmic weaving of the vessel. At first the crowded quarters in the women's sleeping hall and the single common room did not bother her. She loved to walk the small steerage deck or peek out portholes and dream. She spent hours recalling moments with Ramsey and planning their life together. Unlike those who had journeyed from the Old World to the New, here she was, going the other way. But she knew everything would be new for her in England, and she wanted to be accepted and loved there. Carrying with her the cherished memories of her past, she felt secure, until the day she had the problem with the loud Englishwoman.

The woman's name was Xena Coates, and she was forever chattering about how "the lower-class leeches of the world" always wanted more. More housing, more food, more freedom. Her incessant invectives against those from whom Rebecca had come and those whom Ramsey championed began to wear on Rebecca.

Finally, at supper one evening, she had had enough of Xena Coates. She could not resist observing, "Perhaps some ill-informed, selfish cabin class folk literally above us on this vessel are carrying on the same way about us steerage folk. It's sad some are always casting about for someone else to look down on."

Xena's brown eyes widened and snapped. "That accent of yours is pure backwoods. Perhaps you well know those I do indeed look down on, miss!"

Rebecca bit back the words that not only was she a missus, but an English lady. Down here, packed in like this, it suddenly seemed as ludicrous to claim that as it did to take on this woman. She said only, "I do know I admire those who speak out for the rights of the poor."

"Waa—aall, listen to that now," Xena goaded. Her face turned as florid as her hair at being challenged. "A real liberal amongst us."

Suddenly, fury and panic prickled icy cold up and down Rebecca's backbone. A liberal was what those pompous folk at Graham Springs had branded Ramsey when they'd snubbed him, yes, even him! But poor folk were not leeches as this blasted woman said. Rebecca was terrified she would not fit in with Ramsey's life. After all, here she was with two well-worn gowns to her name, sailing steerage class with barely enough coins left to buy her daily bread.

Rebecca rose abruptly from the long table. Everyone gawked at her. "If a liberal is one who cares for those who need help, I am a liberal. And since you obviously need help, Miss Xena Coates, please call on me at any time for a liberal dose of human kindness. Good evening, everyone."

Xena Coates sputtered. Some laughed and some applauded. Rebecca shook with amazement at her own bad manners. She had come a long way from Shaker silence at the supper table, she scolded herself, but that woman had brought out the worst in others and in her. And she'd set loose all Rebecca's fears. Since Xena Coates was English, would others at her new home be like that?

Rebecca wrapped her cloak around her shoulders and strode out into the stiff March wind. She planted her feet firmly and held fast to a small square metal pillar, leaning her cheek against her hands. The wedding ring felt cold against her cheek, but she did not budge.

Ramsey, Ramsey, she thought, as if trying to send him a message, *I'm almost there. I want so to please you and your family and help your people. I want so for us to be happy. We have so much to share.*

The wind whipped her face, stinging her eyes to tears. For the first time, the lurching deck made her feel tossed and alone. Yet she clung hard, staring out steadily into the gray east as the swift ship plunged on.

Part III

Marchioness Sherborne, the Crossbred English Rose
(1837–1839)

All things uncomely and broken, all things worn out and old,
The cry of a child by the roadway, the creak of a lumber-
ing cart,
The heavy steps of the ploughman, splashing the wintry
mould,
Are wronging your image that blossoms a rose in the
deeps of my heart.
       —William Butler Yeats
          "The Lover Tells of the Rose in His Heart"

Chapter Fourteen

Gray rain smeared sky and sea the day Rebecca's ship reached England. She squinted out through the window of the saloon. Spray and her own breath obscured the shoreline, even the so-called white cliffs of Dover, which a kindly crewman called Sam had told her would be the sign they were getting near. During the voyage she had held her love for Ramsey close, so she was terrified when her memory of his beloved face kept merging into mist as the ship docked amid big buildings on the Thames. This was not the London Ramsey had promised her, she realized when she looked around. This was all wharves and warehouses, not wide parks, streets with homes, rows of stores, or churches with lofty steeples. She strode to the door and called to Sam, who had been tossing ropes to voices in the mist below.

"Are we here, Sam? Is this London?"

Sam, who had loaned her an oilcloth cloak more than once as she stood out on deck, turned her way. "Passengers take a ferry from here to London's docks, Mrs. Sherborne. This here's Gravesend."

Grave's end!

The name jolted her. It made her think of finality and death, not the fine beginning she expected here in England. Her Shaker past had made her watch for some welcoming sign that this land would be her happy home—that all she longed for with Ramsey and his family would be bright and beautiful. Grave's end! It had none of the promise of names like Pleasant Hill or Shelter.

Her heart began to thud with foreboding, even as Sam ambled over to assure her the fare to London's downtown docks was included in the ocean passage. She had almost no money left. She had traded her lovely green gown—the first one she had worn with Ramsey at Graham Springs—for her last few weeks' food. Rebecca, she scolded herself, you had more goods when you left Shelter than you do now!

She consoled herself with thoughts of her reunion with Ramsey. She tried to call up memories of the good things of her past. She tried to recall the people who had made her strong. Nervously, she twisted Grandma Mercer's wedding ring, which had been meant for Mama. More than ever now, she understood why old Widow Lang had pretended her sisters were still with her—for company and comfort. She even missed Jeremy intensely.

She left the ship without a backward glance. Sam came down the gangplank behind her, carrying the trunk that contained only her wedding dress and a few other things. Wearing her Shaker gown covered by her cloak, she clutched her battered satchel tight and stepped onto English soil.

Amazingly, her legs felt as if the ship still rolled under them. She had spent weeks walking the tilting deck. They had been weeks too of longing for her new life to begin. And now it had, though not as gloriously as she had hoped—not yet, until she saw Ramsey and became part of his family and his town. Today was Sunday, April 2, 1837. She had been gone from Shelter for twelve years and from Shakertown for more than eight months. But she had only been a bride for one brief, beautiful, blurry night. Now tears of longing and apprehension clouded her vision as Sam set her trunk beside her on the small, crowded ferry and she shook his hand in thanks.

"Mind now," he told her, "give the hack driver that address, and he won't make you pay 'til you get out. With a West End place like that to go to, he'll be willing to take you, no matter if you look . . ."

Sam's rough voice trailed off. He shrugged his sloping shoulders and made a quick exit down the gangplank, waved once, and disappeared into the dusk. Dear heavens, she thought, she must look like a bedraggled, half-drowned rat she'd seen scurrying down the deck one day. Becca Blake, a Shakeress, a lady now, going to join Lord Sherborne as his wife. Going to somewhere Sam had called "a West End place like that." She hurried inside to brush her cloak, scrub and blot her hems, and recomb and tie her blown, damp hair.

As strong as she tried to be, she felt like a wilted flower as she waited dockside in line for a rain-slick black hack. If only she could have let Ramsey know when she would be arriving as he had wanted. Behind her, the Thames stank like a dead thing, making desperation spread through her like some foul disease. She pressed her handkerchief over her nose again after she gave the hack driver the address of the Sherborne town house in Portland Place. He mumbled something she could not grasp, as if he spoke a foreign language that had nothing in common with Ramsey's crisp, clipped English. The burly man frowned at her, but strapped her trunk on the hack and gave her a hand on the elbow to help her in.

"Won' do ta 'ave you out wi' footpads 'n dusties 'bout e'en if the peelers are at their tasks, eh?" she thought he said. But she was so stricken by the certainty that he thought her a servant that she only nodded and pressed her nose to the window. Why did this land have to seem so alien? Surely there was something in Ramsey's land, in Ramsey's London, that would look like home to her.

Street after street, bustling with vehicles and people, row

after row of buildings moved by the hack. This place even dwarfed New York! Stone structures pressed together, hiding the sky; gaslights like disembodied eyes swam out of the fog, and a foul-smelling cloud of sea coal enveloped the city. She had heard that even vegetables bought here at a place called Covent Garden tasted of this smell, which scraped her nose and throat and settled in the pit of her stomach. As for other gardens, if there were any they must be hidden behind the tall stone or wrought-iron fences where the tops of trees reached over, looking as if they were desperate to escape.

She squinted through the murk, picking out boys with dirty faces who swept the streets clean ahead of clumps of people as they crossed. The Shakers never would have allowed this filth, this stench, those ragtag children. She closed her eyes to recall the orderly calm and purposeful bustle of Shakertown, but she could not picture it. She began to panic even more. Her past was gone. This place was not what she had thought; she was not what Ramsey's family would expect!

Her eyes flew open. She had to get to Ramsey; then everything would be lovely again. She prayed he could be here in London and not in distant, rural Sherpuddle. With him, she would change these dark, foul surroundings, make a place here, a lovely world.

"Damn y' blimey birk of a bloke!" her driver cried out to someone as the carriage jolted, jerking her back to reality.

At least, she noted, fewer vehicles clogged the streets in this part of town. But carts and carriages great and small rattled along, amid an occasional coal wagon and an entire herd of mooing cattle with their drovers cursing at them.

"Are there farms near the West End?" she called to the driver.

He barked a laugh. "Tha's fresh beef on the hoof comin' in for tomora's tables."

She sank back against the creaky leather seat. At least she had understood him that time. They halted before a row of tall, narrow, ghostly white stone houses, guarded by squat wrought-iron railings. Each dwelling had a gas lantern like a torch stuck in iron claws attached near the front door. The door of the Sherbornetown house, number ten, was strangely adorned with a dark wreath dripping black crepe ribbons.

She sat frozen with new fear as the hack driver clambered out and disappeared down steps behind the iron railing. Why didn't he go up the steps to the front door?

She scrambled out as she heard him knock on a door below street level. She heard a woman's voice. She gripped the railing and peered below. The people were hidden, but she heard the partly muffled words, "From America? Oh yes, been expecting her for months . . . her husband's not here . . . dead and buried."

Rebecca clutched the iron railing. Ramsey—dead! It could not be! Lights came on above her; the front door snapped open. Rebecca stepped back to look up at an elderly, pale man in black who hurried down the steps toward her. Could this be Ramsey's father? Ramsey—he could not have died! She had come to love him, to help him to . . . She could not get past the horrid shock. She screamed.

"My lady," the man said and reached out to support her, but she clung to the railing. "I say, we'd nearly given up on you. Indeed, if the marquess's father had not been so stricken and then passed on, he would have gone looking for you straightaway in America!"

"He's—he can't be dead."

"Regretfully, yes, several weeks past."

Her head spun. She would be sick. "He can't be! How?"

"Another, graver stroke. The marquess is in Dorset still comforting his mother."

Her head jerked up. Hope sprang alive as the hack clattered off behind her. "But the marquess *is* his father. What of Ramsey?"

"Of course, you could not know. When his father died, the Earl of Blandford ascended to the title," the man told her as he helped her away from the railing. A petite woman with reddish blonde hair, also in black, hurried up from below to assist Rebecca up the steps to the front door. Rebecca walked haltingly, wavering from shock as much as from her unsteady sea legs. She stopped and shook their hands off. Suddenly she did not care what they thought of her. She leaned back against the door, nearly into that ghastly wreath that reeked of moth bags.

"You mean Ramsey's father has died and Ramsey is in Sherpuddle with his mother?" she demanded. Her voice shook at her daring to hope for such salvation.

"Indeed, as I have said, my lady," the man intoned as he studied her, squint-eyed.

Rebecca fought to calm herself. The man's stern face showed disdain at her appearance, or perhaps at her rudeness or the way she spoke. But she did not care, as long as Ramsey was all right. His father had died, and she had to comfort him. But why didn't any of these people speak good, plain English?

"And who is the Earl of Blandford who has become marquess?" she asked, as relief coursed through her. "Hasn't Lord Ramsey Sherborne taken his deceased father's title then?"

The girl answered. "But the new marquess was ne'er called Lord Sherborne, milady. 'Tisn't proper. Don't know what the earl went by in the wilds of America, but he's e'er been the Earl of Blandford here, 'til his father the marquess passed on to his eternal reward. It's the earl you wed, o' course. And I'm to be your maid. Tamar Brimblecomb's the name, milady, and this here is Tellman, the butler. His lordship said you'd come with a maid, but I can care for you, that's sure. If that's all your baggage, we'll go in. You're just awearied from it all, milady, so let's go inside then."

At last Rebecca managed to lift her skirts and place one foot before the other to cross the black and white tiled entryway, then climbed thickly carpeted stairs, up one floor, then another, past dark doors and shrouded furniture. For one moment, she had actually thought she had lost Ramsey before she had even found him again. Despite her relief, everything seemed muted here, unreal, so alien. Everything! Including the man she had married, who had not bothered to tell her his proper English name.

Even the hot bath in a high-sided tin tub and the tea and toast Tamar plied her with did not settle Rebecca's jumbled insides. But they were trying to coddle her, and that touched and warmed her. Tamar had asked her what she would like most of all to make her feel at home. Rebecca had thought of lemonade to rinse the sea-coal taste from her throat, and Tamar had sent for it forthwith. Now Rebecca's thoughts crackled as did her long tresses, which Tamar insisted on brushing.

The girl had explained that Ramsey's father had been buried under the floor in the village church of Sherpuddle—another peculiar practice as far as Rebecca was concerned. The wind-swept Blake family gravehouses on Restful Knob and the orderly graveplot at Shakertown had never seemed farther away. Tamar said that the family's London coach stood ready to take Lady Rebecca, Marchioness of Sherborne, to Sherpuddle whenever she was rested. She would, Rebecca had informed her, be rested at dawn tomorrow, and they would set out immediately. That order too Tamar sent downstairs so promptly that Rebecca began to sense the strange power of being Marchioness of Sherborne.

Ramsey's mother, Clarissa Sherborne, was now to be called the Dowager Marchioness, Tamar informed her, apparently taking more pride in all these confusing titles than Rebecca ever would. Ramsey's—his lordship's—title had indeed been Earl of Blandford. He would not, as his father before him, ascend to the dukedom of Sherborne until the old duke, Ramsey's grandfather, who lived as a recluse at Sherborne House in Sherpuddle, died. Although it was unusual, Sherborne was both the family name and the title of their peerage—and the name of a Dorset village the family came from years ago but had nothing to do with now.

Rebecca thought she would drown in the deluge of facts, though she wanted to learn all she could and was grateful

Tamar was so talkative. Ramsey had been properly called Lord Blandford until his father's death, Tamar added, but now he could be called his lordship or Lord Sherborne or Ramsey or just Sherborne to his friends like Will Barnstable, Lord Richley.

"Will has a title too?" Rebecca blurted.

The pretty girl blushed. Tamar had pale brown eyes in a heart-shaped face and blonde-red hair that reminded Rebecca of Adam Scott's. She was short but shapely, with quick, fussy movements. Her full mouth, which seemed much too sensual for her pert nose and darting eyes, pouted a moment before she responded.

"Sure enough. William Barnstable's father's a viscount, but his heir is Lord Richley's eldest brother, Baron Nunworth, so Lord Richley won't inherit. Lord Richley's his lordship's dearest friend, and we all admire him e'er so much!"

"Of course we do," Rebecca agreed, eager to show she was a part of things here and knew something of these strange matters that made her feel so unsettled. "I came to know Will almost as well as Ramsey—I mean, I knew Lord Richley almost as well as Lord Sherborne before we wed."

As Tamar rattled on about how she favored London and how pleased she was to be a lady's maid, Rebecca wondered at her own fervent claim to know Will well. She recalled more than once how Will had given her those slanted looks that portended she was stepping on marshy ground by marrying Ramsey. And a new worry festered since she had set foot in England—did she even know her beloved Ramsey? Of course, he had chosen to cast his titles aside in America— he had said as much. But couldn't he have more clearly explained to her the way things were here? Will had once told her that part of her appeal for Ramsey was that she was herself and so different. He'd told her not to change. But could she be too different here? Could she fit in with her husband's life and plans when even servants seemed to live in another world?

Rebecca stood and moved away from Tamar's fussing with

her toiletries. She stared at herself—this new Marchioness of Sherborne—in the full-length plate-glass mirror on the hanging wardrobe next to the big bed. Imagine a room of her own with a thick, flowered carpet and striped paper on the walls just like at the Scott house in Shelter. Imagine a necessary room with two walnut seats just down the hall *and* a silver chamber pot in the walnut commode next to the bed!

Wait until she wrote about all this to Christina! Or would she? She must send Christina more money soon. Could she share all this with a friend who was mending linens for survival? She had glimpsed a rainbow of gowns in the wardrobe among the black garb she would be expected to wear. Tonight what she saw in the mirror made her look and feel unreal: the sensually soft swansdown-lined slippers, her ribboned white cotton nightgown, and this nightcap with ruffled lappets that looked like lacy hounds' ears. She was no longer Becca or Sister Rebecca, but—bosh, it was just that she was wobbly on her feet from exhaustion and all these shocks and surprises!

"Don't know what's keeping Tellman or Cook with that lemonade," Tamar's quick voice interrupted her thoughts as she scraped coals from the hearth into a long-handled brass warming pan.

"It's all right. I don't need it. Just a whim."

"Oh, I know all 'bout—I mean about—whims from waiting on the Dowager Marchioness!" Tamar explained with a sage nod.

"I greatly appreciate all you've done to make me feel—at home—and I hope we can be friends, Tamar."

The girl stood abruptly, rattling coals in the pan. "Friends? You and me, you mean, milady? But I'm your lady's maid, you see. Best call me Brimblecomb as ladies do their maids, the way I got taught proper by the Dowager Marchioness's maid Roberts. See, her name's Sarah Roberts, but she's called Roberts."

"Oh," Rebecca said, taken aback by yet another custom that suddenly angered her. No wonder England had some of the problems Ramsey had told her of! Why, folks couldn't even call each other right out by their given names! They had to fancy and foul everything up with all these rules and titles to keep people in their places when it should be the kind of person one was that made the difference. No wonder there were bad feelings between the social classes here! Right then Rebecca, Marchioness Sherborne, made another important decision—besides running right to Ramsey tomorrow.

"No," she told Tamar as the girl folded back the satin coverlet and swept the warming pan between the linen sheets of the high bed. "I'm sorry if it's not seemly here, but I prefer to call you Tamar, though Brimblecomb's a lovely name. It reminds me of adventures in the country, like finding honey in a bee comb and getting one's feet prickled in a bramble bush out on a lark."

When the girl just gaped at her, Rebecca added, "Tamar's shorter too, and it's a proper Bible name."

"Oh, is it, milady? Was Tamar someone special like a queen of Sheba or some such?" she asked, seeming a bit comforted.

"No," Rebecca said, and hesitated a moment. The girl's face had lit again, just as it had when she talked about loving London and how kind Will had been to the family. Rebecca could hardly tell this Tamar that the biblical Tamar was a deceiver who seduced a man—a story Rebecca had read once in Genesis on the sly because she knew Mama had intentionally skipped over it. "As I recall it, Tamar—the other Tamar—became a widow, and then had twins," she explained.

Rebecca knew her voice wavered. She was swimming in exhaustion as she kicked off her slippers and climbed into the tall bed just as a knock sounded on the door.

"Bide still, I'll answer it. Twins?" Tamar said as she hurried away. "I've a twin brother named Brant, but don't see him much no more—anymore."

At the door was someone called an underhouse parlormaid with the lemonade. Perched on the side of the bed, Rebecca saw Tamar close the door and carry in the goblet on a silver tray. "Everything's so lovely in this room," she told the girl as she leaned back in bed. The bounty of these bolsters was a far cry from her flat wool-stuffed pillow in the East Family Dwelling House or her straw tick in Shelter. "The beauty of this room nearly holds the sad things outside at bay," she confided to Tamar.

Tamar's face clouded every time Rebecca hinted she did not like London or praised the country. But she knew she would win Tamar over when the girl saw how beautiful Dorset was—if it was the way Ramsey had said. She took the lemonade Tamar extended to her on the tray.

"O' course, the Dowager marchioness had this chamber when she was in London, but she'll not be back now, I wager," Tamar told her. "Ne'er liked London one whit, only came to please his poor, dead lordship and the old duke. Said her heart was home in Dorset, more'n once, I heard her say it."

Rebecca's fingers gripped the stem of the goblet. New hope lifted her. Her mother-in-law did not like London either but loved the country! Her heart was home in Dorset! Surely they would be kindred spirits, and could build a loving relationship on that. Gran Ida had once been best friends with Mama, her daughter-in-law. Surely Clarissa Sherborne, the Dowager Marchioness, could be her friend and smooth her path to becoming part of Ramsey's family and friends. And Rebecca, in turn, could be a blessing to the older woman in her new widowhood.

Relieved, she took a big gulp of lemonade. It burned her clear down to her stomach. She sputtered and her eyes streamed tears, and she coughed and sucked in air.

"Oh, milady, not too good?"

"Ah—what is it? I never—had—lemon—ade like this."

"Just, well, I think, brandy, white wine, with a lemon or so squeezed in, milady."

"Oh, liquor. Here, take it out when you go, but just dump it and don't tell anyone it wasn't good. I don't want to hurt Cook or Mr. Tellman's feelings."

Tamar gaped at her as though, again, she had said something completely mad. Rebecca fell back against the pillows and slid her bare feet down farther between the smooth, warm sheets. The bed still seemed to pitch and roll as the ship had, as her feelings and fears still did.

Though she and these people all spoke English, they were worlds apart on some things. She was evidently not supposed to be friends with Tamar, who would no doubt be near her most of the time. Lemonade was not really lemonade, not the way Aunt Euphy had made it, or the way the Shakers had. She was not even expected to brush her own hair, and her merest whims were seen as commands. She would wear black for the first time in her life, mourning Ramsey's father whom she had never known, while her own father was now lost forever, maybe dead, and she hadn't worn a scrap of black to acknowledge that. She had to share all this with Ramsey. It took two days to Sherpuddle, they said, but then she'd be with him and never sleep alone or feel alone again.

As Tamar covered her, Rebecca stretched and slid her hand under the pillow and felt a folded piece of paper. "Mm, what's this?" she muttered. Dizzily she sat up again and pulled out the piece of parchment. In Ramsey's hand, it bore her plain, honest name and title on it: *Rebecca, my beloved wife.*

Her head cleared; the tremor in her stomach settled. It was almost like touching him, like hearing his voice saying those words, clear and deep and sure. "A note from Rams—his lordship," Rebecca told the wide-eyed Tamar. "Please bring that lamp over here."

The paper crinkled open in her hands:

My darling.

I regret I may not be here to greet you upon your arrival, but please feel my love as if I held you close to me in this bed. Send word and I shall come by horseback to escort you to Dorset, or the town coach shall bring you to me in two days' time. I have told the coachman he is to hire two men to accompany you and your maid. I hear there has been rural unrest in the west country again. I'm off to Sherpuddle to keep a vigil at my father's bedside, comfort my mother, and care for the estate. I count the days, hours, and minutes we are apart as death. Come soon, my sweet wife and forever my love.

Your husband, Ramsey

"When was my husband last here?" she asked Tamar.

"Not since he came home from America with Lord Richley and went straightaway to his father's sickbed."

The note was old, then. He had written it before he had received her letters from America, before he became marquess, before they spent months apart. But she knew, even in this foreign land that was now her home, the sentiments that warmed her heart had not grown old or cold. She could read Ramsey's powerful emotions clearly; no language barrier kept them apart.

"Be certain to wake me before dawn," she told Tamar. As she lay back, her spirits soared. Surely nothing could go wrong now. All partings and desertions were past. Tamar turned down the wick of the gas lamp, and Rebecca smiled when she heard the girl lift the lemonade from the tray and take a sip of it before she was out the door. She heard Tamar trying to stifle her surprise at the tart flavor. She didn't blame her for stealing a taste, a young girl with all life ahead of her, green as she herself had been once.

On the road to Dorset the next day, everything opened up for Rebecca. She felt free, not confined, even in the black coach painted with the Sherborne family crest and pulled by four fast horses. She rolled up the leather flaps inside each window, even the two narrow ones that had no glass, to let in the breeze. As London had shut her in, the sunstruck sky and leafy lanes drew her out. She sucked in fresh country air when they left the sprawling, gray city behind and sailed the western turnpike road at twelve miles an hour.

" 'Tis a good thing none of those newfangled steam carriages come out this way," Tamar told her with a pert nod. "Heard tell they scare sheep and cows to death and set the crops afire."

"We have steamboats at home, and I've been on them, but they can do terrible things," Rebecca said. Though she would have liked to tell Tamar much more, she held her tongue. She still intended to make Tamar her friend, but it didn't do to rush into heartfelt confessions.

They stayed the first night at a coaching inn near Southampton and plunged on the next day as the fog lifted. Rebecca knew Tamar thought she was daft when she buckled up the flaps and kept peering out one side and then the other, sometimes sliding back and forth along the sleek leather seat. The girl pointedly coughed if dust blew in. Sometimes, with the slanted looks she got, Rebecca thought Tamar ought to be the lady and she the maid.

At another inn where they stopped to eat, Rebecca heard the driver, Phillips, ask, "How does it feel to be going home after all these months?" She spun around, certain he must be addressing her, but he was facing Tamar.

"O' course I favor London over that wretched place, Rob," Tamar retorted with a shake of her black-bonneted head, not aware Rebecca was listening. "Those manor house yew hedges can't e'er be too high for me!"

Rebecca strode over to ask the girl, "You mean you're from Sherpuddle? Whyever didn't you say so? I've a hundred questions about it! And I can tell you're trying to learn to talk better, but I need to know exactly how they say things in the village, so maybe we could trade favors."

As she rushed on excitedly, she saw Tamar's soft face swiftly set to stone. Evidently something sad had happened to her at home in Sherpuddle, and she was unwilling to return. Well, she could understand some of that, Rebecca thought, but that sulkiness beneath the girl's lively surface was most puzzling.

"Tamar?"

"You see, milady," she told her as they climbed back into the carriage, " 'twas my big chance to leave Sherpuddle, maybe like it's yours to come to England. As for the speaking Dorset-like, I am striving hard to get rid—to rid myself, that is—of all my *look see*s and *cassn't*s and *s'hup me John*s. No one worth their salt speaks that way and t'would be scandal sure if'n—if!—you, a lady wedded into the Sherbornes, tried to talk that way!"

"I see," Rebecca said and fell back into the leather seat as the coach started on again. "I see."

Still, as they rolled across the Dorset downs, she questioned Tamar about the bright, bold, twisting river they now followed. Tamar told her it was called either the Puddle or the Piddle, depending where you lived along it.

"See," the girl said, "around here, they can't e'en get that right!"

They passed through the tiny towns of Turners Puddle, Briantspuddle, and Affpuddle and passed a wooden finger of a sign marked SHERPUDDLE and PUDDLETOWN. Rebecca did not need the touchy Tamar to tell her how Dorset people named their villages. To her, the river became a green ribbon of promise pointing straight toward Ramsey. She only wished the horses' hoofs could fly as fast as those darting black rooks in the sky overhead.

She loved the wildness of Dorset; it was so different from other places she had known. Even the sheep that cropped the soft turf of the downs or grazed the ridges into the hills looked unlike her familiar Shakertown merinos. Most had curlicued horns curving down around their eyes that made them look as if they were wearing horn-rimmed spectacles to stare back at her. At least three kinds of clouds bloomed at once in the blustery skies, from big bulbous ones to lacy layered ones. The winds and weather varied too, like a person's moods—like the powerful personality that animated Ramsey's expressions. Yes, now, out here in distinctly different Dorset, she could picture once again his dear, familiar face, which the mists of yesterday had concealed.

Farther on, the countryside nearly overwhelmed her with its wild beauty. She thrilled at the challenge of knowing it and its people. It changed every time she blinked and she persuaded Tamar to give her the names of these new wonders. Secluded dells and steep-sided combes beckoned; green bracken and gold-gorse moorlands looked rusty with patches of what Tamar said was heather, or furze. "But the village folk call it vuzz, and it makes a fierce fire now that the Great Wood's mostly gone."

Still, Rebecca caught glimpses of that once massive forest with its stands of beech and oak and twisted yews. But strangest of all were the stretches of wind-warped heath contrasting with the milder meadows and pale crop fields nearer the river. Each stretch of this unique land was separated by hedgerows and thickets, making a patchwork quilt of the countryside. It was alien but alluring, just the way she saw her new life here.

But a few miles from Sherpuddle, when she was aching to be there, the coach pulled up by a drover's cart tilted half on, half off the road. Rebecca opened the door to poke her head out as the driver called to the old man and the girl standing by their team of oxen. Their heavy load of gravel had evidently broken an axle or a wheel. A Shaker dump wagon, Rebecca realized, would help them unload so that they could repair it.

"I'll see someun's sent," Phillips called down to the man, while the blonde, thin girl stared back at Rebecca, then glanced quickly away. She looked bedraggled and tired; Rebecca knew exactly how she felt. On the seat across from her, Tamar heaved a huge sigh and stared out the other side of the coach.

"Just one moment!" Rebecca called to Phillips. Not waiting for the iron step to be positioned, she jumped down. "We're going to Sherpuddle, if that's where you're headed," she called to the man and girl. "Miss, you could come along with us, and we'll send help back for—"

"Milady," Phillips called out, wrapping the reins and scrambling down while the two hired guards just sat up on the box, looking all around as if they expected others to pop out of the hedgerows. "No problem here. These're village folk, and I'll send someone back to help. It's not far now."

"But the young woman looks tired. Please," Rebecca said, addressing the girl directly, "we'd be happy to take you to Sherpuddle with us. I am the—the new marchioness of Sherborne."

"Oh, thankee, but cassn't, milady," the girl said.

Though she looked fragile, Rebecca could see the determination on her plain, pleasant face and hear it in the timbre of her voice. Her pale blue eyes met Rebecca's curious stare. She was Rebecca's height exactly, though she slumped.

"Look see, more time wi' Granmer Bet, Jen," Rebecca heard the old man whisper to the girl. He had taken off his dusty cap and bowed to Rebecca. He wore a sort of smock over his stained work trousers and scuffed shoes. He looked much too old to be this girl's father. "How d'ye do, milady," he went on. "I be Hollis Wembly and this here my oldest, Jenny."

"I'm pleased to meet you," Rebecca responded. "Well then, I won't intrude here and . . ." she said as she backed away.

"S'hup me John," she heard the girl whisper to her father, and then louder, "Aye, milady, if'n I might. Jest to our cot then."

Jenny Wembly climbed lithely up into the carriage behind Rebecca. It was then, as Tamar stared coldly at the astounded girl, that Rebecca realized she had unwittingly set up some sort of confrontation.

"You two know each other, then?" she ventured. Both young women nodded.

"Long time agone," Jenny muttered.

Tamar nodded. "And how's Charlie then? You see, mi-lady, Jenny's promised to my brother for when 'tis possible."

"Oh, then you'll be family," Rebecca said and smiled at the two faces, which had gone stiff as starched linen. "And just think, you've got a good start by already knowing each other." She felt she was treading on dangerous ground with these two. Jenny's gaze bored into Tamar, who refused to meet either her eyes or Rebecca's.

"Brung up close as sisters. Once," Jenny said and stared out the window in the opposite direction from Tamar. Tamar squirmed, then gathered her black skirts close as if Jenny might dirty her. Ramsey had warned Rebecca of tense feeling between the classes here, but not among people from the same village. And Tamar needed talking to for her snippy demeanor. Rebecca had never put much stock in the Shakers' insistence on confessions, but some of that seemed needed here.

"Jenny, there is so much I want to learn about Sherpud-dle," Rebecca said. "I hope you don't mind if I call you Jenny. Tamar's been kind enough to tell me some things, but I hope I might call on you too for that."

"For certain," Jenny declared, surprise clear on her pale face. "Come to calling at our cot tomorra when you can."

"Thank you. I surely shall!" Rebecca declared, ignoring Tamar's sigh and her shifting on the creaky seat again. "Lord Sherborne and I both, if you don't mind. I'm so anxious to see him. We were wed such a short time when his father took ill and he rushed home to England. Oh, is that the village?"

She peered excitedly out the window again as the coach turned sharply right toward the river and a cluster of buildings.

"For certain," Jenny told her and peered out the same window. "Though some don't give a button for it, there 'tis!"

Small, low-browed cottages—Jenny had called them cots—swept by. Rebecca had wanted Phillips to hurry, but it was

270

all going by too fast. Pairs of hunched dormer windows made the roofs look like thatched eyebrows raised in anticipation. As different as these small, quaint homes looked, they reminded her poignantly of the Crawl Crick cabin. And some of the cots had straggly roses in front in full scarlet bloom!

"Look see, the alehouse, the smithy, the market house across from St. John's church, then the town green," Jenny's voice spoke clearly in her ear as the girl's dirty finger pointed out this and that and Tamar glared at her knees. Rebecca tried to take it all in. They passed between iron gates and rolled up a curved gravel drive between vast lawns encircled by twenty-foot yew hedges making the tallest wall she'd ever seen.

"But which cot was yours?" Rebecca asked Jenny. "I meant to have Rob Phillips let you out."

"I can walk from the manor house—there!"

Rebecca gasped. Sherborne House dwarfed the entire village. Of pale beige stone, it stood in a huge L at the end of two velvet green lawns cropped by sheep. Her heart began to thud harder, faster. She yearned to seize both Jenny's and Tamar's hands for support. Ramsey just had to be here after all this time! His mother had to like her and they all had to work together to make a life for themselves as a family!

Rebecca trembled as Rob opened the door and put down the iron step. She gathered her skirts carefully, gave him her hand, and stepped down. The two hired guards stood like stone sentinels. She squinted into the late-afternoon sun. A black crepe wreath darkened the door of this house too, but an angel was carved in the stone archway. Just as she had imagined, her eyes could not take in the whole place, even if she craned her neck. This could never be her home— never. It made the hotel at Graham Springs seem modest by comparison and the East Family Dwelling House and the Scotts' house in Shelter shrink to nothing.

The front door opened. A striking older woman stepped out into the sun. A wide slash of silver streaked through her dark hair. Her face had been pretty once, but the softness had turned sharp. There was no mistaking who the woman was. The gray eyes, the wide brow, and the high cheekbones showed she was close kin to Ramsey.

"I—I—" Rebecca began as she took two steps toward the woman and the house. Suddenly she did not know how, properly yet lovingly, to address her new mother-in-law. Tamar came to stand close by her side. Jenny and everyone else waited, watching.

Ramsey's mother's mouth dropped open as she, also, was too moved to speak—or was she simply shocked to see Jenny here? But then Clarissa Sherborne held out both hands to Rebecca and said, "My dear, you've come to us at last."

Rebecca ran to clasp her hands. Tears blinded her. She wanted to hug this woman but wasn't certain her embrace would be returned. But then she heard her name shouted by the voice she had yearned for above all others. As Ramsey ran through the door and around his mother, Rebecca dropped Clarissa's hands and rushed into his fierce, crushing embrace. In his arms, she had come home.

Chapter Fifteen

After Rebecca had washed and changed into another black gown, she sat in the upstairs parlor with Ramsey and his mother. She was gratified and relieved when Ramsey reached over the table between their chairs to hold her hand. She could not believe she was here now, looking at him, touching him, living with him.

And living with his mother. She was still not certain how to address Clarissa, Dowager Marchioness of Sherborne. But she did know what she must say to her now.

"I told Ramsey this, but I must tell you too, my lady—how sorry I am to hear of the marquess's death. I was very much looking forward to getting to know and love him too."

"Thank you, my dear. A grevious loss, but not unexpected after his stroke and lengthy illness. Yet after more than three decades of marriage, I feel Lord Sherborne is with me here, and will ever be."

Rebecca nodded with heartfelt understanding as Clarissa poured their tea. She was so pleased to hear something else she had in common with her new mother-in-law besides their distaste for London and love for Ramsey. Rebecca had felt the same way when she had lost those she loved. But there was not time to explain and discuss all that now.

Rebecca followed Clarissa's glance to the portrait hanging over the mantel of a stocky man standing before a shiny black horse. Rebecca could see the resemblance to Ramsey in the shape of the head. The departed Seymour Sherborne carried a fowling gun across an arm bent with easy grace and had propped his other hand, holding a riding crop, on his hip. He looked very much at home and pleased with himself and the rural world that filled in the picture's background. Though he did not exactly smile, his full mouth tilted at the corners with a nonchalance that reminded her of her own Daddy. Rebecca felt another stab of regret that she would never meet this man of confidence and charm who had sired Ramsey. It must have been from his father that Ramsey got his love of teasing and joking. For as Clarissa turned back to pouring tea and passing plates of strawberry tarts, Rebecca realized her mother-in-law was not made from the same mold as her husband and son.

Clarissa Sherborne sat ramrod straight in her chair. It seemed her back and seat hardly touched it, as if she were suspended an inch above it. Her grace and charm seemed studied and controlled. Her hands posed perfectly when not sweeping from one gesture to another. She held her head elegantly high as if it were carved from the same marble as the mantel. She smiled at Rebecca as they talked, but the curve of her mouth never lifted the slanted cheekbones or warmed the dove-gray eyes. Was it that she was stunned by the loss of her husband and the shock of meeting a new daughter-in-law she surely would never have chosen for Ramsey? Or was it even more?

"We must show her the house, Ramsey, attic to cellars," Clarissa was saying. "And I hear, my dear, that you would love to see my roses, so I shall delight in sharing them."

"Time enough tomorrow," Ramsey answered before Rebecca could thank her or tell her how she felt about roses. "You understand she's tired tonight, Mother. And we've really never had a honeymoon."

Clarissa went paler, but Rebecca blushed. She darted a glance at Ramsey. "Oh, yes, I am a bit tuckered from that trip."

"Tired, you mean? Yes, of course," Clarissa said. "But I simply cannot wait to hear your version of your wedding at that Springs place in Kentucky. I've heard Ramsey's side of it and Lord Richley's too, but women always have a finer awareness of such things. Such a rush to wed when we could have done everything perfectly proper for you here."

"I told you, Mother, with several catastrophes, we did not want to part unwed," Ramsey put in, despite a mouthful of tart.

Rebecca appreciated his defense. Yes, she was happily home here with Ramsey. And she would rise to the challenge of befriending this stiffly proper stranger who must now be the second most important person in the world to her.

But there often seemed an undercurrent to Clarissa's words. After she stopped speaking—a kindly enough comment each time—other words seemed to be waiting to be said, tugging Rebecca's spirits down. When Clarissa asked whatever had happened to her lady's maid from America, Rebecca explained about deciding to leave in a rush and about being short of funds. Clarissa nodded and remarked on her "common sense," but unspoken words hung in the air. Rebecca told her tale about leaving money for her newly widowed friend Christina, but the newly widowed Clarissa's "How terribly clever and kind" rang hollow. Where was the rest of her luggage? Rebecca explained about selling some things at the end. But she could not bring herself to explain to Clarissa about earning money at Quinn's Hotel, nor about Mr. Quinn's loaning her enough for her journey. She had learned that Ramsey knew none of this either because he had not received her last letter. But she would explain all of it— at least to him—as soon as she could in private.

"Indeed, I am so pleased," Clarissa said as a housemaid came in to collect cups and plates, "that you are here and that my beloved Ramsey is wed at last."

But not pleased he wed you seemed to ripple between them.

"Thank you, ma'am," Rebecca replied. She could tell that

Ramsey was eager to have her to himself longer than the quarter hour they had managed. She wanted that too, to jump to her feet and run for the door, dragging him behind her.

"And to think," Clarissa concluded, "my only son is wed to a lovely woman with such an interesting and unique background."

And such a terribly common, overly clever one buzzed in Rebecca's head like a swarm of bees. Blessedly, Ramsey took her hand again, though she'd managed to get it and her white linen napkin quite sticky with strawberry tart.

"She *is* one of a kind, and she's mine!" Ramsey declared as he gently pulled her to her feet and threw his arm around her shoulders. "I am indeed delighted to have together the two women in the world who mean the most to me. I am certain you will both be a great help and comfort to each other as Rebecca and I build our dreams here. Mother, I know you will understand if I take my wife off to have her to myself."

"Should I not plan for you at dinner, then?"

"We would like it sent up. All right, darling?"

"Oh, yes, of course. I am weary and—"

"Of course, you'll want Brimblecomb sent up again," Clarissa added.

"No need tonight," Ramsey insisted, his firm voice sending a shiver of relief and admiration up Rebecca's spine. He leaned down to gently grasp his mother's arm and kiss her perfectly powdered cheek. "Not her maid, not my valet, just some food later, if you please. We have so much to catch up on."

"Young lovebirds, I quite understand," Clarissa said. Rebecca sensed she wanted to glance at the portrait of her husband, but she did not. Rebecca's heart went out to her mother-in-law again for the loss of her love. Clarissa reached out and took Rebecca's right hand. Hoping it was not unseemly, Rebecca bent to kiss her cheek. The familiar smell of rosewater made her homesick, though she thought she'd best not bring that up right now. She gently touched Clarissa's right shoulder, only to feel her jerk away.

"Oh, sorry, your lovely gown," Rebecca said. She had felt the padded shoulder give way under her touch.

Quickly, Clarissa puffed out the deep dent in the fabric. "You two run along then. Tomorrow, my dear, we shall show you everything in your new home."

"I am looking forward to it. Thank you ever so much."

Rebecca would have said more, made a little speech perhaps about how she wanted to help here every way she could. About how she hoped they would get on, but that had to be earned, and after all—

After all, her eager husband was propelling her out of the parlor with his hand in the small of her back. He seized her wrist and pulled her down the long hall lined with closed doors, past rows of family portraits and into the suite of rooms they would share as man and wife, lord and lady, as lovers here in the vast house called Sherborne Manor.

Inside their bedroom door, they fell into each other's arms and simply held tight. "You were wonderful, always wonderful," Ramsey mumbled, his mouth muffled by her hair as he began to pull it loose from its combs and pins.

"It's a shock for her. I'm not what she expected or wants—"

"You're what I want. She'll come to love you, as I do . . ."

Hurriedly, standing there by the door, they undressed each other down to their undergarments. He shot the bolt before carrying her to the large canopied bed. As he covered her face with wild kisses, his knees bumped the high mattress, and they both tumbled onto it. She gasped in surprise at the soft, springy depth of it.

"Here I am going too fast when I want to woo and win you all over again," he apologized.

"No, we've lost so much time! I missed you badly, and I've so much to tell you!"

A grin lifted his face. His gaze intensified, his nostrils flared. She had almost forgotten how emotions could light his face, how his deeply felt passions could race across his features.

"Tell me later!" he insisted. "Right now, it isn't our past

that matters, not even the bright future we will build. It's the present, us together like this! Oh, there is one thing!''

She grieved for the loss of his touch when he moved away as far as the bedside table to fumble in a drawer. She sat up, then scrambled across the bed. He held out to her a gold ring with the biggest, shiniest green stone she had ever seen. It was cut in a rectangle and guarded by two big pearls. In the light from the window, the jewel glowed as green as Kentucky bluegrass.

''A wedding ring,'' he told her, his face now boyish and expectant. ''An emerald, a family ring. I hope it fits.''

When he took her left hand, she remembered her grandmother's ring and explained it to him as she moved it to her other hand. Her new wedding ring fit as if it had been made for her.

''It's the prettiest, fanciest thing,'' she whispered in awe, tipping her hand to examine it from every angle. ''But I don't have a thing for you,'' she admitted, ''and compared to all this, never did—''

''You give me all I want!'' he exclaimed, looking almost angry. ''And one more thing I have for both of us. As busy as I've been—I have to go into Dorchester for a brief meeting tomorrow afternoon—I'm going to cancel everything else for a week. We deserve our honeymoon beyond just this one night.''

Her heart swelled with joy. Tears blurred her eyes. She hugged him hard, sitting in his lap in the depths of that soft bed.

''No, not just this one night, but forever!'' she whispered in his ear. And that was the last thing either of them said for a long time.

She swept between exhaustion and exhilaration that night. They loved, they talked, they ate a bite when the butler knocked and left a little wheeled table of food outside their door. By candlelight, they laughed, they nibbled—on each other as much as the food—then loved again. They drank French wine in thin crystal goblets, toasting each other and their future. This brew was so much better than that vile lemonade had been, she told him. She explained all about that, and that she hadn't even known he was once "his lordship, Earl of Blandford," and they laughed again until their sides were sore. Finally, in the dark of the spring-scented night, twined together, they slept. When she opened her eyes again, the sunlight was pale gold and Ramsey was caressing and kissing her.

"Oh, it's broad day!" she cried.

"No better time to see clearly what we are doing!" he teased and pulled the covers down to reveal her ivory nakedness. He began to kiss her up and down her breasts and belly as his hands caressed her.

"My dearest love," she murmured before their lips melded. Their tongues delved deep in each other's wet, warm mouths, their teeth bit lightly at stretches of skin. She grasped his molded back and shoulders as he pressed her down on the bed. She clung to his strong neck and ruffled the thick, crisp hair along his nape. She lifted a sleek leg to stroke his flank. She tickled him behind his knees with her toes—and found herself pressed under him as he moved his mouth down her arched throat to her fluted collarbones and her peaked breasts.

"I am so grateful we are back together—like this!" she said, somehow as out of breath as if she had run miles. She blew into his ear and kneaded his arched back boldly as his knees gently intruded between hers. She felt so vibrant yet so vulnerable, so totally trusting and yet triumphant. She lifted up to meet him as he moved close to make them one again.

"You are so beautiful, Rebecca."

His breath became ragged and she marveled how they could do this to each other over and over. It made everything else perfect. She needed nothing but him, part of her, at one with her. And they had days and nights and years ahead to share this joy.

He lifted his weight from her, resting on his elbows. He smoothed the wild tresses from her face. Their eyes locked as firmly as their bodies did.

"Rebecca Blake Sherborne, I have been waiting for you—for this—all my life."

"And I for you, my lordship of love."

She smiled up at him, dazed that such rapture existed. And then she moved in his strong embrace to satisfy their aching mutual need. Each of them both gave and took, promised and fulfilled.

Awestruck, she watched his handsome face go taut with passion. He threw his head back and gazed at her through half-closed eyes. Tears of happiness blurred her vision. She felt lifted beyond the most thrilling heights of memory. Each time with him, love built and grew, as if she soared over the edge of her lofty mountain refuge again, only wider, higher, before she finally spiraled back to earth.

In late morning, the three of them toured the house. Ramsey and his mother pointed out to her the doors of the rooms which belonged to Ramsey's grandfather, George, the old duke who often slept until noon. A recluse for years, confined to bed or chair, he had earned the Sherborne peerage by helping King George III.

There were many guest bedrooms on the second floor as well as the rooms Clarissa had moved to when Ramsey's father died to give Ramsey and Rebecca the state bedroom suite. For one moment Rebecca wondered if the cold undercurrent she felt could be Clarissa's anger at having to give up the rooms she had shared with her husband for decades. But no, surely Ramsey's mother would not resent her just for that.

This morning they did not enter the upstairs parlor where they had taken tea, nor a room Clarissa referred to as the nursery. At that, Ramsey pinched Rebecca right through her skirts.

On the top two floors were servants' quarters and attics for storage, which she would tour another time. Downstairs was the great hall, now a ballroom and formal dining room. Clarissa told her it had once been vaulted and hung with deer antlers. The house had been built three centuries ago during the reign of Henry VIII before it belonged to the family.

Clarissa seemed very proud of the lowered plaster ceiling and the tapestries that replaced the horns.

The main floor also had a morning room that faced east like the parlor upstairs, but Rebecca liked the library best. It smelled enticingly of leather and held more books than even her old schoolteacher Hortency Hoosier or Adam Scott had probably read. A stiff, flat portrait of the old duke in his white curled wig hung here. Ramsey told her she was welcome to read all the books and that they would meet his grandfather that evening after dinner.

"After I see your rose gardens, my lady, I will walk to the village," Rebecca said. "I promised to call on the Wemblys there."

Clarissa's sleek eyebrows lifted. "When a bridal couple is in mourning, all formal calls to be made in the area are postponed, not that the Wemblys would be on such a list."

"But this is just to the village, to see what it is like," Rebecca explained before Ramsey could swoop to her defense again. But to her surprise, he did not. He only tightened his lips and put his hands behind his back.

They strolled the paneled hall called the long gallery. Painted landscapes and tapestries lined the well-lighted oak walls. She liked this spacious corridor with its curved window seats overlooking the tree-lined back lawn that stretched toward the river.

"Ramsey, I hardly think—about the village—at least until you can be with her . . ." Clarissa began.

"Rebecca's used to being helpful, Mother, and I'm certain a brief walk to the village will be perfectly in order. And in here are the kitchens," he went on, obviously relieved to change the subject. Besides the large, well-staffed kitchen, bigger than any Shaker one, there were smaller adjoining rooms called a bolting room, buttery, and pantry. "You'll like this," Ramsey told her as he showed her yet another room, long and narrow with wooden countertops and shelves built along three walls and two high windows through which sunlight poured in. "It used to be a still room."

"A still room?" she echoed. "Not to make moonshine—corn whiskey like Old Monongahela, you mean?"

Clarissa stared and Ramsey guffawed, while Rebecca went beet red. "No," he told her, hugging her shoulders. "I'll never forget your little distillery for rosewater at Pleasant Hill. In the old days, this was where the ladies of the house used to distill cordials, medicines, and essences from herbs and flowers. Here nowadays, most of those things are bought at the apothecary in Dorchester."

"Even that lovely rosewater I smelled on you, my lady?" Rebecca asked, trying both to include and compliment her mother-in-law.

Clarissa's eyebrows hiked a bit higher. "I have the maids make that."

"Mother," Ramsey said, "since this room is merely used for storage now, perhaps Rebecca might use it to—"

"But her life has changed greatly since the backwoods or that communal living place in Kentucky, my dear," Clarissa interrupted. "She'll be too busy with proper wifely endeavors to be duplicating things we can buy or the maids can make with no fuss. I'll show her the gardens now, since you must be off for town, and we'll delay supper for you."

As Clarissa turned away, Rebecca touched Ramsey's lips. "Later," she mouthed, then replaced her fingertips with a quick kiss. "If I'm still in the village when you get back, I'll meet you there, outside the church."

He nodded. "I shall return by evening, and then let the honeymoon games begin!" He grinned and pulled her back into the still room to kiss her harder, oblivious of his waiting mother.

He waved and was on his way. As the two women strolled along a gravel path behind the house, Clarissa told Rebecca, "I am delighted to have you as an ally to help keep Ramsey from harm's way."

"What harm? You mean this rural unrest hereabouts he told me of? Surely no harm could come to him from that!"

"Now, just let me explain. Those wretched protests from workers' unions, though they've necessitated the calling out

of local or private militia from time to time, will just pass
away as the laboring poor become more used to the inevitabil-
ity of progress. But things may be kept on a boil, you see,
if the local leader—and that is Ramsey now—continues to
publicly encourage their cause. It could even spill over into
the larger arena of things in London. Already the Dorset
gentry are dreadfully put out with him. And after he promised
his father he would not promote violence! Yet for some reason, since he has returned from America, Ramsey seems even
more set on forcing these matters to the fore, of agitating for
change for the poor through publicity and politics.''

She said that last word—Rebecca had come to think of it
as Ramsey's battle cry for rural reform—as if it were a curse.
Once again, Clarissa had implied something she had not quite
said: that Ramsey's new, low-class American wife inspired
him anew in his rebellion.

''But Ramsey believes political change must come to better
England's laboring poor,'' Rebecca argued quietly.

''His grandfather and his father had their hands full and
were quite content overseeing the Sherpuddle area without
such folderol. I can only be grateful the old duke lives on,
for Ramsey will inherit his Lords seat in Parliament when he
passes, and then what will we have? It would be so much
better for us all, dear Rebecca, if Ramsey could be encouraged to simply see to his little projects in Sherpuddle for the
deserving poor. That could be done quietly and circumspectly
without a fuss. Why, even the good Lord Jesus said in the
Gospels, 'The poor will always be with us.' ''

Rebecca stopped and stared at Clarissa's straight back; her
mother-in-law turned to face her. She could probably win the
friendship she so coveted, Rebecca realized, if she would aid
and abet Clarissa in keeping Ramsey busy and quiet here.

''You know, my lady,'' she began, choosing her words
carefully, ''it seems to me the important thing about what the
Lord said is that the poor will be *with us*. And if we are not
poor, maybe even if we are, we mustn't ignore or simply
appease them. We must help them find their own way. I

don't exactly see yet how politics is the way to help either, but if Ram—''

"Good, then we are agreed, my dear!"

"But you see, I think these downtrodden folk need a change of heart, to believe they can better themselves. We can help them find ways to pull themselves up in the world.''

Clarissa blinked once, twice. Her high ivory forehead creased in a frown, then lifted to something between surprise and disbelief. "But charity or not," she said, "one cannot change a cat's stripes." She walked on as if the subject were closed. "Come along then, and do see my roses, for we shall share them, just as we do our concern for Ramsey.''

At first glance, Clarissa's roses, hemmed in, incredibly, by a hedge that was also of roses, awed Rebecca. Besides the familiar apothecary and damask kinds she had known and loved for years, she saw types completely new to her.

"Oh, what are these lovely ones?" she asked.

"They are called chinas. The nice thing about chinas is they are *semper florens*. That is, they flower repeatedly and deepen their color in the sun. And of course, their smell is sweet.''

Sweet was not the word for the intense fragrance that wafted out from them, Rebecca thought. Why had these roses not been used in Shakertown for rosewater? Why, if these plants had not been so severely trimmed, they would spill out in a great bouquet of glossy leaves and a riot of hues.

"And that one in the middle?" Rebecca asked, indicating a sturdy rose that must be late-flowering.

"A portland, named after the Duchess of Portland. It's a cross with damasks.''

"A cross?"

"Crossbred. You know, chinas mixed with damasks or gallicas or whatever. Hybrids. Ramsey told me you knew all about roses.''

"Only certain kinds. You see, crossbreeding is against Shaker strictures, for sheep or anything. They wouldn't even allow mules because they were a crossbreed of horse and donkey and that went against religious rules. But to think of creating new roses by crossing them—even as the hand of God must have once—"

"The hand of my gardeners under my eagle eye, you mean. You do see what my gardeners have made here, do you not? Over there with the rosa odorata tea rose and bourbons?"

Rebecca's gaze followed where Clarissa pointed. "Oh, you forced them into shapes—a wheel and a basket," she stammered, astounded anew.

"A conceit called a rosery," Clarissa explained. "Everything perfectly clipped and controlled. The wheel has a rock-work center with creeping roses trimmed just so. Then, around that hub in spoke-like beds, roses firmly shaped and pruned inside the low boxwood hedge."

Rebecca nodded, but she thought it terrible to cut back flowers that wanted to ramble free and fling their vibrant colors into the air.

"The basket rosery is my pride and joy," Clarissa went on. "Both turf and roses must be trimmed at least once a week. Wood slats make that lattice pattern to imitate a basket of roses. And the handle is of wire to support a climbing rose that takes precise cutting and watching to keep it in its place."

Rebecca's mouth set. Besides creating a look that was completely false, cutting the bushes back so harshly made them compact and dense. That kept the sun and breeze from circulating and kept the roses from really flourishing—from being themselves.

"But don't insect pests or even mold thrive in there? Ramsey says it rains a lot here. At home, I always put rue plants between bushes to keep out pests," Rebecca dared to inform Clarissa.

"Such fussing is not needed. My gardeners care for all that here. But if you would like to help with the roses—"

"Oh, yes, I sure would!"

"Then feel free to clip bouquets from bushes you can reach from the paths, especially from the damask hedges. Take roses to your suite anytime you wish and arrange them too. Brimblecomb can bring you some vases.''

Rebecca looked away. She felt Clarissa was trying to trim her too and force her into the shape she wanted. But she did not want to threaten their new relationship by rebelling more than she already had. Her stomach felt knotted and her lower lip trembled. It was the Shakertown rules all over again, only in a different way. Tears she would not allow to fall stung her eyes. Suddenly she noticed not only the rose hedges closing in the artificially shaped roses, but the tall yews beyond, circling the entire estate, closing her in and closing the world out.

That afternoon, as Rebecca prepared to walk to Sherpuddle, a suddenly sullen Tamar held her cape, tapping a foot. ''It will certainly please your folks to have you stop for a chat while I visit the Wemblys,'' Rebecca said, trying to encourage the girl. She did not mean to push Tamar into something she did not want to do, but Clarissa expected the maid to accompany her. And when did it hurt a prodigal daughter to return home? Tamar had told Rebecca she had had a falling out with her family. Why, back in the old days, Mama would have given anything for this chance Tamar had. ''And I meant to ask,'' Rebecca said as she picked up the gift she intended for the Wemblys, ''could you get me some of that rosewater the Dowager Marchioness uses?''

''It's with your toiletries already, milady,'' Tamar told her and led the way into the dressing room. She reached to unstopper one of the glass bottles lining the shelf behind the ewer and basin. ''For wash water, even your hair.''

Rebecca sniffed it. Again the familiar scent assailed her senses as she inhaled deeply. ''But isn't it for medicine here, or food flavoring too?''

''Mostly to smell pretty, I guess. Never could see what was so good about it myself.''

''Can't you smell all the flowers of the world in here?''

''In that little bottle, made from boiled petals, milady?''

''Come on then,'' Rebecca told her as she let Tamar swirl

the black cape around her shoulders, "and please explain everything we see along the way."

She breathed more easily out here away from the clipped flowers and the big house. They passed the field where the herd of horned cattle—no doubt beef on the hoof—grazed. Next came a meadow, alight with flowers, though not multihued ones like those in Shelter. As it had yesterday, the grass was frosted with pale, bobbing blooms. She pried from Tamar the names of the wildflowers: the beige one was fog grass; the white ones were lady's smock, meadowsweet, the daisy-like ragged robin, and marsh spotted orchid. Rebecca saw that no one could dash freely into and across a meadow here. A man-made hedgerow of live limbs twining through sticks surrounded this one, so one had to unhook and use the gate. But there seemed some good reasons to have hedges. Birds flew in and out of them, and rabbits darted all about. And here, along the lane, a yellow brier-rosebush wove along beside the hedgerow.

"Always did fancy those yellow flowers," Tamar admitted as if to make amends for sulking. "Someone once said they was the color of my hair, so I cut some and stuck them in."

"That must have looked lovely. But didn't you notice they had a fetid smell?"

"Smells just the same as rosewater to me!" Tamar insisted.

Rebecca wondered at first if the girl was teasing her, but evidently she was not. Perhaps Tamar was one of those few people who really could not discern smells. Sister Elizabeth had been like that. So perhaps Tamar loved London because she could not smell the stench of the river or of sea coal. And that meant Rebecca would have to find someone else to help her with the plans for the roses to which she hoped to win her mother-in-law over one way or the other.

"Do folks ever walk through the meadows?" she asked Tamar.

"They'd get their feet wet most of the year. It's a water meadow, fed by sluices and weirs from the Puddle."

So, Rebecca mourned, even the meadows were man-made and controlled here. She asked Tamar about the huge barn which stood on strange, mushroom-shaped stones. "Called stattles," Tamar told her in a droning voice. "Keeps vermin out. Back when villagers had their own fields, they'd come there at harvest to give the landlord his due. It's the tithing barn Captain Owler almost burnt when he lit the ricks in protest, too, 'fore—before—he turned against the laborers and anyone who takes their side."

"What's all this? Who is Captain Owler?"

"Don't know. He rides at night with an owl hood over his head. He used to break up fancy farm machines and burn things to protest the enclosures. But last few years, he's been scaring the village folk pretty bad instead."

Rebecca decided she would have to ask Ramsey about the mysterious Captain Owler. Were the captain's doings part of the unrest which Ramsey had mentioned in the note under her pillow, the reason he had hired guards to ride on her coach? Was Captain Owler part of the protests Clarissa had brought up just today? Could he be the harm Clarissa feared for Ramsey?—for Ramsey certainly took the laborers' side. But right now, everything in the village looked peaceful and pretty.

How quaint and picturesque the cots were, all of cob, a local mixture of mud, pebbles, and straw. Their thatched roofs drooped in muted hues of yellow, brown, and gray, evidently depending on their age. Birds darted into nests under the low eaves where the dormer windows touched the roofs; a body could almost climb out a second-story window to the ground. A few wooden privies leaned along the hedgerows bordering the meadows and crop fields in back. Just behind each cot was a tiny patch of garden with bean poles and a few rows of root plants. She wondered where the larger village gardens were.

The Brimblecomb cot was the first one they came to, so she sent the reluctant Tamar in and told her she would stop for her later to meet her family. She smiled as Tamar stepped inside and she heard a woman's cry of surprise. She so wanted families, even ones with some bad feelings, to get on.

As she walked through the quiet village, she began to hum Gran Ida's old song, "Scarlet Town." Outside most of the cots sprawled scrawny moss-rosebushes, blooming red. The moss roses she'd seen at Graham Springs had had an intense, lovely fragrance. If her mother-in-law would not let her use her roses for her plans, perhaps these would have to do for starters. She could make cuttings and propagate even more.

" 'In Scarlet Town where I was born, there was a fair maid dwelling . . .' " she sang. She'd ask the fair maid Jenny if the villagers used the roses, though they looked neglected. She hoped the people here would learn to trust the Marchioness of Sherborne, who lived in a house big enough to swallow half this village. But she'd win them to her friendship and to her suggestions for helping them. She just had to!

She eyed askance the squat gray church where Ramsey's father lay newly buried under the stone floor. A sudden chill racked her. She preferred the adjoining churchyard with its round-topped, sunstruck tombstones sunk crookedly in the turf. She knew Clarissa had loved her husband; she should have put him there.

She sighed and knocked on the half-open door that must be the Wemblys'. A skinny cat slept in the shade. It seemed so quiet, but Jenny had said to call today.

Jenny opened the door and a pregnant older woman peered out behind her. On a broad bench at a crude table sat a bone-thin, white-haired woman who looked very old. A dirty, wide-eyed boy of about four clung to the pregnant woman's skirts. Awkward introductions established that these were Jenny's mother, Mary, her grandmother, Old Bet, and her youngest brother, Nat. Rebecca saw no others inside the dim cot, though Tamar had said there were four daughters and three sons.

"You came, milady," Jenny said as their eyes met and held. She indicated that Rebecca should step in; Rebecca did, trying not to stare at the single room, much smaller than the cabin at Crawl Crick.

"Of course I came. I was pleased you invited me. Here, I brought you some candles. I hear they are—useful."

"Not stubs?" the girl asked, pleased as she peered into the cloth sack and handed them to her mother. "Aye, these be much better than our rush lights, e'en if the rats like to eat them. Thankee."

Rebecca smiled and sat down on the board bench across from the old woman as she was bidden. "All be out 'til tasks adone," Jenny explained. "Myself, just got back from forking fish out o' the river for Granmer Bet's last night here."

"Oh, she's going somewhere for a visit?"

"The poorhouse in Tolpuddle to live," Mary explained. "Look see here." She pointed out to Rebecca the "P" embroidered, quite beautifully, on the shoulder of the old woman's worn dress.

"P—for 'poorhouse,' " Old Bet said as her bony shoulders slumped even more. "Mustn't grumble." She reached up to pat Jenny's hand, which had become a fist. "The way o' things now."

Rebecca gawked. This could not be what it seemed. An old woman would be taken away from her family to the poorhouse? "But how can you allow this?" she demanded of Jenny and Mary.

"Not us, no other way," Jenny said. Her chin quivered as if she would cry. "You think we want to? Tell true, I ast you to hear it, 'cause you was so kind yesterday."

"I'm glad you did. I can help. If it's money, we can care for that."

"She cassn't work, so it's money. But it's more than that," Jenny said. She sank down next to her grandmother and put her arm around those small shoulders. "We won't take charity!"

Rebecca recalled that Ramsey had told her these people resented and refused charity. But for this tragic case—

"It would not be charity," she floundered. "You said you

will be wedding soon. Surely Old Bet could help you sew things for your new cot, or I'll pay her to—"

"Milady, Charlie and me won't wed for years maybe, 'til a cot be empty or new built. Then there's money for the banns and license 'less we just go to sinful housekeeping."

"Sh. Sh, now, 'nuff, girl," Mary warned and put a hand to her shoulder from behind.

Old Bet said again, "Mustn't grumble."

But Jenny plunged on, obviously choosing her words slowly and carefully now. "Your husband, his lordship, milady. He been tarying to get us better wages, all o' us in Dorset, and that's the best to hope for. Oh, he'd pay us more here but have the squires up in arms. But our field's agone and no gleaning with the new machines. No rabbit poaching, coal too dear. Some places in England, men makes ten shillings a week, the women seven—not in Dorset. Milady, I see you got a good heart. Maybe you can help his lordship make them Dorset and London folks mend their ways!"

"Yes, they must! But right now, there is Old Bet. You see, I intend to be making rosewater and other rose products in the future and hope the villagers will want to help me. And I'll need someone like Old Bet to help me pluck petals from the blossoms, and I pay more than seven shillings a week." She was partly making this up as she went along, but it must come true. She would not let them lose their old grandmother! "I assume the younger of you have tasks, but Old Bet could spare me some of her time for pay, couldn't she?"

Mary Wembly now leaned both hands on Jenny's shoulders. Jenny just gaped. Old Bet's crooked, blue-veined hands twitched on the table as tears fell on them. It was silent in the cot, though young Nat sneezed and sniffled as he played at building a house of sticks on the cold hearth at their feet.

"And, eventually, I'll need other workers," Rebecca added, afraid they would turn her down. "I hope you will consider my offer of employment for Old Bet. And Jenny,

I'm in need of someone to answer my questions about village things too, as Tamar has other tasks.''

At that Jenny sniffed, but a tear rolled down her dusty cheek until she dashed it away with the back of her hand.

"Will you stay for fish and beans, then, milady?" Mary asked in the awkward silence. "Got to save all this thinking 'til my Hollis come home. Fish being stewed next cot at the Brownes'.''

"Another time, I would be honored," Rebecca said. "You see, I'm waiting for Lord Sherborne to return from Dorchester and I thought I'd look at the church."

"Oh, aye, the curate, Mr. Tressler, lives right 'cross the way," Mary said.

"Perhaps Jenny would walk me over." Mary nodded and Jenny got to her feet.

Though the sun was shatteringly bright outside, Rebecca could still see only that dim, barren cot. What she had seen inside had blasted her early impressions of village charm. At first, the earthen floor and ladder-like stairs to the loft above had made her sentimental, as if she had stepped back in time to her long-lost Kentucky home. The family reminded her of her own, with Daddy gone but with Gran Ida, Mama, her and Jeremy there together waiting for his return. But this was not Crawl Crick, and what was here was wrong!

Though she had kept herself from staring, she had seen green mold on the inside walls and felt the dank, destructive chill. The place looked ready to tumble down, with gaps in the cob and rips in the greased-paper windows. The lamps were rushes soaked in fat; the Wemblys' faces were wan. They evidently took turns with their neighbors to cook dinner. No poaching, no gleaning, no hope. Jenny's desperate daring in asking the new marchioness to the cot seemed the only light in their lives, but even Jenny looked stooped and broken.

From afar, the way the Wembly women dressed had reminded her of the deep bonnets, shapeless gowns, and sturdy aprons of her Shaker sisters. But these gowns were tattered, dirty, and old. This was a far cry from the propriety and

292

pride of Pleasant Hill. She had seen the dreary, hopeless look in four generations of eyes in the Wembly cot; she had glimpsed their dark lives.

"You want to know where the old marquess is aburied in St. John's, then?" Jenny's voice came quiet at her elbow.

In the middle of the deserted, dusty road in the heart of Sherpuddle, Rebecca turned to Jenny and took her hands. "No, I want to know how I can benefit this village. I don't offer charity, only hard work using the village's moss roses for profit and for pride."

"Profit and pride," Jenny muttered bitterly and shook her head. "Not here no more. Like Granmer says, mustn't grumble 'cause it's the way o' things."

"But you don't believe that, or you would not have asked me to visit. You took a stand, and I admire you for that. It's not only that I want to help you, but I want you to help me. I'm new here in this place and with these people, including the Sherbornes. My beginnings were not far from this"—she nodded at the village—"from the way you live, I mean. But my folks and friends had independence and pride. They had a chance. And just like you, they hated charity. My Mama and Daddy never wanted to be beholden to those who had more either."

Jenny stared at her. Finally she glanced down at her dirty hands in Rebecca's and tugged them back. She shook her head, and her watery eyes looked away toward the distant, hidden manor house. "His lordship wants to change things too, but it's not so easy. You want our roses with those at the house, they're Sherbornes' to take, just like it all. I best go in now, Old Bet's last night."

"Jenny, she is not to be sent away nor allowed to go! If she is, I shall fetch her back in the same coach you rode in yesterday. And those roses by the cots belong to the village, but I hope you will help me care for them when I buy cuttings from them. I will need workers I can trust."

Without turning back, Jenny nodded, leaving Rebecca wondering what that meant after all that had passed between them. But the girl shook her head as she plodded to the cot next door, evidently to fetch the family's dinner. From the side porch of the church Rebecca watched her lug a small blackened kettle home. As the big bells in the tower clanged overhead, vibrating the stone pillars she leaned against, the village came alive with workers heading home from the fields. Men, women, even children, some far too young to be, as Jenny had said, at tasks. In Shakertown, bells had helped order people's daily lives, but these villagers looked ragged, drooped, and sad.

Sherpuddle seemed centuries away from Shelter or Shakertown, yet she strangely longed to be part of it. Living among these people with no high hedges between them might be the only way to be truly trusted, to make a change in hearts and lives as she had before. She knew all about Kentucky mountain independence and could share the good things the Shakers had taught her. She knew how she herself had grown and changed and fought and won. Ramsey had tried to tell her about the depth of desperation here, but she hadn't understood. She grasped so little about his political cures for all this. But why hadn't he done more? He should have done so much more!

She huddled in the embrace of the cold stone church for how long she was not sure, until she saw Ramsey galloping along the lane toward home. She wiped the tears from her cheeks before she ran out to meet him.

Chapter Sixteen

Ramsey was so nervous he could hardly eat his breakfast, though he was relieved that his mother and Rebecca seemed to be getting on. Clarissa had just given Rebecca a gift, an enameled vinaigrette, one of those fashionable little bottles in which ladies carried their smelling salts or aromatic vinegars to revive failing spirits or stop fainting spells. He could not imagine Rebecca ever having either, but the gift obviously pleased her. Still, he dreaded introducing her to his grandfather this morning.

He had put it off last night. Rebecca had been distressed by what she'd seen and heard in the village, beginning with news of Captain Owler. He had admitted to her that it was a mystery to him why the marauder had turned against the working poor he had once championed. But he did tell her that his strong stand for the right of workers to have labor unions, which the local squires and national government frowned upon, seemed to set off Captain Owler's protests.

"I don't fear him, whoever he is," he had said, trying to calm her, "but the villagers do. They cannot shake off years of superstition any more than they can change themselves in other ways. That is why, even if we share Shaker goods and skills with them, changes must come from the outside at first, not inside them, you see.''

"No, I don't see," she had answered, her face intent. "There is much they could do for themselves, if they just had a boost.''

"Charity, you mean.''

"No, just some suggestions, some guidance.''

"You've lived with the Shakers too long with someone always looking over your shoulder with rule book in hand.''

"But isn't politics just folks in power deciding what the rule book should be for everyone else? These villagers need to change their hearts on their own!''

She looked so passionately indignant that she reminded him of himself before he had learned that, unfortunately, real change had to be made by going through channels with powerful people. "Let's not argue now," he'd wheedled, and tugged her onto his lap to caress her. "Tomorrow we will have all day together, and I'll explain the background of this entire mess . . .''

It was a mess, so much so that, like a coward, he was hoping his grandfather would say something to help him explain things to Rebecca. He wished he could have accompanied her on her first visit to the village, but he trusted the Wemblys. They had been his first real introduction to the village too. And yet he did want her help and support in his struggles. He relied on her optimism and idealism to keep him from plunging into the abyss of desperate, bitter radicalism, those dark depths of himself he feared. He planned to explain today how she could help him—after they survived the interview with his grandfather.

"And I really appreciate the money Ramsey set aside to order Shaker seeds from Kentucky to begin communal gardens in the village,'' Rebecca was telling Clarissa, but smiling at him. "It's a start for the many things we hope to do in Sherpuddle which we were discussing just last night.''

"And we'll order more Shaker farm machinery,'' Ramsey

put in as he managed a smile back at her and pointedly ignored the way his mother's jaw clenched.

He knew Rebecca's personality had pricked his mother's inflated idea of propriety from the first, but he trusted Rebecca to win her over. Rebecca was right to insist he should not intercede for her, but let her do her own convincing.

He supposed others too would view his new wife as an oddity, even more so than they did most Americans. Her vibrant coloring made their creamy English faces seem muted. Rebecca had worn those deep Shaker bonnets for years, but reflected light on the ocean had heightened her color and brought out freckles that were anathema to a proper Englishwoman. He liked her high color, but it took some getting used to. Her wide eyes glowed as green as her emerald ring; her chestnut hair, worn unfashionably loose today, had red highlights in any sort of light at all. Everyone, he thought, both physically and spiritually, paled by comparison with Rebecca.

"I'm so excited about our picnic on the heath today," she told him after they excused themselves and walked upstairs together. She lightly poked him in the ribs. "A whole honeymoon week of funning and frolicking!"

Despite his tension, he was amused by the way she put things. Blast it, he hoped Rebecca still felt it was fun and frolic after she met the old duke and understood the mingled curse and blessing the man had been to him and the Sherbornes!

In the dim doorway of his grandfather's bedroom, they whispered to the faithful valet, Maxwell, then approached the bed. On good days, Maxwell got the old man up to sit in a chair by the window overlooking the rose gardens or at the table where he took most of his meals. His living as a recluse, emerging only several times a year for family occasions, was his choice, despite their proddings and pleadings. And now, with Ramsey's father dead, he wondered if the old duke would ever darken the halls of Sherborne House again.

Ramsey cleared his throat. He clasped his hands tightly behind his back.

"Grandfather, as promised, I have brought my new wife to meet you. This is Rebecca."

The glassy eyes opened just below the woolen skullcap. It seemed to Ramsey the man spent most of his hours now just drifting in and out of sleep. But his heart beat strongly and his mind was sharp—though more often with memories of the past than awareness of the present. And so Ramsey hoped the old duke would reveal to Rebecca what he had not yet brought himself to tell.

"A pretty one, isn't she, boy?"

"Yes, indeed she is, Grandfather."

"I am very honored to meet you, sir," Rebecca said, and briefly clasped the withered hand on the bed.

"Find her in London, boy?"

"From America, Grandfather, remember?"

"Rebels, the lot of them, but then, you'd like that."

"I love her very much."

"Hmph. Did you tell her how the Sherbornes got the peerage, tell her how your father's not restful in his grave the way you carry on?"

"I thought perhaps you would tell her for me, Your Grace."

"You young pups are all the same with your ideas of progress. By damn, real progress was enclosing all the land, turning out more food faster during the wars with that Napoleon fellow. Your father tried to bite the hand that fed the Sherbornes, but you want to out and out cut off that hand, my boy. Now, I've told you to bear up. Bear up, that's all."

"Yes, Grandfather. But there are some things too hard or too wrong to bear up to."

Ramsey glanced at Rebecca. Surprise and confusion made her frown. With one more long look at her, the old duke closed his eyes and seemed to sleep instantly. Ramsey knew better, but he took her elbow and guided her away.

"What was that all about?" she asked him in the hall as they strolled toward their suite. "Does he always scold and fret so?"

"He's scolded and fretted people all his life one way or

the other. But, as we told you, it was his service to King George that earned us the peerage.''

In their bedroom, she spun to face him. ''Exactly what service was it?''

Ramsey could see the quick brain working behind her lively face. He was trying to form the words to tell her when she blurted, ''You mean he came up with this idea of enclosing folks' land that is at the root of all these rural problems?''

He pulled her to sit beside him on the bed. ''It wasn't his idea, but yes, he oversaw its implementation in the entire west country, including Dorset in the 1790s. He used his own estate as the model for it, turning the forty farms leased to his workers into one. It increased the output of food for England, whatever it did to those who were now just laborers. All over England, men who loved but lost their land had no choice but to work for whatever poor pay was given or go to cities to work in the wretched new factories, or to starve.''

''They're practically starving now. And for that your grandfather earned the Sherborne dukedom?''

He could only nod.

''Oh, Ramsey, then your zeal to see this injustice undone is a quest to destroy your grandfather's great accomplishment!''

He crushed her hands in his when she reached out to him. ''And,'' he choked out, ''I lust for his seat in the House of Lords, which he hasn't filled for years. Then I would really struggle against that which gave us the seat in the first place! Even more than now, I'd be a traitor to my own class, my friends here in Dorset, my heritage and family!''

He searched her face. Did she frown because she grasped that they might have to live in London someday and mingle with those who she feared would not accept her? Was she disappointed in his ingratitude? He knew what family loyalty meant to her. But once again, the woman he adored surprised him.

''Your desire for rural change—your fierce need to protest—is it partly because you feel guilty for what your family has done?''

"Partly. But I am motivated by much more than guilt. That's a weak, pitiful thing compared to what I feel!"

"Yes, but in your desire for change and protest, and your wanting to make a public, political statement that you care for the rural poor—I mean, that isn't why you wed me, is it?"

He gaped at her. "No, never!" he exclaimed and gathered her into a fierce embrace. "I wed you because you were the most wonderful, unique woman I'd ever met! I knew your goals and spirit matched mine in what I valued most. I wanted and wed you not to make some statement, but for you!"

He felt her nod, her head pressed against his shoulder. She gripped him as tightly as he did her. But he felt her body heave with a huge sigh. Relief because she believed him? Resignation because she could not believe him? Recognition of the irony of their cause? All he knew was that, as before, he could not stop touching her, kissing her. He needed to possess her again, so that she, too, could possess him. As he tumbled them onto the bed, he knew they would begin their picnic in the depths of the wild heath very late.

As Rebecca held tightly to her horse's reins—Ramsey had promised to begin her riding lessons himself this week—they plodded slowly along into the heath. Each area seemed different from the one they had just passed. Here it was half heather and gold-tufted broom. Farther on green bracken vied with purple gorse. Occasional thickets of pines and fir guarded hollows where rainwater collected in ponds. Only the main road itself seemed straight and sure; random footways and bridle paths twisted off into thick foliage. Over the centuries, travelers had sunk droveways between steep banks. They passed ancient Celtic earthworks and barrows where Ramsey said festival fires had once burned in honor of their gods. Rebecca decided she must explore the books in the library. Just as she had suspected, Ramsey's education at the English schools called Eton and Cambridge outstripped her Shelter and Shaker learning.

"Oh, Ramsey, over there, a fox!" she cried and pointed at a flash of red disappearing into the depths of heather.

"That's what my father and grandfather used to chase here," he told her. "We'll stop at their old hunt lodge farther in. And there's another surprise I have for you—the heath is full of surprises."

It was indeed. It seemed to her that winds rose from it rather than from the turbulent sky above. Much of its vegetation was dark and seemed to breathe out coolness. But they spread their blanket in a sunny clearing before the old stone hunt lodge and lay in each other's arms after they had eaten their fill of the local Blue Vinney cheese with bread, cold fowl, and strawberries.

She took the opportunity finally to tell him about her difficult journey to be reunited with him. He had received her letter from Graham Springs, but something had gone awry with the one from Cincinnati. She explained her trials in visiting the Mercers and then in Cincinnati working at the Quinn Hotel to earn her passage to London. She told him how John Quinn had helped her and how she had almost come to blows with Xena Coates on the ship. Ramsey looked more stunned at each adventure she revealed, but he held her close and marveled at what he called her "Yankee ingenuity."

"John Quinn meant the money as a gift to me, but I'd like to pay him back," she said, pressed tightly against Ramsey.

"We will," he vowed, his voice muffled as he began to kiss her. "And we'll write your Mercer family too, so they know you are indeed wed to me as you claimed!" He pulled her down on the blanket into his arms and kissed her until she felt dizzy.

"It would be strange to really love out here," she told him, breathless, as she struggled to sit up. Her heart was racing, but something held her back from luring him on as usual. "Don't you ever feel this place has eyes and ears?"

"Don't you like it?"

"I do, but it feels alive with—sad memories or something."

He sat up beside her, his right arm thrown over his bent

knee. He raked his fingers through his tousled hair. "Sometimes," he admitted, "I think I feel the presence of ancient people who passed through here. The pagan tribes, the Romans who built the main road, the one that goes straight to Dorchester. I'll take you into town someday this week, if you'd like. It's only seven miles straight through the heath, but longer if you ride around."

She knew Ramsey would always prefer the direct, fast way. She went back to weaving a chain of trumpet flowers she had been working on while she had been talking earlier. "I'd like that. I want to see it all and understand it all."

"Such as? More about the enclosures?" he asked, his eyes still warm on her.

She nodded, pleased he had read her mind. When they had first met, she had felt she could discern his deepest thoughts and feelings, but here in the heath, she was suddenly not so sure. It was the only rural place where she had ever felt unsettled. Yet it was a fine escape from the manor house. With Tamar's sharp looks and her mother-in-law's assessing stare, she felt there were eyes and ears watching there too.

"Jenny said yesterday," she explained, "that she hoped I could help 'his lordship' get the Dorchester and London folk to mend their ways. So I'd like your *political* explanation of it all."

He explained a great deal more to her. How just one generation ago, love of their own plots of leased land bound the villagers to their landowners and the nation. Small farmers tithed—paid one tenth profit—from their crops or livestock, but they were proud and free. Working hard profited the farmer as well as the landowner, for men could save to buy their own land and, through several generations, perhaps work their way up to becoming rural squires themselves.

But after the enclosures, hope and loyalty began to die. No one could lease the small farms now surrounded by hedges. There was no gleaning, no more common fields and pasturage. Men were forced to labor for set fees on the master's fields, which were worked by increasingly modern machinery. Riots resulted in London, Wiltshire, Hampshire, and

Dorset. The gentry hired irregular armies backed by cavalry to put them down. So anonymous protestors like Captain Owler led rick burnings and left threatening letters for land-owners—until, for some reason, Captain Owler had turned against the workers.

"Maybe the landowners caught Captain Owler and decided he scared the superstitious villagers so much they would turn their own version of Captain Owler against them."

"Whatever happened, blast it," Ramsey cursed, gesturing as if he were making a speech, "this chaos never should have occurred in the first place! Parliament made slavery of Ne-groes in the British possessions illegal four years ago, but still promotes the enslavement of our own yeoman farmers, the backbone of this country!"

"I know your grandfather's part in this," she said quietly, "but what about your father's?"

"He tried to speak to his friends against the destruction of the little man. You heard the duke say he bit the hand that fed him. But his heart wasn't really in making a difference. Later, he agonized that I went too far. He was relieved to have me go to America with Will to seek economic methods of change."

"How did he think you went too far?"

"I spoke out in support of rural labor unions which were asking for better wages. I helped organize several protest marches in Dorset and one in London. Prime Minister Mel-bourne claimed I promoted violence and betrayed my class and the Whig party. Now King William is an old, ill man. His throne will no doubt soon go to his niece Victoria, who is but eighteen."

"So young for all that responsibility. And everyone will look to her with great hopes for signs of what's to come. You see, I know how it is for a young woman to have some-one else lay out her life with their rules and beliefs. And, sometimes, even though she disagrees, she goes along for what she hopes is the common, 'political' good. I suppose," and her voice grew very quiet, "it's why Jenny Wembly hesitates when her family tells her not to grumble. It's what the duke means when he tells you to bear up. I pity the young Victoria already."

"Exactly. Rebecca, I'm so glad we are in agreement on all this!" His warm hands grasped hers so hard she crushed her flower chain. His words echoed his mother's assumption that Rebecca agreed with her motives and methods, when she did not. "You recall," he interrupted her musing, "I mentioned that the Wemblys were the ones I first knew in the village. My grandfather said to bear up then too. Let me tell you about it, so you know my cause is not just fueled by the fact that my family led the Dorset enclosures."

He told her how he had been thrown from his horse when he was thirteen, trying to vault a hedgerow in a field. The fall had broken his leg and his nose, and his mount had run off. Jenny's father, Hollis, had seen it and ran to help him. Hollis put Ramsey into his wheelbarrow and took him back to their cot, where Hollis's mother, Betty, and his wife, Mary, sponged his face and tended him while a man was sent to the manor house with the news.

"Was Jenny there then?"

"She was a child barely walking. That day, even though I was in pain, I got a good look at the inside of a cot and the meager meal of horse beans—hoss beans, they call them—on the table. My parents were away, but my grandfather rode out to the village on one of his fine mounts and told me to 'bear up' while they put me in a cart and hauled me home to send for Dr. Mulvaney to set my leg and nose." He rubbed the crooked bridge of his nose as he spoke. "But I yearned to stay there longer with the Wemblys. They had tears in their eyes for my pain. And later, when I learned that the Sherbornes had been the cause of all *their* pain . . ." His voice trailed off and he looked away, biting his lower lip.

"I understand you better now. I'm so glad you told me all this, my love, the political and the personal," she said and hugged him, tucking her head up under his chin. "And thank you for understanding about my working to get to England.

We've both done things that rile others, but we had to take the risk to get where we were going."

"Then let me explain something else to you," he said. "How you can really help me get where I—where we—are going."

"Yes, I want to help! In the village, you mean."

"No, I mean with my friends, the local squires and their wives. Since I've spoken out, there have been rough spots between us. Rebecca, you have such a way with people. They need to be convinced to side with me, and thereby with the unions and the people in this struggle!"

"But perhaps I'm too different—"

"They will love you!" He seized both her hands in his again, his face impassioned. "I'm just asking you to be yourself. There is Geoffrey Prettyman and his wife, Penelope. They have four children and live in Higher Burton. Squire Randolph Viscint-Hewes and his Emmalyn have two young ones and hail from nearby Stinsford. Family mourning or not, we will call on them soon, and you will be such an encouragement to me. People are drawn to you!"

"Thank God, you are, at least," she said, trying to tease him, but her heart wasn't in the jest. She felt trapped between what his mother wanted, what he wanted—and what she felt was right. And now she must try to please and win over these friends of his, when what she wanted most to do was help the villagers!

"The heath will be an even more special place for me, Rebecca, now that you are here."

"Then let's explore the hunt lodge, even if it hasn't been used for years. Maybe we could even clean it up and make it our own special retreat!"

"Actually," he told her as they got up and walked around its wind-worn stone façade, "my father let Geoffrey and Randolph use it to hunt several years ago, back when we were all on better terms. Let's see if we can unboard the door."

They did and walked through the four-room hulk, but sneezed so much they did not stay long. The sun was low. She thought they would be going, but they lingered.

"What is the surprise you wanted to show me?" she asked.

"It has to get dark first."

"We're going to stay here in the dark?"

"Are you frightened or intrigued, my darling?"

"Both, but the moon will be a mere sliver tonight."

"We are going back on the road a way, up on an ancient barrow to see better. Besides, my horse knows the way back in the dark, even through the heath."

Her curiosity built as they packed their things and rode slowly toward home. Before the place where they would emerge onto the turnpike, Ramsey led them off the Roman road. They tied their mounts and, hand in hand, climbed a low Celtic barrow to wait, for what she did not know. But she appreciated the slightly elevated aspect. With a little imagination, she could almost pretend they were home on Concord Peak and she had brought him up here to see the moonbow. But all that felt so long ago and far away.

He stood behind her, his arms around her, his lips nuzzling her blowing hair. His hands caressed her waist, her hips, her breasts. She reveled in his touch. And then he lifted his hand skyward and tipped her back.

"Look up, my darling."

She did and saw the wonder of it all. She had never seen Concord's moonbow, but surely this would rival it. The clouds had cleared. Not only had the stars come out in the black silk sky, but each had a misty circle of light around it. And most marvelous of all, the stars shone different colors!

"It's like a meadow at night filled with glowworms!" he said.

"You mean lightning bugs? It's better than that. All those rings interlock with other rings of stars. But what makes the colors and the halos? Why, each one might be an angel watching over earth."

He chuckled. "I've heard it is a phenomenon caused by high mists drifting from the Bristol Channel. This place used to be my escape when I was a boy, whether things went wrong or right. I'd even sneak out here at night alone sometimes and never have a fear."

She understood completely. "What colors!" she murmured. "Pale yellow like honeysuckle and bright gold like daffodils."

"They are called daffydowndillies in Dorset."

"And lavender like chive blossoms."

"Or English lilacs. I've a notion you'll soon be distilling all the flowers in the gardens and using all the herbs. You'll win Mother and everyone over."

Though foreboding filled her again, she moved back against him. But she could not drag her gaze from the splendor of the skies. She felt so deeply moved that Ramsey had wanted to share this marvel with her. It was more precious than her other gifts, the vinaigrette bottle and even the emerald ring. It made her love Ramsey's heath with a fierceness she could not fathom. It was as if in showing her the stars above their Dorset home, he had given her the heavenly patchwork meadows and guardian angels of her girlhood once again.

"Will's just ridden in from London!" Ramsey called to Rebecca two weeks later. He had been out all morning working with the estate overseer. She looked up from reading one of Ramsey's favorite romantic poets on a sunny window seat in the long gallery. Tamar, hemming printed calico sweetbags in the next window seat, scrambled to her feet as Ramsey stopped to peck his wife's cheek.

"Come on then, milady," Tamar urged, "we'll have to fix your hair and change your gown."

"We'll be right there," Rebecca promised Ramsey. "You go on ahead. I know how much you've missed your best friend, even with those visits to see the local squires."

Those visits, polite and proper as they had been, had almost made Rebecca ill. It was worse than having to keep her mouth buttoned shut at Graham Springs. She had tried so hard to live up to her husband's expectations of her, but when anyone got onto the topic of the villagers staying in their place where they belonged, she guessed she hadn't kept quiet enough.

"Of course," she had gently protested last week over tea at the lovely Georgian brick home of the Prettymans, "I doubt if *we* would sit by and never protest such living conditions if we were in their shoes."

"But we're not in their shoes," Squire Prettyman put in.

"Sometimes they don't even wear shoes," his wife added.

"But they would wear shoes if they weren't in their shoes!" Rebecca had insisted before she realized she was ridiculously arguing in circles. Then too, she caught Ramsey's warning expressions, which said he had brought her here to charm and warm them, not plow them under with criticisms and wit.

She sighed at the memory as Ramsey went to greet Will and Tamar hurried her upstairs. How much she missed her own dear ones here amid these English people! She often wondered how Jeremy was getting on and what he thought of her for being a "lost sheep seeking the flesh in the world." She had written Christina and sent money. She hoped her big Shaker family would forgive her for her betrayal. How she longed for them to change their harsh attitude toward those who were different. She gripped the poetry book so hard to her breasts she bent the thin binding.

The library had turned out to be a treasure trove. She had read many things and had a long list waiting. Clarissa did not set foot there, so it seemed a safe haven where she could be herself. Ramsey had asked her to help clean out his father's desk there, and in doing so, she had learned more about the father-in-law she would never know. But that reminded her, too, of how much she still missed—and yes, loved—her own Daddy.

But despite these feelings and her efforts to help Ramsey and get on with Clarissa, she had carefully moved her plan ahead to try to aid the villagers. With Jenny's reluctant help, she had pruned the moss-rosebushes and planted cuttings along the church walls and back hedgerows behind the cots. She had paid the different families for each cutting she took, despite their evident mistrust of her motives. She had Old

Bet, who, she had discovered, was the widow of the village molecatcher, plucking petals with several other ancient dames. She dried the petals on netting nailed to wooden frames, which Jenny's betrothed, Charles Brimblecomb, had made and been paid for. The frames were spread along the unused shelves in the still room of the manor house, though Clarissa had ignored her hints that it would help to have the barrels cleared out.

Clarissa still insisted that roses were for gardeners to care for and that herbs were for cooking only, not medicines or sweetbags. Ramsey had offered to reason with his mother; Rebecca said no. After all, Clarissa at least was kind to her, and Rebecca must be grateful for that much, no matter how those echoes of the way her mother-in-law really felt rattled Rebecca. Tamar had not helped her confidence the day she blurted in dismay, "Oh, no, milady, I'm starting to say things like you, like Ken-tucky, when I'm trying to speak proper like the Sherbornes!"

Each time she opened her mouth, Rebecca wondered, was everyone but Ramsey thinking she did not belong? Would her attempts to help the villagers by making rose products for them to sell alienate her from Clarissa and Ramsey's friends—and thus from Ramsey too? Still, the first chance she got, she hoped to conquer Clarissa and the villagers by using rosewater for a flavoring as well as a sweet smell.

"You been walking slower and slower, milady!" Tamar protested, bumping her back to reality. "Don't you want to hurry down to greet Lord Sherborne's best friend? I hope Lord Richley's biding for a few days, as my brother Brant will be ever so glad to see him again!"

"I came to see how things are going with the bride and groom," Will told Rebecca and surprised her by kissing her cheek and taking her hands. "I was terribly pleased to hear you had made it all the way here from the wilds of Kentucky!" His piercing blue eyes swept her and seemed to approve.

309

"We've been very happy, Will, as no doubt Ramsey told you."

"I dare say; he seems almost too happy for his own good," Will teased. "Mistress Brimblecomb, how have you been?" he inquired of Tamar, who stuck to Rebecca's side like a glove to skin. "Have you seen Brant or your family?"

"Most times I go to the village with milady," she said, blushing at Will's attention. "But don't feel much home there anymore—but with Brant, o' course. After months awaiting the new marchioness's arrival in London—"

"Have you seen your maid's twin brother, my lady?" Will interrupted as the three of them went into the dining room to join Clarissa for luncheon. As the door closed, Rebecca caught a glimpse of Tamar's expression as it swept from sun to cloud. The girl's excitement at Will's visit—that intent look on her face even when she did not appear to look his way—she had seen it before in her own mirror and hardly needed to ask the reason.

Over luncheon, the four of them chatted about the king's ill health and the imminent probability of a new queen. Rebecca could tell that Will was taken aback to find she knew all about it, as well as about Whigs, and Melbourne. Will told Ramsey news about friends they had in common from Cambridge. He passed on the tidbit that someone named the Duke of Wellington belonged to his London club, called Crockfords.

Rebecca wondered why London clubs were permitted if people looked down on the villages' having workers' clubs, but she held her tongue. Still, it annoyed her when Will mentioned he'd lost money gambling at "Crockies" and paid as much as forty pounds a year for tobacco. She almost demanded how he could afford it. Ramsey had said Will had to make his own way in the world. Besides, weren't he and Ramsey supposedly trying to help the villagers, who were desperate to earn ten shillings a week for food and fuel? But she certainly did not want to criticize Ramsey's best friend when Ramsey was always so generous to her own best friend, Christina.

"The meal, as ever, was delicious," Will told the Dowager Marchioness as he patted his mouth with a linen napkin. "I have never seen a home and grounds so beautifully run as here, my lady. My visits almost, but not quite, make me want to find a lady to come home to myself."

"Do you have a favorite dish you'd like to have during your visit?" Clarissa asked, aglow with his compliments.

"I remember some delicious pancakes I had here," he reminisced after he had asked permission of Clarissa to light a cheroot. "Terribly thin things indigenous to Dorset topped with sugar and lemon and brandy, I recall. I dare say I could have ignited that sauce with a lucifer!"

"Mother's Shrovetide pancakes," Ramsey said. "You're only supposed to eat those before the Lenten season when you've been shriven of all your sins, my friend."

They both chuckled. "Sinfully delicious, that's all I recall," Will added.

"Have you ever eaten pancakes flavored with rosewater, Will?" Rebecca put in. "Remember that delicious flavor in some of the Shaker food? Ramsey, you remember! If the Dowager Marchioness wouldn't mind, perhaps I could have some pancakes made with rosewater. Then we'd have more than one flavor to enjoy."

Fortunately, Ramsey encouraged her, and Will joined in despite Clarissa's loud silence. After they ate, Ramsey and Will went out to ride the estate and Clarissa retired for a nap. It was later, upstairs, after she had told Tamar why she was going down to speak to Cook in the kitchen, that Rebecca's second idea about rosewater and pancakes blazed across her mind. It excited her so that she decided not even to question the girl just then about her interest in Lord Richley.

"Oh, you're going to talk to Cook about *those* pancakes," Tamar had said. " 'Twas a favorite dish when I was a wee one in the village. And heard tell the villagers used to make them years ago with sugar, cream, and eggs too."

Rebecca had stopped on her way to the door. "But that's

how they're made now. You mean, because villagers can't afford those ingredients anymore, they don't eat them?''

Tamar sniffed. '' 'Spose they still have them with oatmeal flour 'stead—instead—of wheaten flour and water with a pinch of ginger when they get it.''

"But the older folks would remember how good the earlier ones were,'' Rebecca prompted.

"That's right. I think the seasonings used to be tansy or rosewat—'' was all Tamar got out before Rebecca shrieked and clapped her hands.

No, she still did not exactly believe in Shaker signs, Rebecca told herself, but she knew now how she would show the villagers how much they meant to her and how her plans to make rosewater could profit them all. And surely this would be one way to convince her mother-in-law to let her make rosewater in the still room too!

"Come on, Tamar, I need you to help me carry some things from the kitchen to the village,'' she said as she headed to the door.

"But I thought those pancakes were just for Lord Richley to try!'' Tamar protested.

"And bring that bottle of rosewater in my dressing room in case we can't find any in the kitchen,'' Rebecca added as she darted back to scribble a note to Ramsey. She rushed out, not waiting for Tamar. She had to talk to Cook about exactly how old-fashioned Dorset pancakes were made. She had not been so excited about doing a good deed since the old days when she had hauled healing herbs up the heights of Concord Mountain.

The rosewater-flavored pancakes turned out as perfectly as Rebecca knew they would. She had insisted on helping Cook—whose name was Ellen Markwood—make the pancakes to her specifications. When she tasted one, it was wonderful. With the pancakes as a starting point for discussion, she could convince the villagers and later her mother-in-law to accept her help with the roses. They would grasp how it would benefit the village to sell rosewater for food flavoring. In covered baskets, she and Tamar hauled thirty pancakes with sugar and lemons to the Wembly cot.

Fortuitously, the Wemblys, Brimblecombs, and Brownes were all crowded into the cot. More people to win to her way of thinking! Rebecca thought excitedly. The Brimblecomb brood numbered six, not counting Tamar. Her twin, Brant, who had been in the fields the day Rebecca visited, was easy to pick out, as he looked so like Tamar. Charles Brimblecomb, Jenny's betrothed, nodded to her. Robert Browne served as the village smith and ironmonger when he was not laboring in the fields. He and his wife, Pamela, had four ragged-looking children. Then there was Old Bet, the only one who smiled at Rebecca when she entered.

Rebecca watched the surprise on the faces as she produced her pancakes and passed them around in their linen-lined basket. She sliced lemons to squeeze on and set the sugar jar on the plank table for all to share. Why, Aunt Euphy must have felt this thrilled the day she invited the mountain girl Becca Blake to partake of the wonders of China tea and nut bread! That had been one of the most momentous days of her childhood. If she could only be an Aunt Euphy to these people, or persuade them to trust her and let her help them the way Shelter folk used to trust Gran Ida and Mama!

She was relieved that there were enough of the pancakes to go around. The children gobbled theirs down and then ate their lemon pieces coated with sugar, rinds and all, before their elders grabbed the sugar jar back and Mary Wembly pointedly replaced it in the basket.

"Pancakes flavored with rosewater to mark the beginning of our partnership to produce rose products here in the village!" Rebecca told them with a smile when she noticed that the adults were barely partaking.

She watched them shift their feet and eyes; a few barely nibbled. "I wanted to remind all of you how good rosewater tastes in food, which we can make to sell. This is the recipe from Shrovetide, an old Dorset tradition . . ." her voice trailed off.

"Lent's agone, like lots o' things," Robert Browne whispered.

"Wha's she know of Dorset?" Mr. Brimblecomb hissed.

"You said you understood no charity, milady," Jenny said to her.

"Oh, is that it? This is not charity, but hospitality. You invited me to dinner the other day, and I could not stay. But I'm simply returning the kindness."

No one moved; no one smiled. She had overstepped somehow. They didn't understand that she wanted to help them and reach out for their help too. She wanted them to work with her, not for her. "Please, I did not mean to upset you. Charles, you helped me by building me some drying racks. Please explain what the problem is here."

He looked at Jenny, who nodded. His delicate pancake looked silly in his big hands. "Men's wages for men's labor's what's needed, milady, not fooling with roses."

Hollis Wembly spoke next, his voice controlled but his face a stone wall. "Cassn't be your life started out like us, like you told my Jen, milady," he explained. "Not an' be wed with Lord Sherborne!"

Rebecca stared at their sullen or sad faces. It was like trying to see through a hedgerow or into the tall, clipped yews encircling the manor house. They were shutting her out. They did not believe her, trust her, or like her. It was like standing before her Shaker family after she had betrayed them, but she had betrayed no one here! It was like the real feelings beneath her mother-in-law's gifts and "my dears"!

She yearned to stay to reason with them, even to argue. But all the pain of past rejections came pouring back to panic her—even that tearing agony when Daddy thought she had caused her baby sister's death, when she lost Mama, when Daddy gave her away to the Shakers, who turned on her because she was made to love Ramsey.

"I regret it mightily if I have offended you. Tamar, kindly bring the things," she managed, then hurried outside.

When she started back to the manor house, a voice behind her called, "Milady!" She turned, expecting to see Jenny or Tamar, but it was Tamar's mother, Martha, wadding her coarse apron in her hands as she approached. She had been blonde and pretty once, but it seemed her beauty had fled, living on in her children's faces.

"Yes, Mrs. Brimblecomb?" Rebecca said, trying to keep from breaking into sobs at the ruin she'd made of things.

"Been wanting a word 'bout Tamar. So fine she be at the house, aworking as your maid and all. But, milady, please doan make her come visit. Sh'up me John, that girl do make me wild if'n she lords it o'er her old mother, just the way she be, milady. Naught to do for it, cassn't be changed. Well, I be done with talking—save my breath to cool my soup."

"I'm sorry," Rebecca apologized again. Her voice broke. "I thought it would be good for her to make amends. But I wish we could change Tamar, working together, Mrs. Brimblecomb, just like I wish with all my heart we could change other things here in the village."

The woman nodded and backed away before she turned to hurry to the Wembly cot. Voices buzzed loudly inside now; they were probably furious with the new Marchioness of Sherborne for trying to force charity down their throats while she "lorded it over them" and lied to them about her past. But she had not done any of those things, had not even wanted the status her title evidently afforded her.

Her legs shook as she turned away. She felt shut out. Her plans to work with roses on both sides of the tall yew hedge seemed doomed. Her attempts to be the wife Ramsey wanted, the daughter-in-law Clarissa wanted . . . Fighting tears of utter defeat, she plodded back toward Sherborne House.

Chapter Seventeen

As if it would cool her temper, Rebecca sat on the banks of the River Puddle with her feet in the cold water. She had finally exploded at her mother-in-law. Fortunately Ramsey had not been there to see it, even though it was not an argument about him. It was about the housemaids—at least in the beginning.

Rebecca supposed it had started building in her that first day when Lily, the underhouse parlormaid, came in to light the fire in her bedroom. Lily White was another Sherpuddle girl who deemed herself fortunate to be a house servant. Imagine, Rebecca thought, a name like Lily White when the girl worked so hard at scrubbing she always had dirty hands and face! If times were better in the village, Lily would not think it so fine at the manor house. House servants weren't allowed to wed, and what young girl—including Tamar—did not want a husband?

When Rebecca had talked to Tamar about blushing when Will looked her way, Tamar had confessed she had always admired him. But she claimed she knew full well she could never set her cap for him. Tamar said she was only grateful that Lord Richley had offered Brant a position as a valet at his London town house. Rebecca knew well what it meant to be grateful when someone was good to one's brother. Adam Scott's kindness to little Jeremy was one of many reasons she had admired him. But Rebecca had felt a bit guilty that she had Ramsey when young women like Tamar, Jenny, Lily, and their countless sisters in service were trapped by economic hardship and manor house rules to be as celibate as Shakers.

She recalled Lily's sweet, sad face again. "Evenin', milady," the girl always said with a bob of her capped head.

"I could have lit the fire myself, Lily," Rebecca had told her, "but you do it best." She had watched the girl perform her many tasks. Besides emptying slops and chamber pots, Lily spent an hour each morning burnishing the steel fireplace furniture—grate, fender, shovel, poker, tongs. To clean it all, she used oil, then emery, then scouring paper on each inch of each piece. Rebecca's blood boiled at such unnecessary drudgery.

"Are you glad summer's coming, Lily?"

"Oh, yes, milady. 'Specially 'cause then all these things for ten hearths is just rubbed with goose grease and put 'way."

Goose grease and cold hearths, Rebecca mused now—pitiful reasons to be happy to see summer. She had also watched the painstaking way the girl dusted the carved furniture with a paintbrush, then removed any spots with stale beer. She had seen her dust with a goose quill the rows of library shelves, careful not to "meddle the books." Sometimes Rebecca read aloud to Lily as she dusted or as she labored to make the big beds upstairs, beating and turning the feather ticks and heavy mattresses and refusing to let Rebecca help her.

In the five weeks she had lived here, Rebecca had been deeply bothered by the exacting way Clarissa ran her household. Each task was a tiny spoke in the great wheel that repetitively revolved to keep that little world clean and perfect—and buffered from the real world of dirt and pain outside. Like anyone reared in a Shaker village, Rebecca appreciated cleanliness. But she thought it a sin that the servants were expected to complete such elaborate tasks every day. At least rotating their tasks would give their lives a bit of variety.

And so she had said to her mother-in-law this morning, "I wonder if I might free Lily from her dusting to work with me in the still room once or twice a week, my lady."

Clarissa peered at her over a triangle of toast. "White, you mean." Clarissa was still appalled that Rebecca stubbornly called servants by their given names.

"Yes, Lily White. I thought, really, she could just do the dusting—at least in our suite—less frequently. A few hours of her time would be so valuable to my plans to help the village, and I could teach her the alphabet while we're together."

"The alphabet? Whatever for? Besides, her days are quite full enough."

"What about those two scullery maids Cook Ellen oversees? They spent three hours yesterday whipping eggs and sugar with birch-twig whisks to get that icing to set, and everyone was too full to eat dessert."

"But that is their job and they are expected—expected by themselves, too, I assure you—to do it. This sentimental softness toward the servants will not serve you well as you begin to learn to run this household, Rebecca."

"*Am* I to run this household, my lady? No more than I'm to run my marriage, as far as you're concerned, or have a say in our relationship, I wager!" She jumped up from the table and started for the door.

"Rebecca, since we are clearing the air all round, it seems, I insist you not dirty your hands further by fussing with the village roses."

"By midsummer I'm fixing to make rose products from them."

"Dare I hope you intend them simply for the manor house or little gifts to send to your American friends?"

"For the villagers to sell, once they see it will work. Back home, the Shakers sent out peddlers and the profits were good, besides allowing folks to see the countryside."

"But my dear, *this* is your home now, and it simply is not done. Not the wandering about the countryside by those who have hardly been ten miles from home. And certainly not to *peddle* things, especially rose products, as you call them. I am certain Ramsey's friends with whom you have begun to associate, not to mention his London acquaintances, would be quite taken aback if they heard the young Marchioness of Sherborne was actually *laboring* with village girls to sell things, let alone helping Cook prepare pancakes and the like with rosewater in the kitchen. I realize, Rebecca, with your— ah, unique—upbringing, you are not accustomed to having servants and village girls to command, but, quite frankly, I, at least, expect to be able to tell the difference between you!"

Instead of digging herself in deeper, Rebecca ran out of the room. She tried to convince herself that she was proud Clarissa realized she didn't lord it over the servants. But the way Clarissa meant it, it was the worst insult. Clarissa's face and voice had stayed so controlled, Rebecca fumed, that it made her own outburst seem even more heathen. Ramsey would be so vexed at his mother!

Or would he? Rebecca mused. Who would he side with, if she told him? Blast it, she was not going to tell him! She did not want him torn between the two people he most wanted to please, even if she was. He already felt pulled asunder by his desire to help the villagers directly and the need to do things indirectly—politically, as he always called it. For all their sakes, she had to patch things over between her and Clarissa. But oh, how she would like right now to push her mother-in-law into this river!

She held her skirts and petticoats up to her knees and kicked at the water until it frothed. Though she felt close to Ramsey, she was divided between her desire to help him further his ideas and her lack of faith in them. But she supposed he felt the same about hers. He encouraged her plans for the village but urged her to go more slowly until everyone would "come round."

"Darling," he'd said just last night, "I'm not ignoring your suggestion we get everyone quickly involved in producing Shaker goods to sell. But it's too much to plan a communal hall, workshops, and a house for us in the village. Besides the expense, all that would threaten the progress we've made in convincing the local gentry to see things our way. It would be political suicide to make too many radical moves at once!"

"Just call me radical Rebecca, you mean. Ramsey, you say to be myself, but when I am—"

"I'm the one torn in two here! I want to do things your way, and I—we—will. But not yet. It will make me seem too eccentric, too separate from those we need to get backing for better wages. It's obvious the so-called Friendly Society of Agricultural Laborers needs support from the top, not the bottom."

"Then you see the workers you are striving to help as being the bottom of the heap—and me too if I stand with them."

"That isn't it at all, my darling. But this is not freewheeling America, and certainly not Shakertown where minds are open to equality and to bettering the community."

"I know it isn't," she snapped out before he pulled her into his arms. She kissed him back and held him tight, but in her own quick words she heard an echo—like Clarissa's— of an unspoken accusation: *I finally know my life here working at your side isn't what I had dreamed of and hoped for at all.*

But perhaps, she scolded herself, as she sat quietly now with her feet in the river, she was just too impatient with her new home, even with Ramsey and Clarissa. After all, Mama had not felt close to Gran Ida at first and they had turned out best friends. And it was obvious even the best marriages—

like hers!—needed fixing up sometimes. She sighed and lifted her feet out to dry.

Again as she sat there she tried to battle bitter homesickness for her past, for Christina, Jeremy, even Adam. But she was not going to give up! And she was certainly not going to solve any of her problems by just "staying to home" the way Mama had done to try to hide from pain. Bosh, that was just as good as locking it up inside you when it should have been dragged out and tackled somehow.

She yanked her stockings back on and jammed her feet inside her new riding boots. She lengthened her strides toward the house. "Never did to fret and sulk, best to talk it out," she chanted to herself in time with her steps. At first, she meant to avoid Clarissa's roses, for it annoyed her that mildew had attacked them. They had no room to breathe, any more than she did! Clarissa permitted things to flourish, but only according to her rules. But then Rebecca saw some bustle by the roses and walked over to gain more time to calm herself.

She peered over the waist-high damask hedge. Not only the two gardeners, but three other men whom she did not recognize were bent among the tightly packed bushes in Clarissa's roseries. She walked around to the gate and in. "Are you trimming them again?" she called to Turner, the head gardener. "I suppose with all the rain that mildew—"

"Plant lice, milady," he told her. "Mildew's one thing but these is worse. We're to brush them off and haul them away to be burnt."

"Plant lice?" she repeated and pulled her skirts tight to move among the bushes. She was familiar with most pests that could harm her Shaker roses, but lice? She bent to a china bush. She saw that the men were tending to individual leaves with soft brushes like those Ramsey's valet used on his coats. She squinted at the small, greenish bug the gardener showed her before he dropped it into a hemp bag tied to his waist. And then she saw the flaky white cast on the leaves the little pest had left. "Oh, aphids," she said. "But you'll never get them all that way."

"Dowager Marchioness's orders," Turner mumbled without looking up again. "Then we'll use lime water."

"But you won't get them all, and they'll come right back. The bushes should be dusted with leaves of powdered tobacco or sprayed with strong tobacco water. We did that in Kentucky, even once after smoking was forbidden for the brethren and we had to buy it special."

"Milady's orders."

Rebecca headed for the house again. Her cuttings in the village were flourishing. This time, Clarissa would have to listen to her and let her help. She even knew where to fetch tobacco, for she and Ramsey had bought some for Will in Dorchester last week and would not give it to him until he visited next time. If she could only think of a way to spread the tobacco solution on each crammed-in, severely cropped bush.

She knew where Clarissa would be this time of the morning. Rebecca hardly ever entered her rooms, but today of all days she must. She knocked on the door. When Clarissa called, "Enter," Rebecca thought to take off her bonnet, pat her blown curls into place, and shake out her black muslin skirt. Whyever wasn't the woman at least out overseeing the attempted salvation of her roses!

"I'm back, my lady, and regretful I lost my temper," she called as she strode into the prettily appointed sitting room with its blue-striped silk wallpaper. Not even glancing out at her roses, Clarissa sat erect at the oval table near the window. Her gray eyes narrowed as Rebecca came closer.

"I am sorry too, Rebecca, but at least we know where we both stand now. Actually, when you knocked, I thought it was my maid."

Rebecca bit back a retort about Clarissa's still not knowing her from the servants, but she forced herself to keep calm. "My lady, I want to help with the aphids—the plant lice— on the roses. At home—my former home—I oversaw their rescue from that pest more than once with tobacco water or powder sprayed right on."

Even as Clarissa gaped at her, Rebecca noticed she had been busy at a task. With a tiny pair of silver scissors, she'd been cutting a shape from black paper. It was—Rebecca could not believe her eyes—a silhouette of Rebecca herself, from the upper arms up, like the marble bust of Caesar in the library. In neat rows on the table were other profiles of her, evidently rejected for some flaw. And on the table lay a large open book displaying silhouettes of Ramsey and some other people Rebecca did not recognize, stuck right in little cut-out black frames the shape of tombstones.

"Oh, you are right clever!" she said.

"Now you've ruined my surprise for you," Clarissa muttered, pursing her lips. "I planned to give Ramsey one of you and vice versa when they were perfected."

"Are they black for mourning? Wouldn't they be so pretty in bright colors too!"

"Cutwork like this is never done in colors. And as for the roses, if it would make you feel better to take a brush to them with the gardeners, fine. I'm through chiding you. As for tobacco juice or powder dumped on them like some ruffian taking aim at a vile spittoon, I think not, though if you try something like that on the ones you're fretting over in the village, what can one say?"

Rebecca opened her mouth to announce that her roses were healthy. But she knew that each time she protested, she got into deeper trouble with Clarissa or with the villagers or with Ramsey. Her desire to be close to them all was tearing her in pieces.

"Thank you, my lady," she replied, fighting to keep her voice pleasant. "Rather than lose your lovely roses which all live and grow so tightly together, I will make an exception and help the gardeners."

She spun away and strode outside. This gown was just a walking dress, so it would have to do. But she knew the puffs over the elbows, which bloomed from the fashionable dropped shoulders, would be snagged by thorns. And the close-fitting sleeves with tight wrists, not to mention the boned bodice, would be a terrible bother for reaching.

All afternoon she struggled to brush each tiny insect into the bag at her waist. Her back hurt, her neck ached, and she silently cursed the cumbersome gown. But she was working among some of the most fabulously fragrant flowers she had ever smelled. Soon she moved by rote, her eager eyes and mind lost amid Clarissa's roses.

Their remarkable shapes and hues seduced her senses. A few big blooms billowed like ladies' skirts; the buds looked as delicate as folded butterfly wings. They ran from muted, pearly shades to lusty romps of color. But the roses seemed to grieve for their lost liberty—as tightly packed and forced into artificial shapes as they were, they were not leafing out or flowering as they might. She could tell the canes wanted to ramble, swoop, and soar. Despite the attacks by aphids and mildew, the flowers yearned to be free.

If she could save them, there must be a way to convince Clarissa to let her have some cuttings or try the crossbreeding she had mentioned. This brushing at them was interminable and, in the long run, ineffective. Something needed to be changed! She ached almost as much for the roses as she ever had for herself.

That night, cramped and exhausted, twisting and turning, Rebecca plunged in and out of sleep. Beside her, each time she woke, Ramsey breathed deeply. He had rubbed her muscles with something called Daffy's Elixir, though she protested it was not half as good as her Shaker marigold balm would have been. He had held her tenderly. But that did not save her from descent into dark dream after dream.

She was dressed all in black, the color of death. No, all of her was black, her hair, her face, her entire form, like a cutwork silhouette. She wanted to be brightly colored, but she was mourning the loss of her hopes and the death of the roses.

She tried to brush death away, but she stumbled and fell toward a huge open grave. She tried to cling to the bushes, but the thorns tore her skin. She bled black. She tumbled down the deep hole, twisting and turning.

At the bottom of the blackness, she heard the sound of scissors coming close. Snip, snip, they sliced at her hair, her head, her heart. Clarissa! The woman she should call mother, not my lady, was snipping her to make her fit some wretched shape.

She tried to climb back up, clawing at the soil lining the grave. Snip, snip sounded behind her. She screamed Ramsey's name; he reached down for her. He pulled her up, but she still bled.

"I love you, my darling," he shouted to her with grand gestures as if he made a political speech. "My Dorset smock is so tight, I almost could not reach you."

She saw now that they lay together in the heart of the heath, but no colored stars blinked above. She cried and cried. But then it was another man who came and opened his black bag and took out instruments to stitch her patchwork of wounds.

"You fell down a molehole in the village," the other man said. She could not see his face, but she thought she should know him. "Did you write Christina that Old Bet's husband was once a village molecatcher?" the warm voice asked. Shaking, she still held tightly to Ramsey. "Here, let me care for those hurts. Pretty sights and sweet smells hiding rose thorns, everyone catches it," the doctor pronounced.

She knew he was not making sense, but she felt sheltered now. "I tried to save the dirty, ragged moles in their cots once," he assured her, "but it's hard to help the creatures if they won't let you."

She smelled tobacco smoke on Ramsey, or perhaps on the doctor too. Was he healing her with smoke? It was not black but white and lovely, and she opened her eyes and found herself clasped tightly in Ramsey's arms amid the twisted sheets of their bed.

"My darling, you groaned and cried my name," he murmured, his mouth in her wild hair. "Are you all right?"

"Oh. Yes. Yes, just a nightmare."

They held each other close. Already she could not recall the dream, but she knew what she must do tomorrow.

"Ramsey, you said you've been pleased at my effort to get to know the local squires' families. More pleased, I think, than you've been when I try to befriend the villagers."

"It's only that village friendships might work at cross purposes, my darling. I think the scales of your efforts are best weighted on the side of convincing the squires that the villagers deserve help through support of the unions and better wages."

"I've been doing as you wanted, despite the fact I don't agree."

She felt him stiffen before he sighed. "I know. Was that what the nightmare was about?"

"No. But I want to ask you to help me save the roses tomorrow, even though your mother will not want me to, even if she gets angry." She looked into his eyes in the darkness. Their breaths entwined. If he would just give her this, perhaps later she could win more of his support in the village. "Ramsey, will you help me?"

"Of course, my love. It's only roses. I can handle Mother if she's piqued. And I trust my Rebecca to be sure everything will come out all right."

She relaxed in his arms. At least in this he was with her. And as for the other, she still believed she could win him to that too.

The next morning they were up before dawn. She explained her idea to Ramsey, and he made several useful suggestions. When Tamar came in, Rebecca sent her to the village to buy a Dorset smock, then turned to ripping the bodice and sleeves of her least favorite mourning dress from its skirt. She belted the skirt to her waist and donned the loose-fitting smock. Ramsey met her among the roses with a large iron kettle on a tripod in which they built a fire so they could move it from place to place among the bushes.

They worked steadily. Ramsey ordered the five men who appeared, brushes in hand, to stand by with old tablecloths he'd fetched to funnel and fan the smoke toward the bushes. Rebecca made the fire and crumbled the tobacco they had bought for Will into the flames. The breeze was just right to fumigate first the wheel rosery and then the basket one.

The smell and smoke soon brought Clarissa from the house. "Whatever are you doing?" she cried, addressing Rebecca, though Ramsey stood right beside her.

"Tobacco smoke will stun or kill them, my lady," Rebecca told her, hands on hips over the big smock. "You said no tobacco water or powder, so I took your advice. It's not like spitting now, you see, but like breathing heavenly clouds. These bushes are so cut up and jammed in here, nothing else could save each one."

Without waiting for further questions—or a scolding—Rebecca turned back to her work. The gardeners raked aphids an inch deep from the ground. When a bee stung Turner, Rebecca sent him to fetch comfrey from the herb garden so she could tend the sting. Her muscles hurt more than ever, but she reveled in every movement. It thrilled her to be working amid the roses and with Ramsey. She was touched to see how moved the men were that the Marquis of Sherborne labored alongside them. And once, when she put her hands to her hips and arched her back, she caught the pale face of the duke pressed to the window in his room before it disappeared. Well, she thought, he was always preaching that people should "bear up," and she had done just that!

Five hours later, when the task was done, she called the workers to her, including Ramsey, and washed their scratches in marigold and savory water she had secretly made from the herbal beds. She herself, as usual, had hardly a scratch.

"How d'you keep from it, milady?" Turner asked her, amazed.

"I don't know, Mr. Turner," she admitted. "Roses have

always been my friends." It was only then that she saw, on the other side of the hedge, Clarissa watching from the shade of a tree. In a flick of skirts and black shawl, she was gone.

Late that afternoon, Rebecca and Ramsey collapsed on the low stone balustrade behind the house. They reeked of tobacco smoke. It was in Rebecca's hair, clothes, and stomach; she was certain she would never forget the acrid smell.

Ramsey kissed her, then stood slowly. "I've got to go to the necessary, and then I'll send for something for us to drink."

"Mmm, thanks. I don't think I could move right now."

"As ever, you are a great success, my darling!" he called over his shoulder as he went inside.

She was pleased to hear his praise, but his *as ever* hurt. In a way, this was the first thing she had made a success of here. But she was doubly grateful to him because she knew he was tired. He had been working hard, not only overseeing the estate but speaking at local labor union meetings. She had even accompanied him twice, though that had been another burr under Clarissa's saddle. She sighed and leaned back against a stone urn. She breathed in the afternoon air, free of smoke. Her eyelids felt very heavy.

"Rebecca, you look a sight."

Her eyes flew open. Clarissa had come right up to her; the older woman's shadow fell across her feet. She stood quickly to not feel at such a disadvantage.

"But I'm a far sight happier than yesterday, when I thought you would lose all your lovely roses," she replied and dared a brief smile. "But plant lice, mildew, even black spot will come to kill them if they aren't planted farther apart to get some sun and air, my lady!"

"They have died before, and I've simply looked in the gardening magazines from London and sent for more."

Rebecca gasped aloud. "But roses are like longtime friends. They grow like family—if they are allowed to flourish."

"Yes, so I overheard you say earlier. Indeed, I see now you do know a great deal about growing things. If you think we need to take out a bush or two or trim them differently, just have the gardeners do so. And if you would like to have a plowman turn up a bit of the back lawn to plant a cutting or bush, that would be fine."

"Oh, my lady, that would be right fine!" Rebecca cried and almost lunged to hug her mother-in-law before she remembered she was dirty and reeking of smoke. "I'll plant garlic and rue among the new roses to keep pests off, if you'd like me to put in some for you."

"I suppose we could try it," Clarissa admitted with a sniff.

Rebecca's heart soared. Not only would the Sherborne roses heal, but perhaps her relationship with Clarissa would too!

"But one thing, my dear. You simply must find something else to wear than a laborer's smock."

"All right. Perhaps I can have a gown made with looser sleeves and waist. Could I perhaps borrow your maid Roberts for that? I notice that she has cleverly padded the shoulders of your gowns . . ." She trailed off when she realized from Clarissa's expression she had somehow spoken amiss again, when she had only meant to give in to Clarissa's wishes and to compliment her.

"My gowns are made to my preference, not to make some sort of protest that the Sherbornes can labor with the working poor!"

"I didn't mean—I am so grateful for your kindnesses, especially about helping watch over your roses and tending my own from your cuttings. You have given me several gifts, but the chance to share the roses is one of the best—a blessing."

"You are welcome," Clarissa replied, her face still as stiff as her stance. "Now perhaps you will be busier here where you should be and not flitting about the village or encouraging Ramsey's little speaking tours. Ah, here he comes, but I shall chat with him later."

Rebecca stood agape at being bested again, this time apparently by having accepted a bribe. She almost called after Clarissa to reject her gift. But for the first time Rebecca saw that, though Clarissa held herself erect and her gown was skillfully made, both shoulders were not padded. Her misshapen right shoulder rode much lower than her left.

Ramsey smiled as he surveyed the cluster of busy food booths on the Sherpuddle village green. Some of his happiest memories were of country fairs held here, which he had enjoyed with his boyhood friends Randolph Viscint-Hewes and Geoffrey Prettyman, who were here with their families today. Although they were only two months into the year of mourning for Ramsey's father, the old duke had decreed this traditional celebration in honor of the new queen.

" 'This day, Saturday, June the twenty-fourth, the year of our Lord, 1837, shall be a blessed day of celebration,' " the old man had dictated in the announcement Ramsey read to the restive crowd. The numbers were large today, because Squires Viscint-Hewes and Prettyman had brought in their own laborers in big harvest wagons, just as in the old days. After all, Sherpuddle was a larger estate than either of the ones at Higher Burton and Stinsford.

It was a sobering day for Ramsey, the celebration of the first ascension of a new monarch he could recall when his father and grandfather were not present. His mother had made a brief appearance on the village green and then had returned to the house, complaining of the bright sun and a headache. Ramsey was pleased to have his gentry friends here, for he was certain it was a sign that they were being won over to his position. Rebecca was apparently making headway with the wives, who seemed at least as curious about her as they were surprised by her American openness. Unfortunately, he thought, she was determined to win over the noisy villagers today too. He recalled that June twenty-third in the old days had been the raucous celebration of Midsummer's Eve, and he wondered how passions long pent up would find what Rebecca always called "releasement" today.

*   *   *

Rebecca felt torn between overseeing the table of rose products she was offering the villagers and tending to Emmalyn
Viscint-Hewes and Penelope Prettyman. She felt desperate to
convince the villagers to trust her, however much it meant to
have the goodwill of these gentlewomen and their husbands
to raise wages. These two new friends seemed very impressed
with her rose delectables, but perturbed to see her offering
the same to the villagers.

"Actually, you see," she explained to them, "I'm having
the villagers barter with village roses for these products, but
yours are *gratis*, gifts to friends."

"But Rebecca," the pale Penelope pursued, "did I not
overhear you might ask the villagers to sell these things outside Sherpuddle for profit? Even these conserves named for
the new queen?"

"If our husbands can urge others to raise wages," Rebecca
replied, "perhaps there won't be such desperate need for
folks to sell the work of their hands to survive."

"Dear me," Emmalyn huffed from the shade of her parasol, "they've already, obviously, survived for centuries!"

Rather than argue, Rebecca craned her neck again to see
how Tamar and Lily were doing, supervising the table of
goods. Despite Clarissa's coldness when she had heard this
plan, Rebecca had relieved Lily of her dusting duties yesterday, appropriated the still room, and prepared several rose
products to try again to prove her point to the villagers. Even
today, she was afraid it was seeing these items that had given
Clarissa a sudden, raging headache. Laid out on the long
linen-covered table she had ordered hauled from the house
were small jars of rose petal jam, rose drop candy, sweetbags,
and small bottles of rosewater for food flavoring. She had
cooked up a Shaker conserve of rose hips spiced with lemon,
ginger, and cinnamon and called it "Queen Victoria
Conserves."

"Four flowers for this here, or you not speaking down to
the likes of me?" Rebecca heard Jenny challenge Tamar in

a loud voice. Rebecca yearned to run over. Not only did she want those two to get on together, but she knew Jenny could be the bridge to the other villagers, persuading them to accept Rebecca and her ideas.

"Excuse me for one moment, please, and I'll be right back," she assured the squires' wives and hurried to the table.

Old Bet sat on a low empty ale keg at Tamar's side. As if to demonstrate how such tempting wares were made, she was madly plucking bartered flowers right on the spot. Rebecca laid her hand on the old woman's shoulder. She never flinched away when Rebecca touched her as her own mother-in-law did. So far, Old Bet was really her only village friend.

"Hello, Jenny," Rebecca said and shot Tamar a warning look. "I could certainly use your help when we produce more of these items."

"Cassn't. Too busy in the fields trying to feed the family and put a penny by to wed my Charlie. Not all can go to housekeeping in a big house—or any house."

Another worry Rebecca had been brooding over racked her: of course Jenny must resent her and Ramsey's having so much, as well as each other, while the wretched conditions in the village kept her from wedding her Charles. Rebecca saw Jenny's face set even harder as Penelope and Emmalyn trailed over with several of their squirming children and lady's maids in tow.

"I'm thinking," Rebecca told Jenny, not wanting to lose this opportunity, "in the beginning, these new endeavors would be done in the evenings or late Saturdays."

Jenny hesitated, her hand on a sweetbag. "You don't give up, milady."

"Nor do you, Jen. And I think that's one of the good traits we share."

"Well, really!" Rebecca overheard Penelope whisper to Emmalyn before their talk turned to buzzing she could not make out.

While their mothers were talking, several of the Prettyman

and Viscint-Hewes children ducked under the table. With giggles and squeals, they exploded out from under the white linen cloth. Women shrieked. Jenny shouted a warning. Visiting maids tried to grab for the rose products and the youngsters. But two large jars of potpourri bumped off the end of the table and broke on the storage boxes standing there.

The village women gasped and froze. The children quieted.

"Oh, bother," Penelope said. "Dear me, such a fuss over village flowers!" She pulled her children away, brushing at a soiled skirt.

"They could have been cut!" Emmalyn announced as if to scold them all, especially Rebecca.

"But fortunately their funning didn't cause any real harm," Rebecca managed, though she too was boiling with anger.

The crash had been loud enough to draw a crowd. Ramsey took it all in with a glance.

"No one hurt?" he asked.

"Thankfully, no," Rebecca told him with a beseeching glance at Penelope and Emmalyn that did nothing to soften their indignant faces as their husbands joined them and more whispering began.

"Good, no harm done then," Ramsey declared loudly. "Squires, with everyone here, perhaps it will be the best time for our mutual announcement." He gestured to Randolph and Geoffrey to join him. Their wives stood looking up at the men as they mounted a nearby wagon bed.

Rebecca felt relieved that the incident was past. She did not want to be the cause of dissension on this day that she and Ramsey had worked for so hard. It was essential for the landowners to stand together, showing the laborers that they were working for change. This announcement must mean the men had come to an agreement on better wages or at least on the idea of presenting a petition for them to Dorchester City Council.

Squire Prettyman took the lead, lifting his hands for quiet, and Squire Viscint-Hewes bellowed out, "Wages to be paid today, in honor of the new queen!"

Several people huzzahed, but the crowd seemed strangely quiet. "God bless'r, but what we needs is better wages every day!" someone called out in the hush.

Mutterings. More cheers than for the earlier announcement. A hubbub began to build.

"Who can bargain with such ingrates?" Emmalyn hissed behind Rebecca.

Men began to shout from the crowd. Fists shot aloft. Now it was Ramsey who put up his hands for silence, but he was mostly ignored.

"When we gettin' help to fill yer promises, Lord Sherborne?" someone shouted.

"Through the peaceful actions of your agricultural labor union and the backing of men like the three of us, change will come!" Ramsey shouted in return.

"When?" a woman's shrill voice demanded. It was Jenny, standing on a box and pushing Charles's restraining hand away as she cried out, "The only one here really understands us is the Marchioness of Sherborne! Least she tries to put doings with her words! 'Sides, she was araised up like us!"

How grateful Rebecca was for those words; how horrified at the faces of Ramsey and the men with him. She dared not even glance at Penelope and Emmalyn; she shoved away the thought of what Clarissa would say. But her eyes focused on the village women. Mary Wembly was nodding. Mrs. Brimblecomb had tears in her eyes!

"My wife believes in helping you, and I do too!" Ramsey's voice rang out even more strongly. "But we need a bit more time. And we would not be here with you today if we couldn't promise we will put 'doings' behind our words too!"

Rebecca clasped her hands tightly together, hoping, praying. They just had to believe and back Ramsey, all these people, especially the squires, who muttered behind his back. The crowd still seethed. Some yelled out random challenges that became a raucous chant. Rebecca recognized the swelling song of their Society of Laborers which she had overheard more than once in the village: "We raise the watchword Liberty. We will, we will, we will be free!"

From somewhere, her rose candies began to pelt the men. Gingerbread and meat pies followed. Ramsey stood there, shouting back, gesturing, while Randolph and Geoffrey jumped down from the wagon and made their way to their wives.

"This crowd's a headless monster!" Randolph shouted. "Get the children in the carriage, wife! This is the end of this asinine political coalition Ramsey wants!"

"He's worse than ever, as dangerous as these bastards! He's got to be stopped one way or the other," Geoffrey cried as they ran past, "or we'll have another damned French Revolution here'bouts! We'll have to raise our militia again, and—"

Abandoning their workers to ride the wagons back, the two families departed in the general chaos. Instead of trying to stop them, Rebecca fought her way through the crowd toward Ramsey. The food had stopped flying, but shouts and insults roared around her. Finally Henry Brimblecomb, Tamar's father and head of the Sherpuddle workers' union, jumped up on the wagon with Ramsey and shouted down the crowd.

"Go on back to yer cots now, go on! Peaceful, like Lord Sherborne says! The fair's done! Go on now!" he screamed and waved his hands.

When he saw Rebecca, Ramsey jumped down and pulled her tight to his side. "Our friends have fled!" she told him.

"I saw! And with all my hopes!"

But not mine, she thought. The politics of this tragedy might be done, but perhaps now Ramsey would see there was another way.

Chapter Eighteen

"S'hup me John," Martha Brimblecomb declared, "we been busy as a cat in a tripe shop."

"Cassn't say tripe when it smells like heaven in here!" Old Bet put in from her perch on a keg in the corner. This afternoon the other women had delivered Bet, whom Rebecca had come to think of as Sherpuddle's guardian angel, to the kitchen door of Sherborne House in a wheelbarrow to help with the bottling of rose hip jam and a sauce Rebecca had concocted.

The crowded room fell silent as each one bent to her tasks again: Jenny and her two younger sisters, Clara and Betty; Martha Brimblecomb; Lily White's mother, Dara, and sister, Sally. Rebecca had requested that Tamar join them, but the girl had not appeared yet—perhaps, Rebecca thought, to protest the amount of responsibility her mistress had given Jenny lately. Wonder of wonders, Cook Ellen even came in for a proprietary sniff, for she had let the skullery maids stir the two mixtures over her big wood-burning range after breakfast. Now the women carefully ladled the liquids into small glass jars and pasted on the labels Rebecca had lettered last night. Old Bet gave orders from time to time as if she, instead of the young Marchioness of Sherborne, oversaw the workshop.

"What's this one called?" Dara White asked as she held up a jar.

Once again Rebecca reminded herself that the school she wanted to establish now that the communal hall had been built in the village must welcome adults too. It was obvious none of these women could read the clearly written labels. She heaved an inward sigh at the turmoil the village school would cause between her and Clarissa, but it must be done.

"That one's Sauce Eg-lan-tine," she told Dara, pointing and sounding out the words. "The deeper-colored one is Rose Hip Jam. Jenny, you—and your Granmer Bet, of course— please watch over things here. I'm going out to the stables to see how the men are coming with learning to make brooms and hangers. I think his lordship meant to go out to look things over there."

Jenny nodded and even smiled. Her despondent slump was gone. The completion of the community hall meant she and Charles were to be wed in a fortnight, for they could live in two rooms on the top floor and oversee activities there. The hope of such happiness had changed Jenny's life and made her the link to the villagers Rebecca had hoped for. But for Rebecca and Ramsey, the price of that victory had been steep outside the village.

She seized her bonnet and wrapped her cloak around herself to ward off the brisk February wind. She longed for warm weather when the first Sherpuddle products could be sold by peddlers at fairs and when her first crop of crossbred roses would bloom.

As she neared the stables, she saw a lone rider rein in before the manor house. Even from here, she recognized Will. He had not visited since Christmas and wasn't expected.

"Ramsey, Will's ridden in!" she shouted. "Ramsey, are you out there?"

"Not here, milady!" Charles Brimblecomb called to her as he ambled to the stable door. "Gone to the village for somethin' or other."

She called her thanks to Charles and strode toward the front of the house. When she rounded the corner, Will had dismounted and Tamar was holding the reins for him. Will removed his hat, Tamar leaned closer and lifted her face, and they kissed.

Rebecca gasped and strode toward them. Will looked up and Tamar went red.

"I was giving your maid a kiss from her brother Brant," Will said. "He sends all of you his regards, but he's had a chill, and Ramsey and I can always share his valet, so I didn't bring him. Tamar, though, is grieved I delivered only a kiss from him and not the lad himself."

" 'Tis true," Tamar agreed and stood her ground between them as if challenging anyone to say more.

Rebecca looked from one to the other and decided that speaking to Will privately would be better. She could hardly call Ramsey's best friend a liar or a seducer, but she had the strangest feeling about these two.

"Welcome, Will. I just heard Ramsey's in the village. I'll send someone for him while you rest and wash up."

"No need. I will just walk out there and find him. I dare say we've a good bit of catching up to do."

"I was just looking for him too," Rebecca said. "I'll go with you. Tamar is late for helping the other women anyway."

At least Tamar knew better than to argue. With a pout and frown, she pulled Will's horse toward the stables as Will and Rebecca walked down the lane together. Outside the tall hedge, as always, Rebecca breathed more easily. At first they chatted about the weather. Blessedly, spring came early in mild Dorset. The meadow was alight with flowers peeking through the patchwork of snow: yellow primroses, snow-drops, and carpets of golden daffodils. She pointed out to Will an early-flowering quince. She did not tell him that

Tamar had annoyed her by telling her it meant bad luck this year: "If'n both buds and flowers pop at once," the girl had said, "something bad's coming our way." But even the flowers did not lift her heart, and it was not because she felt she must ask Will about Tamar. She dreaded his learning how much worse things were among the members of her family. He was sure to see it in the house, so she and Ramsey might as well warn him first.

"Will, I've been meaning to ask you something about Tamar."

His head jerked around. "I know she misses her brother and favors London," he said, "but with my meager bachelor household, I do not need another maid. She is best off with you."

Relief flooded her. She didn't know whether to laugh or chide herself for her foolish fears. Will actually looked afraid that she would suggest he take the girl on. Had Tamar been hinting at that to him? She saw now that the attraction was all on poor Tamar's side. If Will had designs on the pretty girl, he would hardly want her kept here. She felt guilty that she had mistrusted him; she must make amends.

"Rebecca," he put in before she could think what to say, "Tamar gets notions above her place. Second sons with gambling debts hardly need entanglements like that!"

"Yes, that's right. Only in America could a match like Ramsey's and mine happen. You see, I've become a realist here in England, Will. It's just that forbidden love always seems the sweetest, and Tamar is so impressionable, and quite taken with your—grandeur."

His expression changed from wariness to amusement. "Grandeur?"

"To her way of thinking. Like Ramsey was to me at first— grand."

"And not anymore?" he inquired as he drew out his flat filigreed box of cheroots. "No problems between you and Ramsey, I dare say?"

"No. I'm so grateful Ramsey never blamed me for the

chaos at the fair last summer. He said he had done as much to stir up the workers as I had, if in a different way. We're closer than we've ever been, since we are both working with the villagers to bring in the best Shaker ways. We've vowed to share everything now. And we've been fixing up the old hunt lodge for a retreat. I'm afraid we need it at times,'' she admitted with a shake of her bonneted head.

"An escape from his mother, you mean? Things are still tense in the house?''

Rebecca's voice snagged more than once as she began to explain. "Worse than you saw during the holidays, when we could all at least pretend to be preoccupied with the celebrations. Of course, she is unfailingly polite, proper—even pleasant at times, but she's bottled up her real feelings. She won't let me get close to her at all. She's furious with us for pursuing both his politics and my mountain and Shaker ways. She blames me even more than she does him. We both suffer for it.''

He struck his match on the sole of his boot and stopped to cup it in his hands and light his cheroot. He exhaled a plume of smoke which the wind snatched away. "She'll come round when things calm down and she has a grandchild to coddle,'' he said.

She walked on, then spun to face him again, tugging her shawl closer.

"Rebecca, sorry if I spoke out of turn,'' he said.

"We want a child desperately, it's true. But that isn't—well, right now, it's not working out any better than anything else.''

"What other things are not working out?''

"Our relationship with Ramsey's mother isn't the only one we've sacrificed. The Prettymans and Viscint-Heweses are barely speaking to us, and they're still stirring up other land-owners. I was trying so hard to be friends with them as well as the villagers, but poor Ramsey has lost his childhood friends, and I know how that hurts. At least he has you!''

"Yes, he has me and you do too.'' Will squeezed her

shoulders with his free arm as they started off again. "But if you've been accompanying Ramsey on his local speaking tours, as he wrote me, no wonder his mother is fretting and the landowners are up in arms."

"I just want Ramsey to know I haven't abandoned his ideas even though he's supporting mine now. I don't want him going off chasing his rainbows alone the way my daddy did once. I just—I don't want any more folk I love bolting like these blasted skittish cows always do!" she protested even as the cattle shifted away from them along the fence.

He eyed the herd with a nervous sideways glance. "Now, listen, Rebecca. I will certainly support anything you and Ramsey do, but I think you will lose his mother and *all* Ramsey's friends if you become part of the new London protest march he's planning. There are powerful factions in London dead set against it too. Even—especially—Prime Minister Melbourne."

"Ramsey's really considering London again? Are you certain? He didn't tell me."

"Sorry again. I assumed, since you said you were even closer now and shared everything—"

"He probably didn't want to worry me. But I should have known he wasn't really content to change the hearts of individuals in a small village. He still wants sweeping, far-reaching results, but the impact of that here would be awful. What would Captain Owler do then, let alone Ramsey's mother?"

"What has that sneaky bastard—pardon my language, Rebecca—been up to lately?"

They were about to walk into the heart of Sherpuddle, where others could overhear, and she slowed her step. "You know, I've not yet laid eyes on him, as if he wasn't even real. But he's been trampling village gardens at night. Breaking church windows and pulling up rosebushes. If only his visits were at all predictable, you and Ramsey could lie in wait for him while you're here this time! And Will"—she grasped his sleeve—"I worry that Captain Owler could actually be one of the local squires. He sits a horse well, the villagers say. He obviously targets my works and Ramsey's now rather than riding farther afield as he used to. But when I brought up the possibility that it could be someone close to us, Ramsey lost his temper, and . . ."

"And what?" Will prompted.

She shook her head. She could still hear Ramsey's roaring protest now: "Don't you think I know that, Rebecca? It could be anyone in this entire blasted area, anyone who is in league with my old chums! For all I know, the way mother is acting lately, *she* could have hired Captain Owler!"

"You don't mean that! She would never do something so—so improper! I only brought it up because I overheard Randolph and Geoffrey's threats when they left the fair that day. I'm just trying to help . . ."

But she could not help him when, after that argument, he descended to the depths of depression. It took two days for his black mood to lift. Yes, they were united in purpose and in love and in their determination to conceive a child. But when he sank into such despair, she almost felt she'd lost him, as if she wandered the thick heath on a starless night, searching for him—

"Rebecca, you look as if you are going to cry. Cheer up for an old friend. After all, it is St. Valentine's Day."

"It's what?"

"I dare say you've still a lot to learn. You just ask Ramsey about it then if he has forgotten. And here is something to cheer you. I brought you that colored paper for the Dowager Marchioness you asked me to find. She will know you were thinking of her with love and concern. And I have been distributing your Queen Victoria Conserves around a bit, and the London ladies love them."

"Do they? That is good news! If there's a broader market for them than Dorset—after Penelope and Emmalyn evidently refused to recommend them—that could mean more money for the village! And that could ease the pressure of having to get money through higher wages. Now I can tell Ramsey about that!"

"You mean he did not know already?" he said and gave her a narrow-eyed look.

"He told me that what I did with the rose products was fine with him and he would oversee the rest," she protested. Still, Will was right to look askance on her claims that she and Ramsey shared everything. He had not told her about his London plans. And she had thought he was too busy to hear about her roses.

She glanced up and saw the two youngest Browne boys swinging on the sheepyard gate. "Now keep that closed, you two!" she shouted angrily. "I told you more than once before the sheep will get loose again!" Too late she realized she had taken her feelings out on them. But they only giggled and scampered away.

She proudly invited Will into the new communal hall, built between the Brownes' and Wemblys' cots. When she did not find Ramsey there as she expected, she showed Will around. The ground floor encompassed a large combined workshop and dining room, with several smaller storage rooms in back. No separate working or dining facilities here for men and women as in Shakertown! She explained that Jenny and Charles would be overseers here as soon as they were wed.

They glimpsed Ramsey behind the hall and went out to join him. With several village men, he was proudly surveying the first two dump wagons, which village carpenters and the smith had built to the Shaker specifications brought back from America.

Ramsey was so happy to see Will, Rebecca thought as she watched them greet each other. Again she sympathized with his feeling that his local friends had abandoned him. Will admired the wagons with the clever dumping device, then helped cover them with canvas before the village men left for other tasks.

"I fear I've gotten you in a bit of trouble with your wife," she heard Will say. "I let it slip that today is St. Valentine's Day, and you have evidently not bought her a thing!"

Ramsey smiled guiltily at her. "I have planned something

343

special for her later,'' he said and slapped Will's shoulder. "Something private, so don't be asking what it was tomorrow at table with Mother sitting there, old chum!''

Their laughter mingled with hers. It was good to have Will back.

"And, pray tell, where are we going, deserting our guest so early after supper?'' Rebecca asked Ramsey as he led her upstairs to their suite after only four hands of whist with Clarissa and Will and a hasty good-night.

"Will is almost family, not a guest. He and Mother enjoy each other's company. Besides, maybe he will put in a good word for us with her,'' he said lightly.

She smiled at his joke, then giggled as he shooed her up the stairs with his hand on her hip. It had been so good at supper to have a new conversationalist who knew to avoid touchy issues. Even her Valentine's gift of colored paper to Clarissa had not gone over as well with her mother-in-law as Will's clever compliments about the meal.

"Shall I call for Tamar?'' she asked Ramsey in their bedroom.

"I am lending Will a valet, so I shall lend you one too—me,'' he told her with a mock leer at the bodice of her black gown. She laughed again. She turned her back to him and let his big fingers fumble with the tiny hooks while she unpinned her hair.

"I'll wager,'' she said, "we'll be long out of mourning before your mother gets to any of that colored paper—unless she uses it because Will delivered it.''

"Now, no fussing about anything tonight,'' he said sternly and gave her bottom a slap as he sat down on the bed to remove his shoes. "Behave, or you'll not even get your surprise before I take it off you.''

"What surprise?'' she demanded. "Something to wear? But I had the distinct impression I had no need of garments right now!'' She dropped her gown in a pool at her feet, untied her petticoats, and kicked it all away. "What did you manage to think up for me when Will said it was Valentine's Day and there you were without a gift?"

"Without a gift?" he said with a laugh as he tossed his garments to the floor after hers. "I believe my sweet American didn't even know there was such a thing as a day for lovers."

"Don't try to change the subject, English! In America, every day is for lovers!" she insisted and pushed him back on the bed.

He hooted even more loudly and she did too. It had been too long since they had frolicked like this, she thought. Whatever Valentine gift he had promised, they both promptly forgot it as they kissed. Naked on the bed, which the maids had not yet turned down, they rolled over and stared deeply into each other's eyes.

There was as ever between them that hush before they loved, when all the possibilities between them crackled in the air like summer lightning. She thought of that day before the storm when they had first declared their love in the Shaker meadow.

"You have made me so happy, my love," she told him as they lay skin to skin and soul to soul. A single tear of joy ran from the corner of her eye. "Ramsey, you have made me whole. Often I feel we are really one person, one desire. If only we could make a child!"

"But if we never do, our love will be complete. Our love will be enough," he whispered in her ear as he began to move against her with sharp desire.

Their lips lingered together, then parted so their tongues could delve deeper. They gave love, which fed passion. Their hands clasped and caressed; curves to angles, softness to strength, they blended bodies and hearts and hopes. She wrapped her arms and legs, her entire life around him. Their mutual demands and needs magnified and burst to shards of brilliance in her body and her brain.

Later she lay in his arms, sated, drifting. He had tugged the coverlet up over them as their bodies cooled. She was not certain he was asleep, though his eyes were closed. She studied the heavy lashes smudging his high cheekbones. It was dark outside; she had heard Will walk along the hall to his room long ago.

"I'm not asleep," he answered her unasked question. "What are you thinking?"

"That that was the only Valentine present I ever want from you—your love, I mean."

His eyes flew open and focused. He shoved the coverlet away. "But I really do have one for you!" he said and groggily got up. She reached for him too late. "I bought it for you in Dorchester last week and was going to give it to you some special night like this. It matches your eyes and your ring," he added as he produced a jade-green *robe de chambre* from one of the drawers of his bureau and padded back to hold it up for her. Even in the wan lantern light, it shimmered like the green bluegrass hills. She slid across the bed and touched his cheek as she stood next to him on the soft carpet. Then she slipped into the cool sleekness of the robe and pulled the sash tight around her waist.

"In our bedroom, together," he said, his voice gone husky again, "we will not wear mourning. And Rebecca, even if we never have a child, I rejoice in our marriage. We share all things and always will."

She nodded as she stared wet-eyed up at this man she so adored. "I have a little confession, then," she said. "I asked Will to take some conserves back to London last time, and he said the ladies loved them."

He did not seem a bit surprised or upset. "Of course they did," he declared. "They are delicious. You should send some to their namesake."

"The queen, you mean? Now, that would be something! But I thought if we could only open up a London market that might mean folks here would want them—even if Penelope and Emmalyn are probably telling everyone they're choking on them. So, I guess, I too thought London is the place to try things out on a bigger scale."

She held her breath, waiting to see if he would tell her about the new political plans for London Will had mentioned. But he seemed not to be listening. His eyes were skimming the new robe. His hand lifted to stroke her hip, where his eyes held. Her insides coiled tighter again. That look from him, a touch, the love that leaped eternally between them was all it took.

She leaned into him where they stood beside the bed. He cradled her curves against his strong body. Then he set her gently back and slowly untied the robe. He parted it, and the silk whispered down her shoulders to the floor. Whatever she had asked him, whatever he had not answered, whatever doubts she had about him faded. They were always one, whatever different thoughts and hopes they had.

"Come over to the window and let me see you in moonlight like this!" he said.

Like a sleepwalker, she went. She looped her arms around his neck. She stood proudly for him, then—

"Ramsey, what's that glow in the southern sky? It can't be the moon."

Slowly he turned to look out. He bent low to press his face to the window. Over the line of tall hedge beyond the front lawns, the sky was golden like a sudden dawn.

"I don't know," he said and ran for his scattered clothing. "It looks like fire in the village. Get dressed and wake the servants. I'll get Will."

In trousers and shoes, carrying the rest, he ran out in the hall bellowing for Will. Feeling in her wardrobe, she found her work gown, the easiest to get into. She covered the mostly unhooked back of it with a cape and jammed her feet into shoes. But by the time she was out in the hall, Will and Ramsey had yelled up the steps for the servants.

"Takes too long to saddle horses!" she heard Ramsey yell as they clattered down the stairs, holding lanterns. She started down behind them as she heard the front door bang and the servants moving about.

Outside, the moon and the glow in the sky made enough

347

light to see by. The men had abandoned their lanterns on the gravel drive. Holding up her skirts, she raced after them. Without stockings, her shoes soon rubbed her heels raw. Despite a light frost, she kicked them off and tore on. The hedges loomed larger, blocking out the unearthly light, but when she ran through them, she saw. At the far end of the village, a building burned. As she raced closer, she saw that it was the Wemblys' cot blazing like a torch next door to the communal hall.

In the village, folks shrieked and shouted. "Captain Owler, he done this!" she heard someone scream. "Saw him clear in moonlight on that same black horse with the white feet!"

She felt the next shock like a fist to her stomach. Not only the cot burned, but the first floor of the communal hall seethed inside. When she arrived, breathless, she saw that one of the two front windows had been broken and a torch tossed in.

"More water buckets! Water!" Ramsey and Will were shouting.

People already ran with kettles, skillets, anything to slosh water on the flames. Rebecca seized Ramsey's arm. "The Wemblys?"

"They're out! The son of a bitch woke up the whole village riding through before he torched things!"

"But if the cot's gone, we've got to save the hall!"

"Thank God there's no wind. But if the thatch on the next cot goes, the whole village might! It's only the wooden floor of the hall aflame so far! It will have to wait!"

She found a washtub and carted it back and forth with Dara White, but their efforts seemed futile. The fire ate away at the cot and leaped to the thatch of the Brownes' next door. If only she could cover the roofs with something wet. If only they had a river of water to douse the flaming floor of the communal hall before it devoured all their dreams for the village! As she and Dara raced for another tubful of water, she saw Old Bet silhouetted against the conflagration, wrapped in a tattered blanket. To have so little, Rebecca thought, and then have it taken away . . .

And then it came to her. She dropped her side of the tub and lunged for Ramsey; Will turned toward her too, his face demonic in the leaping light.

"The canvas over the dump wagons," she screamed. "We can wet it and cover the thatch. And if the wagons would just hold water long enough to drive them to the front door and wet that floor—"

She ran behind the men as they tore away. Ramsey seized on some of the villagers, shouting orders. Charles Brimblecomb appeared at his side. Men shoved and pulled the wagons toward the well. Women, children, everyone drew water to wet the canvas, and the men dragged it away to drape over the smoldering thatch. But when they tried to fill the wagon, its boards so tightly fitted to hold grain, water trickled out. It ran through the dump gate like a sieve.

"Was there more canvas on that roll?" Ramsey shouted to Charles.

"Aye, enough."

"Line the wagon with it! Some of you get on board to hold the sides up to make a big sack!"

They worked on, men and women, all of them together. When it was over and the fire's glow gave way to red dawn, they surveyed the damage Captain Owler's torches had wrought: the Wemblys' cot was smoking rubble; the Brownes' charred roof had tumbled in. The floor of the new communal hall was devastated and smoke had blackened the walls and ceiling, setting back the building's use for weeks. And a crudely lettered note nailed to a tree by the church warned, "NO MORE RABBLE-ROUSING. BE CONTENT OR BURN!"

Exhausted, wet, soot-smeared, Ramsey, Will, and Rebecca huddled over the note. Finally Ramsey cleared his throat and wiped his dirty hand across his forehead as he handed it to Rebecca. "Keep it safe for evidence when we find the wretch and hang him!"

" 'Rabble-rousing,' " he said in a low voice to Will. "A

word that blasted *Dorchester County Chronicle* has used more than once lately when they weren't accusing the union of treason.''

''That clue narrows down the search to anyone in the whole damned bloody area,'' Will muttered. ''Hiring your own militia to catch this villain will cost a pretty penny.''

''No militia, but I am going to hire guards, I'll tell you that!'' Ramsey said, his voice both weary and angry.

''Maybe Captain Owler has done his worst,'' Rebecca whispered, but neither of them responded. She looked up to see Jenny standing some way off, wiping her eyes on the sodden, soiled skirt of a too-small gown someone must have loaned her. Rebecca went over to her and took her hands. She looked slumped and stooped again, and Rebecca knew it was not only from exhaustion and loss—at least not the loss of her old family cot.

''We will repair the hall as soon as we can, Jenny. And all our hopes, too, all we were starting to believe in together! I see no reason for it to delay your wedding.''

''Thankee, milady, but Charlie and I cassn't go to housekeeping now, my folks without a place.''

''Until the villagers can build a new cot, your family can use extra rooms at the manor house.''

Jenny's head jerked up. ''At the manor house? Oh, cassn't, milady, no matter what!''

Tamar appeared by Rebecca's side as if she'd been listening. ''My mother says the Brimblecombs and others will take them all in, milady. To make my mother happy—and his lordship's mother, too—perhaps 'tis better than their staying in the house.''

Rebecca's eyes met Tamar's. She was so glad to see the girl helping, and she had to admit it was good advice. It lifted her spirits to know that Tamar had obviously been talking to her own mother, and that she cared how Rebecca was getting on with the Dowager Marchioness. She almost hugged the girl. All her dark feelings about Tamar and Will, all the anger about her snobbish stubbornness evaporated with the rest of

Rebecca's strength. Right where she was, she sat down hard on an upturned bucket.

"And the Dowager Marchioness sent down coffee and bread and jam," Tamar said and pointed at the family market wagon being unloaded before the church.

"If she didn't send it for everyone, we don't want it," Rebecca said sharply, then regretted her words and tone. What was wrong with her? She felt dizzy with exhaustion. "Or at least, be sure the Wemblys and Brownes are tended to first, please, Tamar," she amended.

"No, her ladyship sent enough for everyone, near most all the coffee and bread in the house. And she said she'd be here soon herself."

Rebecca looked back at the wagon. Tears blurred her vision. Lily and her mother poured a huge, steaming tub of coffee into an urn while men unloaded boxes of cups. Piled plates of toast and mounds of butter appeared.

Clarissa, Rebecca thought, did care about the village. She had opened her larder and her heart. Tamar was talking to Jenny, who had stopped crying. Will and Ramsey and the village men had worked side by side.

Rebecca smiled through her tears as Ramsey came over to take her hand. "I don't suppose," she choked out, "that fiend Captain Owler would be pleased to know that bonds of human kindness came out of his blasted conflagration."

Ramsey gripped her hand more tightly. "I swear, I could kill him with my bare hands," he muttered between clenched teeth as Will came to join them, but even Ramsey's hatred could not dim the brightness of new dawn for Rebecca. Surely now, after this tragedy, everyone would get on much better.

Chapter Nineteen

"I am certain I can trust the flower arrangements to you, my dear," Clarissa told her with the merest glance at the sketches Rebecca had labored over. "You do such a nice job with that."

The two of them sat in the morning room going over plans for the dance at Sherborne House next week, Saturday, August third. They had been planning it since the end of formal mourning for Ramsey's father, but there were many last-minute tasks yet to do.

This large gathering of Dorchester gentry was supposedly to celebrate Clarissa's birthday and had been her idea: she wanted to return her family to everyone's good graces. But the occasion was partly for Ramsey's benefit too. He still felt ostracized by his old friends, and this would be a conciliatory gesture to them. He had seemed willing enough that the dance should take place, Rebecca noted, once his various endeavors to discover Captain Owler's identity had failed.

Then she learned why. Not only did he hope for a reprieve with his friends, but he hoped someone with knowledge of Captain Owler would give himself away in the elegance of a social affair. Since Ramsey had hired village guards, the night marauder had lain low of late, but no one believed he had given up.

Rebecca felt this dance was for her too, though no one said so. She wanted to reestablish neighborly ties to the Prettymans and Viscint-Heweses. She wanted to show Clarissa that she could shine in a social situation. And with her roses on display and village products for favors, she hoped the fledgling Sherpuddle industries would receive a boost. How sad that her rose sauces and Queen Victoria Conserves were doing better in distant London than hereabouts! Even the brooms, hangers, and dump wagons were selling better outside Dorset, because a local ban on Shaker products was a ban on Sherborne politics. At least her infant crossbred rosebushes were flourishing, but sadly, there was still no sign of a human infant to love. As ever, she tried to push that disappointment from her mind.

"I'll be happy to take care of the flowers, my lady, but I want to discuss it all with you," Rebecca persisted. "You do such a fine job decorating the house, and I'm hoping to enhance that by working with you."

"I do strive to make things perfect, but it's been quite impossible since Ramsey's father died."

Rebecca sighed inwardly. Once again, did she imagine the unspoken import of Clarissa's words? In her inimitable way had she not implied that striving to make things perfect had been quite impossible since Rebecca had come? This time, despite the demands they faced this week, Rebecca decided not to let the implication pass.

"I'm afraid, my lady, I will never be perfect. The world's not that way either, you know."

"Indeed not. How very strange those Shakers of yours thought they could earn heaven on earth. Quite impossible. And don't fret that that blackguard Captain Owler will dare to make a shambles of our lovely party!"

Rebecca's eyes darted to her mother-in-law's. "You act as if you have privileged information."

"Hardly. It is only that after all this work we've done, he dare not intrude! Besides, Ramsey's convinced with all the invitations that have been accepted that the culprit will be here on his best behavior partaking of our hospitality and not abusing it!"

At least, Rebecca thought, they shared their detestation of Captain Owler, if not their anticipation of the occasion. Nearly sixty people were coming, and having even a few guests about always made Rebecca realize how different she was. Whenever she met people here, their reactions ranged from mild amusement to smothered outrage at her past, her speech, her ideas. And she knew there would be more provoking if polite inquiries about when she was going to "stay home to start a family." But for those she wanted to please here, she would give her all for this momentous event.

"I'm sure everything will be a success, milady," Rebecca said as she gathered up her things. She excused herself and walked slowly toward her suite. The long, empty hall echoed with her footsteps. Maybe, she thought, it was bothering her too that this gala would make any Shelter frolic or Shakertown celebration look pitiful. Gilt-edged invitations, silver and porcelain, a hired orchestra from Dorchester, and new garb for everyone seemed to make the gatherings in her memories fade away to nothing.

Her eyes misted as she went into the bedroom and gazed out the window from which they'd seen the fire last winter. The cot and hall had been rebuilt and repaired; Jenny and Charles were happily wed. She felt eternally blessed to have Ramsey. But, just as with Mama, who had loved Daddy so, there was pain mixed in too, and longing for things she might never have.

The night of the dance was warm. Tamar guided Rebecca's mint-green and pale pink satin gown carefully down over her elaborate coiffure. The massive weight of her auburn hair was combed back, then coiled up into loops and braids on her crown—she needed no fashionable false hair. Curls flourished at her left temple, and pale pink china roses adorned her right one. Pearl drop earrings and a matching necklace seemed to weigh her down, but she stood straight and tall, hardly breathing while Tamar fastened her into the garments. She was so used to her loose-fitting garden dresses that she felt trapped in the off-the-shoulder gown, boned bodice, and petticoats. When she walked, the tiny heels of her silk dancing slippers clicked as if to announce her approach. She glanced once into the long looking glass, then hurried downstairs to be certain nothing would go amiss at the last moment to upset Clarissa.

The strain of preparing everything perfectly these last few days had brought Clarissa nearly to her breaking point. Rebecca bit her lip at that image as she hurried downstairs. She could not picture her stiff, stern mother-in-law ever breaking, but the closer today had come the more she had ordered everyone around with snappish comments. Rebecca pitied the poor housemaids, but she had no time to pity herself.

To complete frenzied last-minute preparations, servants bustled across the vast parquet floor of the great hall. Gleaming silver and glassware, pyramids of fruit, platters of cold meats, breads, salads, and desserts covered the linen-shrouded tables. At the far end of the hall the six-piece orchestra tuned their stringed instruments. Rebecca made the rounds, complimenting housemaids and scrutinizing again her rose decorations swagged above doorways and windows and arrayed in massive bouquets. When she finally glanced out a window, she saw lanterns lined the approach to the house as if to reflect the glitter of sconces, gas lights, candles, and candelabra within. All looked in readiness for the onslaught at seven, after which the duke would be brought down to meet the guests.

She smiled at Ramsey as he escorted his mother downstairs and bent to kiss his wife's cheek. He had been dressed and nervously pacing for over an hour. He looked very handsome in dove gray to match his eyes. His embroidered waistcoat and narrow trousers strapped under his soft Wellington boots looked so elegant that, for one moment, she could not believe he was hers. His turned-down wing collar, white satin cravat and bowtie made his sun-browned face look especially ruddy tonight. Let them all know her freckles and Ramsey's color showed they worked outside among their people, she thought. She flipped her fan to calm herself and smiled at Clarissa, gowned in the pale lavender of proper half mourning. In her décolletage, she wore a nosegay of tiny white rosebuds Rebecca had chosen especially for her.

Ramsey winked at Rebecca, then glanced around the room. "A riot of roses," he observed.

"I just hope," Rebecca said and tapped his arm with her fan, "it's the only sort of riot we see tonight."

"Don't either of you—you too, Lord Richley," Clarissa warned Will as he joined them, "dare to allow a single thing to go wrong this evening!" Then she strode stiffly away to make yet another appraising circuit of the rooms.

Soon the crowd swelled and buzzed inside while, at the door, Ramsey and Rebecca greeted arriving guests and presented them to Clarissa. A few took a quick turn at dancing or quaffed punch, but no one touched the food yet. When everyone had arrived, the Sherbornes mingled with the crowd.

Rebecca breathed more easily when Penelope Prettyman nodded and spoke, but it annoyed her when the woman said, "Whoever that Owler rogue is, at least he seems to focus his attention on you and yours alone now."

"Whoever the rogue is," Rebecca replied, "he seems afraid of laborers earning their own way in the world. That, in my book, does not say much for Captain Owler."

"No political talk, only social chatting!" Clarissa smilingly scolded both of them as she walked past. But soon enough Rebecca's social chatting got her into her first muddle of the evening.

"I do declare, Lady Rebecca, it is indeed fascinating the way you drag out your words," Sarah Swithins said to Rebecca when she stopped to join the group surrounding the woman.

Sarah was the wife of Samuel Swithins, the wealthy owner of the influential *Dorchester County Chronicle*. The paper had been hostile, and Ramsey and Rebecca were hoping to win the Swithinses over tonight.

"My, mi-yiy," the woman was saying in a poor imitation of Rebecca's drawl, "it takes a goodly while to know whatever are you going to say next, which, perhaps is just as way-ell for the rest of us."

Rebecca was astounded and hurt at being mocked to her face. She did not think for one moment the woman was funning her. Whatever, then, were they saying behind her back? She forced a tight little smile. "I do declare, Mrs. Swithins," she retorted, "I've always thought you English talked much too fast to really have anything to say. We Kentuckians believe, since our ideas are worth the saying, we might as well give them enough time."

Mrs. Swithins gaped like a fish. The moment Rebecca excused herself and walked away, she regretted making another enemy. No matter what happened tonight, she wanted everyone to feel welcomed and appreciated. Gran Ida and Mama had taught her that, and here she was stooping to meet some of these snobbish people on their ground. But how could dear, wonderful Gran Ida and Mama ever have known their Becca would be facing these fancy people in faraway England? Gran's old English songs of queens in castles and their gentlemanly lovers had almost come true since Rebecca had become Ramsey's Marchioness of Sherborne.

Once the Sherbornes partook of food, people began to eat and dance in earnest. Ramsey and Rebecca whirled about in a waltz most Dorset folk called the turning dance. She realized she and Ramsey had not danced since the days she was his "country cousin" in Graham Springs, but tonight they were too nervous to enjoy it.

Later she strolled about again to talk to guests about village products and pride. It seemed either Clarissa or Will was ever hovering, as if they'd made a pact to keep her out of trouble. But it was Ramsey she feared would get into deep trouble when she realized he was asking the gentlemen to write down the Shaker farm implements or wagons they would like to have a look at—and he was having them print their lists, "so my workers who are just learning to read can decipher them too."

"I really can't see for the life of me why they need to read," Rebecca heard Geoffrey Prettyman complain to Ramsey as she joined them. "Your church curate reads, doesn't he? The workers can go to him."

Rebecca held her breath. Ramsey was not only *not* catching flies with honey, but might be about to kick over the beehive. No wonder just last night before they went to bed he had been studying the hand-printed note of Captain Owler's which they had saved. He was obviously hoping to match the printing with a guest's.

"What say you, Rebecca?" Randolph Viscint-Hewes inquired to draw her into the growing circle of men. Will, too, drifted over. "All Americans think they have a voice in everything." Randolph said, looking down his long nose at her. "But here, as I hope you have learned, my lady, it is quite different and shall ever be."

"It is indeed different," she agreed. "but how sad that human beings, whom God made all in His image, should be thought low or high because of their family situation. Why, the little man is only little when the big folk try to keep him down to make themselves look and feel bigger."

"But you see, Lady Rebecca," Samuel Swithins said as he stepped forward, evidently to assume the role of spokesman, "those whom you are calling 'the big folk' need to protect themselves from the dirt that often clings to the 'little folk,' and I am hardly speaking of their working the soil." He spoke so loudly now, he seemed to be addressing the entire room. The orchestra had taken a respite, so the buzz of guests was all she heard. Suddenly, to Rebecca, this portly man embodied all the people at Graham Springs, and on the ship, and here, who had looked down at her and hers.

"A wretched outlook," Ramsey challenged before she could respond. "Explain yourself further, sir!"

"Let us face facts, Lord Sherborne, standards and morals are indeed different in the social classes. Why should the classes mix when they are so radically different?"

At that moment, Clarissa joined them, tightly grasping Ramsey's arm, as if to keep him from a brash rejoinder. That furtive, frightened look on her mother-in-law's face suddenly reminded Rebecca of her own Mama's face years ago, a face hiding some secret fear of loss. But there was no time for that now. She knew this man was attacking her right to be wed to Ramsey. But if she publicly recognized his accusation, would she not be lending it credence?

"All I can say," Rebecca declared as Ramsey hesitated, "is ever since I arrived, I have greatly admired the villagers who work so hard to profit those *supposedly* above them."

"Utopian hogwash," a man's voice behind her whispered.

"I don't doubt you admired them, considering your past," Mr. Swithins said as his wife approached with Penelope and Emmalyn.

Rebecca saw Ramsey shake off his mother's grip and flex his fists. Surely he would not use physical force here! Quickly she stepped forward to fight her own battle.

"Oh, yes," she said, "I admit I came from humble beginnings, but the only dirt that clings to me is good, productive American soil!"

"She'd best not continue in the same vein, however high her marriage has taken her," Mr. Swithins warned Ramsey, "or we'll all have to hear about her tippling."

"My what?" Rebecca asked so loudly that the man jumped. Was he making light of her dancing? Had he said *tripping*?

"Tippling, drinking to excess," he declared. "I don't own a fine investigative newspaper for nothing, you know."

Clarissa gasped. Ramsey stepped forward before Will pulled him back, but Ramsey shook him off as he had his mother. "I hope, sir," Ramsey said, "you have not taken advantage of our heartfelt invitation for hospitality to slander us in our own home. If so, I shall personally throw you out.''

"Heathens all," Mr. Swithins muttered, but he stepped back behind Randolph and Geoffrey before Ramsey could reach him.

"Wait, Ramsey," Rebecca said. "I have no notion what the man could mean. Let him speak.''

"Can you deny that you came reeling drunk to England?" he asked.

She had gone red, but she could not allow such sordid lies to go unchallenged before all these people. And, at this worst possible moment, she glimpsed, across the sea of whispering heads, the servants carrying the old duke into the room in a chair to meet the guests.

"That I what?" Rebecca demanded, hands on hips.

"That you could not even stand straight on the street when you arrived at the Sherborne town house in a hack straight off steerage class on a ship and that the first thing you demanded was hard liquor," he accused, pointing to punctuate each accusation. "That you sang and who knows what else for pay in a common Cincinnati tavern where women's services were bought and sold? And this is the woman," his horrid voice continued, dripping with disgust, "who implies the lower classes have morality equal to ours!"

Rebecca could have fallen through the floor. How could he know all that about her and distort it so dreadfully? No one in all England but Ramsey knew of her dancing at Quinn's Hotel, and he never would have told these people! And as for these other twisted half-truths, who could have known about that night she arrived in London? Clarissa—perhaps Tamar had told Clarissa! But, surely her mother-in-law could not want to shame her, and therefore the Sherbornes, publicly like this!

"Lies and distortions, all of it!" Ramsey shouted as he strode closer to Mr. Swithins with clenched fists. "But what would I expect from you, all of you, hanging on this liar's every word? After all, you are the ones who would do anything to discredit honest, hardworking people. Men like all of you who feed on your own pride have no social soul!''

"This love feast tonight was at your bidding, and we'll not be insulted here again, even by an old friend!'' Geoffrey cut in.

"I say,'' Ramsey went on, his face livid, "there is someone in attendance here who is the ultimate insult. Someone who hides behind the hood of the despicable Captain Owler!''

"You're as demented as you are dangerous, Sherborne!'' Mr. Swithins shouted. "If you want to know what some of us think, we think *you* are behind Captain Owler! Interesting, how he just harasses you and your people lately. Gets you sympathy and loyalty and keeps your unwashed underlings in line, doesn't it? For all we know, you *are* Captain Owler, just looking for ways to draw the headlines of the *Chronicle* your way!''

Ramsey gaped at him, obviously astounded. But Rebecca, as shocked as she was at the attack on her, feared the guests would think Ramsey was astonished at being caught. She shook like a leaf in a gale, but her voice rang out strongly.

"That accusation against my husband is ridiculous. Ramsey and I were together in our bedroom the night Captain Owler started the fire in the village. Even though it was so late, we were both awake, so I know he didn't slip out!''

Someone behind her dared to titter at the implications of what she'd said.

"Ah, then, if *you* are an eyewitness, my lady,'' Mr. Swithins mocked, "we all must accept your word for it.''

Clarissa stepped forward and took Ramsey's arm again. "Your grandfather has come down to meet the guests,'' she said. "How unfortunate that some of them have disagreed tonight when the Sherbornes have extended this hospitality. No more, please, from any of you.''

"There will be no more, ever!'' Geoffrey spat out as he pulled Penelope away. "It was folly for us to try to offer forgiveness here. Come, wife.''

The room went very still. Some left; some stayed. A few

guests drifted off to the buffet tables, their heads together. Samuel Swithins and his wife saw fit to leave with much huffing and puffing, though they first went to bid farewell to the duke in his chair. "No doubt they are recalling the good old enclosure days!" Rebecca heard Ramsey mutter bitterly to Will.

For Rebecca, after that, even when the orchestra began to play again and a few dared to dance, the glorious hope of reconciliation—with neighbors, perhaps even with Clarissa—was dashed. She felt frozen where she stood. Why did Ramsey not come to comfort her, to at least give a show of solidarity? She had tried hard to protect him—could he not return the kindness? But Ramsey was fuming, she feared, and at her. He had come to her defense and yet had seemed so angry when she had stood up for herself and for him. Now people kept away from both of them as if they had some dread disease.

But Rebecca refused to run. At the door, she forced herself to help Clarissa bid farewell to the guests. The two Sherborne women did not speak to each other. In charming shepherd-esses' gowns, Tamar and Lily handed out baskets of favors to each departing lady. Rebecca could just imagine those goods being dumped from carriage windows or trampled on the road home. And all the time, her mind raced over Samuel Swithins and his so-called "investigative newspaper" which had discovered and distorted so much about her. At least he had not printed his claims, though that might well be next.

At last Rebecca could not bear Ramsey's brooding any more than she could Clarissa's ignoring her. Without a word to her mother-in-law, she crossed the room to him and Will.

"Your mother—she couldn't have discovered things from Tamar about the night I got off the ship, could she, Ramsey?"

"And have told that blowhard Swithins so he could shame the Sherbornes further?" he clipped out and tossed down his drink. "Are you speaking of the same woman I know?"

"I have to find out how that man learned about my actions in America."

"How in bloody blazes would I know? I'm the last to know or speak up for anything," he muttered and strode away as if he could not bear to look at her.

She held her head up, but her shoulders drooped. She stared helplessly into Will's eyes. Right now, as he was to Ramsey, Will seemed her only friend.

"Things couldn't have gone worse," she admitted. "Well, none of this fancy foolishness tonight was my idea!"

"Buck up, Rebecca. You've ever been the idealist, the optimist. Both Ramsey and the Dowager Marchioness will need that more than ever now."

"I think not. You told me once my uniqueness drew Ramsey. Now," she got out before her voice broke, "it repels him, like it always has his mother!"

"That is ridiculous!" Will insisted and took her hands. "He is just furious that he did not flush out Captain Owler and people turned the tables on him."

Tamar came over. "The Dowager Marchioness has gone straight up to bed with a raging headache," she told Rebecca, but her eyes darted to Rebecca's hands, clasped in Will's. "Will you need me now, milady?"

Her family—Ramsey and Clarissa—that was all she needed, Rebecca mourned, but she had evidently lost them. She pulled her hands away from Will. She nodded to Tamar. "Good-night, Will, and thank you for everything." Will went upstairs; she looked around the room to see whether Ramsey had returned. She saw only servants clearing things away. "Has his lordship turned in too, Tamar?"

"Oh, no, milady, thought you knew. Heard him tell Jensen he was going out."

"Now? Out where?"

Tamar only shrugged. The girl was obviously exhausted; she said nothing upstairs as she divested Rebecca of her gown and draped the green silk robe over her shoulders. "I'll be fine, Tamar. You can leave me now," she told her.

"If'n you want me to stay, milady . . ."

"No, you've been a big help to me—always, Tamar. But you never told Mr. Swithins about the night I first came to London, did you, or someone else from around here who might have told him?"

Tamar's eyes widened. "No, milady. I heard tell of what he said tonight, but no, I didn't."

Rebecca nodded and sank down on the bed as Tamar went out. Her head hurt, but she would not hide behind that as her mother-in-law did. And how dared Ramsey race off like that without a word about where he was going!

She jumped to her feet and tore off her robe. She dashed to her wardrobe and pulled on her riding habit, stockings, boots. If he had gone to the hunt lodge in the heath to escape her—unwilling to discuss either her mistakes or his—she would not allow it. The lodge was their lovers' place, their refuge, and he had no right to go there alone. The moon was full; she and the horse knew the way. And nothing either she or Ramsey had ever done—nothing!—was enough to keep them apart.

But as she dressed, she realized where he must have gone. His words that night in the heath, when they had shared the stars, came back to her: "This place used to be my escape when I was a boy . . . I'd even sneak out here at night alone and never have a fear." Yes, somehow, she knew that was where she would find him.

She strode out to the stables and roused the boy who slept there to saddle her mare. "Did Lord Sherborne tell you where he was going, Timothy?" she asked.

"Just out. His lordship used to go ariding at night lots 'fore you came, milady."

She opened her mouth to ask more, but why? She trusted Ramsey. She would ask him. The old Celtic barrow was but a short way into the heath, and she would be on the village road and turnpike the rest of the way. She doubted anyone beyond the estate and village guards would even see her.

She slowed the horse to a walk through the village, so as

not to alarm anyone. The guards Ramsey had hired, who kept to positions at both ends of Sherpuddle, called out to challenge her each time, as she expected. Ramsey had told them to be vigilant tonight even after all the guests departed.

"It's me, the marchioness, riding out to join his lordship," she told the guards. "He passed this way?"

"Good hour ago, milady."

That comforted her as she rode on. No one who had a thing to do with Captain Owler would let a stable boy and his own hired men know when he was riding out. But how foolish she was being. She might as well accuse Lord Melbourne himself, even if he lived in London! The way things had gone tonight, she'd place her bets as to Captain Owler's identity either on Ramsey's boyhood friends or on someone hired by that horrid Samuel Swithins with all the money he made on that wretched newspaper of his.

A low-hanging mist swallowed her horse's hooves as she plunged into the heart of the heath. She had not ridden far before her determination deserted her. She had never heard anything about dangers in the heath at night, but this was not wise. Clarissa would be shocked. Besides, the heath always made her nervous, even in broad day. Ramsey would surely cool his heels by tomorrow, and they could settle everything then. She reined in just before she reached the barrow. She squinted up, but there was no starry beauty in the sky this night.

She heard a horse whinny nearby. The hair on the back of her neck stood up; gooseflesh prickled along her arms and legs. Her horse answered, then walked a few yards and stopped where another horse was tethered.

Ramsey's! Thank God, it was not that midnight-black horse with four white feet which the villagers always claimed carried Captain Owler. She had found Ramsey.

"Who's there?" came from the darkness.

"Ramsey, it's me."

He emerged from black thickets in shirtsleeves that

gleamed stark white as a ghost. "I heard your horse. What in bloody hell are you doing out here? Isn't Will with you?"

"You rode out alone, so I guess I can too. I had a feeling where you'd be."

"Get down then." He strode over to reach up for her.

"Not until you explain a few things."

"Come on, I said," he muttered, and half lifted, half dragged her down into his hard embrace. She smelled liquor on his breath.

She became very angry again. That's what Daddy had always done when he wanted to escape—hide his sorrows in wandering and drinking. She squirmed and elbowed Ramsey. "Let me go. I don't care if Captain Owler himself rides out of the dark!"

"That was just another farce tonight, my plans to unmask him. And of course, you and Mother had to leap to my defense and not let me settle things myself, as if I were yet some lad at play. Damn, I've done some stupid things!"

She wondered if he now thought one of those things was marrying her. She pushed his restraining hands away, but he yanked her back with a hard grip on her arms.

"Stop struggling for once, Rebecca!"

"I've decided I'd rather go back alone! I've been a fool about a few things too."

"That's obvious."

She tried to pull away again, only to be hauled back and headed up the hill instead of toward her horse.

"Ramsey, I'm regretful if your family's plans exploded in your face tonight, but it's your fault too."

"*My* family and *my* plans, is it now, separate from yours?" he muttered.

"Yes! It could be *your* mother who intercepted my lost letter or distorted what happened my first night in England! If she hadn't had one of her convenient little headaches, I'd have cornered her on it after folks left tonight. Tamar claims it wasn't her! And I assume it wasn't you, or should I not assume anything about you lately?"

"Meaning what?"

"Meaning I thought we made a heartfelt vow to share everything. But even when I told you about sending rose products to London and gave you an opportunity to reveal your plans for new protests there, you didn't see fit to tell me until weeks later."

"Back then, I had other things on my mind, and Will said he told you. You didn't need me to tell you, just as you didn't need me to defend you tonight. But let's not cloud what's important with the little things. You heard all that rubbish from Swithins. What about all that?" he roared.

"All what?" she shouted and tried to stop before he shoved her on so that she had to argue back over her shoulder. "My being a drunkard and tavern girl, or worse? You mean you believed him?" New anger raged through her at the thought that he had abandoned her because of a falsehood.

"Of course not as he said it, but I don't give a damn right now if someone found the lost letter or someone just dug up dirt about your days alone in Cincinnati when you should have been here with me. I demand to know if there is anything you haven't told me about that!"

"How dare you imply such a thing! I tried to tell you everything shortly after I arrived, after struggling to come to you, but you said never mind, only our future mattered. And now you've ruined that!" she cried and turned back to strike his shoulders once with both fists.

He seized her wrists in an iron grip. How was everything falling apart like this? She should never have come to England, never have trusted his vows that she could fit in here! Had he been disappointed in her from the first, only standing up for her to protect the Sherborne name? If so, he was his mother's son indeed! She tried to shake loose, but he pulled her on with him up the hill. They stopped and confronted each other on the ridge like sparring partners.

"Let's face facts, Rebecca. Why would some strange man just give you the money to come to England when you had only been leading good old mountain songs at his hotel?"

367

She lifted her arm to slap that smug face, then brought her hand down against her own thigh. "Because he did. He liked me and he gave me the money. And I liked him, because he believed in me, which is more than I can say for my own husband right now."

She began to pace, just to be moving, just to keep from striking him again or throwing herself flat on the ground and screaming. Her own Mercer family had not believed she could be wedded to an English lord. Why had she ever believed it herself? The Dorset gentry knew better—Ramsey's mother knew better—Will, even Tamar and Jenny had always known. Back home, Christina and Adam had known, though, staunch friends that they were, they had supported her and wished her well. Now it was over. Now Ramsey too knew she could never belong.

As she paced, she stumbled over Ramsey's coat. He must have been sitting here watching for stars, but there were none. His hands clasped her shoulders from behind. "Rebecca, I do love you and need you. Don't turn on me too, though, God knows, sometimes I deserve it."

She stood still; she felt surprised by his firm, gentle touch. "I thought you were turning on me," she said.

"Never. It is only that you are so—so different, special. You were on your own in Cincinnati and desperate. And I was trapped here and no help to you at all and detesting myself for that. I blame myself, then get bitter and strike out when it's not your fault at all."

At that apology, she turned to him. "I won't tell you again I did nothing wrong, Ramsey. I see now you only believed *in* me but did not believe me. No wonder we have made no child between us with all our fervent coupling! We weren't really one at all," she choked out and crumpled to her knees on his coat.

He sat beside her and held her hand even when she tried to pull it back. "That's not true! My darling, I am trying to explain this confusion I feel inside. I just desire you so desperately I can't bear to think you could survive and triumph without me. I even suppose I was thinking you would need me more in England because I knew things would be hard for you. But even tonight, under attack from that pompous bastard Swithins and the rest of them, you stood up for yourself. I have always wanted to be the strong one, your protector, and yet you have been that to me instead.''

"Ramsey, I—"

"You think it's easy for me to accept that I gave you money in Graham Springs to come to me, but then you gave it away to someone who needed it more and still got here on your own? You think it's easy for me to accept—as proud as I am of you—that it was your clever efforts, not mine, that have begun to pull the village out of the depths of despair? Your ways, your strength have accomplished miracles in Sherpuddle, when I long yearned to be the village savior. These hidden places in my soul—my aspirations and bitter guilt, Rebecca—in bringing those to light, your brightness has made my shadows seem so much darker. Rebecca, I need you so!''

Ravaging emotion contorted his handsome face. Tears matted his thick eyelashes. Such confessions! Yet it was her own need for him that frightened and stunned her now. Yes, with her own desire for acceptance warring with her stubborn mountain pride, she understood him. Understood and could forgive.

They reached toward each other and embraced intensely. They rolled over on the ground, not caring that they lay upon a hill in the deep heath under heaven, kissing and caressing fiercely. She ran her hands down his back and waist, gripping sinew and muscle. He seized her buttocks to pull her closer; she trapped his thigh between her knees as her skirts rode higher. They matched each other move for move, slowing in wonderment as passion stretched even tauter between them.

Soon they lay naked together on the mass of her black riding habit and his clothes. The cooling August night lay sweet on their perspiring limbs. Their skin was bathed in starlight, for, as if in blessing, the colored rings had appeared overhead. They almost slid down the hill on the pile of clothes that was their bed, but they did not laugh or stop. Tongues and lips lingered; hands explored and discovered, enticed, incited. He lifted her astride him as if he were her powerful stallion and they would go pounding off across the heath together.

"I shall always see you this way, goddess not of the family hearth, but of my refuge in the heath," he whispered. "You have conquered me and your world here. Poor, pitiful folk who get in your way—"

"Who get in *our* way. Pity anyone who has never loved like this—oh, Ramsey!"

He began to move under her, in her, to lift and lure her on. She moved too, her hair swinging free. She gazed deeply into his eyes, but saw the colored lights of the sky reflected there, luminous and lovely.

Afterward, as they lay close together in the nighttime chill, he whispered, "We'd best go home."

She nodded, but she knew she would always feel more at home in the village than at the manor house. Old Bet seemed more like family than Clarissa did. But she had chosen to love this man and live with him here. Even when, someday, they built themselves a house in the village, she must remember to live in and to love both worlds. She would build bridges, she vowed silently, not make the hedgerows higher.

Part IV

Rebecca, Long-Blooming
American Rose
(1839–1842)

You may break, you may shatter the vase, if you will,
But the scent of the roses will hang round it still.
                                    —Thomas Moore
                                        "Farewell! But Whenever"

Chapter Twenty

Rebecca felt she made progress as she and Ramsey planned the Sherpuddle Country Fair to display Shaker-inspired products. For various reasons, her mood soared on the day of the fair, about three weeks after that night on the heath. She felt a bit better about Clarissa since her mother-in-law had assured her that she had never seen the missing letter, though she admitted "Brimblecomb" had told her about Rebecca's arrival in London. Clarissa had said she understood how Rebecca had been misled that night to think Ramsey had died, and that lemonade was a non-alcoholic drink. And Clarissa had also said that the behavior of their guests at the dance was "entirely, utterly abominable." Still, though she had made no comment about Rebecca's own behavior, once again Rebecca wondered what her mother-in-law was really thinking of her.

Another reason for Rebecca's raised spirits was a letter from Christina telling her things were going well in Harrodsburg. She was now helping the widow whose house she shared in her dressmaking business, and Rebecca's little namesake, Becky, nearly three years old, was thriving. But what lifted Rebecca even higher was that the letter included a warm note from Adam's Aunt Euphy, whom she had not seen since the day Daddy had taken her and Jeremy away from Shelter.

Aunt Euphy was now keeping house for Adam in Harrodsburg, where he had been building up a medical practice with Dr. White. Aunt Euphy said she was finally adjusting to widowhood and saw Adam's sisters and their families when she could. Despite her weak leg, she traveled all over town, she declared proudly, riding a beautiful white mare. She thanked Rebecca again for suggesting the mule so long ago, though that hadn't worked out so well. Adam had taken to going out west to Indian country off and on, Aunt Euphy wrote, because epidemics were killing off the tribes; Adam was immunizing them. Rebecca recalled the horror of epidemics and the regal sadness of the Indians she had met on the steamboat heading for Cincinnati. She was so glad Adam was still helping others, just as they had promised each other to do so long ago on Concord Peak. How proud she was of her Kentucky friends, just as she was of her Dorset ones.

Then too, she and Ramsey had decided to begin building a small house for themselves in the village, no matter what the local gentry or the newspapers or Clarissa thought. Someday, Rebecca dreamed, people at the Sherpuddle fair would be invited into their village home to visit, just as they were viewing the communal hall today. Meanwhile, she and Ramsey planned to go out to other villages to discuss the establishment of cottage workshops. And he had even asked her advice on another march he was planning in London this autumn. To Rebecca, no day had ever looked lovelier, no future brighter.

Rebecca squeezed Ramsey's arm and smiled up as him as they surveyed the busy scene. Sherpuddle and Dorset people from miles away had walked or ridden in on big Dorset wagons. The green and both sides of the street were dotted with booths displaying and selling products; there were open places with plank tables for eating and the competitions. Will

had said the Prettymans and Viscint-Heweses had arrived together. Evidently they were curious about the goings-on, even
if they weren't speaking to the Sherbornes. Their presence
had worried Rebecca at first, but she and Ramsey decided
that perhaps they had come to make amends, and that if they
met in the crowd, they would offer a welcome. Clarissa was
coming out soon with the house servants. And best of all,
the old duke had asked to be brought out.

In the middle of the village street before the church, the
old man sat in the place of honor in his faded red leather
sedan chair. He wore the only wig here today, and his finest
clothes no longer fit his shrunken frame. But he had come.

"Wouldn't want to miss such a thing," he had told Ramsey and Rebecca when they explained it all last week. "Want
to see the village once again, my boy. If there be more of
your wife's roses there, like the ones under my window, it
will be a fine thing to see."

But the fine thing was that near the old duke's sedan chair,
Old Bet sat on a tall barrel with a board back as if to oversee
things herself. It looked as if Bet had perched upon a makeshift throne to challenge the patriarch's fine chair. As usual,
she had arrived in a wheelbarrow, with no less pomp than
the duke.

"It's like they've been named official king and queen of
the fair today, Ramsey," Rebecca whispered.

"I was thinking much the same," he told her, his voice
rough with emotion. "It is as if the old enclosure acts somehow are reconciled at last with the new model village we are
building."

But to Rebecca, the most exciting visitor at the fair was
the one nobody could see. Never in all the years since she
and Mama had celebrated her first monthly flux together had
she ever missed it or been late. But she'd missed it for weeks
and at breakfast time she felt as if she could toss up her
insides. She remembered what that meant from hearing Gran
Ida talk. Conceived that night under the stars, a child grew
within her. She had only decided for certain today, and things

had been so hectic she had not told Ramsey yet. But tonight, after the shared triumph of the day, she would.

She and Ramsey judged the wheelbarrow races and visited the booths. People came up to chat with them or just to meet the woman the Dorset people had named the "Shaker Rose." She had heard that the villagers thought it good luck to receive a rose from her hands, but she was careful to foster no further superstitions. She and Ramsey waved to Jenny and Charles across the crowded green. They bid a stilted welcome to the squires and their families. When Clarissa joined them, the three of them watched the grinning contest, where people thrust their heads through horse collars to see who could grin for the longest time. Rebecca thought she had never laughed so hard when Jenny's brother Nat won and kept right on grinning.

"I've never seen the villagers so happy," Ramsey told her after Clarissa had returned to the house and they were strolling about. "And I haven't forgotten my promise to take you back to your town of Shelter to see if some of the same things would help there. Perhaps next year."

"That would be so wonderful, my love!" She almost blurted out that they would have to take the baby too, but stopped herself, wanting to save the announcement for tonight when they were alone. If Will stayed on, she would let the proud future father tell him, though she longed to be there when Clarissa heard the news.

Later, Ramsey and Rebecca took turns mounting a tree stump to give speeches of dedication and encouragement. "When word gets back to Samuel Swithins or even Lord Melbourne that the Dorset workers are united in pride and purpose," Ramsey defiantly told the crowd, "we must and we will be ready for the challenge!"

The crowed roared.

When the hubbub subsided and Ramsey stepped down, he seized her arm. "What's that strange rumbling?" he asked and glanced up to scan the sky. "No thunderclouds." They heard shouts from the edge of the village nearest the manor house. Ramsey leaped back up on the stump. He shaded his eyes and peered down the street.

"Run!" he shouted to the crowd, gesturing wildly. "Run! The cattle got loose somehow! They're bolting!"

Screams shredded the air as people seized their children and scattered. Booths down the way flew apart; tables toppled. And then, at the same moment, as Ramsey and Rebecca turned to flee, with the long-horned herd funneling up the narrow village street, they saw that no one had taken the duke and Old Bet out of harm's way.

"Get Bet!" Ramsey screamed and tore toward his grandfather.

Rebecca ran after Ramsey, crashing into the fleeing villagers. The ground thumped and leaped under her feet. She seized the old woman as if she were a rag doll and dove the other way from Ramsey, hurling herself and Bet into a cottage where Jenny and Charles held wailing children in their arms. Only then did she fear she might have hurt the baby she carried. A dust cloud choked them as the first animals crashed past, then the rest, hooves flying, eyes wild.

"Catastrophe!" Rebecca muttered to Jenny as the girl held Old Bet. When the cloud began to clear, they ventured out. Despite the villagers' frightened cries, Rebecca's first feeling was relief that Clarissa had gone back to the house. Today she had almost forgotten that Sherpuddle was not a perfect place. She coughed in the dust, and her eyes watered as she looked for Ramsey beyond the chaos of broken booths and trampled tables. Across the street by the churchyard, she saw Hollis Wembly bent low in the rubble and thought he might be hurt. She hurried to him, and then she saw.

The old duke's sedan chair had been smashed. She raised her eyes to search for Ramsey. If he had not been able to save his grandfather, it would only deepen the guilt he felt because he both hated and loved the old man. She saw two legs protruding from under the heavy chair, which Hollis was trying to lift.

"Get back, milady," he told her. "The duke! Here, boys, to me!"

But when the village men lifted the rubble away, there were four legs trapped beneath. Two bodies, trampled and twisted.

"Oh, dear God in heaven," she heard a woman scream. "Not Ramsey too!"

She threw herself down and clawed at the debris. Blood seeped through Ramsey's clothes; his arm encircled the old man. "Ramsey!"

"He's breathing, milady, he's breathing," someone said. Jenny knelt now too, trying to hold her when she only wanted to hold Ramsey. She was dreaming; this was another nightmare. "Ramsey!" a woman wailed.

"Fetch the doctor from Dorchester! Someone ride now. The old duke's dead and the marquess bad hurt."

It was Will making her stand up, Will with his tobacco breath smothering her when she had to help Ramsey breathe. Some woman kept screaming, "Ramsey, Ramsey!" in her ears.

"Rebecca, we have to be careful how we move him." That was Will again. "Damn! Those cattle—I can't believe they did—all this."

She shook her head and surveyed the broken booths, the wide-eyed faces in a circle around them.

"Took care o' him when he was a lad and broke his leg," someone was saying. "Took him to our cot, 'member the story, Jen?"

"Here, Rebecca, sit over here in this cottage while we cover him until the doctor comes. He's alive, Rebecca, just his legs maybe. He will be all right."

She shoved Will away with a strength she did not know she had. Ramsey was really hurt. She knelt beside him again. Men carried the duke's body into the church entry and covered it. Ramsey would inherit his grandfather's House of Lords seat, she thought. They would live in London. Melbourne could not stop him from speaking out for all these people now.

"Ramsey," she cried and bent over him to tuck Will's coat tenderly around his shoulders. "I have something very special to tell you. I should have told you earlier today, but we were so busy and I wanted it to be private and special. Ramsey, please hear me, please talk to me. Ramsey!"

She huddled there in the street to protect him. Someone fetched the sobbing Clarissa and they knelt in a silent vigil in the center of Sherpuddle until the doctor came.

Day and night, as she sat by Ramsey's broken body in their bed, voices whispered far back in Rebecca's mind. *The Widow Lang and her sisters just flew off to heaven,* the voices said . . . *Mama, the little mite, my sister, she isn't breathing . . . Mama's got the milk sick . . . Daddy, don't leave us here . . . Christina, I'm so sorry, but there's been a steamboat accident. Another irony of life and pain and joy and death.*

No, she thought, trying to fight the voices. No! She was not going to lose Ramsey! If she sat here day and night and held his hand and stared at him and prayed and willed her strength into him, he would come back to her! She prayed hard. She knew the curate and the villagers were praying too.

"His legs and backbone, my lady," the doctors said. "He might never walk again." She nodded and thanked them for telling her. Imagine, thanked them for that!

They had dosed him with laudanum for the pain. He drifted in and out of reality, even as she did. But the first time she thought he could hear her, she told him her precious news.

"Ramsey, we are going to have a child. I'm certain of it, and that's another reason you must get well."

His face, blurred by pain, went very still. His eyes opened and blazed. "A child!"

"Yes, our child we made that night on the heath, I am sure of it!"

"A fine idea," he murmured as he drifted away again, and she wondered if he'd understood at all.

Clarissa, weeping but still stiffly erect, came and went. "I am so pleased about the child you carry—Ramsey's son for the Sherborne future—" she got out before she choked with tears. She put her arms around Rebecca, who returned her embrace, careful not to touch her ruined shoulder. But what did all that matter now when Ramsey's whole body—their whole lives were ruined? Would she and Clarissa be able to abide each other if Ramsey was gone?

Will came and went too, asking her what he could do. He helped Clarissa plan the old duke's funeral and escorted her to it when Rebecca would not leave Ramsey's side. The rector from Dorchester and the local curate had eulogized Ramsey for trying to save his grandfather's life and his grandfather's village, they told her. The words did not even sink in. Fearful of disturbing Ramsey, they held no funeral banquet at the house.

Clarissa wore black again, but Rebecca refused. She would not have Ramsey think she was in mourning for him when he opened his eyes the next time. She did not care what anyone else thought: she wore her pink wedding gown. Roses filled the room; Tamar brought them in, then tiptoed out. Rebecca bathed Ramsey's face and wet his lips. The doctors said he was slipping, and she saw her sanity going with him.

She heard whisperings again late the next night, perhaps this time not the voices in her head. In the hall. Men's voices, the doctors.

"But Captain Owler's never done his work during the day!"

"The gate was not only deliberately opened, but someone had to run them out and head them down the lane. There should be some sort of investigation."

"Plenty of powerful people hate and fear his radical ideas. No one will want all that brought out."

Their words did not matter to her. Nothing did. She did

not leave the room. She prayed harder. At night, she brought lanterns closer so it would not be dark around Ramsey.

"Are there stars tonight?" he asked once, his brow furrowed, his eyes still tightly closed, in pain or in concentration on his labored speech.

She jolted into alertness. "Yes, my dearest love. And I am here with you."

"That's all that matters, my Rebecca. You're singing that song again—aren't you? True lovers' knots—like our lives—entwined . . ."

She leaned close over the bruised face and brushed a kiss upon his lips. He did not respond, but she spoke anyway. "Ramsey, you are the most beloved person I have ever known. My life with you has filled my heart with joy. Whatever happens, please know my love will always be with you. Our child, my dearest, stay to see the child we made together in our love!"

"I meant to take—you back to Shelter," he whispered in a broken voice. "But you will go there—someday. I'll still be with you then . . ."

"Yes, my love. Yes, when you are better we will go together and take our child."

He opened his eyes for the first time since she had told him of the baby. She could tell it pained him terribly to speak, and each word grated across her very soul. He seemed to look not at her but beyond.

"Rebecca, our child, bright stars . . ."

He settled back with a sigh she could almost call contented. But he never spoke, or moved, or breathed again.

She fought the voices and tried to stay strong until they buried him. She could not believe God had let him die. She needed him! Clarissa, their unborn child, the villagers, all England did too! She could not understand God's reason for letting him leave her.

She refused to let Clarissa lay him under the cold church stones with his ancestors. She refused to wear black, no matter what Clarissa said. She had him buried in the old church-yard among villagers and amid her scarlet roses in a spot where sun and stars would always find his bed. On the day of the funeral, she graciously greeted everyone who called. She spoke to them all, villagers and gentlepeople, about Ramsey's goals and dreams. She asked each person—even those of the gentry who had let him down—to do what he or she could to keep Ramsey's legacy alive. They murmured their replies, shifting their feet. Sometimes they did not meet her intense gaze. She almost screamed out that their selfishness had killed him, but she looked across the room at Clarissa and said nothing. She was afraid that if she tried to discover who had opened the gate, she might find that it had been the village boys playing again, and she could not have borne that.

Through it all, the voices in her brain tormented her. Now they sang to her the very song she had sung the day she met Ramsey Sherborne among her Shaker roses, the song he had remembered on his deathbed:

> *They buried her in the old churchyard,*
> *They buried him beside her,*
> *And from his grave grew a red, red rose,*
> *And from hers a green brier.*

> *They climbed and they climbed up the churchyard wall*
> *'Til they couldn't climb any higher.*
> *And there they formed a true lovers' knot,*
> *The red rose and green brier.*

And when it was all over, she closed herself in her room and wept.

She ate only for the sake of the child she carried. She tried to comfort Clarissa and get some sleep, but the voices would not let her rest. She pored over her few years with Ramsey, reliving laughter, embraces, dreams. Those first forbidden days at Shakertown, the week at Graham Springs, the honeymoon, the triumphs in the village, even the sadder times. She could not believe he was gone.

One day, after forcing herself to eat breakfast with Clarissa—she was keeping food down better now—she decided to reread some of Ramsey's favorite books. She carried several volumes of romantic poetry from the library back to bed, but could not read. She lay there on the bed Lily had remade, the place where he had died, and stared up at the blank ceiling.

Tears rolled down her temples. If only their child was more real to her, perhaps swelling her belly or even making her sick again. What if the child were not really here? At least Ramsey had understood there was a child before he died. But what if she had hurt it running and falling with Old Bet that day and never knew she lost it?

Ramsey had abandoned her, the voices in her head tormented her. Left her here as surely as Daddy had left her and Jeremy at Shakertown so long ago. Bitter bile choked her. Damn Daddy for that. Damn him! And curse herself that she loved him still!

But then she remembered her own words to Christina when she had claimed that her parents had deserted her and poor Travis had left her to rear her child alone. "These people did not choose to leave you," Rebecca had comforted her. "You still have Travis and your future in this child." Sisters—she and Christina were sisters of the heart again, more than ever! And Clarissa. If only something could be made of the ruin of their lives, she had an earthly mother yet.

She felt Ramsey's books pressing against her. Suddenly she knew there was a poem she needed, one by Shelley which Ramsey loved.

Desperate, she scrambled to find it. Unlike the song of Scarlet Town, this one was not hidden in the voices in her head. She found it and stared down at the last verse:

Rose leaves, when the rose is dead,
Are heaped for the beloved's bed;
And so thy thoughts, when thou art gone,
Love itself shall slumber on.

"That's it!" she said aloud. "How could I have forgotten?"

She remembered now certain things she had known since Shelter. Everything in life moved in a cycle, a circle, like petals and thorns, triumphs and tragedies; like buds and blooms, and the circles of herbs in healing mountain meadows; like the rings on the Widow Lang's marriage and burial quilt. She held up her shaking hands and stared at the emerald ring from Ramsey and the thin gold band from her mother's mother. Such things—such wisdom—were keepsakes of life.

"Love does not die, but stays sleeping inside you until you take it out and use it again." She spoke the words in wonderment. After all, it had been that way when she had lost others she had dearly loved. She had felt dead inside then, until she reached out to need and to help people again. If she tried very hard, perhaps it could be that way now, and then the baby would come to help her face the future. After all, carrying and then tending Ramsey's child, she could never feel dead inside, never for one moment.

She gently pressed her hands to her belly. Yes. The child must be there. The voices in her head had finally stilled. She felt only deep calm pouring over jagged pain. Gran Ida, Daddy, Christina, Aunt Euphy, and Clarissa had survived such loss. Yes, somehow, some way, even through the agony of separation from her beloved Ramsey, she must and would go on.

Yet six weeks after Ramsey's death, Rebecca still felt torn between her fantasies and reality. She found solace in her imagination. She was not ready to let him go; she bade him walk and talk with her daily in her thoughts and dreams.

But she also strove to carry on his work in the real world:

she attended local labor rallies in his name and wrote letters which several London papers printed in support of the coming protest march there. She continued with their projects in the village.

She felt torn too about Will, whom she considered her friend and adviser now, as he had been Ramsey's. Yet each time Will visited, he triggered both memories of happy times and constant reminders of her loss. And Will's closeness to Clarissa, a closeness she longed for but seemed unable to obtain, cut her deeply, though time and again he tried to smooth things over between her and her mother-in-law.

Her attempt to stabilize her fluctuating spirits suffered another setback when the Dorchester magistrate called for an inquest into Ramsey's death. The judge summoned Squire Prettyman, Squire Viscint-Hewes, Rebecca, and several villagers to testify. In town, people dogged her steps and stared; some harassed her for the stand she dared to take for the workers as she testified. The hearing was reported in minute, if slanted, detail in the *Chronicle*. No one had seen the cattle loosed, though it came out that several boys had been swinging on the gate that morning. Rebecca feared the crime would be laid at the feet of the villagers. But a verdict of accidental death was handed down and the herd of "killer cattle," as Swithins's snide paper put it, was sold for meat in town "as just and righteous punishment."

Tonight, as the October wind howled in a dreadful storm, Rebecca felt the weather suited her. She tossed and turned in bed. There was a bitter, cold finality about the fact of Ramsey's death which she must accept, but she had not found the way. She considered Will's suggestion that, as Ramsey had wished, she might return to Kentucky, at least for a visit. She feared it would devastate Clarissa if she left, despite their lack of intimacy. Still, she yearned to see the people in America, the people who accepted her as she was. She even missed Jeremy, and yes, even some of the other Shakers she was at odds with. Christina and little Becky, Aunt Euphy, Adam . . . she would like to see them all. And the folks of

Shelter beckoned like a cry from her past. She must return to help them, to show them there were ways to pull themselves out of grinding poverty.

This battle between her duty to remain and her desire to go home was wearing her down. Blast it, she had never really slept well since Ramsey had left her alone in this big bed—alone but for the child she carried. Sometimes she would wake, thinking she heard the thunder of hooves again, coming closer and closer, but it was only the pounding of her heart.

This night it was also real thunder outside and the pounding of rain on the windows. She lay still, curled up in bed, remembering the howling wind and blizzard at the Crawl Crick cabin when she had lain in bed next to Mama. Had lain there and tried to comfort her, those days when Mama was heavy with child and Daddy had left her alone. Swirling through her dreams and thoughts, Rebecca did not move when she first heard the knocking.

Then the door opened and Tamar came in. Lately Rebecca always left one lamp burning low. "Whatever is it? Can't sleep with the storm?" she asked Tamar, sitting up.

"It's the Dowager Marchioness, milady. Roberts says she took sick and wants to send someone for the doctor in town, but the roads'll be mud and there's trees down."

Rebecca's feet hit the floor. She had her robe on before Tamar could reach it. "She seemed peaked at supper. What's amiss?"

"Bad chills like the agues, milady. She said not to fret you, but I knew you'd want to know."

"Yes. Thank you for being on my side, Tamar," Rebecca told the girl, ignoring the puzzled look on her face. She took the lamp and swept out into the hall, her hair flying.

In Clarissa's suite, she sailed right by her mother-in-law's elderly, protective maid, Sarah Roberts, and the cook, who stood there in her robe holding an empty tray. Rebecca sniffed at, then set aside the cup of tea on the bedside table: pekoe, not herbal.

"My lady, if we're to be without a doctor for awhile, what may I do to help?" Rebecca asked, perching lightly on the side of the bed to lean over Clarissa.

"I didn't want to wake you. I'm so cold my teeth are rattling, and my head hurts so."

"Sometimes violent changes in the weather bring headaches, but not chills. Now, if you were my mama, I'd dose you with lemon balm tea and have you chewing mountain mint leaves. Then I'd cover you up good and let you sweat it all out."

Rebecca ignored the servants' muted protests as she felt Clarissa's forehead and cheeks. Burning hot, though she shook like a leaf in a mountain gale. Gently Rebecca pushed her back onto her pillow, careful to touch only on her good shoulder. She tucked the covers in, hoping that Clarissa's silence meant acquiescence.

"Sarah, I'll need more bedclothes to cover her," she commanded. "Ellen, please fetch hot water and lemon balm and mountain mint leaves from the still room. They are in clearly marked tins. They're herbs I grew in the village from Shaker seeds, my lady," she said, "and you're beginning to shake so hard I think they're just what the doctor would order."

Clarissa's eyes watered, whether from pain or gratitude Rebecca was not sure. Silence stretched between them as Clarissa seemed to ponder her words and actions.

"You're certain it won't harm your child to doctor me?" she asked through chattering teeth.

"No more than it will harm you to help me when this grandchild of yours comes calling. I hope you will be willing to help me then. You and I must stick together now in everything."

"Well, Roberts and Cook, do as she says!" Clarissa commanded before she heaved a huge sigh and gave herself over to Rebecca's care.

The sweats began before Rebecca could even get the diaphoretics—the herbs that would make Clarissa perspire—

down her. Strange how that fancy word came back to her from Mama's old herbal book, which she hadn't seen for years. Perspiration poured from Clarissa, and Rebecca gave her more tea. Still, she shook so hard that Rebecca held her like a child to warm her, daring to cradle the weak shoulder only to find it not so very different from the other. In the delirium of her mounting fever, Clarissa rattled on in a strange, disjointed way: how her sister was so pretty, about swinging by her neck when she was young.

Finally, near midmorning when the fever broke, she bathed Clarissa's face and neck in refreshing rosewater. Clarissa's eyes opened; the confusion on her face cleared. Rebecca smiled at her, but Clarissa started and reached for the damp square of flannel with which Rebecca was sponging her neck.

"Only Roberts does that!" she croaked out.

"Not anymore," Rebecca declared and went on sponging. "I'm honored you let me help."

Clarissa sank back against her pillows. "Yes," she murmured and closed her eyes. A single tear squeezed out, though Rebecca dared not blot it. "Everyone," Clarissa whispered to the hovering servants, "leave us alone." The maids went out and closed the door.

"It is queer," Clarissa said, "but I half knew I was talking balderdash last night. I did, didn't I?"

"That's the fever talking. Besides, lots of folks in their so-called right minds talk nonsense too."

She meant to reassure Clarissa and to lighten her dark mood. But Clarissa reached for her hand and held tight.

"You saw my bad shoulder, didn't you?"

"I saw it months—years ago, my lady. It's not bad, just a bit lower. And I always thought how clever you were to cover it so fashionably, but how sad it was that it grieved you."

"It never grieved my husband. He said so!"

"It never grieved me either. All that grieved me was that you were disappointed in me, and I wanted so to be not only part of your family but your friend."

"My dear, I admire you so! I always have!"

"You do—did?"

"Yes, for your boldness and bravery, your fierce love for and loyalty to my son, whatever he did. It makes you so beautiful."

"My first thought about you—that day you met me at the front door—was how striking you were, my lady. You have boldness and beauty too."

Clarissa shook her head slowly. "My sister was the pretty one. I heard it time and again. My sister was pretty, but I was clever. But you are both."

"I'll cherish that as a compliment. You know, you spoke last night of your pretty sister and something so strange about swinging by your neck. It must have been a nightmare and—"

"It was a nightmare, all of it, Rebecca. Mother said I was deformed, and it was her fault. But she made me pay for it. She strapped me in a shoulder brace with pins that pricked me if I slumped. She said she would make me perfect. She used to have the butler and my father's big valet stand on chairs and swing me by the neck to straighten that shoulder—oh, the pain of body and spirit! I begged Father to make her stop, but he did nothing. I felt abandoned by them both! But Mother said a man would never want to wed me otherwise," Clarissa managed before she was racked by sobs. Again Rebecca held her as she would a frightened child, and Clarissa did not pull away.

"It's all right," Rebecca said, her voice rough. "Your husband loved you just the way you are, Ramsey and I too, and so will your grandchild. Your mother was very much mistaken."

"Yes. Yes, I never wanted to be like her, and I'm so afraid I am!"

"No, that's not true. Even if you seem to follow in your parents' footsteps, you can be yourself. I am. And—I've felt deserted sometimes because my mama died and my daddy took me and my little brother and—and left us—and never came back . . . and now Ramsey . . .''

She stopped so that she too would not burst into tears. She realized she had never even told Ramsey all that. And now she had told Clarissa and they were comforting each other.

"Oh, my lady,'' she choked out, "I have wanted us to be so close from the first. And here, though we came from different pasts and different places, we both felt abandoned and needed each other.''

"And now we have found each other!'' Clarissa declared, holding tight to Rebecca's wrists. "Even without our dear Ramsey, we can be family and—if you want—friends!''

"Yes! Yes!'' Rebecca cried, but now, for the first time in long weeks, her tears were joyful.

Soon she found herself telling Clarissa that last night had reminded her of the snowstorm that had trapped her in the cabin tending Mama when her sister was born. Words tumbled from her about how she had feared for years she could have done more, saved the baby. About how terrified she felt sometimes that Daddy blamed her and even little Jeremy, and that was why he didn't want them. About how afraid she was sometimes that she would lose her baby the way Gran Ida and Mama and her friend Christina had lost theirs. About how her Shaker family had cursed her for going to the world because she loved Ramsey, and how she wanted them to change their unforgiving ways. Even about how the frightened look in Clarissa's eyes above her smile had reminded her of Mama before Rebecca had found out that Mama longed for the family she had left behind at home, just as Rebecca longed for Kentucky people, however much she liked it here.

"In your heart, you still have your own mama to love. How I wish I'd met the woman who made such a fine, strong, dear girl,'' Clarissa said before exhaustion claimed her. "But if you could find it in your heart to call me Mother . . .''

"Oh, yes, Mother!'' Rebecca cried and held hard to Clarissa's thin hands long after she had fallen asleep.

Chapter Twenty-one

After Clarissa's healing, the grief of Rebecca's widowhood and the fear of childbirth she had buried deep inside were easier to bear. But the stronger bond she and Clarissa shared forced her to put off thoughts of going home to Kentucky for now. A week after her mother-in-law's illness, she heaped compost around the stems of her churchyard roses. A splash of sun warmed her and fell on Ramsey's grave. Just as she had once chatted with Gran Ida among the gravehouses above the cabin, just as the old Widow Lang had conversed with her departed sisters, she talked to Ramsey as if he could hear her.

"And your mother and I are getting on so fine, you would not believe it, my love. I knew that would please you. I'm going to name a new perpetual hybrid after her, too, call it Clarissa. I've named others Ann, Sherborne, Jennifer, Tamar, Christina, Euphemia, Amrine, and Old Betty. You know, long-blooming crossbreeds for my long-blooming friends." She chattered on until Tamar came running around the corner of the church, leading Rebecca's saddled mare.

"What now?" Rebecca asked.

"Some men on the road told our workers there's smoke coming from the hunt lodge chimney," Tamar told her. "Since it was your special place with his lordship, I thought sure you'd ride out to see about it, and I could go with you."

Rebecca hesitated. The hunt lodge and the heath had been the only places she had not forced herself to visit since she'd lost Ramsey. But she had been meaning to face the lodge and close it up for winter; she had not wanted to send anyone else to do it. This would be a good opportunity to secure it and make sure strangers were not occupying it.

"All right," she said, wiping her hands on the grass. "It's a lovely day for a ride, and I'll appreciate your company."

She mounted carefully. Tamar held on behind with her hands on her mistress's shoulders. Soon, Rebecca knew, she would have to forgo riding. Strange, how she thought of Aunt Euphy now. She pictured the pretty woman riding free about the Kentucky countryside on her white horse, perhaps with Adam riding fine and strong beside her.

The heath seemed dull now, as if Ramsey's passing had changed it for her forever. Colors were muted; the wind wailed weakly. Tamar seemed jumpy. The heath used to make Rebecca uneasy too, before Ramsey showed her how to feel a part of it. There was the barrow where they had shared the stars and made a child. She turned the horse off the main road toward the hunt lodge, and already she could see that Tamar had been told the truth. A wisp of smoke rose from the chimney; probably poachers, transients, or even gypsies. She didn't want to oust anyone who needed shelter, but the lodge must not be harmed. Too many happy memories were enshrined in it.

When they dismounted, the door stood ajar but the place was silent. Calling, "Yoo-hoo!" and carrying a stout piece of firewood, Rebecca tiptoed in with Tamar right behind. In the light from the open door and a dying wood fire in the grate, they could see that the interior had been ransacked. They peeked into the nooks and crannies to be certain the lodge was deserted.

"Now who would do this?" Rebecca demanded, tossing the wood onto the fire. "Captain Owler hasn't made a move since Ramsey died."

"The village folk say it's because he's the one loosed the herd, and he's laying low," Tamar said, her voice quavery.

"Mere supposition. His ilk never acts by day."

"Well, since it's such a mess here, you want me to go back for folks to help clean it up?" Tamar asked, clenching handfuls of skirt in her fists. "You know, fetch some of those fine Shaker brooms and all? If you can bear to be here alone with your thoughts for a few minutes, that is."

"Of course I can. I should have come weeks ago. But can you handle the horse?"

" 'O course, though wish I could ride as fine as you, milady."

She helped Tamar mount and watched her start nervously away. Poor girl, striving to speak like the Sherbornes, yearning to ride like a lady, when her life here in hidebound England would never allow it. At least she hoped Tamar's foolish dreams about Will were over. Things like that happened only in Gran Ida's old songs or in magic Kentucky meadows.

Slowly Rebecca meandered back inside, adrift in beautiful yet painful memories. Despite the chaos here, she could almost see Ramsey leading her through the dusty place that day of their honeymoon, when they had sneezed and laughed. She recalled nights they had spent here. His voice had rung out so strongly when he told her how much he loved her, for there had been no Clarissa and no servants to overhear in the heath.

A scuffling sound behind her. A shadow on the floor. She spun, pressing her hands to her mouth to stop her scream. Not Ramsey's ghost, but a caped man with an owl's head hood!

"We meet at last," the muffled, whispering voice declared.

At first she simply stared. She stood her ground. Her heart

thudded as Captain Owler entered and closed the door. But as he came closer in the dim, shuttered lodge, she backed away until she found herself trapped against an upturned table.

"You!"

"Of necessity. To deal with a woman who does not know when to cease, when her dead husband's cause is dead too. No more attending labor meetings and no more letters to the London papers! You will swear to this now or suffer consequences."

She began to tremble. She squinted to see Captain Owler's eyes, as if to assure herself the disguise concealed a flesh and blood man and not an apparition. His eyes were exposed, though in shadow. But that voice, even if rough and slow— and a smell that enveloped him and his garments even from this distance. It was tobacco smoke, the smell the same as it had been that day when she and Ramsey saved the roses . . . the smell of the tobacco they had bought for Will in Dorchester to help with his debts . . . the smell of his cheroots since then.

The man's height, his build—everything fit but the fact that this could not be! He had been sleeping in the next room the night of the fires in the village! Her insides twisted; she thought she would be sick. She locked her knees to stand when the rest of the horror hit her. Tamar had brought her here; Tamar had led her into this trap. He had lured the girl to this! Her mind scrambled for reasons. She had to know.

She stepped suddenly away and unhooked a shutter to swing it open. The move obviously surprised him. She saw sunlight shine on familiar pale blue eyes.

"Dear God, no! Will?"

He started. And drew a pistol from the depths of his cape.

"Why, damn you, have you had to ruin everything from the start?" he demanded in his own voice.

"I? You're evidently the traitor!"

He yanked off his hood and threw it to the floor. "Are

you demented, woman? Unless you swear to desist, you have doomed yourself!''

"Will, how could you? Let me pass! Go back to London to your gambling and poor deluded girls like Tamar or whatever else you do there to ruin your once-good name!"

"My name? You're the one who encouraged Ramsey to drag the Sherborne name through the dust! Even Lord Melbourne—"

"That's it!" she cried. "I cannot believe it of you. Ramsey loved and trusted you. Betrayed by one even closer to him than the local squires! But you—you are working for Melbourne."

"I dare say you might as well hear it all now. I should have known there's no bargaining with Shaker Sister Rebecca. Melbourne was kinder to me than my father ever was. Only one son for a father, evidently, as mine was only too happy to cast me out after he had his heir. I have served Melbourne for years. He appreciates me. I wrote him from America when I went with Ramsey there. I keep him informed and—''

"And you never did a thing to help our cause. You worked against it! How clever of you to just happen to be in the next room that night you must have had someone toss those torches in the village. How did it feel that night to be a hero helping to put out the destruction you had caused?"

"If I had not cared for you and Ramsey, I swear, I would have had my man torch the entire village!"

"Who is it that helped you? Not one of the Sherpuddle—"

"An associate from London you don't know."

"But it does nothing to exonerate you!"

"Judge and jury now, are you sane? Don't you realize you stand alone with the stupid, superstitious villagers in this? I should think you would accept by now that most intelligent people are against Ramsey's and your head-in-the-clouds ideas! Even your mother-in-law, let alone the local newspaper, the squires, the powers that be in Dorchester. The first

Captain Owler, the one who tried to stand up to these powers, was caught and killed by Squire Prettyman's estate guards, but the idea to terrorize the superstitious villagers was such a good one—"

"I knew it!"

"What?"

"That the squires were in on this!"

"Not on the Captain Owler tactics, though Squire Prettyman inadvertently gave Melbourne the idea when he wrote to him that Captain Owler had been secretly killed. Melbourne sent me to tell him to keep it quiet—and I turned the idea to our benefit."

"You know," she said, aghast, "I'm glad Ramsey never knew."

"Rebecca, I cared for him, I swear I did. But he would not listen to reason, to warnings. I tried to save him from his own destruction in this, but he was driven by devils."

"You are the devil, you foul—"

"Enough!"

"It's not enough. And now you try to cloak your motives by blaming your father or implying you were just serving Melbourne, and 'the powers that be.' How very grand and noble! But I think you did it for your own selfish ends! Did Melbourne underwrite your gambling debts? And you've been cajoling Ramsey's mother for years, fixing to get the Sherborne heritage that now belongs to Ramsey's child!"

"Ramsey's *unborn* child," he said so acidly her fear conquered her anger again. She tried to ignore his threats and the pistol that wavered in his hand. But still, she had to know the truth.

"You had someone take the letter I sent to Ramsey from Cincinnati, didn't you, Will?"

"How clever of you."

"No, I've been very stupid where you were concerned. It's only that I could not fathom your deceit any more than did poor Ramsey. I'm only hoping you haven't been deluding

Tamar too. She's the link here, the one who took my letter, your little spy, like you are Melbourne's, isn't she?''

He looked sad and tired. Perhaps she could reason with him, plead with him if he felt guilty about Tamar. But it was obvious that the girl was in on this and would be bringing neither sweepers nor saviors to the lodge today.

''Yes, with coaxing and for the promise I'd save her brother from Sherpuddle, Tamar gave me the letter and told me things about the night you arrived in London,'' he said quietly as he came closer. ''Pity she got ideas beyond her station about me.''

''You sound just like Samuel Swithins, but then you're the one who gave him information about my struggles to get to England so he could discredit me before our guests!''

''But I did it all for what I believed in, Rebecca, not money, not Melbourne. You, of all people, ought to grasp risking all for what one believes in! We must stamp out the radical, dangerous ideas you and Ramsey espoused. Liberty for the laboring poor will shred the moral fabric of this country if it is not ended. But even Ramsey's death did not end it for you. No, the Shaker Rose becomes a martyr's wife with explosive power you cannot begin to realize. I am sorry, Rebecca. Sorry Ramsey died. I didn't mean for that to happen any more than I did what must happen now. I only meant to draw you here, to warn you.''

Her knees went weak as water; she sank to the floor. Will had loosed that skittish herd that trampled Ramsey. She had once told Will those cattle liked to bolt! He had killed Ramsey!

She was so horrified that she could not demand to know if it was true, could not accuse him. But he seemed to read her thoughts.

''I only meant to break up your bloody fair and scare people off. I had no idea he would not rescue the old duke in time—that was the only risk of it, in case the old man was trampled and Ramsey inherited his House of Lords seat to

397

speak out, but accidents can always happen to people in busy London.''

Rebecca wrapped her arms around her middle as if to shield the child. He meant she must die too. He was going to kill her, kill her child. Still, she huddled there as Will fished out a jar of lamp oil from the pile of rubble on the floor. He splashed it on the upturned furniture, the jumbled bed linens, the rug. The smell of it bit deep into her, mingling with the tobacco stench.

"Will, let me go," she said, amazed at her calm voice as she slowly stood. "Do not compound your sins."

"Sins! I would expect a Shaker to say it that way, so I will proceed with my confessions." His voice cracked with emotion. "I do not want to burn this lodge with you in it. But again, necessity rules. Poor Rebecca, so distraught without her husband, she took her own life. But I have marveled at and admired you, really, Rebecca. At first I thought your— uniqueness—would ruin Ramsey's cause here, but it actually resurrected it. You drew people to you and embraced the village. When Ramsey was cast down, you were not afraid nor ashamed. Now I see that an Englishwoman of his own class could have scuttled all his dreams, but not you!''

She continued to stare at him, but she was no longer seeing him. Clarissa had told her that same thing when they had reconciled: *I admire you.* Ramsey had told her that. Mama had said much the same on her deathbed, and the Shaker elderesses had expected so much of her. But she had only been herself. She had not intended to be admirable or clever or anything but herself, loving and needing and reaching out to others. Now this wretch was going to rob her of that. Take away all her memories, her future, her child.

Will dared to produce one of his damned cheroots with that stomach-turning smell and light it from the ashes on the hearth. But as he backed toward the door, the strangest thing happened. She knew he would toss the cheroot into the room to make a holocaust that would trap her here, but she felt very calm. Pictures of her life flowed through her brain like a cascading crick. Not just her own life, but parts of Gran Ida's too, parts of Mama's when she left the Mercer farm to marry, parts of Daddy's when he was keelboating down the rivers of his dreams, even the part of Clarissa's sad childhood which she had shared with Rebecca. And the life of her unborn child too, growing up beautiful and bold and brave in the land of Rebecca's beginnings, the land she had missed so much.

She moved forward to face Will down, to defy and stop him. But then the air outside swelled with chanting voices that made Will grasp both his cheroot and his pistol tight to his chest.

" 'We raise the watchword liberty. We will, we will, *we will* be free!' "

The labor union song! Then other shouts, her name and Will's.

"How in hell!" he snapped. Pointing the gun at her, he darted to the window she had unshuttered and peered out. "Surrounded—the whole damned union—pitchforks and scythes. Tamar too. And here for you!"

"They know, Will. Put the cheroot out and drop the gun. They have you now, Captain Owler, and Melbourne will have to do his worst without you!"

The noise came closer. She saw Will waver. She feared he would yet drop the cheroot to engulf them both in an inferno. She edged to another window and opened the shutter. She would go through the glass if she must. Will blinked at her in the light.

"I am so sorry—about Ramsey. About this," he floundered.

She saw tears dribble from his dazed eyes. He leveled his gun at her while their gazes held. She put one hand up as if to ward off the bullet. He ground his cheroot out against its handle, then lifted the pistol barrel to put it in his mouth.

"Will, no!" she screamed and covered her eyes with her hands. The gun exploded, sprinkling her with crimson rain. The villagers flooded the room as she began to scream.

Outside, they washed Will's blood from her skin. She sat with her back braced against a tree, with Jenny on one side and a sobbing Tamar on the other. She stared at the smoking hulk that had been Ramsey's and her retreat. Although she had thought Will had snuffed his cheroot out, somehow the oil had ignited as the villagers carried her and then dragged his nearly headless body out. Now, too late, she realized that Will had burned everything and everyone he had touched.

"Some of the men saw a hatted rider go by on a horse that looked like Captain Owler's," Charles told her. "And 'sides, Tamar came screaming for us, saying there was someone at the lodge going to hurt you, but we were halfway there by then."

Rebecca reached out to take the crying girl's hand. "You had a change of heart about Will, just in time," she said. "A change of heart about me."

Tamar nodded wildly. "You always stood up for me, even called me a friend and appreciated me, milady. You believed me and thanked me. Honest, he just said he was going to talk some sense to you about visiting America and I should bring you out to the lodge by telling you there was a mess. He—he kissed me like he did that other time he told me I was special and it was Valentine's Day. But today, I got to thinking when I saw the horse he had, he could be Captain Owler, and he never told me that. And then I saw him put the cape and hood on in the bushes, 'fore I rode farther away. I started thinking he just wanted to use me, and you were always so kind and true—" Sobs racked her again.

Rebecca was too shocked and drained to cry. But deep inside, she mourned for Will, covered by someone's coat on the ground, waiting for the magistrate's men to arrive from Dorchester. She could have cried for such treachery, for the tragedy of Ramsey's friend who had betrayed him. She could have wept for the loss of the lodge, but maybe it was best it was gone with Ramsey. She could have sobbed for joy that the village labor union was united still and had come to save her, or that now she had a chance with Tamar, or that Jenny and Tamar comforted each other too. She could have wept with sorrow and joy for all those things, but tears finally streamed from her eyes in relief for just one reason. She knew, when the baby was here and she and Mother Sherborne had a chance to share the child, what she was going to do. She would take the child and go home to the Shakertown and Shelter folks she had left behind too long.

29 October 1839

Lord Melbourne,

Through admissions of William Barnstable, Lord Richley, just before his unfortunate death last week, I have learned of your plotting against the rural laborers of Dorset and my family. If you or those who do your evil bidding try to harm me or my family again, letters exposing your treachery will be sent to the London newspapers to show you for what you are.

If you wish to avoid this, you must publicly confess your sins or exile yourself from politics. I should like to know your answer soon, sir.

Rebecca Blake Sherborne,
Marchioness of Sherborne

"Rebecca, my dear, you will not believe what just arrived." Clarissa called to her the entire length of the long gallery and hurried to meet her, waving an envelope in her raised hand.

"Not a second letter from Lord Melbourne! I had hoped, as he vowed, he is long gone."

"A message from the queen herself!" Clarissa cried.

Rebecca was big with child, but she moved as fast as she could. "Oh, not bad news, I hope. Now that that wretched man has announced his retirement, I hope he hasn't said something and Her Majesty is blaming me!"

Trembling, she broke the red wax seal. The stiff vellum crinkled in her hand. She read aloud to the hovering Clarissa:

28 March 1840
Buckingham Palace

Marchioness of Sherborne,
Sherpuddle, Dorset

The Queen wishes to compliment you on the high quality
of the Queen Victoria Conserves that a lady of the bedcham-
ber offered to the Queen last month. Please send a goodly
supply forthwith. It is a great favorite with the Queen and
her husband, Prince Albert. Henceforth, it may be noted
upon all labels of Queen Victoria Conserves that such is
approved by 'appointment to her Majesty the Queen.' Your
Sherpuddle village folk are now 'suppliers of provisions and
royal household goods.'

We hear that the fame and the village products of the
Marchioness of Sherborne have now spread far and wide
in our beloved land. The Queen recognizes and praises the
skills and heartfelt strivings of stout British souls to elevate
themselves and inspire other rural folk. You and your peo-
ple have helped heal wounds from previously embittered
and dangerous labor disputes in your area which have
sometimes spilled over even to London. We hope that our
royal approval of your philosophy of rural independence
shall enhance the profit and pride of even wider endeavors,
toward which you and your brave late husband have led
the way.

Signed,
V.R.

"Oh, my dear, what an honor for the family!" Clarissa
said, clapping her hands. "It justifies the work you've done
here for the villagers—you and Ramsey—and with your own
hands!"

"It's wonderful all right, but why does she refer to herself
as 'the Queen' and 'we' and this V. R. if she's writing the
letter herself? Isn't her name really Victoria Hanover?"

"Well, more or less. But she has used the plural 'we,'

formal third person, and the initials in Latin for *Victoria Regina*. It's proper for a queen, of course.''

''Yes, I should have known,'' Rebecca admitted with a shake of her head. After all, she reasoned, if a marchioness was not to call servants by their given names, it was pretty obvious that the queen could hardly refer to herself in a real common, friendly way to a marchioness. She'd lived here for three years and still didn't think like these fancy folks did! And Clarissa was still fussing over this letter as if she'd known from the first that working with one's own hands and with the villagers, no less, was proper and perfect! How proud Ramsey would have been of his mother's approval and the queen's, for it was he who had first suggested she send her conserves to Her Majesty. But it was poor, bitter Will's circulating them in London society that had evidently brought them to royal attention. So in the end, perhaps Will was not a traitor in all things. Rebecca blinked back tears to smile at Clarissa.

''Shall the 'royal we'—that's us around here, Mother Sherborne—go in for tea and have some of the queen's favorite conserves, then?'' she asked and gave her a big hug.

''Oh, yes, let's. But let's send someone for your women workers too and lay out a bigger spread so we will all be together when you tell them the good news!''

Rebecca nodded, tears in her eyes again. Though she still missed and mourned Ramsey terribly, her cup overfloweth.

Rebecca's labor pains began late at night on April 6, a week after the queen's letter arrived. Both Clarissa and Tamar tended her until the Sherborne surgeon, Dr. Mulvaney, arrived posthaste from Dorchester.

''I'm in the early grinding pains,'' Rebecca informed him through clenched teeth, while Tamar blotted the sweat from her face. ''And I'm going to get up and walk a spell again.''

''Walk, my lady?'' the obviously startled man said. ''Best save your strength for the bearing pains later.''

''Mother Sherborne and Tamar,'' Rebecca said, ''please

help me. I want this baby to drop proper and soon. And, Tamar, keep that feverfew tea close, because I plan to drink a lot of it.''

At that, the doctor helped her up too. As time went on, she could tell he was perturbed that she kept drinking cold herb tea, but Clarissa stood up for everything she wanted. At least this baby was not early, Rebecca thought, as pain more intense than she had ever imagined tried to turn her inside out. Her belly was so swollen that she knew this baby would have strong lungs and would scream right out—the way she was going to scream soon, she feared, as they eased her back onto the bed and her legs into stirrups secured to the bottom bedposts.

Her mind wandered. Blast it, why couldn't she have a good mountain midwife here like Gran Ida, or a country doctor she trusted, like Adam? Still, this man's father had brought Ramsey into the world. Everything went in circles, she thought, and that comforted her a bit. But Dr. Mulvaney had also attended Ramsey before he died. He had told her Ramsey might never walk again. Unfortunately, that had been only part of the truth. And the doctor hadn't wanted her to walk today, and she just wanted to scream at him—

She cried out and pulled the tether lines tied to the headboard. It went on and on. She was not really frightened, but felt herself getting more and more anxious to have it over and her baby in her arms. How could women like Jemima Tucker, Prudence Johns, and Mary Wembly do this over and over? No wonder Adam's mother took to her bed permanently after having too many babies too close together! Not only should this world change its laws about not letting house servants marry, but it should find something to ease a woman's pain besides the laudanum the doctor kept offering her. She knew laudanum sent a person off into the clouds, and she wasn't going to be somewhere else while this man and these women—as much as she trusted Mother Sherborne and Tamar—delivered her baby!

"Is the head crowning yet?" she asked between her fierce panting and cries.

"If I ever need an assistant, I shall know where to come," she heard Dr. Mulvaney tell Clarissa. "Yes, my lady, you are doing splendidly, and it is crowning. Lots of black hair. Now will you not take some of this laudanum?"

"Nothing but herbs! Be sure its cord is not around its neck—" she got out before the next twisting pain tore away all thoughts. It sliced her in two like a huge knife. Pain screamed at her, pain nearly as terrible as when Ramsey had died. He had left her, that was why she was screaming. Screaming without him, screaming to have this over, to reach out freely and—scream again to drown out Clarissa's words of encouragement and comfort. She did not like waiting for this to be over. She wanted to be the one helping, not the poor soul in desperate need!

"Oh, it's a girl!" Clarissa's voice floated to her. "A lovely girl for my lovely daughter-in-law!"

"I knew it, milady," Tamar said either to Clarissa or to her. The girl sounded so excited, or was she crying? "Saw three magpies this morning, milady. You know the villagers say, 'One for sorrow, two for joy, three for a girl, four for a boy.'"

"Yes, I've heard they do," Clarissa said.

Rebecca tried to swim up from the depths of exhaustion. More village superstition, but she felt "to home" hearing it, as Shelter folks had always said. How many times had she heard Gran Ida say some mountain woman had put an ax under the childbirth bed to cut the pain? But Gran Ida was dead like Ramsey, and Mama was not here. Rebecca was not in Shelter now, and the woman washing her hot, wet skin was her other mother. Still, her anger at the pain and at not being in control of her body began to ebb slightly.

"She did so beautifully, didn't she, Doctor Mulvaney?" Clarissa demanded.

"Especially with such a big child for a first birth," he announced and heaved a great sigh.

Why were they all carrying on as if she had no part in this? Rebecca fumed. She forced her eyes open. And where was her baby? She was so tired. Then she heard a strong, lusty cry and saw her squalling red-faced, black-haired daughter, naked as Tamar washed her in rosewater, just the way Rebecca had made her promise she would. Why, the child looked as angry as Rebecca had felt a moment ago! What if all her pent-up feelings had flowed into that tiny, innocent baby?

"She's all right?" she asked, trying to count the tiny fingers and toes from across the room. "She's not hurt?"

"She is just telling us it is not the easiest thing to be born into this life," the doctor said as Clarissa wrapped the baby and placed her in Rebecca's outstretched arms.

"And not the easiest thing to live it," Rebecca murmured as she held the precious bundle to her, the last but most perfect gift her dear Ramsey would ever give her. And that it was a girl was like a sign from him, too, she reasoned. Since these English folks set such stock on having male heirs, it would be easier to take a Sherborne daughter away from Dorset to Kentucky.

Rebecca nursed her daughter the next afternoon while Tamar fussed over the ruffled, canopied cradle next to the bed and Clarissa sat in the chair, watching and smiling. Rebecca could tell she was remembering Ramsey all over again in a new way.

"We've discussed names, but you have never quite decided," Clarissa said.

"I had to see her first to know for certain," Rebecca explained, stroking the child's soft hair with her free hand. "Her name is Ann, for her maternal grandmother, but there's more. Her entire name is Ann Clarissa, for her other dearest gran too."

Clarissa and Rebecca clasped hands. Their eyes held; they smiled. Years, even months ago, Clarissa probably would have fretted at being called a gran instead of a grandmother.

But now she saw Rebecca just as she was and loved her that way.

"I am moved and honored," Clarissa told her hoarsely. "And though I was saving this until you were more rested, I believe it is time to give you a little something I worked on until late last night. Just too happy and excited to sleep, you know," she added as she rose and hurried from the room.

"Another present, my darling," Rebecca whispered to the blue-eyed child. Handmade gifts of every description had been pouring in from villagers today. "A gran who is going to spoil you and a lady's maid who wants to be a nursemaid instead, don't you, Tamar?"

"Oh, yes, milady. She's so lovely. I tell you, if you'd just trust me—though I know I don't deserve it for things I've done—I'd be the finest nursemaid in the world for her."

"But I don't intend to live here or in London, Tamar. I may go back to Kentucky someday, and you'd have to come too."

"Oh, for an angel like that—and you, milady—I would be glad to go, parting from my mother and Brant or not!"

"Sh. We'll speak of it later then," Rebecca told her as Clarissa bustled back in with something flat in her hands. Rebecca was surprised; she had been expecting another embroidered baby's gown.

Then she saw what it was. A piece of cutwork, which Clarissa had given up since Ramsey's death. The silhouette was of the baby's tiny profile, but it was not in the black paper she had always used. It was white, with the paper petals of a pink and mauve rosebud, just opening, for the background. Clarissa had used the paper that Will had brought at Rebecca's request from London so long ago.

"It's a lovely keepsake, Mother Sherborne. I shall frame it and cherish it, and Ann Clarissa will too!"

"Wherever either of you take this someday, a bit of me will be there!" Clarissa declared. "Even, eventually, if you go—back."

"But for now our home is here, and we are a family, all of us!"

Clarissa nodded so fiercely that the lace lappets on her house cap bounced. "It's you who have made it so," she got out before all of them—except the very contented baby Ann—cried together.

They were a family for a wonderful fourteen months before Rebecca arranged to head home for America, Kentucky, and Harrodsburg in June of 1841. There she would buy a house with some land for the roses and invite Christina and her four-year-old Becky to live with them. But until then, the three generations of Sherborne women were often together; the two eldest treasured each moment. When Rebecca was out in the village or visiting in the area, either Clarissa or Tamar cared for baby Ann. The rose trade and other workshops in the village flourished; Sherpuddle even grew with outsiders who came looking for employment. They built more cots, another workshop, and a separate building for the school when the teacher was hired from Dorchester.

With royal patronage of village products, visitors from London sometimes came to view the communal buildings and buy goods or the crossbred roses. And yet times were hard in most rural areas and in the manufacturing towns where the same poverty and pain had sent Mother Ann Lee, the founder of Shakerdom, to America almost seventy years earlier. Now Rebecca and her daughter, Ann, were leaving with their nursemaid, Tamar, and more than one hundred rose seedlings for America, on a different sort of pilgrimage.

Rebecca simply had to go home to the land and the people who had made her what she was. She had to see the places of her past again. She needed to be reconciled with her Shaker family, including her brother, Jeremy. She wanted to see Christina and have her child play with her friend's child. She wanted to see Aunt Euphy, and her old friend Adam once again. She dreamed of helping the poor of Shelter increase their productivity and pride with roses and Shaker work ways. She was frontier American, not proper English. She was simply Mrs. Rebecca Sherborne, a twenty-eight-year-old widow with a child; she no longer felt like the Marchioness of Sherborne now that Ramsey was gone. She had to go home.

But she had been dreading the parting from all she loved here. It was more painful than the day Daddy took her and Jeremy from Shelter, or the day she was cast out of Pleasant Hill. Now, of her free choice, she was the one deserting, though she could have changed her course with a single word to her tearful, dear mother-in-law. She was uprooting herself, with no prodding from anyone but Christina and Aunt Euphy, who were so excited that she was coming home.

Rebecca bit her lip and blinked back tears as she watched the wagon being loaded behind the carriage that would carry her, the baby, and Tamar to Poole Harbor to board the ship. Boxes of rose seedlings, samples of products, crates and trunks of goods were stacked in the wagon. She was taking so much more with her than she had arrived with. It was not the same Rebecca going home. She was now a wealthy woman, in so many ways beyond these items being stowed or the money she had put aside. But most of her funds were in trust for little Ann or already reinvested in the village. She intended to earn her own way at home.

She could see villagers beginning to gather down the lane as Tamar bounced the baby and she lingered at the front door with Clarissa. "My dear daughter," Clarissa told her, "I could never have let you go if you had not taught me not to be selfish. And I am trying to be brave, just as you said I have been."

"We have both had to be in losing Ramsey," Rebecca said. "But now we have little Ann Clarissa as well as his memory to bind us together wherever we are. And we will both write every week!"

"Yes, yes, of course. And I will visit Jenny in the village. She's patterned herself after you there, you know, just as you've taught her, so I shall try to be a—friend to her."

Suddenly, sniffing back tears, Rebecca knew something else she must leave with Clarissa, besides all the time and thoughts they'd shared. Quickly she slipped Grandmother Mercer's wedding ring from her right hand.

"Mother Sherborne, I want you to have this ring—a farewell gift, though I will be back to see you someday."

"My dearest, not your mother's wedding band."

"No, my Daddy has—had—that. You said the night we really became a family that you would have liked to have met my mama. But this circle of gold means more than that. It was my mama's mama's, you see. It's a keepsake, a link between generations of mothers and daughters who understand special things and love deeply—as we do."

"Yes," Clarissa whispered fervently as Rebecca slid the ring onto her thinner finger. "As we do and ever will!"

Rebecca hugged Clarissa hard, not worrying anymore about touching her shoulder. She turned quickly away. She took little Ann from Tamar so that Clarissa could kiss her good-bye again, then lifted the child up to Tamar in the coach. Tamar's cheeks were wet from her parting with her own mother, with whom she had gradually reconciled since the village fire.

Rebecca climbed up into the coach, but stared back out the window at the sprawling manor house, with Clarissa at the door, as if she were seeing it all again for the first time. No, she could not, perhaps would not, go back to that first day, but how fresh and fragrant that moment seemed to her now. Then, she had climbed down to see Clarissa standing stiffly under that stone angel above the door, and then Ramsey had come running—

"We are ready!" she called to the driver. "Let's go!"

She waved out the window until the tall hedges swallowed the house. People lined the village lane, waving, shouting, crying. Some sang Shaker work songs she had taught them; the voices and faces blurred as the coach rolled on. Boys waved brooms; girls threw cuttings from the village's old moss roses—yes, that's what these folk were like, their sturdy and fragrant common moss roses. And Tamar was like the vibrant, rambling brier rose the girl loved, even if it bore sharp thorns and had a sour smell at first. Clarissa was like her own roses, delicate-looking chinas and gallicas, but with hardy blooms that flourished once they were cut free of restraints. But Ramsey, she thought, as the coach rolled by the churchyard where he lay forever, Ramsey had been the very essence of the rose's precious beauty to her.

She began to cry then, though she'd tried to smile and be brave. A very pregnant Jenny, standing in Charles's embrace, caught her eye. Smiling through her tears, Rebecca shouted to her, "Write me as soon as it's born, Jen!" Why, she thought, to console herself, the baby news in England was fine. The queen herself had borne a daughter just last November.

The entire assembled Wembly, Brimblecomb, and Browne families cheered the coach on. And there, outside the communal hall, perched on a bench, sat Old Bet, waving more wildly than the rest.

"You gave me my future!" the old woman shouted. "You gave me my life!"

Rebecca thrust her head far out the window. Though she had already said her farewells to each of these people, now she almost could not bear the pain of parting. She nearly shouted to be put down, to turn back. But she heard her own future calling in Kentucky. She waved and waved like a girl until the coach swung onto the turnpike and Sherpuddle, but for its cherished place inside her heart, was gone.

Chapter Twenty-two

"You'd think at least one of them would take a nap, even if it is Christmas!" Tamar exclaimed as she led the toddling Ann slowly downstairs with little Becky cavorting behind them.

Ann ran to Rebecca, who picked her up to look out the window. "See the little lace handkerchiefs from angels in heaven," she told her daughter as they watched the snow fall. The grass and rows of rosebushes looked pristine white, as did the roofs of Harrodsburg beyond.

Rebecca was pleased with the progress she had made in barely six months here. She had purchased an old Georgian house on the north end of Main Street with a large backyard, garden house, and carriage house. The last had been converted to a rose products workshop. She had hired seven local women, mostly poor widows, to work a few hours each week. One or two of them took turns tending the children not yet in school while the others worked. Christina helped too, but mostly oversaw the house. Aunt Euphy, who lived two streets away, dropped in almost daily to lend her warmth and charm. She was here now to spend the day with them.

But Rebecca would head home to Shelter to start cottage and communal industries there as soon as she had established things here to support Christina and her endeavors—and as soon as she had somehow managed to see Jeremy. When she had ridden to Pleasant Hill last autumn, she had been recognized by Brother Phineas and turned back at the village boundary. She knew he had not given Jeremy the message that she longed to see him and Sisters Faith and Alice before she went home to Shelter.

But today, for once, it was not the hope of seeing Jeremy or going home, nor even Christmas, which excited her. They were all awaiting the return of Adam Scott from his journey out west. He had written his aunt he would be home by Christmas, so they had set a place for him at the table.

As the day dragged on, Christina, Rebecca, and their girls delivered gifts to their neighbors. Already such new products as rose honey, rose syrup, and sweetbags had become popular with Harrodsburg's citizens. Rebecca knew her royally approved Queen Victoria Conserves, vinegars, and sauces would be snapped up by the pleasure-loving, prestige-hungry people of Graham Springs next summer. Still, most of the profit would go toward new endeavors for the folks of Shelter.

As Aunt Euphy bustled in from the kitchen, Rebecca saw that the usually calm woman was as rattled as she was, waiting for Adam to appear. "Perhaps his steamboat got iced in somewhere or the snowy roads are worse to the west," Aunt Euphy fretted. "I described in my last letter where you live and, if he should not have received it by chance, my maid will send him here. For goodness' sake, we cannot have these little sweethearts getting fussy waiting for their meal. Now, Tamar, you go fetch your dinner guest, we shall have a prayer for Adam's safe and quick arrival, and then we shall partake."

Tamar seized her bonnet and cloak and hurried off. Rebecca was pleased to see Tamar blossoming. She had a beau, a strapping lad named Chester Corwin, who lived next door.

Chester owned a dry goods shop on Water Street and insisted on giving them bolts of material for sweetbags and gowns. It moved Rebecca deeply that Tamar had said more than once, ''Chester treats me like a real lady!'' She knew Tamar would not be heading to Shelter with her; she and little Ann would be on their own. But that did not frighten her. The challenge warmed her as much as the blazing fire did this room.

They sat to eat, seven of them, but Adam's empty place loomed large. Ann chattered from her tall wooden chair and five-year-old Becky sat importantly on a cushion placed on the seat of an adult chair. It struck Rebecca that the day of Becky's birth had been the last time she had seen Adam. Now he was gone so much that old Dr. White had also taken on a second young assistant. And Adam was never paid for his months out west; Aunt Euphy said he worked day and night when he was home to make up for it and would never let her give him money. Despite the delicious food, Rebecca's stomach tightened. How would it be to see her old friend after all this time, now that Ramsey was gone, and with two separate, different lives between them?

Amid the clatter of pewter on china and the buzz of conversation, they heard a flurry of knocks at the door. Everyone froze, then jumped up. Despite her bad leg, Euphy made it to the door as fast as Rebecca. With her heart pounding more loudly than the knocking, Rebecca swung the door wide open.

Adam stood there, hat in his big hands, so solemn, taller than she'd remembered, gaunter, darker-skinned from sun and wind.

''Adam, welcome!'' Rebecca cried as Aunt Euphy exploded past her to embrace him. Adam kissed, then set Euphy back, replaced his hat, and took both Rebecca's hands tightly in his. As ever, despite the cold day, his big hands were warm holding hers.

Tamar crowded behind with Ann in her arms. Becky clung to Christina's skirts. ''This here's the real fine doctor what brung you into the world with Aunt Rebecca's help,'' Christina said to her child. That jolted Rebecca into speaking again.

"Come in. Come in,'' she managed, her throat tight with emotions she could not begin to name. She tried to pull him through the door, but he did not budge. She let go of his hands. He took off his hat again and brushed melting snow-flakes from his thick, shaggy hair and broad shoulders.

"Becca, there's someone else—an old friend I met on the Missouri this trip. I asked him to come back with me, so—''

"We can set an extra place,'' she assured him. "Where is he? Bring him in.''

"He was a bit shy about it and wanted me to ask you first,'' Adam said and stepped aside. "I don't exactly know how to prepare you for this after so long . . .''

Rebecca squinted out into the snowy dusk. A man stood amid the snow-shrouded rosebushes, looking tired, old. His shoulders slumped. Then, even as Adam continued his explanation, she knew.

"It can't—can't be . . .'' she floundered, pressing her clasped hands to her breasts.

Adam reached out to steady her by both elbows. "I know it's been years, and it's a bit of a shock. He hoped you'd forgive him and be happy to see—''

She pulled away from Adam's kindly touch and stepped across the porch and down the steps. She ran no longer from her big house in Harrodsburg, but from the small cabin on Crawl Crick. She was nine again, not twenty-nine. She threw her arms out and flew toward the man.

"Daddy, Daddy, you're back!'' she cried and ran so hard into his trembling arms she almost knocked them both off their feet.

After Daddy and Adam ate their fill of oyster soup, ham studded with cloves, vegetables, biscuits and jam, and pumpkin pie, they took turns telling their stories. Rebecca hung on every word; her avid attention bounced from one to the other: Adam so quiet, sure, and strong; Daddy talkative, but unsure and jumpy yet. But she would make him feel at home here. He had said he'd stay the winter with them, help with the rose products or drive the delivery wagon. He said he'd been to Pleasant Hill two years ago, but the Shakers had told him Becca had gone away and Jeremy was too busy to see him. Her heart soared. He had tried to come back for her! He hadn't really deserted her! Since the day of the fair, before she had lost Ramsey, she had never been so happy.

"It was Adam here first told me you was a fine lady in England, but come back widowed," Daddy explained, dandling his granddaughter on his knee. "So much for a young girl to go through, Becca."

"But you and Mama bred me strong. Besides, I'll turn thirty next week, Daddy."

"Well, now, don't time have a way of slippin' past? But little Ann here"—his voice snagged in his throat—"guess she's proof of that."

"And Daddy, I'm going back to Shelter to set up a business and help folks there. It's my dream now, what I've always been meant to do."

"And I've told her she can live in the old Scott house," Aunt Euphy put in with a sharp look at Adam which Rebecca caught.

"That place used to seem a palace to me," Rebecca admitted and reached over to take Aunt Euphy's hand.

"But now, I suppose," Adam said, "after living in that big manor house Tamar's told us of—and with special recommendation from the Queen of England herself—it won't seem like much."

"It will to me, Adam. Have you ever thought of going back? I'm sure they could use a doc—" she got out before she realized what she seemed to imply.

"I'm sure they could, Becca," he admitted, frowning down into his coffee cup. "Only, you know I was never happy there. If I'm going to support myself, I've got to stick close to the practice here, so I can return out west to the Indians.''

"I admire you, Adam," she said. "I really do."

"The feeling's mutual, Becca. I—well, I had hoped you'd be settling here in Harrodsburg.''

"My dreams are calling, Adam, just like yours," she said, and he nodded before looking down at his cup again.

Silence settled over the table. "Well," Daddy said. "Now and then when I come back through, maybe I'll come acalling at Shelter, just like the old days, Becca.''

Rebecca almost said something harsh, but she must let all that pain go now. And she must evidently let go of her hopes that Adam would—

"All right, you two young ladies, Becky and Ann, upstairs to bed!" Tamar interrupted Rebecca's musings, and conversation swelled again.

Even after the excited children were tucked into bed, Daddy regaled the adults with yarns of the wild stretches of the Missouri, Platte, and Yellowstone rivers. He had keelboated first, then worked for the government—"the Treas'ry Department inspecting steamboat hulls and boilers.''

"That must have paid quite well," Adam observed, looking so surprised, Daddy must not have told him that before.

"Well, sure, got me a nice nest egg left with a friend at Fort Leavenworth. You know, Becca, never trusted them damned steamboats. Glad to do what I could to make them safe, 'cause I'm afraid they're the way of the future.''

"I'm so proud of you, Daddy," Rebecca said and reached over to squeeze his hand. His dark hair was dusted with silver now, but it was as unruly as ever. His cheeks looked a bit sunken, but then so did Adam's. She and Aunt Euphy had already agreed they were going to fatten the two men up this winter before they set out again.

"I sure do admire you for making steamboats safer, Mr. Blake," Christina put in. "My Travis died when a boiler blew just before little Becky came along.''

"How well I recall the night she was born," Adam said,

with a glance at Rebecca that made her feel warmer than ever. It was amazing, she thought, how she and Adam fell back into the same old friendly intimacy each brief time they met, but there was something different in his eyes this time. Something hungry and hot, not just warm and comforting like the time they delivered little Becky together.

When Daddy took a breath, Adam explained that he had vaccinated Indians, but that tribes to the north of the Platte River Pawnees had been decimated by the white man's epidemics because the government had stopped funding immunization too soon. With a shake of his blond head he told them, "The hardest hit were the Arikaras, Hidatsas, and Mandans, beautiful people, all of them."

To Rebecca the Indian names almost sounded like a foreign language. It made shivers run up and down her spine to think of all the strange things Adam and Daddy had seen, but then she told some of her tales of England, and realized she had seen a foreign thing or two herself.

Finally Daddy went up to bed, long after Christina had turned in and Tamar had bid Chester good-night and retired. Aunt Euphy had gone to peek at the children and fetch her cloak. Adam and Rebecca stood close together, staring at each other, waiting in the front hall for Aunt Euphy to return so they could say formal good-nights.

"I know it's a bit late for condolences," Adam told her, "but I'm very sorry you lost your husband, and so young."

"Your kindly words are much appreciated, Adam."

"Appreciation and admiration, is that what's left between us, Becca?"

"I—it's always been more, Adam. But with you set on staying here and heading west and me dedicated to heading to Shelter next spring right after I get out to Shakertown to see Jeremy somehow . . . Adam, I have to do those things!"

"I do understand," he said matter-of-factly, as if he were making a medical diagnosis. He turned his profile to her, his features strong in shadow. "Mostly happy days for you in Shelter, Becca, but not for me. I not only will never have my father back, but I never had him in the first place. There was such bad blood between us that not even Aunt Euphy could ever heal the wounds.''

''I'm sorry for that. But it didn't keep you from becoming a fine, caring doctor, even helping the Indians at great risk and hardship to yourself. You are still a loving person, Adam.''

''Yes,'' he whispered, turning to face her. ''Yes, I'm still loving.'' His eyes held hers. She looked away first. ''And I have a Christmas gift for you,'' he said in a rush. ''I've been out to doctor those Shakers of yours. When someone breaks a bone, they'll summon what they call a worldly surgeon. So next time they call me, I'll take you as my assistant to mix herbs and such. That will get you past their boundaries, and there could be no one better at herbs than you. Then you can see Jeremy and your old Shaker friends before you head east and I head west.''

''Oh, Adam, I can't thank you enough. I'd love to show them I have no hard feelings, and then they'd have to let me see Jeremy!'' she cried and flung her arms around him.

He hugged her back so fast and hard, it startled her. But when Aunt Euphy appeared, he cleared his throat and moved away to help her don her cloak. Aunt Euphy winked at Rebecca, but did not let on she'd seen. Then, at the door, after Euphy kissed Rebecca's cheek, Adam bent to put a kiss there too. The touch of his warm lips lingered as she watched them go out to the workshop to fetch Aunt Euphy's horse, which they both mounted. Rebecca stood in the dim doorway as the white horse disappeared into the swirling snow.

That spring, Rebecca got her chance to go to Pleasant Hill, and not just to help Adam set a broken bone. There was a virulent outbreak of measles and the Shakers had lost two children to it already. Both Becky and Ann had come through all right when they'd contracted the disease last February. Now Rebecca was packing to ride out with Adam, and more afraid than ever that they would refuse to let her onto the grounds.

"I should have known you wouldn't give up on them, even after how they treated you," Adam had said just this morning when he told her he'd been sent for.

"*You* don't give up," she had challenged.

"I'd like not to," he had said, leaving her with the clear impression that they were both talking about themselves, their different dreams, their fierce attraction to each other.

But neither of them were children now, letting their hearts rule their heads. Still, she kept hearing Mama's words in the back of her head, "Becca, when it's the right man . . ."

She jumped when a knock sounded on her bedroom door. It was Daddy. He leaned against the wall just inside the door while she sat down next to her satchel on the bed to give him her full attention. He stuck his hands under his armpits in his old stubborn stance, so she knew something unpleasant was coming.

"You know, I always had the itchy foot, Becca, so I'll be setting out tomorrow too."

"I wish you wouldn't, Daddy. We'll all miss you. Besides, as soon as I've been to Shakertown and the river goes down, I'm heading for Shelter. Soon I'll need a regular keelboatman to take goods back and forth on the river."

"Just might come back for that all right. But I came now to tell you something—to clear the air."

He was silent a moment. One eyelid twitched. "I see how important it is for you to go back to see Jeremy and those Shaker sisters you said used to care for you. Becca, your mama would be right proud of you if not of me."

"Now Daddy, she always loved you deep—"

"Hush and don't make what I'm fixin' to say harder. I just got to tell why I left you and Jeremy there years ago. 'Course I couldn't of earned a decent living staying at Shelter like you wanted, but the thing is, I wasn't up to taking care of you—not anywhere we would of lived. See, I know I was bad to your mama by leaving her so much—that hurt look in her eyes, Becca. You was so like her that way, I couldn't face lookin' at you and seein' that again over the years."

She gaped at him. "Oh, Daddy, no! All these years, I thought you were angry with me for not helping save Mama or the baby—"

"No, nothing was your fault, but there's more. Told a lie bigger'n most of my yarns," he went on, "and just 'tween you and me, gonna set it straight. There's no nest egg at Fort Leavenworth I left with a friend. Truth is, never trusted another friend since I sent that man with money to your mama years ago and he just skedaddled."

She grieved for him, betrayed by a friend. Her scattered thoughts flew to Ramsey and Will before she concentrated on Daddy's Shaker-like confession again.

"Never worked for no Treas'ry Department inspecting no steamboat hulls nor boilers," he plunged on. "For years after I left you and Jeremy at Shakertown, worked keelboats offloading from steamships run aground on sandbars or snags."

"You always were a right fine keelboat man, Daddy."

He shook his head, squeezing his hands hard under his armpits. "A right fine dreamer and a highfalutin yarner, that's me. In the winters I'd lay to or hire out to load sugarcane or cotton on bayou boats down south. And, Becca, the worst is I never went calling at Shakertown to see you and Jeremy— too ashamed to face them stiff-backed Shakers and you after what I done. As much as I hated myself for leaving your mama, girl, it was worse I felt about leaving you and Jeremy, but I just couldn't help myself. I was—never worthy of your mama's love, Becca, and not yours neither."

She saw his chin quiver. She could not bear it. "That's not true, Daddy. People hurt each other real easy when they love, that's all. We've been a family since you came home!"

"Oh, Becca, Becca girl," he said, so low she hardly heard him. He sniffed hard and stepped forward to pull her to her feet. "Don't you see I can't bear to be beholden to you even now, but I know I always will be?" He hugged her hard, turning loose the bottled-up pain and fear of little Becca at last.

In the first four days Rebecca spent in Shakertown, she learned a great deal, but saw neither Jeremy nor Sister Alice Triplett as she had requested. Sister Faith, she heard, had died last year. Still, though what Rebecca wanted most here was denied her, she worked hard. She waited for someone to rail at her that her husband's loss was her just punishment for going to the world, but no one said anything like that.

Actually, none of the Believers said much of anything to her here in the East Family Dwelling except "Thank you kindly" when she tended them. Sister Sally, who had escaped the measles, brought her food every day. She always bustled back to her labors, but it was Sally who finally explained that Sister Alice was working in the Children's Order, caring for the worst cases.

It felt so strange to Rebecca to be working in this building that had been her home for almost ten years. She was glad it *was* only a building to her now and not a place she yearned for as she did the old cabin at home. She was relieved to realize she felt Shaker no more. Perhaps it helped that much had changed here since she had gone away. The Harrodsburg-Lexington Turnpike Road came right through town, bringing the world's people closer. There was an impressive new red brick Trustees' Office. And the Shakers, sadly, were much more dependent on signs and visions, called "Mother Ann's Work," than they had been before.

But beyond the chance to help here and to convince Jeremy and Sister Alice to meet with her, she looked forward to something more. Each evening, she saw Adam in the Central Family Dwelling House nurse's shop, a tiny office with three nearby rooms currently set aside for the worst male cases of measles. In the office, they tended their supplies and made plans for the next day. Each night they slept exhausted across the hall from each other in the new Trustees' Office retiring rooms, where visitors were allowed. She reveled in helping him, in her physical and emotional closeness to him, and simply in the sound of his voice.

She battled her need to go to Shelter. Perhaps once she started things there, she could return to live in Harrodsburg. But she knew that would be like putting a high yew hedge between her and the people of Shelter. As she and Ramsey had once dreamed of building a small house in the village to be closer to their friends, she must live where she meant to heal hearts. Besides, that had long been her own heart's desire. After all, Adam clung to his dreams too; he would return to roving west through dangerous territories where a wife and child could not easily go. Then why, *why*, did she have to long for this evening again to hear his voice and know he was near?

But just after Rebecca returned to the nurse's shop this afternoon, Adam walked in. His eyes were bloodshot, his hair tousled from the horseback ride. "How are the children?" she asked, surprised to see him this early.

"The vapor baths and inhalations help, but the pleurisy pills don't stem the virulence as they do for an adult. The poor little things just have to suffer it through."

"Did you try the strong nettle tea I brewed?"

"Yes, Dr. Sherborne, and came back to get more." She thought at first he was funning her, but he did not look amused. He opened wider the window of the office and leaned out on stiff arms while the curtains whipped around his shoulders in the breeze. It was against Shaker rules of order to let curtains flap out a window, but Rebecca knew not to say so. Adam was not only tired but especially testy lately.

But, strangely, the gruffer he was toward her, the more she desired to placate him—in fact, desired to please him. She longed to tease him, to smile at him, to touch him, to care for him in the most intimate ways. Sleeping so close to him at night, she even dreamed of him, of reaching out to him. But she had once fallen under the allure of a man in Shakertown where it was forbidden, and it had spelled catastrophe here.

Now, especially when she was trying to prove herself to the Shakers, she could not allow it to happen again no matter how much she wanted Adam.

"And how are the ill brethren?" she asked him as she got busy pulling more nettles for him from the neatly numbered drawers.

He turned back from the window and leaned against the sill, arms crossed, just watching her. "Most are mending, but there's one named Deacon Drury who is ailing so bad I think we may lose him before nightfall."

Rebecca's hands stilled. "Deacon Drury Triplett from the West Family?"

"Yes. You know him?"

Rebecca sank into the single chair at the worktable. "He's actually Elderess Sister Alice's son—illegitimate, conceived before she came here. She claims she's never thought of him as more than another Shaker brother. She told me once she seldom even sees him, but I wonder . . ."

"Wonder what?"

"If you'd tell her about him when you go back to the Children's Order where she's nursing. Tell her I say if she won't reconcile with me, she might at least want to see the Shaker brother who is her God-given son."

But Adam returned alone from the North Lot long after dark.

"I suppose," Rebecca said when she saw Adam's taut expression, "Sister Alice won't see Deacon Drury."

"When I repeated your exact words, the news seemed to stun her, but she didn't say a thing. I swear I don't understand these Shakers of yours, Rebecca." Adam rolled up his sleeves and bent to wash his hands at the sink. "They may be brilliant enough to have running water, but they're crazy enough to claim they've had spirit visitations of entire Indian tribes lately. The brothers were very impressed to hear I knew a few Indians too, never mind that mine actually exist. But I do admire some of their philosophy. The idea of life being a united entity, physically, intellectually, and spiritually, intrigues me. I do believe that an unclean mind or heavy-laden guilt can affect bodily health, but this idea of theirs that disease means they have sinned is—"

"Is one reason I have been so unbending about not seeing you, Rebecca," a voice from the door said. Rebecca knew it was Sister Alice before she turned. The old woman stood there with a big muslin-wrapped package in her thin arms. Adam straightened, his hands dripping water, his eyes going from one woman to the other.

"You mean you thought my earlier attempt to see you, as tainted by the world as I must be, brought this plague here?" Rebecca asked. She had been relieved that no one had said her sinful defection had caused Ramsey's death—only to be accused of this. She did not flinch, though she felt Sister Alice's sharp stare stab her.

"I always thought you were special, Rebecca, that you were a sign sent by Mother Ann for renewal of the faith here. I was sadly mistaken," Sister Alice said. "But you have been an angel of mercy to us these last few days, and perhaps this virulent disease is visited upon us for our own sins. The community has become too rich, too big, too worldly with this public road passing through its very heart. We must become stricter, more wary, or suffer for our sin of savoring worldly success."

Rebecca felt both relief for herself and deep sadness for the Shakers. Many of their beliefs seemed wrong to her, but she wanted to tell Sister Alice other things. That the world was not all bad, even for Shakers. That she had missed Sister Alice. That she had not regretted leaving, even though she had not kept her beloved Ramsey long. That she felt honored to help Adam nurse the sick here. That, as strange as it seemed, she had once again discovered desire for a man where it was strictly forbidden. But she stood speechless as Sister Alice extended her heavy package to her.

"For me?"

"I thought since you have left us, it was only seemly and proper that you have your old Blake family Bible and your herbal book returned. The copy of *Pilgrim's Progress* we shall say was Brother Jeremy's contribution and should stay.''

Rebecca cradled the books. Tears blurred her vision. Her voice wavered. ''Again, for many things, I am grateful, Sister Alice. And I hope you came also to see Brother Drury.''

''I have prayerfully decided that, since I was with him when he came into this world, I shall be with him when he departs it.''

The stern face did not soften. But the burden of deserting the Shakers when she had chosen Ramsey and the world lifted from Rebecca's shoulders. Perhaps now she would even have the strength to leave without seeing Jeremy. She stood unmoving as Adam dried his hands and escorted Sister Alice down the hall to see the son she had so long denied. Rebecca moved to the door and watched as the old woman wavered a moment before stepping out of sight into his sickroom.

''My poor, dear boy . . .'' she heard the gentle words.

Rebecca stepped back into the small office and leaned against the wall. She knew Sister Alice would not cry, but she cried for her. For all the years this mother had lost with her child. It made her miss Ann so much more. It made her miss Daddy again, and Jeremy—and Shelter. And it made her want to keep Adam in her life.

The next day near noon, the day the brothers' burial detail laid Deacon Drury to his eternal rest, Rebecca heard a commotion in the street between the Trustees' Office and the Center Family Dwelling. Instead of heading back to the nurse's workshop, she walked over to see what was amiss. Few visitors had stopped to ask for a free meal lately, which the Shakers gave so willingly, because local people knew of the contagious disease here. No Shakers staffed the Trustees' Office kitchen now. Yet two covered wagons pulled by oxen had disgorged four men who shouted at Sister Lorana, who was in charge here. Because, according to Shaker rules, Sister Lorana could answer only ''As you kindly wish'' to the raucous demands assailing her, Rebecca dropped her things and hurried down the street. She noted crudely scrawled signs reading "TEXAS OR BUST" nailed to the backs of both wagons.

"Wal, lookie here. Another of them prim and proper Shaker ladies to do our biddin'," a burly man shouted. "We hear we can get grub here, 'long with a little Shaker sweetness."

"I'm afraid we have a measles epidemic here," Rebecca explained, "so you'd best move on. Ordinarily, we'd be glad to give you food, but—"

"Just hand it out the door then. We heard all about you Shakers and your weird ways, dancing real crazy like. Wanta dance for us, gals?"

Rebecca's temper roiled. How dared these men barge in here to mock and criticize these kind people! "Then perhaps you had best leave before you catch those weird ways, sir," she dared.

"Got a real smart mouth, don't she, Hal?" the burly man asked one of his companions. "And here I thought Shaker gals was real shy. And the men, I hear, are yellow-bellied cowards got no backbone to fight this nation's wars neither!"

When several of the men advanced on Rebecca to back her out into the street, Sister Lorana came around to stand shoulder to shoulder with her. Rebecca glanced back toward the Central Family Dwelling House. She knew Adam was out on the North Lot, but perhaps if someone saw, they could run and fetch him. She knew he would have no qualms about taking on these men.

"I am not a Shaker, sir, but a resident of nearby Harrodsburg," she said, trying to keep her growing panic in check. "And if you do not push on, you will have law-abiding citizens of that town after you, even if the Shakers live far above such crudities."

"Crudities, says she!" the man bellowed and snatched at her skirts. Just then, from the dwelling, out strode ten brethren with brooms in their hands as if they meant to sweep the

427

street clean of such scum. Silently they stared the intruders down, advancing like a living wall with the sturdy wood handles clasped horizontally before them. The outsiders quickly retreated to their wagons, cursing every step of the way.

But it was not the visitors' hasty departure from the village that excited her. The man who had led their rescuers out of the dwelling was Jeremy.

"That was good of you, Rebecca," he told her as though they had never been apart. He kept a distance from her.

"It was—needful," she managed. "Thank you for coming to my aid, Jeremy."

"As you have come to the aid of the Believers," he replied. "Though I have not been ailing, it put me to mind of that time you and Mama nursed me through the canker rash."

Two other brothers stayed with him. He came no closer. She did not dare either, though she longed to. It seemed they were nearly shouting at each other to be heard.

"Oh, Jeremy, you think dearly on—on things we once shared too!"

"Of course, but I am ever thankful our worldly father brought us here. You made a grave error leaving, Sis—Rebecca."

She squinted into the sun to stare deep into his burning eyes under the shade of his Shaker hat. His gaze was clear, distant, beyond her. He was content. He was home and she was not, and never would be until she set foot on her Concord Peak refuge once again. She wanted to tell him she had seen Daddy, tell him about her child, tell him it was her dream to go home. But already he had turned away and disappeared into the brethren's door of the dwelling house. She hurried around the back entrance she and Adam used, and saw him galloping up on his horse at breakneck speed.

"The trouble's over?" he demanded as he dismounted. "You're all right?"

"Thank goodness, they sent for you. But of all people, Jeremy led my rescue."

"I'm glad you saw him," Adam said as he escorted her into their office. "I asked him to speak with you, but he seemed so distant. They're all caught up in seeing visions. I think that's a way they can rebel with no risk," he said as he closed the door behind them. He came close to take her gently by her arms. She gazed up into his eyes, which blazed with desire. She nodded. He gave a tiny tug and she pressed closer to him.

"I'm like that, Rebecca," he admitted, still out of breath. His mouth was so close. "I see visions of my own and want to rebel."

His lips covered hers. They felt and tasted so good, so strong. Fierce joy and expectation churned through her. He had kissed her more than once back in Harrodsburg, but so restrainedly, as if he had been waiting for something from her she could not give. Now, his arms crushed her to him and she felt the power of his body, the rapid rise and fall of his chest. She began to kiss and embrace him in return.

She could not—not here! Not after trying so hard not to admit she loved him among the Shakers, who could only tarnish such lovely longings for a man. If someone came in, word would run riot in the village that the worldly sinner was in love with another man. And if they both gave in like this, she would give up her dream of Shelter for him, as she had given up her dreams to do things Ramsey's way, making things so painful!

The moment she pulled back even slightly, he let her go.

"I've been meaning to tell you, I think you should leave," he told her, his voice crisp and commanding now. "After all, you've seen the two folks you deeply care about here." He turned away, not looking at her, wiping his hands on his shirtfront, then riffling through the herbal drawers as if he were instantly busy. "The river's gone down, and I think it's time for you to take little Ann and your roses and head for Shelter. Funny, each time we're together for a while, there's something calling you away—last time a husband in England, this time the dream you've always had inside you."

"Adam, you have your calling, too, and I—"

"No, I understand. I want you to go, the sooner the better for both of us. It won't be long until I'll be heading west."

"Yes, I know."

"Look, Becca—Rebecca, all grown up now—just take my buggy back to town and I'll borrow a horse. Things are better here now and I'll be back in a day or two. I know you miss Ann. I'll try to see you before you go."

She nodded numbly. She would hold to that promise at least. Back in Harrodsburg, away from here, she could convince him there was some sort of future for them, if he wanted it. Could they divide their time between the places they must be? There must be some way!

"Please don't cry, Rebecca. Please, just take my buggy and go!" he said, still not looking at her.

She stood stunned as he seized something from a drawer, then stepped forward to squeeze her shoulder with his free hand. His eyes stared down into hers. The lips she longed to kiss pressed into a tight, hard line.

"Adam, please, listen—"

"It was just never meant to be," he choked out and banged through the door. She stood rooted to the spot, even as she heard him ride away.

Before Rebecca left Shakertown that afternoon, perhaps forever, she had one more thing to do. She traversed the raised steps where she had first entered the village with Daddy and Jeremy seventeen years ago. She walked out to the herb-embroidered meadow where she had declared her love to Ramsey. She went this time not to recall the past here or with him, but to say farewell to it. Ramsey had been dead for almost three years. She had probably ruined things with Adam, at least for now. She only dared to hope that someday something better could be built between them.

She meandered just to the fringe of the riverside meadow. Beneath the wooded cliffs, she felt the Kentucky calling her upriver toward home. She leaned her hands and chin on a sturdy black locust fence post that, with others, now cut this field off from plowed and planted ones. Just like in England, foolish men thought they could hem in God's great meadows.

She stared dazedly across the lilting roll of grass and herbs like yellow-blooming life everlasting and blue lobelia she used to gather here. The scene blurred before her to become that old quilt of Armine Lang's with the never-ending circles of gold and blue. Her memory circled back to the folks she thought of as her guardian angels—Armine, Mama, Gran Ida. But Sister Alice had called her an angel of mercy, and now she must fly away home.

She ran back to borrow Adam's horse and buggy. She was going home to Shelter. And this time, like Daddy, she was not looking back.

Chapter Twenty-three

Rebecca put off her departure for a week, waiting for Tamar's wedding—and for Adam—while she packed for the journey. But Adam did not return to Harrodsburg. Then, at Tamar's reception at the house, Aunt Euphy told her Adam had been summoned to Lexington by a doctor friend to help with the measles there. He had said Rebecca was not to wait for him. That message was clear enough, she thought. But perhaps next year when she came back to visit Aunt Euphy and Christina, if Adam was here then, she could make him understand how much she had always loved him and they could find some way to put their two worlds together.

She hired a flatboat and loaded it with rosebushes and supplies. Though another family now owned the Scotts' brewery, the key to the old Scott house hung by a chain around her neck. The June river was still a bit frisky, but they made good headway to Boonesville, where she stopped to see her mother's family again.

As she had thought, her Grandma Mercer had died shortly after she had visited. But her cousin Sarah greeted her more kindly now, and they got on fairly well. The Mercers and their kin doted on Ann and urged Rebecca to tell stories about England. They had been convinced she had wed her English lord by the letter she and Ramsey had sent and their gift of a crate of Wedgwood tableware in thanks for the Mercers' hospitality. Rebecca planted four perpetually blooming bushes called Sweet Ann around the corners of her maternal grandparents' graves, but was eager to push on. She promised she would stay the night whenever she traveled to and from her house in Harrodsburg.

And then, after two days' journey, majestic, purple Concord came into view, then gray-green Snow Knob. She gasped at the way Shelter had grown, though it was still pitifully small compared to other river towns. But the Scott house looked so much smaller than she had recalled it. Surely not everything had shrunk so from her girlhood memories! She stood awestruck as her two hired boatmen began to unload burlap-balled rosebushes at her feet on the bank. That old, haunting song of Gran Ida's lilted through her head; "In Scarlet Town where I was born, there was a fair maid dwelling . . ." But today the song felt happy, not sad. It was Ann who finally broke her reverie.

"Home, Mama?"

"Yes, home, my sweet girl."

The afternoon was wearing on, but she had to see the cabin and her refuge today. She gave the men the key to the Scott house with instructions to place the bushes in the yard and the other things inside. She waved and cried greetings to a group of curious youngsters, wondering who their parents were. She couldn't wait to see everyone, but right now she was in a hurry. She gathered just two items, as she had planned, and took Ann's hand. Then, on a whim, she removed her shoes and lifted the child for the long climb up.

Wind tugged at her hair and skirts. She did not look back at the town but ever upward. It had been so long since she had walked this way. How desperately filled with loss she had been that day Daddy took her and Jeremy downward; now, she still missed Adam. Sometimes she shifted arms, switching Ann and the single rosebush she carried. Pebbles hurt her feet. She had become a tender city girl, but her soles would toughen up this summer and she'd let Ann go barefoot too.

She passed the chestnut snag and then the large rock that marked two corners of the Blake claim here. She set Ann down while she pulled the family deed from the bodice of her gown. It had remained in the family Bible all these years, and she had brought it back in case someone questioned her right to the land and cabin. She meant to replant Mama's herb beds and intermingle her new perpetually blooming roses with the original apothecaries. She meant to do so much here.

Crawl Crick rattled along beside the path, some of it greatly overgrown. It only meant people had not moved this far up, she thought, relieved that the places she sought would be untouched. Pulling Ann by the hand when she tired of carrying her, Rebecca hurried on. They halted under the big white sycamores that had once been her sturdy friends. Then she saw the cabin, weather-worn, memory-worn. It stood empty, yet full of fragrant thoughts of those she loved. Both its doors and the single window were gone, letting the wind wail through. But for one moment she almost believed that Mama would come running out to welcome her home as they had Daddy so many times. No, Rebecca warned herself, no grieving, only happy memories to build the future. For her own Ann stood smiling up at her.

At the cabin door, Rebecca put the rosebush down and whirled her daughter in her arms. "This is where we dance and sing!" Rebecca told her while the child squealed in de-light. "I'm going to teach you the Virginie Reel and the waltz and we'll have our own frolic on the brow of the hill, just Ann and Mama. But someday when we've got these folks making rose and Shaker products, we'll invite everyone up here . . ."

Her voice trailed off as she approached the west cabin door. She let Ann play in the old garden, now gone to weeds, leggy rosebushes, and a riot of untended herbs. "Pretty, Mama!" Ann pronounced the tangled mess.

Despite the slant of the sinking sun, the silent shell of the once bright cabin was dim. No echoes of voices or feet. But there were the footpegs up to Jeremy's and her sleeping loft; a piece of string dangled that had once held drying herbs, pumpkin rings, and shucky beans. Chimney chinks had grown to huge holes. The corners of the puncheon floor had snagged the debris of years; vermin had made nests here. Well, she thought, perhaps these critters were descended from Adam's broke-boned animals Jeremy had to let loose the day they left. Like her own heart after losing Adam this time, this place needed more than to be cleaned and swept; it needed to be rebuilt. And she would do it, maybe not to live in, but for a retreat as fine as the hunt lodge in the heath ever was for her and Ramsey.

Carrying Ann and the rosebush, she climbed higher. At the old family graveyard on Restful Knob, she paused, holding Ann so tightly she squirmed to be set down again.

"You should have known them all, my dearest," she whispered, gripping the child's hand. "But I'll tell you all about them as you grow." Before the grown-up Rebecca could stop her, the old Becca shouted toward the worn gravehouses sheltering their tombstones, "I love you all!" Someday she'd sit here and sing songs and tell Mama and Gran Ida everything that had happened, but not today. They turned and went on.

Now she became very nervous. She had been afraid for years that the first rosebush she had taken from the Widow Lang and planted up on her refuge would not have survived the harsh wind and scant soil, as Mama had warned. But it just had to be alive!

Besides, as she put the first foot on the ledge, she feared she would picture Adam here. She could envision how he had looked that day she had showed him this special place. He had embraced her and called her "beautiful Becca, wild mountain rose." It pained her that he didn't love this place and its people as she did. There was just no changing some folks, no reconciling with them, no matter how desperately you wanted it.

"Mama cry?" Ann asked as Rebecca bit her lip to stop its quivering.

"Yes, Mama cry, but Mama's glad you're here!" Then, "How you keepin'?" she shouted the old mountain greeting to her favorite place to hear it echo off the rill-washed rocks.

"How you keepin'?" Ann called, drowning out any other echo there might have been.

No swinging in on the vines today, Rebecca thought. This climb seemed to steal her strength, and her feet and back hurt. And then her heart caught in her throat.

Her refuge was adorned with roses, leafed out and budded in rich profusion, though it was too early for their pearly pink or sunset flowerings. But, even wind-whipped, her very first rosebush had lived and flourished! She fell to her knees beside her daughter to look up at the extent of it, climbing the once barren rockface.

"Mama cry?" Ann repeated.

This time Rebecca only nodded as tears washed her cheeks. She pulled Ann into her embrace, and for the first time, as she had planned, surveyed the sweeping scene below.

Again, as ever, it took her breath away. The green ribbon of South Fork still wove its way through the curly heads of trees. In the circle of the seasons, the apple green of spring had merged into the moss green of summer. The rainbow valley of meadows was cradled by the loving arms of the mountains, making one perfect whole. She sucked in a breath and heard the shriek of Whistling Peak below. And something else.

"Re-bec-ca! . . . bec . . . ca . . ."

Someone had seen her and come up this way! Old Claib Tucker out on a hunt perhaps, or—

She stood and turned, gripping Ann's hand. The wind ripped her chestnut hair loose, coiling it in tendrils around her face. Her skirts brushed the tops of her scratched, dirty

436

feet. Tears stained her cheeks. She stared at the stone arbor entrance and gasped.

"Adam!"

"Adam, hello!" Ann called to him.

"Am I welcome here?" he asked Rebecca as he walked out onto the ledge. His eyes locked with her wide, green gaze; he fluttered his fingers in a wave to Ann. Rebecca's heart thundered so hard she could not even hear the wail of the wind.

"You have always been welcome here, but I think I'm dreaming."

He came slowly closer. "Not having a nightmare after how we parted?"

"I can't believe you're here."

"I knew where I'd find you when you weren't at the cabin. We promised each other once to meet back here."

"Yes. But I thought you were avoiding me."

"I was avoiding myself even more. My past and the way I felt about this place. I was letting my hurt over what my father did to me make me bitter."

She nodded at that. They had so much to share!

"But there were good times and good folks here too," he went on. "You and your mama and Jeremy, my sisters, Aunt Euphy."

He came even closer. He was so handsome. Still, coward that she was, she picked up Ann and held her between them, when she wanted to throw herself into his arms.

"Adam, it took me so long—to know—to admit—I love you enough to make you my dream, and not only this place and its people."

"All I want now is to love you—share my life with you, even here."

"In a way, you've always been part of me, Adam. We're more alike than different. If you want to go out west, Ann and I could try to go too."

He grinned like a boy. "To help me with my doctoring? To plant rosebushes across the country the way Johnny

Appleseed did trees? The west is not a good place for women yet, Rebecca, but it's going to be. But for now, I think we're better off here.''

She smiled, though tears blurred her eyes and she saw two Adams putting big hands on her shoulders. He stroked his thumbs tenderly up and down her throat. Wild joy coursed through her veins at his touch.

"Actually," he said, "I should take up doctoring in one place to build a practice. Dr. White's at his wits' end with my comings and goings. Besides, the government has some doctors for the Indians now, even though they cling to their tribal medicine men. I should settle someplace where there are no doctors. A place where I can heal bodies while my wife heals hearts."

"Seeing my folks years ago, I'd be worried about wedding someone whose mind and heart was elsewhere."

He pulled them both to him; she felt his strong arms trembling. For once, Ann kept quiet between them. "No one fortunate enough to take you to wife, Rebecca Blake Sherborne, would ever have his mind, heart, or body elsewhere. I know. I've tried it these last couple of years, even when you were married to another man in another country. But now, I think we've both come home."

They looked off down the valley. Rebecca leaned her head back against his shoulder and sighed in utter contentment. His arms around both of them, Adam caressed Rebecca's windblown temples with kisses. Ann squirmed and pointed off down the valley at a soaring bird. Bursting with love, Rebecca had to have the last word to mark this new beginning.

"From the high up heavens to the low down earth, it's a right fine day!"

Author's Note

Most of the characters in this book are fictional, although they are inspired by historical research. Exceptions include two minor Shaker characters, the schoolteacher Hortency Hoosier and preacher Brother Benjamin Dunlavy, and, of course, Lord Melbourne and Queen Victoria, who do not actually appear "onstage." Otherwise, any resemblance to people living or dead is purely coincidental.

Shelter, Kentucky, is fictional but is based on research into such early mountain communities. As I mention in the book, my Sherborne family has no relationship to people living in the Dorset town of Sherborne. Sherborne House is loosely drawn from such grand Dorset homes as Athelhampton near Dorchester and Parnham near Bridport.

Shakertown at Pleasant Hill actually existed and can be visited today as a "living tourist attraction." Buildings have been restored, crafts are demonstrated, Shaker singing and dancing can be enjoyed, bounteous Shaker food is offered, and visitors can sleep in the original dwellings. And on the Kentucky River below the village, visitors can take riverboat rides.

The Shakers should not be confused with the Amish or Mennonites. The cult of the Shakers, more exactly called Believers in Christ's Second Coming—their belief was that Mother Ann was Christ come again in female form—was spread from New England to Kentucky during the years in which this novel takes place. It is estimated that in 1840, six thousand Shakers lived in the nineteen Shaker villages. But after the Civil War, such diverse cultural changes as mass production of goods, the opening of state orphanages, and the lure of the world spelled doom for Shakerdom as much as did the Shakers' belief in celibacy. Today only a handful of Shakers exist. But that does not lessen the impact they had on our culture. I hope my story shows that these innovative people gave us much more of a heritage than today's expensive antique furniture.

The rural unrest in the Dorset of this era is well documented. However, I have taken fictional liberties to base the town of Sherpuddle, the Friendly Society of Agriculture Laborers, and Lord Melbourne's machinations on actual happenings in Tolpuddle, Dorset, three years before the events in the novel. Today, Tolpuddle is a sort of shrine to the early labor union movement. During this rural upheaval, an anonymous Dorset night marauder named Captain Swing frightened local landowners and superstitious villagers. Captain Owler is loosely drawn from this hooded terror.

This was also the era of both American and English reform movements such as Chartism and Robert Owen's far-flung international socialism. Although I did not use these movements per se, some of Ramsey's ideas and Rebecca's deeds were inspired by the period's atmosphere of utopian experiments.

Visiting the sites for this novel helped me greatly. I am deeply indebted to the following people and institutions, who helped me during my several years of research into the Shakers, Kentucky, London, and Dorset: In Shakertown at Pleasant Hill, Larrie Curry, curator; Bill Kephart, researcher; and Debbie Larkin Pope, herbalist and horticulturalist. In Harrodsburg, the staff of the Harrodsburg Historical Society and the Mercer County Chamber of Commerce. Alberta Moynahan, assistant director of the McDowell House, Danville, Kentucky, a home and museum of a Kentucky doctor of this era. In England, researchers and local Dorset citizens at the tourist information center in Dorchester and especially the Dorset County Museum. In London, the Victoria and Albert Museum and the London Museum were two of the locations that educated and inspired me.

As always, I am appreciative of librarians at my home research sites, the Columbus Public Library, the Upper Arlington Public Library, and the Ohio State University Library. Also, thanks to the Rose Festival, the Columbus Recreation and Parks Department, Columbus, Ohio, especially for the antique roses on display in the park.

I would like to express special, heartfelt appreciation to my agent, Meg Ruley, who believed in this story from the beginning, lent continual encouragement, and helped the book find a wonderful publishing house and editor. As always, my love and gratitude to my husband, business manager, proofreader, and travel companion, Don Harper. And to my mother, Margaret Kurtz: thank you for reading me all those fairy tales when I was young. Attentive, supportive mothers help adult, real-life fairy tales come true. Rebecca knows that, little Ann is about to discover it, and I have seen it too.

Karen Harper

Prologue

The Scottish Island of St. Kilda
March 20, 1851

Long after the silver gloaming had deepened to darkness, Abigail
heard her lover's secret signal, nearly swept away by wind: "Yo-
ou, you, yo-ou!" Douglas imitated the long-beaked curlew's cry
so perfectly, she thought, not even a canny fowler would ken it
was a lad calling his lass and not a bird its mate.

Abigail's half-darned stocking tumbled from her hand. She
lowered the wick of her lamp, seized her plaid shawl, and peeked
out the door to be certain no one was in the street at this end
of the village.

She fled on her familiar, fleet-footed way, fretting that there
must be more to this summons than the usual invitation. She had
bid Douglas goodnight a scant hour ago at their lofty trysting
place they called the castle, tucked in the rocky folds of Mullach
Sgar. In his calling her again, so soon and so late, she scented
danger or disaster. He should be home, helping his father mend
the climbing rope for the old man's journey tomorrow. Surely
their meetings had not been discovered, else his mother or village
folk would have been at her door ere now. For years she and
Douglas had been, of necessity, skillful at stealing hidden hours;
now, Douglas had said, finally freedom was but a week away!

She felt the silent sprawl of village street and took the upland
rise easily in stride. She could hear the muted boom of breakers
crumpling against cliffs below; her heart boomed as hard. She
had forgotten bonnet or kerch, and her waist-length hair whipped
free. Crisp air bit deep into her lungs, and soon her muscles
heated with the ache of a climb.

Ignoring the meandering path, she scrambled higher. The
stalks of new heather under her feet merged with the pebbly

slide of rocks from the peaks of Mullach Sgar to make footing more perilous. She knotted her shawl over her breasts to free her hands should she skid or fall. But she was only to the first big boulder when she heard "yo-ou, you, yo-ou" again. She turned toward the sound.

Douglas's broad-shouldered form loomed large against the gray arch of sky. His straw-blond hair glimmered white, but his deep-set eyes and slash of firm mouth hid in black shadow. Balanced on the steep slope, he came closer, clasping her upper arms, then pulling her into his embrace. She held to him, her face pressed against his wool jerkin. He clamped her closer, his chin against her temple, his powerful arms and thick wrists like metal bands around her.

"Abby lass! I'm in a rush, so we shalna go up to the castle."

"My love, what's amiss?"

"All of a sudden, father says I must go to Boreray with the men tomorrow, and for so long without ye! But Parliament decided one young cragsman should go too. Edmund Drummond put my name forward, and they gave approval to a man."

Abigail heard the pride in his voice rise above his disappointment. She heaved a sigh of mingled relief and regret. When St. Kilda climbers went for gannet feathers on the nearby outlier of Boreray, they stayed for several days, as there was no place to land a boat. The fowlers leapt ashore and the crew came back for them later, depending on weather and tides. She was proud her lad had been selected, but grieved he would, no doubt, be gone next week.

"I'm glad for you, my Douglas," she murmured as she drew in the manly scent of him, mingled with salt air. "At least, your news isna someone saw us, as I feared."

"To tell true, but for leaving ye, I'm glad to try those cliffs. 'Tis a test of even braw climbers' skills to get ashore with waves rising and falling so high at every pitch!" he said, as if he saw it all this very moment. "The gannets must be taken at night, ye ken. Aye, the cragsman's at his best there, and it's no sabbath stroll! But," he lowered his voice and pressed his lips to the wild hair at her temple, "to be there and ye here, the very day we been waiting for so long . . ."

He tugged her above a nearby outcrop of rock so he could lean on it and she, full-length, against him. She reveled in his hunger for her; her own need swelled. The bittersweet lure of their yet unfulfilled passion made her knees go weak, but she wondered if his desire was not right now more for his grand adventure than for her.

"Time will crawl without the hope of seeing you, even for a stolen moment," she told him.

"Ye'll stay busy as I. I couldna just have ye surprised to see me depart tomorrow with everybody standing by. I had to say a right farewell, even if for a wee while."

"But when—" she got out before his lips covered hers, and she opened her mouth willingly to tempt him deeper.

Since their youthful friendship had bloomed to adult love, they had struggled with themselves and each other to be clever, controlled, and careful. They had fought plunging themselves in the familial act for which they so longed. Often they had been a step from that precipice but had not fallen completely. They had vowed to await the blessed day next week when Douglas Adair turned twenty-one and when, as a Far Isles man, all things were then possible.

The reasons their love and union were frowned upon, and thus forbidden, were a twisted skein: his peoples' pride, her parents' past—and Douglas's lofty perch in the islanders' regard she feared she could topple, however much she loved him.

His breath came harsh as he broke the kiss and tipped her back in his arms. "I wanted us to be together on my manhood day. I wanted to decide and share everything then, whatever they do!"

"What can they do when you are a man and sit in the island Parliament? Only, I fear that—"

"Fear naught, lass! Only that we have had to wait so long for the real loving, the thing that would bind ye even tighter to me!"

"And maybe make a bairn before 'tis proper, my own dearest," she reminded him. She poked him in the ribs but her voice sounded sad and heavy. "I want a child with you more than life itself, Douglas Adair, but not 'till everything is right. Life is hard enough for bairns here even when their parents not be tempting the way of things."

"True enough," he agreed, "but when I ask ye right and proper—well, just ye practice reciting yer 'Aye, my love!' while I be gone then. And, think of this!"

He crushed her to him again, lips and limbs. Though she fought to keep her head for both of them, passion louder than the sea roared in her ears. His beard stubble rasped her chin and upper lip, but it was a thrilling ache. Her mouth felt sweetly swollen when he finally, slowly set her back; she wet her lips to taste him yet again.

"And when I return," he vowed, his voice gone rough, "we'll be done with this blasted burrowing about like puffins to mate! And things shalna ever go wrong for us again! I'll send ye home alone now, and, for the last time, I swear it, Abigail MacQueen. Tomorrow, ye'll get a mere nod and wink when I set off, but there will be much more when I return, no matter if they think we must have tricked them all these years!"

She squeezed his hand as they started back down the slope. She prayed all would be well so they could walk and talk together in daylight as well as darkness. But she still feared, deep down, what she had been terrified to tell him lately, the one thing her braw lad had never fathomed. If St. Kilda folk frowned upon Douglas Adair's bold decision to take Abigail MacQueen to wife, for his sake and that of the islanders, though it would be the very death of her, she must find the strength, the love, to tell him no.

Chapter One

St. Kilda's far isle,
Bold-browed, spray-swept,
Crags, clefts, winds, waters,'
Snared from sky and wild sea.
Old hearthsongs sang thus to me.

Questions questing,
Awestruck astonishment
Snare me and my lad,
Till hand-in-hand we fly free.
My heart-wings sang thus to me.

Tall, red-haired Abigail MacQueen leapt from slick boulder to boulder above the swirl and shift of foaming green water. Her long legs were bared to half-thigh; her toes skillfully gripped the slick surface of the stones. She had removed and knotted her stockings about her hips and caught up her hems to save her skirts from a sloshing. A wool belt of rainbow hues cinched her brown gown at her waist. Tied back from her oval face by twisted heather, her long hair whipped free. She had stuck her small, sheathed dirk behind her ear for safe keeping. She held a cloth sack in her teeth so both arms were free to balance her bounding progress across the low-tide inlet between St. Kilda and the rocky ridge of Dun.

Her rich, deep voice hummed her song through the sack as if to challenge the cacophony of wind, water, and birds. To set free the words of her own making, she seized the sack in one hand and let the song pour forth. Then, she seemed to fly across the boulder bridge with freedom and exuberance, like a flapping, soaring bird of brown and russet plumage.

Reaching her destination, she propped her bare feet on a boulder and leaned back against the sheltering rock drapery of Dun. She untied her stockings, and wriggled into their knee-high, thick wool warmth. She thrust her dirk into her belt, then pulled a chunk of cheese and a barley bannock from her sack and devoured them.

She tried to tell herself that the day was too lovely and life too wonderful to let her great trial turn her hopes to black stone like this rock against which she rested. She breathed in deeply, then began to sing again. But that drifted to humming, then silence. Her heart was as heavy as the old hearthsongs, and she soon turned to brooding again.

Abigail was two months from age twenty-one, but her beloved Douglas reached that venerated age today. Though St. Kildan folk made no great show of birthdays, twenty-one marked the time a lad formally became a man and eligible to sit in the daily decision-making gathering of island men called Parliament. And a man could marry whatever lass he willed, no matter what his folks, kin, or the other men counseled—and therein lay her dire dilemma.

"Aye, Douglas, my love, wish you were here to turn my head, but 'tis my burden to decide too, and that's the way of it." She glanced in the direction where the steep-sided cliffs of Boreray, which her Douglas climbed, lay, four miles off St. Kilda. But broad granite Oiseval Mountain blocked her view just as she feared the St. Kildans might block her way to Douglas. She shook her head and deftly climbed to rocks above the high-tide line where she would find lichens for her dyes.

She knew she would be alone here today to make her momentous decision, for none of the other women ventured out this far. Still, she always offered to share these lichens which produced the unique rose and crimson dyes the islanders would not use for tradition's sake. To forgo a life with Douglas would be a thousand times worse than forsaking her dreams and desire for brilliant-colored clothes!

"I ken you St. Kildans fancy the bright hues," she muttered, "so why let the old ways keep you from wearing or selling them, you stubborn Scots!" Her high brow furrowed as her thoughts fled to Douglas again.

Abigail had loved Douglas as long as she had memories, and he loved her in return. They had been reared next cottages, and though their folks had never kept company—to say the least of it—the children had. As mere bairns, Douglas and Abigail had protested heartily when they found they were expected to act differently because lads and lasses had separate paths to tread.

Like all island lads, Douglas Adair had learned the bold skills of a fowler and climber. At age three, he clung to the rough, rounded cottage stones; as a lad of twelve, he skillfully clambered up clefts to leave other boys far behind; at fourteen, he scaled sky-high cliffs to harvest birds. Now, he was admired as one of the island's youngest of a select group of fowlers called cragsmen, a hero soon worthy of his own hearthsong. But always in his ascent to manhood, though Abigail had heavy, earth-bound woman's work to do, she and Douglas had smiled and shared whispers in the dusk between their cottages at day's end.

Even in lamp-lighted rooms with the others, their eyes had met, eagerly then shyly, in the years of their youths. When his parents subtly then stringently forbade them to keep company, they secretly defied them. Today, Douglas no longer needed his family's nor Parliament's approval for anything. Only, now, nearly too late, Abigail realized that for him to ignore this might mean disaster for his reputation and his future—and endanger the island's welfare too.

Lately, as reality had come home to roost, she saw their union might hurt him more than help him. It would probably cause a rift in the Adair family, and she could not bear that, even if Margaret, his sister and her best friend, sided with her and Douglas. Some villagers, though none said it to her face, evidently still saw the stain of her parents upon her, and would, no doubt, think she was unsuitable to wed him. She feared that she would not be the dutiful and sweetly meek wife Douglas needed as he rose in St. Kildan admiration over the years. If people disapproved of her, Parliament could cut back his duties, though that would endanger the food and other supplies a great cragsman would harvest over the years for the island's profit and very survival. No one had ever been exiled from the island, but they might be ostracized: to be an island on an island as her father had once been—she could not face that for herself not consign her beloved to such a fate.

And yet, if she told Douglas he should wed another, even the bonny Flora Fergusson, whose green eyes followed him everywhere, she feared his fierce anger and bitter agony as well as her own desolation. He might claim she had led him on and betrayed him. She kenned well how hurtful words flowed from a man's wounded pride by listening to her father after he was abandoned, even by her mother's death. And if Douglas did not understand it was all for his own good and turned against her, she might as well cast herself off the cliff of Oiseval as some folks said her mother had one stormy night.

"Blast, my dearest lad, I fear I wilna have the strength to tell you no!" she fervently admonished the slick rocks, but she saw only Douglas's beloved face before her again.

She heaved flat, gray-green lichens into her sack so hard some bounced back out. Finally, she turned to rest her elbows on an outcrop of rock, frowning in concentration until the beauty of the outer weather again lured her attention from her inner storm.

Though clouds often clustered to blur then blot the scene, today the sky was brilliant blue and the sun warmed her. Its mid-afternoon heat beat down on the passage from the southwest, illuminating a green-walled cave carpeted by ruffled, sun-gilt sea. To her left, the far end of the passage took the fury of the westering waves; the east end, which emptied into the curved harbor of Village Bay, ebbed with the gentle flow of waters protected by the bold, black breakwater of the Dun, which once had been part of the island. These far isles, called St. Kilda, were comprised of this island, its smaller outliers, Soay and Boreray, and several now stranded stacks of stone. St. Kilda lay forty miles farther west from Scotland than the Outer Hebrides and seemed to those few outsiders who ventured here to be the rocky roof of the world arising from the depths of the north Atlantic.

From this sheltering arm of Dun, the view was spectacular, even to one who was used to it. Above and around her, goldheaded, white-bodied gannets darted and dove for fish. She wondered how many Douglas had gathered on Boreray; it took nigh on two-hundred-forty of them to provide feathers for one good mattress in Glasgow. From her view here, graceful, gliding fulmars, on which the island greatly depended for its food and other supplies, seemed to drench St. Kilda in a blizzard of bickering bills and wild wings. Feathers floated in the air like strange-shaped snowflakes. On this side of Dun's serrated spine, she admired green grass cropped by sheep and the spongy turf burrowed by puffins, which were just now returning from their winter migrations. For centuries, the arrivals and departures of the many birds that made the isles their home had governed the St. Kildan calendar.

Beyond the sheltered arc of dark blue Village Bay lay the islanders' homes in a sweep of a single street overlooking all this God-given wonder. From this distance, the thirty-two stone cottages that comprised the island's only inhabited town of one hundred ten folk seemed a crescent of fairy-size buildings: church; the minister's gray stone, slate-roofed manse on the far end; then the factor's house before the curve of smaller, lower thatched cottages; hers, called Lady Grange's cottage, one of the oldest, was at this end nearet Dun and lofty Mullach Sgar.

Above the village, the irregular stone sheep fanks and the walled cemetery climbed the rocky hillside toward clouds encircling the stony steeps of Carn Mor and Oiseval mountains. Beneath the village lay the strips of fields which, in its windy wrath, sea-savaged Dun doused with spray like rain. Abigail licked her lips and tasted the familiar salty tang. The villagers were used to it, but not the crops, meager and sporadic most years. The seasonal harvesting of birds was for survival as well as feather rent to their landlord, the laird, MacLeod of Harris. The man himself never set foot here, but each June he sent his factor for a month to land his smack on rough rock to collect the woolen cloth and feathers that were his due.

"Abby! Ab-i-gail!" floated to her on the wind. Her head jerked up. She squinted across and up the boulder-strewn gap she had crossed. Margaret Gillies waved to her from the last grassy height before the rocky shore below began. Margaret was Douglas's younger, married sister and Abigail's boon companion. Theirs was a frowned-upon friendship too, for Margaret's mother approved of it only a bit more than she did Abigail's so much as speaking to Douglas.

"Wha-at?" Abigail's strong voice lilted back across the gap. It was those bell-clear tones more than the talent of her heart-wings—her imagination—to create new songs that had made her the only woman hearthsinger at her young age. Quickly, just to be certain Douglas's boat had not appeared, Abigail shaded her brow and squinted across the harbor. No sign of any craft yet, so Margaret had not come to tell that. She scrambled to strip off her socks before leaping back to the mainland.

THE INCOMPARABLE MAX

A play by Jerome Lawrence and Robert E. Lee
Based on Sir Max Beerbohm's
trips beyond reality

A SPOTLIGHT DRAMABOOK

Hill and Wang   New York
A division of Farrar, Straus and Giroux

The younger generation is knocking at the door;
and as I open it there steps spritely in
the incomparable Max.

    —G.B.S. in his valedictory as drama critic
      of *Saturday Review* (May 21, 1898)

Max Beerbohm, Incomparable Critic

WE ARE BORN CRITICS. The first yowl of a neonate is not a protest against a sinful world; it is a review of the birth canal.

A critic does not need to be right, erudite, scholarly, or even able to spell (especially if he phones in his review or does it in front of a TV camera).

A critic needs two things: (1) an editor who will hire him and (2) the style to win a following. In the matter of *style,* few critics of any age are a match for Beerbohm. But Sir Max was not likely to enter a match with anyone. He was a watcher of matches, the onlooker supreme.

Max wrote sparingly. The prolific Somerset Maugham complained that while he himself was writing more and more to a diminishing reputation, Max kept writing less and less to expanding acclaim. True, there is not much "bad Beerbohm." (He must have tossed it in his own wastebasket!) But his slim little volumes, illuminated by impertinent strokes of the pen or pencil, leave no doubt: he will always be "Around Theaters."

Criticism today is a different kettle of hot lead. Whereas Max had dozens of compeers, the ranks of Broadway and London have so thinned that, even as Max himself wished, the audience may be compelled to make up its own mind. Max was constantly running down the power and ability of critics to make and break authors and "mimes" (his word for actors). One of his favorite stories told how Aubrey Beardsley got back at the art critics who had disparaged his drawings in the initial issue of the *Yellow Book;* one even went so far as to say: "This kind of thing should be made illegal by an act of Parliament!" In an essay after Beardsley's death, Max recalled:

> In the third number of the *Yellow Book,* two pictures by hitherto unknown artists were reproduced, one by Philip Broughton, the other by Albert Foschter. Both the drawings had rather a success with the reviewers, one of whom advised Beardsley "to study and profit by the sound draughtmanship of which Mr. Philip Broughton furnishes another example of his familiar manner." Beardsley, who had made both the drawings and invented both the signatures, was greatly amused and delighted.

When Max was in America with his actor-brother, Sir Herbert Beerbohm Tree (as his press agent, for God's sake!), he went to see the Paul Potter dramatization of du Maurier's *Trilby.* Max told his brother it was a terrible play and advised him against producing it in London. But Herbert stayed over an extra day and went to a matinee himself. His profits from playing the part of Svengali went into building one of London's most lavish and spacious playhouses, Her Majesty's. Max held to his guns. It only went to prove, he contended, that a play could be both penny-dreadful and a resounding hit. On the other hand, Max protested continuously that popularity with the public didn't automatically condemn a work to the dustbin of trash, maintaining always that Shakespeare, Molière, and many other working craftsmen of the theater would never have existed without love and cheers from the pit.

Max was a critic not only of the theater but of life as a whole. (The two are, or should be, related.) His *scope* makes Beerbohm interesting as play material. This is not a play about what Max did. It is about what he imagined. In some cases, it is about what we have respectfully imagined he imagined.

Current conceptions of Max are of a soul-eyed patriarch, sunning himself at Rapallo. We tend to forget that everything old was young—once. In the days of Socrates, the Parthenon was new. Bernard Shaw was once a beardless schoolboy. Every junked car had its hour in a showroom; and even Methuselah wore diapers, or an equivalent apparatus. The late Victorian era was not always distant, dusty, plush, and velvet. The air was electric with the scarcity of electricity. The natural exhaust from engines of authentic horse power delighted the flies but did not eat out the lungs and scald the eyes. London at the turn of the century was prosperous, aglow with the flush of empire, bristling with challenges for young men.

And Sir Max was young in that bright world.

On the stage, we have tried to catch both its newness and its universality. (Youth is not a matter of years; it is simply retarded disenchantment.)

Life—and theater, which distills the keenest in life—enchanted Max. This is why he was and is enchanting—as a critic, a wit, a raconteur. The creatures of his inventive mind were bizarre but believable; grotesque, perhaps, but never gross. He had both frankness and charm. When Shaw relinquished a critic's seat on the aisle to create what he had spent half a lifetime criticizing, an assistant editor of *Saturday Review* found Max. And Max found a following—greater today than when he wrote his first notice in May, 1898 at the age of twenty-five. Unlike so many of his successors in the trade and despite his protests to the contrary, Max loved theater. That is why we have written a play about him. And that is why he remains . . . THE INCOMPARABLE MAX.

J.L./R.E.L.

The Incomparable Max was presented by Michael Abbott, Rocky H. Aoki, and Jerry Hammer at the Royale Theatre, New York City, October 19, 1971, with the following cast (in order of appearance):

MAX BEERBOHM   Clive Revill
USHER   Christina Gillespie
WILLIAM ROTHENSTEIN   Michael Egan
LEWIS, A WAITER   Louis Turenne
ENOCH SOAMES   Richard Kiley
THE MAN   Martyn Green
LIBRARY CLERK   John FitzGibbon
GIRL LIBRARY ATTENDANT   Fionnuala Flanagan
PORTLY MAN   Claude Horton
HIS WIFE   Betty Sinclair
USHER   Fionnuala Flanagan
YOUNG MAN   John FitzGibbon
YOUNG GIRL   Christina Gillespie
A FRENCHMAN   Louis Turenne
HOTEL CLERK   Donald Marye
A. V. LAIDER   Richard Kiley
MAID   Christina Gillespie
UNCLE SYDNEY   Donald Marye
COLONEL ELBOURNE   Martyn Green

The Incomparable Max

MRS. ELBOURNE   Constance Carpenter
MR. BLAKE   Rex Thompson
MRS. BLAKE   Fionnuala Flanagan

Directed by Gerald Freedman
Settings by David Mitchell
Costumes by Theoni V. Aldredge
Lighting by Martin Aronstein
Special Sound by James Reichert
Associate Producer, Donald Sheff

The first public performance of *The Incomparable Max* was presented by Robert Porterfield at the Barter Theater, Abingdon, Virginia, June 24, 1969, with the following cast: Jerry Hardin, Cherie Elledge, Robert Foley, Ginger Guffee, G. Leslie Muchmore, Walter Williamson, James Farmer, Lisa Galloway, Roy Clary, Dorothy Marie, Robert Fortune, Betsy Cornell, John Gilpin, Thomas Rowland, Henry Strozier, Marlene Caryl, Harold Herman, Linde Hayen, Stephen Levi, and Diane Hill. Settings by Michael Stauffer. Costumes by Johorne. Lighting by Henry Millman. Sound Consultant: Jonathan Lee. The production was directed by Jerome Lawrence.

Act One

MAX AND ENOCH SOAMES

(There is no curtain.

As the house-lights slowly dim, there is a "sound-overture": the distant clop of horses' hooves on cobblestone, the singing of buskers, a faraway, euphoric strain of strings, suggesting the elegant days when Edward VII was still Prince of Wales.

There is a false portal; upstage, another portal—actually a projection screen—seems to represent the proscenium of a late Victorian theater.

A lone theater seat is down center, facing upstage. A spotlight burns down upon that crucial critic's seat-on-the-aisle.

In a moment of black, MAX *moves to stand jauntily beside the seat, looking upstage.*

A projected self-portrait of MAX, *back view, appears on the screen, which has been lowered into place in the black. Lights come up to model the living duplicate of* MAX *himself in the same pose.*

He takes off his top hat, removes his gloves, sits.

The sketch vanishes from the screen, replaced by a projection on the fire curtain: FOR THINE ESPECIAL SAFETY.

MAX *crosses his legs, as if waiting for the play to begin. Then he squirms a little and recrosses them. Impatient, he looks back over his shoulder, sees the audience for the first time.*

The projection vanishes as a smile of relief crosses MAX's *face.)*

3

MAX (*Delighted.*)

Oh, thank God, there's somebody else here!

(*He spins the theater seat around to face front.*)

I despise being alone. Of course, I may very easily be alone *to-morrow* night. If the damned critics don't take to this thing. I know how those damned critics behave. I'm a damned critic myself.

(*He rises, leaving his hat and cane in the seat, which he spins around again.*)

Do seats make a theater? Certainly not. It's the people sitting *in* them.

(*He settles smugly into the seat again, facing front.*)

What happens onstage doesn't make a play. It's what happens in the heads of the people watching it. Every theater is empty—dark—until each god in his own seat whispers: "Let there be light!"

(*Another theater seat slides on, suggesting an aisle. A pretty* USHER *comes down to* MAX's *seat, hands him a program.*)

USHER

Tea or coffee at the interval, sir?

MAX (*After a quick glance at the program.*)

Hemlock.

(*He hands her a sixpence, but she declines it.*)

USHER

Oh, no charge for the program, sir. *Critics* don't have to pay.

(*She goes off with an automatic smile.*)

MAX (*Wryly.*)

"Critics don't have to pay." We have to sweat ink, that's all! You have no idea what we go through sometimes. You've heard of the Iron Maiden, which punctured its victims with spikes? Or that Pit and Pendulum of Edgar Allan Poe?—I think he's British; he writes too well for an American. And of course, the rack! Where a poor devil's limbs were torn from their sockets. Terrible?

(*A little laugh.*)

Playthings for children—compared with *this*.

4

(*He taps the arms of his theater seat, then recrosses his legs.*)
My predecessor in this chair—a George Bernard Something-or-other—had a theory that people who go to the theater have a disease. They are infected with optimism. Some foolish fever leads them to think that theater may someday become a place of light and laughter and—who knows?—perhaps even *entertainment!*
(*Shakes his head.*)
Can't happen. The whole contraption's rattling in the other direction.
(*He pauses. He sees a sketch pad and pencil on the other seat; he picks them up.*)
Sometimes, to break the monotony, I doodle.
(*He notices someone in the front row, narrows his eyes, begins sketching intently. He speaks to the subject.*)
Turn slightly, please. Do you mind? So the light catches your chin. What there is of it. Of the *light,* I mean . . .
(*He has been sketching busily, then holds it up, squints at it disapprovingly, then crumples the page.*)
Doesn't do you justice. By "justice" I mean it doesn't catch your most fascinating faults. Perhaps you don't have any faults; in that case, how can I sketch you? Angels are for Michelangelo, and I'm not that good. Besides, I prefer to do people from memory. I don't have a very good memory, but it's devastatingly *nasty!*
(*The portly and fecund figure of* WILLIAM ROTHENSTEIN *enters at the top of the aisle, in time to hear* MAX'*s last few sentences.*)

ROTHENSTEIN (*Cruising past the* USHER.)
Two teas. A great deal of sugar. And cream, not milk. If I leave before the interval, give the entire mess to Mr. Beerbohm, who will tip you handsomely. Max, how are you?
(*A little dazed, the* USHER *gives him a program, accepts the sixpence, and goes up the aisle.*)

MAX
Better. Seeing you.

ROTHENSTEIN
May I criticize a critic?

5

MAX

If you'll let me sketch a painter.

(MAX *recrosses his legs and begins to sketch.*)

ROTHENSTEIN

You critics are two-faced bastards. On the one hand, you wail: Why can't theater give us light and entertainment? And on the other hand, you say that only *faults* are interesting.

MAX (*Sketching.*)

Head a bit higher.

ROTHENSTEIN (*Posing.*)

You needn't flatter me.

MAX

You needn't worry.

(MAX *squints, makes a monumental slash with his pencil.*)

ROTHENSTEIN

Question: Are you going to damn tonight's play for its faults? Or will you damn it for its lily-pure perfection? What was that . . .

(*He imitates with his hand and a noise in his throat the "monumental slash" of* MAX's *pencil.*)

MAX

Your stomach.

ROTHENSTEIN

I was afraid it was.

(MAX *scratches some more lines, hands the sketch across the aisle to* ROTHENSTEIN, *who puts on spectacles to examine it.*)

I've been assassinated with a pencil!

MAX

Caricature!—that's the *true* art. It has the two most essential elements: truth and economy.

ROTHENSTEIN

But where's the depth, the color, the light and shadow? If a playwright dared to put stick-men up on that stage, you'd hoot him out of the place. Caricatures instead of characters!

MAX

Happens all the time. Nobody wants to see *truth* in the theater,

6

they get enough of it on the pavement outside. I abhor "drama-of-the-dustbin." I didn't coin that phrase; I *never* alliterate!

ROTHENSTEIN

But, Max——

MAX

Besides, nobody *believes* the truth. You have to give it an edge to make it interesting. When a theatergoer hands the man at the door his ticket, he expects to *go* someplace. He wants to take a *journey*. To leap beyond himself. To some higher truth. Or higher falsehood. But you don't even need a theater. It's *what* happens, not *where* it happens.

(*Waving his cane, almost like a magician.*)

Any place, any room can be dramatic. It doesn't have to be a stage; it can be a waiting room, a dressing room, a bedroom. What could be more dramatic than a bedroom?

ROTHENSTEIN

Depends on the person you're in bed with.

MAX

Take the Cafe Royale, the Domino Room. Sometimes there's more drama there than at Drury Lane.

(*Thinking back.*)

The first time we met.

ROTHENSTEIN

Even before you were illustrious.

MAX

Wasn't I always?

(*A table slides on, replacing the theater seats.* ROTHENSTEIN *moves grandly into the cafe.*)

ROTHENSTEIN (*Calling to the* WAITER.)

Lewis! A vermouth for my young friend!

(MAX *follows him into the restaurant. The action is continuous.*)

MAX

Thank you, sir.

(*They sit. The* WAITER *scurries for drinks.*

MAX *seems to be younger, more eager and impressionable—rather humble in* ROTHENSTEIN'S *regal presence.*)

7

ROTHENSTEIN

Now, young man. What do you intend to do with your life?

MAX

I'm not entirely sure, Mr. Rothenstein. I may be a critic.

ROTHENSTEIN

Isn't everybody? Oh, you don't have to say "Mr. Rothenstein."

MAX

What would you like me to call you?

ROTHENSTEIN

Rothenstein.

MAX

Thank you. I—I intend to write much more than just criticism. Essays, of course, and short stories, and a few novels. Very few. Novellas, probably. I have a theory, Rothenstein. Most writers these days confuse their inkwells with their bladders. As a result, they urinate the English language.

ROTHENSTEIN

Oh, very good. Write that down.

MAX

I have. But I relieve myself sparingly of words. Instead of wetting the literary bed, I'm trying to develop restraint.

ROTHENSTEIN

Restrict your output. Splendid! You'll end up with a charming little reputation and everybody will want to take your books to bed.

(MAX *flips the menu and starts to sketch on the back of it.*)

MAX

I also draw.

ROTHENSTEIN (*With distaste.*)

Draw? Draw?

(MAX *holds up the pencil.*)

My boy, you *draw* a pistol. An artist sketches. Are you any good?

MAX

Not yet. I'm practicing.

ROTHENSTEIN

Well, that's a waste of time. Practice is fine if you're a quarter of a string quartet. That's art through industry. Most pure geniuses flower young and go to seed in their teens. Thank God, I'm not so pure and I've taken longer about it.

MAX

How did you learn to paint?

ROTHENSTEIN (*Expansively.*)

Life classes, and all that. I spent a few years in France looking at things—usually nude models. Wasn't too painful.

MAX

And you copied them.

ROTHENSTEIN

In a sense.

MAX

What if you dared to play God? To create Eden entirely from inside your own head? What if you imagined Eve, with no old Edens to copy from? Might you get the perfect woman on your canvas?

ROTHENSTEIN

If I did, I'd be ruined.

MAX

Why?

ROTHENSTEIN

I might spend the rest of my life looking for her. The woman I'd created. And that would spoil me for any model after that. Perhaps any woman after that. I'd never find her, of course. And where off-canvas do we ever brush up against perfection?

MAX

How do you know she doesn't exist?

ROTHENSTEIN

Hm?

MAX

Perhaps more than any flesh-and-blood woman. How do you know that what you imagined is not a truer truth—and what you merely *see* is false as false teeth?

(LEWIS *has come on with two vermouths.*)

9

ROTHENSTEIN (*With a laugh, lifting his glass.*)

All right. To imagination.

(*They touch glasses and drink.* ROTHENSTEIN's *eye wanders to the back of the menu where* MAX's *pencil has been working. He takes it, studies it.*)

You're proving your point. You couldn't sketch this from life.

MAX

Why not?

ROTHENSTEIN (*Holding the menu at arm's length.*)

What are your chances of ever running into a creature who looks like that?

MAX

I think they're rather good. He's standing over there.

ROTHENSTEIN

Where?

MAX

By the swinging doors. I've been trying to draw him without staring at him.

(ROTHENSTEIN *looks off, compares what he sees with* MAX's *sketch.*)

ROTHENSTEIN

My God, you have caught the fellow! But suppose you were to put him on paper with words alone? Or, with your caricaturist's economy, in *one* word. What would you call him?

MAX

Hungry, I think. Yes . . . hungry, that's the word. How would you describe him, Rothenstein?

ROTHENSTEIN (*Staring off.*)

Dim. Merely dim.

MAX

Do you know him?

ROTHENSTEIN

Good God, no!

MAX

Well, your "dim" man is on his way to this table.

ROTHENSTEIN

Don't look at him. Try to act as if we haven't been talking about him.

(MAX *quickly hides his drawing, sitting on it.*

ENOCH SOAMES *comes in. He is a stooping, shambling person, rather tall, very pale, with longish brownish hair. He has a thin, vague beard—or rather, a chin on which a large number of hairs weakly curl and cluster to cover its retreat. In short, he is a Bohemian—a Victorian hippie.*)

ENOCH (*Stopping at the table.*)

Hello.

ROTHENSTEIN (*Very casually.*)

Oh? Hello.

ENOCH

You don't remember me, do you?

ROTHENSTEIN

Remember you?

ENOCH (*Loftily.*)

Soames is the name.

ROTHENSTEIN

Soames?

(*Searching his memory.*)

Edwin Soames!

ENOCH (*Insulted.*)

Enoch Soames.

ROTHENSTEIN

Enoch Soames. Didn't we meet in—in——

ENOCH

Paris. Several times. And I came to your studio once.

ROTHENSTEIN

So sorry I was out.

ENOCH

But you were in. You showed me some of your paintings. I heard you were in London now.

II

ROTHENSTEIN

How clever of you. I am.

(*He turns back to his drink.* ENOCH *takes a chair and sits down at the table.*)

ENOCH

May I sit down?

ROTHENSTEIN

You already have. This is Max Beerbohm.

MAX

How do you do?

ENOCH

Not very well, thank you.

(LEWIS *comes on.*)

LEWIS

A vermouth for the gentleman?

ROTHENSTEIN (*Trapped.*)

You wouldn't care for a vermouth, would you?

ENOCH

Absolutely not. Absinthe.

ROTHENSTEIN

It's bad for you.

ENOCH

Nothing is good and nothing is bad. Nothing is anything.

MAX

I don't quite follow you there.

ENOCH

I explain it all in the preface to *The Ultimate Nil.*

ROTHENSTEIN (*Startled.*)

The Ultimate Nil? What in the devil is that?

ENOCH

My first book. I gave you a copy of it.

ROTHENSTEIN

Oh, yes, of course. That thin thing. Green, wasn't it?

ENOCH

Poets do not write encyclopedias.

MAX

You've written a book. How wonderful.

ENOCH (*Pompously.*)

Several books. My second volume is about to be issued.

MAX

May I ask what kind of book it will be?

ENOCH (*Grandly.*)

My poems.

ROTHENSTEIN

Is that to be the title—*My Poems by Enoch Soames?* It rhymes!

ENOCH

Certainly not. Though you are a very good painter, Mr. Rothenstein, you have a very bad ear for phonic values. "Po-*ems*" does not rhyme with "Soames."

ROTHENSTEIN

Oh?

ENOCH

As a matter of fact, gentlemen, I had rather thought of giving the book no title at all.

(LEWIS *returns with an absinthe on a tray, and, before he has a chance to put it on the table,* ENOCH *takes it and downs it in one gulp.*)

Another please.

(*Turning back to the two men.*)

Why burden a book with a title? If a book is good in itself——

ROTHENSTEIN (*Interrupting.*)

But don't you think a book without a title might be difficult to sell? If, for example, I went into a bookseller's and said simply, "Have you got . . . ?" or "Have you a copy of . . . ?" how would they know what I wanted?

ENOCH

My name will be on the cover, of course. And I rather want to have a drawing of myself as frontispiece. Do you happen to know a painter who might like to perform such a commission? I feel certain it would bring that artist great honor.

13

ROTHENSTEIN (*Quickly.*)

Well, *no*. I don't happen to know such an artist. I rarely associate with other painters. I feel it hurts my work.

(*He glances quickly at his watch.*)

Oh, dear. Look at the time. We really must be running. Come, Max.

ENOCH

But . . .

(ROTHENSTEIN *hastily takes out his wallet and puts a bank note on the table.*)

ROTHENSTEIN

There. That should pay the reckoning.

ENOCH

But, Mr. Rothenstein. I was about to order another absinthe.

ROTHENSTEIN (*Getting up and moving away from the table.*)

There's no law against that.

ENOCH

There is if I don't pay for it. And I don't have a single copper.

(*Sighing,* ROTHENSTEIN *places another bill on the table.*)

ENOCH (*Calling.*)

Absinthe!

ROTHENSTEIN

Goodbye, Mr. So-*ems*.

(MAX *gets up, bows slightly to* ENOCH, *then moves to join* ROTHEN-STEIN *outside the cafe.*

Inside the cafe, ENOCH SOAMES *finishes the drinks left by* MAX *and* ROTHENSTEIN, *then takes a large volume from his pocket and settles down to read. The light dims slightly on* ENOCH.)

ROTHENSTEIN (*Sighing with relief.*)

Whew!

MAX (*Looking over his shoulder.*)

Quite an interesting character.

ROTHENSTEIN

Interesting! My dear boy, he's impossible.

MAX

Why were you so determined not to draw him?

ROTHENSTEIN (*Correcting him.*)

Sketch! Sketch him? Him? How can I sketch a man who doesn't exist?

(*They start to move off, but* MAX *turns and stares at* ENOCH, *still seated in the cafe.*)

MAX

But he seems a rather tragic figure. I suppose a man like that might literally die for want of proper recognition.

ROTHENSTEIN (*Laughs.*)

My dear Max, you are trying to get credit for a generous nature and a kind heart—

(*Taking* MAX's *sketch and jabbing a finger at it.*)

—and I suspect you have neither one.

(ROTHENSTEIN leaves.

A hat tree slides to the edge of the portal. Clothes hang on it. MAX *moves to it and changes from full evening dress to dandyish afternoon clothes of the period, topped with a carnation in his lapel. He speaks to the audience as he changes.*)

MAX

Still, Soames had written a book—and I rushed to buy it. After all, I had met the author face to face. I kept a copy of *The Ultimate Nil* lying around my room, and whenever a friend picked it up and asked what it was about, I would say casually, "Oh, it's a rather remarkable book. It's by a man I know." But the truth of the matter is, I never *did* know what it was about. The words were all on the page, marching along like good little nouns and verbs and prepositions. But none of them seemed to have been introduced to each other. It might have been written in Esperanto or Serbo-Croatian as far as I was concerned.

(*He reaches up to an offstage bookshelf and picks up an extremely thin, green volume.*)

The stuff went something like this . . .

(*He flips open a page and lowers his voice, as if telling a great secret, as he reads.*)

Lean near to life.
Lean very near.
Nearer.
Nearer.
Life is a web
And therein nor warp nor woof is . . .

(*He looks at the audience blankly.*)
"Nor warp nor woof is . . . "? Yes.
(*He closes the book and studies the binding.*)
Now, here's the question: Was Enoch Soames an ass—or was *I?*
(*He tosses the book offstage.*)
I met him again in the same cafe.
(MAX *walks over into the scene.*)
Hello, Soames. I hope I'm not interrupting you.

ENOCH

I prefer to be interrupted. It's the best way I know for a genius to prevent himself from *over*writing. Would you care to buy me a drink?
(MAX *sits, beckons to the* WAITER.)

MAX (*To* ENOCH.)

Do you often read here?

ENOCH

Yes. Things of this kind I read here.

MAX (*Glancing at the book.*)

The Poems of Shelley.

ENOCH

Second rate.

MAX (*Taken aback.*)

Oh, of course. Shelley's very uneven.

ENOCH

I should have thought *even*ness was just what was wrong with him. A deadly evenness. That's why I read him here. The noise of this place breaks the rhythm. He's endurable here.
(LEWIS *appears.* MAX *looks up.*)

MAX

A vermouth for me. What will you have, Soames?

ENOCH

An absinthe, of course. Now that I can afford it. Bring the bottle. And take away this deadly tea.

(LEWIS, *shrugging, takes off the teacup and disappears.*)

MAX

Do you approve of Keats?

ENOCH (*Grudgingly.*)

Well, there are *passages* in Keats. Of the older men, I only like Milton. Milton wasn't sentimental. I can always read Milton in the Reading Room.

MAX (*Puzzled.*)

The Reading Room?

ENOCH

Of the library. The British Museum. I go there every day.

MAX

You do? I've only been there once. I'm afraid I found it rather a depressing place. It—it seems to sap one's vitality.

ENOCH

It does. That's why I go there. I prefer having my vitality sapped. It makes me even more miserable.

MAX

You *like* being miserable?

ENOCH

Of course. A happy artist is a hack. Masterpieces spring from a seed-bed of agony.

MAX

Oh. So you devitalize yourself in the Reading Room and lose paradise with Milton?

ENOCH

Usually Milton. It was Milton who converted me to diabolism.

MAX

Diabolism? I've never thought of Milton as a missionary for the Devil.

ENOCH

Not a missionary, perhaps. But he and the Devil were on extremely good terms, there's no doubt of that. I myself have gone far beyond Milton. Milton wore the impurities of Puritanism. *I* am a confirmed diabolist.

MAX

Take up much of your time? I mean, is there some Black Mass you have to attend every morning—or you'll be forever doomed to heaven?

(ENOCH *looks at* MAX *disdainfully, crushes out his cigarette, takes his tattered cape and starts out, stepping over his cape as he walks.* MAX *quickly apologizes.*)

Did I offend you? I'm sorry. But I'm really interested. Please sit down.

(*Guardedly,* ENOCH *settles back into his chair.*)

For example, do you have some special gospel? The Book of Lucifer, perhaps?

ENOCH (*Steadily.*)

We use the same Bible as the Anglicans. As you may have heard, the Devil's very good at quoting Scripture.

MAX

But do you actually worship the Devil? "Hallelujah Satan" and all that?

(LEWIS *returns with their drinks, a bit appalled at the conversation.*)

ENOCH

It's not exactly worshiping. It's more a matter of trusting and encouraging. Most of my new poems are about the Devil.

MAX

When does your new book come out?

(*There's a deathly pause.*)

ENOCH (*Hardly any voice.*)

It's out.

MAX

Congratulations. Did you publish it without a title?

18

ENOCH

No. I found a title at last. I'm not sure it entirely satisfies me, but it's the best the language provides. It suggests something of the beauty of the poems: strange growths, natural and wild yet exquisite—and many-hued and full of poisons.

MAX

You must have been tremendously influenced by the French. It sounds as if you're a literary cousin to Baudelaire.

ENOCH (*Scornfully.*)

Certainly not! Baudelaire was very commonplace! France has had only one genuine poet—François Villon. And two-thirds of Villon was sheer journalism.

(*As he tosses off this remark, he unconsciously tosses off the drink as well. When he puts the glass to his mouth, it is empty.*)

You want to see some truly creative originality?

(ENOCH *dramatically digs into the depths of his cape and lifts a very thin purple volume from his lap and brandishes it in front of* MAX's *face.*)

Here. Here is my masterpiece.

MAX (*Taking it, reading the title.*)

Fungoids. Yes. Yes. That's quite a title. I hope *Fungoids* is selling splendidly.

(*There is another deathly pause.*)

I'll rush to my bookseller's and purchase a copy.

ENOCH (*Ungratefully.*)

Thank you very much. That's very charitable of you. You will be in extremely select company. My publisher has just informed me that a grand total of *three* copies has been sold.

MAX

You're jesting.

ENOCH (*Snarling.*)

You don't suppose I *care,* do you? I'm a poet—not a tradesman.

MAX

Well, an artist who gives truly new and great things to the world always has to wait a long time for recognition.

ENOCH (*Lashing out.*)

I don't care a sou for recognition! Book buyers are all stupid sheep who baa their way to a book shop whenever some sheep-dog of a critic barks at them.

MAX

Well, I agree the act of creation is its own reward.

(*Suddenly* ENOCH *drops his high-flown, flamboyant manner.*)

ENOCH (*With fierce sincerity.*)

I'm a liar. A damned liar. You know that, don't you?

MAX

I don't know what you're talking about.

ENOCH

You think I haven't minded?

MAX

Minded what, Soames?

ENOCH

Neglect. Failure. But what would you know about the feelings of a great poet? You imagine that an artist's faith in himself is enough to keep him happy. You've never guessed at the bitterness and loneliness.

MAX

Perhaps you'll get your due from posterity.

ENOCH

Posterity! What use is it to *me?* A dead man doesn't know that people are shedding tears at his grave—visiting his birthplace, putting up tablets to him. A dead man can't read the books that are written about him, or hear the unborn school-children reciting his works in unison. A hundred years from now! Think of it!

MAX

We shall not be here.

ENOCH

No. But the library will still be here . . . the British Museum. And the Reading Room just where it is. And people will queue up to go in and read.

MAX

To devitalize themselves.

ENOCH (*Warming up to his dream.*)

Hundreds of books about me. Thousands perhaps. If I could come back to life *then*—just for a few hours—and go to the Reading Room and touch copies of my books, honored and treasured by a more enlightened generation! Or better still, if I could be projected, now, at this moment, into that future, into that Reading Room, just for this one afternoon! I'd sell myself body and soul to the Devil for that!

(*A looming shadow appears on the back wall.*)

Think of the card files! Drawer after drawer after drawer, and every card headed up: "SOAMES, ENOCH." Endlessly. Endless editions in exquisite bindings, commentaries, bibliographies, critical studies, tributes by great literary figures!

(*A sinister* MAN *in a black cape and a smartly trimmed Vandyke beard appears.*)

THE MAN (*With a polite apology, and just a trace of a Continental accent.*)

Excuse—permit me. I have been unable not to hear. Might I take a liberty? Might I, as the phrase goes, "cut in"?

(MAX *nods.*)

Though not an Englishman, I know my London well, Mr. Soames. Your name and fame—Mr. Beerbohm's too—very known to me.

MAX

You're a Frenchman, of course?

THE MAN (*Elusively.*)

On occasion.

MAX (*Puzzled.*)

German, then?

THE MAN

Perhaps more often than French. I am in fact a citizen of the universe, so to speak.

(ENOCH *is looking at him with penetration and a little bit of fright.*)

MAX

May we know your name, sir?

THE MAN

I have had many.

(*He lowers his voice and glances quickly over his shoulder.*)
Shall we dispense with the fancy ones?
(*He reaches into his waistcoat pocket, draws out a pitch-black calling card, which he tosses on the table in front of* MAX.)

MAX (*Glancing at it.*)
Black on black? I can't read that.

THE MAN
Oh, dear. My printer is always singeing them.
(*Awed,* ENOCH *reaches with his lean hand, picks up the card—then drops it with a small cry, as if it were something very hot.*)

ENOCH (*Staring at* THE MAN.)
I know you.

THE MAN
Know me! You *worship* me!

ENOCH (*Leaning close to* MAX).
It's the Devil!

MAX (*Openly.*)
The devil it is!
(*Starting to laugh.*)
Are you with some local theatrical company?

THE MAN (*Indignantly.*)
Theatrical!

MAX
Playing Mephistopheles perhaps? And you're practicing your latest role on us.
(*Laughing, applauding.*)
Well done. Oh, good show!

THE MAN
Show! I am a gentleman. I thought I was in the company of *gentlemen.*

MAX
You've been paroled from a matinee. You've escaped from Covent Garden. *Faust.* Not one of my favorite operas.

THE MAN
Please.

MAX

We don't even tolerate that nonsense on the legitimate stage any-more. It's endurable as opera only because of Mr. Gounod's melodies.

THE MAN (*Tremendously insulted.*)

Curious, *nicht wahr?* There is a type of person to whom the very mention of my name is—oh-so-frightfully funny. In your theaters the dullest comedian needs only to say "the Devil" and receives a roar of laughter. Is it not so?

MAX

Go on. Go on with your act.

THE MAN (*Totally insulted, turning to* ENOCH.)

I shall address my remarks only to you, Mr. Soames. I am a man of business and always I would put things through "right now," as they say in the States.

MAX

You've been there?

THE MAN

Many times. My kind of country.

(*To* ENOCH *again.*)

Mr. Soames, you are a poet. *Les affaires*—you detest them, yes? So be it. But with me you will do business, eh? What you have said just now gives me curiously to hope.

ENOCH

Hope?

THE MAN

I am prepared to make—as they also say in the States—the *deal*.

ENOCH

Go on.

THE MAN

It will be the more pleasant, our little deal, because you are—I mistake not?—a diabolist.

ENOCH

A *Catholic* diabolist.

(*He glances nervously at* MAX, *who has now become deadly serious and is listening intently.*)

23

THE MAN

You wish to visit now—this afternoon as-ever-is—the Reading Room of the British Museum, yes? But a hundred years hence, yes? Time—an illusion. Past and future—they are as ever-present as the present. Or at any rate, only what you call "just-around-the-corner." I switch you on to any date. I project you—pouf! What is today's date? June 3, 1897. Yes? You wish to be in the Reading Room just as it will be on the afternoon of June 3, 1997? You wish to find yourself standing in that room, this very minute? Yes? That you stay here 'til closing time? Am I right?

ENOCH

That was my wish.

(THE MAN *takes out a large pocket watch, clicks it open. Flames leap out of it.*)

THE MAN

Ten past two. Closing time in summer same then as now—seven o'clock. That will give you almost five hours. At seven o'clock—pouf!—you find yourself again here, sitting at this table. This evening concludes my present visit to your great city. I come and fetch you here, Mr. Soames, on my way home.

MAX

Home?

THE MAN (*Lightly.*)

Be it never so humble!

(*Nervously,* ENOCH *lights a cigarette.*)

MAX

Soames! I believe this creature really *is* the Devil.

ENOCH

But of course he is.

(THE MAN *gestures toward* SOAMES's *cigarette.*)

THE MAN

A hundred years hence, as now, no smoking allowed in the Reading Room. You had better, therefore . . .

(ENOCH *removes the cigarette from his mouth and drops it into his absinthe glass.*)

ENOCH (*Rising.*)

Shall we go?

MAX

Don't be ridiculous, Soames. Think of the consequences.

ENOCH

I would prefer the truth.

(THE MAN *turns cordially toward* MAX.)

THE MAN

And you, my dear Mr. Beerbohm, will have something rather remarkable to write about, yes?

MAX

It has been written about. H. G. Wells did it admirably in *The Time Machine.*

THE MAN

You are pleased to sneer. But it is one thing to write of an impossible machine. It is quite another thing to be a Supernatural Power.

(THE MAN *turns pleasantly toward* ENOCH.)

A hundred years hence. Ready?

ENOCH (*Taking a deep breath.*)

Ready.

MAX (*A little panicky.*)

Soames. It's your own business, of course, but I strongly advise— Soames!

(THE MAN *places his hand calmly on the tablecloth.*

The lighting becomes suddenly unreal, streaked with intense, unnatural colors. ENOCH *seems to be whisked away toward a questionable eternity.*

When the lights become terrestrial again, ENOCH *is gone.* MAX *stands gaping at the empty chair.* THE MAN *smiles, bows with a Continental superiority.*)

THE MAN

Auf Wiedersehen . . . ?

(*The lights fade.*

The lights come up on a world-of-the-future as imagined by a world-of-the-past. It is a blend of Melies, Verne, H. G. Wells, and the sputter of spark-gap electricity. It is a future unburdened by the futuristic. The restaurant has slid off, replaced by the control board of a computer. The projection screen shows some gibberish equations in a sterile, pale-green light.

The LIBRARY CLERK *enters.*

A GIRL LIBRARY ATTENDANT *rushes across, pointing off stage, terrified.*

ENOCH *comes on, looking around, bewildered. The* CLERK *behind the desk stiffens.)*

ENOCH

You! Listen to me. Why does everybody in this room move away from me in terror when I come near? I shan't bite your head off.

CLERK *(Very clipped, no wasted words.)*

Your dress. Strange.

ENOCH

I'd say *you're* the one who's strange. Tell me quickly. What's the date?

CLERK

Date? June third.

ENOCH

I know it's the third of June. What year?

CLERK

One-Dub-Nine-Seven.

ENOCH

Nineteen ninety-seven, sure enough.

(Staring around.)

This is the Reading Room of the British Museum. Right?

CLERK

Read-room. Brit Muse. Right.

ENOCH

But where's the catalogue? Where are the books?

(There is laughter and tittering from the GIRL ATTENDANT.*)*

CLERK

All on compute.

26

ENOCH

I don't understand. This is a library—I want to see some books.

CLERK (*Shaking his head solemnly.*)

Books? Paper perish. Books old-fash.

ENOCH (*Pale.*)

My God.

CLERK

All lit on mike-film. One, two books in Muse. Preserve in inert gas.

ENOCH

That's dreadful. Nobody reads anymore?

CLERK

Read. Yes. Any film—any libe in world.
(*Pointing to the row of buttons on his computer.*)
Lon? Par? Mosc? Bos-Wash?

ENOCH

They've stripped the language naked!
(*Wrinkling his brow.*)
Let me get this straight. Lon must be London. Par—Paris. Mosc—Moscow. Correct?
(*The* CLERK *nods.*)
But where and what the devil is Bos-Wash?

CLERK

In U.S. One megalop. All coast. Old-fash Boston to old-fash Washington.

ENOCH

What happened to New York?

CLERK (*Gesturing, making a sound of "swallowed up."*)

Pst-sssshp!
(*This does not displease* ENOCH.)

ENOCH

How do you read?

CLERK

Press butt.

ENOCH

(*Waving a finger shakily at the computer.*)

You mean—you can press one of those buttons and reproduce any book—or what used to be called books? Where does one read them?

(*The* CLERK *points silently to the screen.*)

And you're trying to tell me that I can read in those picture frames not only any book in this library but any in America and France and Russia?

CLERK

Four hundred libes. Tok. Johan. Hong. San-San. Mex. Chi.

ENOCH (*Puzzled.*)

I understand Tok and Johan and Hong and Mex and Chi. But where on earth is San-San?

CLERK

Last cench San Francisco to last cench San Diego. One megalop.

ENOCH

Wasn't there some little town in between?

CLERK

Los Angeles.

ENOCH *and* CLERK (*Simultaneously.*)

Pst-sssshp!

ENOCH (*Eagerly.*)

Can I try your machine? Do you mind?

(*The* CLERK *nods.*)

Before I begin, tell me something. Do you know the name Shelley?

CLERK

Yes.

ENOCH

Keats?

CLERK

Yes.

ENOCH

Milton?

CLERK

Yes.

ENOCH

Which of my contemporaries do you know? Hardy?

CLERK (*Puzzled.*)

Hardy . . . ?

ENOCH

Thomas Hardy.

CLERK (*Thinking for a moment.*)

Uh—yes.

ENOCH

Wells. H. G. Wells.

CLERK (*Enthusiastically.*)

Yes!!!

ENOCH

Swinburne, Algernon? Rossetti, Dante Gabriel?

CLERK

Not read, but know.

ENOCH (*Holding his breath, then plunging.*)

And do you know the name Soames? Enoch Soames?

(*The* CLERK *looks blank.*)

CLERK

Soames? Soames?

(*He presses a button. A buzzer sounds off. The* GIRL ATTENDANT *appears, still frightened.*)

You know name "Soames"?

(*She shakes her head "no."*)

No. Don't know.

ENOCH (*Insulted.*)

How in the world did you two get jobs in this Reading Room? You are both obviously very ill-read.

(*Impatiently.*)

Go ahead! Press some of your blasted buttons and do what you have to do to contact somebody with superior intelligence!

CLERK

How spell? S-O-M-Z?

ENOCH

Don't be ridiculous. S-O-A-M-E-S!

(*There is another offstage titter.*

The CLERK *presses several buttons. The screen bursts into life*

29

with a scrambled pattern, which quickly unscrambles and produces an almost instantaneous answer:

ENOCH *stares at it, puzzled and indignant.*)
   ENOCH (*Continuing.*)
What the devil does *that* mean?
   CLERK
Lon. No info.
   ENOCH
No info?
(*Realizing.*)
No information?
(*Accusingly, attacking the machine.*)
Something's wrong with your machine. It's stupid. It's broken!
   CLERK
Hume error possible. Compute—*no!*
   ENOCH (*Appalled.*)
In all of London, not one copy of my poems, my thoughts, my creations?
   CLERK (*Sterile.*)
No info.
   ENOCH (*Staggered.*)
Oh, God. Poor England. Sacked. Laid waste. Finished. Turned into a race of illiterates.
(*Suddenly.*)
Try Paris—the City of Light!
(*The* CLERK *nods obediently, slightly frightened of* ENOCH, *and*

30

presses more buttons. The pattern scrambles again then comes up
with a similar result.)

ENOCH
The States, the New World. Bos-Wash!
(*More buttons, another pattern.*)

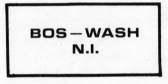

ENOCH
San-San—the West. That's where the brains have gone!
(*Obediently, the* CLERK *presses more buttons, but the screen gives*
the same response.)

ENOCH (*Hopefully, in a small voice.*)
Chi?
(*Again, the* CLERK *presses some buttons. There is a squeal and*
some printed letters flash on.)

31

WHO'S WHO IN MIDWEST
SOAMES, JULIUS 678945396
TEKNIK RITER

SOAMES (*Disappointed.*)

Julius?

(*Angrily.*)

Turn it off. Who gives a blast about some unborn technical writer? I'm interested in the poets. The great poets!

(*A sudden idea.*)

If they've forgotten my name, certainly the fruit of my mind survives. Try my titles: *The Ultimate Nil. Fungoids!*

CLERK (*Puzzled.*)

Spell please.

ENOCH (*With angry impatience, rattling them off.*)

T-H-E U-L-T-I-M-A-T-E N-I-L. F-U-N-G-O-I-D-S.

(*Simultaneously, the* CLERK *presses buttons. Quickly a series of answers appears.*)

ENOCH

Stop! Stop it!

(*The* CLERK *snaps off the screen.*)

What the devil have you done—*burned* all the books?

CLERK

All books on mike-film.

ENOCH

Well, get me some decent critical study of the late nineteenth century. How about the *Dictionary of National Biography* or the *Encyclopaedia Britannica*?

CLERK (*Nodding.*)

Dicksh Nash Byog, Encyk Brit. Yes. Which?

ENOCH

The *Encyclopaedia Britannica*. Certainly they'll have something.

(*The* CLERK *presses some buttons. There is a scramble on the screen. A page of type lights up.*)

**INGLISH LITRACHER 1890-1900
LEEDING RITERS:
GALSWORTHY, JOHN
KIPLING, RUDYARD
SHAW, G. B.
STEVENSON, R. L.**

ENOCH (*Squinting at the screen.*)

Galsworthy? Below-stairs pap! Kipling? Barroom poetry. Shaw, G. B.? Who the bloody hell was he?

(*Despairingly.*)

Stevenson? They're joking. Tiddly-bosh for children.

(*Turning impatiently to the* CLERK.)

Go on! Go on! Is that all?

(CLERK *nods.*)

I've changed my mind about your damned Encyk Brit.

(*Quickly he takes out a tarnished pocket watch and glances at it impatiently, realizing that time is passing. He laughs dryly.*)

Nothing?

(*Refusing to abandon hope.*)

There must be something. A paragraph someplace. A mention, even a *bad* mention. On all your worldwide mike-film, or whatever the bloody hell you call it——

GIRL ATTENDANT

Kloz time!

(*Big Ben begins to strike and a flashing pattern of KLOZ TIME appears.*)

ENOCH

No, not yet! Tell me quickly. What's the best book on late nineteenth-century literature? The last ten years.

CLERK (*Thinking.*)

Uh . . . Nupton. T. K. Nupton. Brit Litracher. One-Eight-Nine-Oh to One-Nine-Dub-Zero. Page?

ENOCH

The index, of course. Under S-O-A.

(*The* CLERK *presses some buttons and an index page appears.*)

SNOW, ELIZA ROXEY, Pg. 96
SNOWDEN, PHILIP, Pg. 137
SNYDERS, FRANS, Pg. 11
SOAMES, ENOCH, Pg. 234
SOANE, SIR JOHN, Pg. 371
SOAPLY, OSBERT, Pg. 101
SOCIALIST WRITERS, Pg. 11
SODERBLOM, NATHAN, Pg. 49

(ENOCH *mutters the names, then practically leaps off the floor in delight when he sees his own.*)
Grazie Diavolo! Can you show me page 234? Right now?

CLERK

Yes.

ENOCH (*Taking in a deep breath.*)

Wait. First get me a pencil and paper—or whatever you monsters use these days to write with. I want to copy down exactly what it says and take it back to my own time.

(*The* CLERK *hands him a greenish-white clipboard and a strange luminescent writing instrument. He poises the writing instrument and stares up toward the screen.*)

Now!!!

(*The* CLERK *presses buttons.*

The screen begins to scramble. As ENOCH *prepares to write, the whole area fades out. In the darkness, the Reading Room slides off.*

A spotlight hits the opposite side of the stage where MAX *is standing thoughtfully.*)

MAX

I tried desperately to get Soames out of my mind during those five hours of June 3, 1897. Or was it June 3, 1997? All I could think was: Is it possible, was it possible, will it be possible that book lovers of the future will find bread for the spirit in: "Life is a web, and therein nor warp nor woof is"? Precisely at seven o'clock . . .

(*Without invitation from* MAX, *the Domino Room slides into view. At the table sits a downcast and desolate* ENOCH. *The table is now set, with silverware and a breadbasket.*)

. . . he reappeared. There he was. It was as though he had never moved—he who had moved so unimaginably far.

(*Raising his voice as he walks into the scene.*)

Soames!

ENOCH (*Still in a daze.*)

I can't believe it. I can't believe it.

35

MAX (*Grasping his arm.*)

Soames. You need a drink.

(*Calling.*)

Lewis! Bring Mr. Soames an absinthe.

ENOCH (*Waving dispiritedly.*)

No. I shall never drink absinthe again, or anything.

MAX

Soames. Did you find anything?

(*No answer.*)

You mustn't be discouraged. Maybe it's only that you—didn't leave enough time. Two, three centuries from now, perhaps.

(*With urgency.*)

And now—now for the more immediate future. Where are you going to hide?

ENOCH

Hide?

MAX

From him—from the Devil. Catch the Paris express from Charing Cross! Almost an hour to spare. But don't go on to Paris. Stop at Calais. Live in Calais. The Devil would never think of looking for anybody in Calais.

(*Slowly* ENOCH *lifts his clenched fist from under the table.*)

ENOCH

It's like my luck to spend my last hours on earth with an ass.

(*He opens his fist, and there is a crumpled bit of greenish paper in it.* MAX *glances at it, puzzled.*)

MAX

This is gibberish.

(*Disregarding the paper.*)

Soames, pull yourself together. This isn't a mere matter of life and death. It's a question of eternal torment. You don't mean to say that you're going to wait here limply until the Devil comes to fetch you?

ENOCH

I can't do anything else. I've no choice.

MAX

But surely, now that you've seen the brute——

ENOCH

It's no good abusing him.

MAX

You must admit there's nothing Miltonic about him, Soames.

ENOCH

He's rather different from what I expected.

MAX

He's a vulgarian. The sort of man who hangs about the corridors of trains and steals ladies' jewel cases.

ENOCH

Careful—he'll hear you.

MAX

My God, if Goethe had ever met *this* one face to face, he'd never have written *Faust*. And a good thing, too! Imagine eternal torment presided over by *him*. He has no *taste!*

ENOCH

You don't think I look forward to it, do you?

MAX

Then why not slip quietly out of the way?

ENOCH

How can I?

MAX

For the honor of the human race, you ought to make some show of resistance. At least give it a go.

ENOCH

What has the human race ever done for me? Besides, can't you understand that I'm in his power? I've no will. I'm sealed.
(*Muttering.*)
Sealed.

MAX

Eat some bread, Soames. You've been on a very long journey. You must be starving.

37

(*Halfheartedly,* ENOCH *takes a piece of bread and chews at it a bit viciously.*)
Are you sure you looked in the right catalogue?

ENOCH (*Numbly.*)
There wasn't any catalogue. There weren't any books.

MAX
No books! In a library?

ENOCH
No books.

MAX
I don't believe it.

ENOCH
But everything's preserved—all the worthless stuff anyhow. On some kind of celluloid. And you manage to read it wherever it happens to be in the whole blasted world.
(*Suddenly remembering.*)
There was one work by T. K. Nupton. Not very easy reading. Some sort of phonetic spelling. All their stuff was phonetic.

MAX
Then I don't want to hear anymore, Soames, please.

ENOCH
Except the proper names. If it weren't for that, I mightn't have noticed my own name.

MAX
Your own name? Really Soames? I'm *very* glad.

ENOCH (*Accusingly.*)
And yours.

MAX
No!

ENOCH
I thought I'd find you waiting here tonight, so I took the trouble to copy out the passage.
(ENOCH snatches the *piece of pale green, half-crumpled paper and thrusts it at* MAX.)
Read it, you bastard.

(MAX *is baffled. He scowls at the paper.*)
There it is. All written in their crazy phonetic language. Read!
Read it, you scavenger!

MAX (*Puzzled.*)
Scavenger?
(*He tries to read, and then turns the paper over and sideways.*)
This *is* very queer.
(*He reaches in his pocket for a pair of reading glasses and puts
them on; then he puzzles at what he has in his hand.*

Slowly deciphering it.)
"From page 234 of Brit Litracher 1890–1910 bi T. K. Nupton,
published bi th stait, 1992." Literature spelled L-i-t-r-a-c-h-e-r, for
God's sake!

ENOCH
Read on! Read on!

MAX
"A riter ov the time, naimd Max Beerbohm, rote a stauri in which
he pautraid an imajanri karakter kauld Enoch Soames—a thurd-
rait poit hoo beleevz imself a grate jeneus an maix a bargin with
th Devvl in auder ter no wot posteriti thinx ov im."
(MAX *looks up, scowling.*)
Thinx? T-H-I-N-X???
(*He continues reading.*)
"It iz a sumwot laibud satire but not without vallue az showing
how seriusli th yung men ov the ainteen-ninetiz took themselvz.
Nou that th litteri profeshn haz bin auganized az a department
ov publik servis, riters hav lernt ter doo their duti without thot
ov persnl gayn. Th stait alows no Enoch Soames amung us to-dai!"

ENOCH
What a nightmare!!

MAX
It's horrible. And very baffling. What do they men—I-m-a-j-a-n-r-i
. . . imaginary, I suppose that is. But you're no more imaginary
than I am.

ENOCH

But the future thinks I am.

MAX

Are you sure you copied this correctly?

ENOCH

Quite.

MAX (*Peering through the paper toward the light, then dropping it on the table, a bit revolted by it.*)

Think of what's in store for the art of letters. Heaven preserve us.

ENOCH

Who cares about the art of letters? Think of what's in store for me!

MAX

Soames, don't look at me like that. It's this wretched Nupton who must have made—must be *going* to make—some idiotic mistake. Besides, I don't write stories. I'm an essayist. You must see . . .

ENOCH

I see the whole thing.

MAX

Run. For God's sake, run! If this is true, and I am destined to write about you, the story should at least have a happy ending.

ENOCH (*With intense scorn.*)

A happy ending. In life and in art, all that matters is the *inevitable* ending.

MAX

But an ending that can be avoided isn't inevitable.

ENOCH (*Suffering.*)

You're such a bad writer that instead of imagining a thing and making it seem true, you're going to make a true thing seem as if you'd made it up. You're a miserable bungler. And it's just my luck.

MAX (*Helplessly.*)

The miserable bungler is not I—is not going to be I—but T. K. Nupton. Don't you see that?

(ENOCH *is staring at an offstage door.*)

ENOCH

Save your arguments. Here's my guide to the Nether Regions.

(THE MAN *enters. He is very cocksure.*)

THE MAN

Ahhh, good evening, gentlemen. Enjoying yourselves? What a pity I must disturb your pleasant party, but——

MAX

Mr. Soames received absolutely nothing from his journey this afternoon. The whole thing is a common swindle. The bargain is off.

THE MAN (*Starting toward* ENOCH.)

On the contrary, a bargain is a bargain.

(*Suddenly* MAX *picks up two dinner knives, makes them into a cross and brandishes them in* THE MAN's *face.*)

MAX

Stand back! You're not taking him!

(THE MAN *steps back, cowering a little before the crossed knives.*)

THE MAN

Mr. Beerbohm, that sort of thing went out in the Middle Ages.

MAX (*Smiling.*)

Then why are you frightened?

THE MAN (*As if speaking to a servant.*)

Soames! Put those knives straight! Immediately!

MAX

Mr. Soames may be a diabolist. But he is a Catholic diabolist!

(*Like a zombie,* ENOCH *leans over, takes the knives from* MAX's *hands, uncrosses them, and they clatter to the floor.*)

ENOCH

It's no use arguing with the Devil. You should know that.

(*Slowly.*)

Goodbye, Beerbohm. I ask only one thing.

MAX

Yes?

ENOCH (*A plea from the depths.*)

In your blasted story, *try* to make them know that I *did* exist.

(THE MAN *takes* ENOCH'*s arm. They start out.*)

MAX (*Protesting.*)

Soames!

THE MAN

Shall we be *off?* It's a shorter trip than you think.

(MAX *watches helplessly as* THE MAN *swings open his wide cape, swirls it around the limp* ENOCH, *enveloping him.*

THE MAN *raises his red cane, signally off, as if to an elevator operator.*)

THE MAN (*Calling.*)

Going *down!*

(SOAMES *and* THE MAN *disappear.*)

MAX (*To the audience, numbed.*)

I've got no choice. I have to write this story. It's fate. Pre-ordained. Now, there's one way to prove who's going to be right—myself or T. K. Nupton. Enoch Soames will appear again in 1997. A lot of you will be alive then. I shan't. So, why don't you put it down on your calendar pad? Go to the Reading Room of the British Museum. A visitor from a century past will be there—a dim man with a hungry look . . . sometime on the afternoon of June third One-Dub-Nine-Seven.

(MAX *puts a cigarette in his mouth, then strikes a match. Through the flame, he sees* THE MAN *approaching. By the forced habit of courtesy,* MAX *greets him.*)

Hello . . .

(THE MAN *looks at* MAX *with an appraising but disdainful air, then glances away as if he didn't think much of the market value of* MAX'*s soul. Without the courtesy of a reply,* THE MAN *goes off.* MAX *is indignant.*)

Did you see that? To be cut—deliberately snubbed—by *him!* That's insufferable! What do you say to a character like that?

(*He turns, shouts off after* THE MAN.)

Go to hell!

(*The match flame has burned to* MAX's *finger. Wincing, he shakes it out. Cautiously,* MAX *strikes another match, lights his cigarette, and blows a puff of smoke out at the audience.*)

Do you realize what that means? They don't *want* critics down there! By God, it must be absolute heaven!

(*The curtain falls.*)

Act Two

MAX AND A. V. LAIDER

(The lights come up on a row of five red-plush theater seats, the stalls of a London theater. They face directly front, as if the audience were the stage. Number 1 is an aisle seat. A PORTLY MAN *and* HIS WIFE, *both in evening dress, are ushered into seat numbers 2 and 3 by a young lady, the* USHER, *who accepts sixpence for the program. The* PORTLY MAN *has to search several pockets to fish out the coin.)*

USHER

Thank you, sir.

(The WIFE *is aflutter at attending an actual opening night. The* PORTLY MAN *is already sorry they bought the tickets.)*

Tea or coffee at the interval?

PORTLY MAN

Neither. We'll be at the bar.

WIFE

You'll be at the bar. I want to remain alert. After all, Eric, how many first nights do we see?

PORTLY MAN

Too many.

(An epicene YOUNG MAN *in Edwardian coat comes down the aisle and is ushered to seat number 4, so he must pass in front of the already seated couple.*

The PORTLY MAN *looks over his program.)*

I don't like this one already.

WIFE

That's prejudice, dear. You mustn't dislike it until the critics *tell* you to.

(MAX *appears upstage, as if at the top of the aisle. He is smoking. He is ushered down the aisle to his seat.*)

USHER

The management respectfully requests no smoking in the stalls, sir.

MAX

Oh? Would you respectfully tell the management I detest the theater; it's becoming more and more uncivilized.

USHER

Yes, sir. Tea or coffee at the interval?

MAX (*Sitting.*)

What makes you think I'll still *be* here at the interval?

(*He takes a program from the* USHER. *He looks around for some-place to dispose of his cigarette; finding none, he hands it to the* USHER.)

USHER

Thank you, sir.

(*The epicene* YOUNG MAN *leans forward, gasps.*)

YOUNG MAN (*A hoarse whisper.*)

It's Max Beerbohm!

(*The* WIFE *is also excited.*)

WIFE

Eric! Eric, don't *look*. But do you know who's sitting next to you?

PORTLY MAN (*Looking.*)

Who?

WIFE

Max Beerbohm!

(*The* PORTLY MAN *looks bluntly at* MAX, *who looks bluntly back.*)

PORTLY MAN (*To his* WIFE.)

No. Can't be. Beerbohm's a much bigger man. More impressive. And funnier.

(*No reaction from* MAX. *The* WIFE *turns to the epicene* YOUNG

MAN.)

WIFE

Is that *really* Max Beerbohm?

YOUNG MAN

Of course, it is.

WIFE (*Poking her husband.*)

Ask him!

PORTLY MAN

Ask him what?

WIFE

Ask him who he is!

PORTLY MAN

I don't care who he is.

(MAX *recrosses his legs.*)

WIFE

You've *got* to ask him. I won't enjoy a minute of the play unless I know.

(*Unwillingly, the* PORTLY MAN *speaks to* MAX.)

PORTLY MAN

Excuse me—uh—beg your pardon. My *wife* wants to know if you, by any chance, happen to be—uh—Max Beerbohm.

(MAX *stares at him.*)

MAX

Do *you* want to know?

WIFE (*Leaning across her husband.*)

You *are,* aren't you! You're the Incomparable Max!

MAX

Well, I think of myself more as the *comparable* Max. That is, I'm constantly comparing myself with what I was yesterday and what I'm likely to be tomorrow—if anything.

(*The* WIFE *laughs with nervous excitement, turns triumphantly to the epicene* YOUNG MAN.)

WIFE

Do you know who that is? That's Max Beerbohm. I wonder what he's thinking.

49

MAX (*Flatly.*)

She wonders what I'm thinking.

(*The lighting narrows on him slightly.*)

Why the hell did I get here so early! That's what I'm thinking.

(*He opens his program, wrinkles his forehead.*)

I've seen this play before.

(*Studying the program more intently.*)

My God, I saw it last night! In another theater, of course—and with a different cast, and a different title. But I have the sickening feeling it's the same play! Perhaps last night is tonight, or v`` versa—and I've slipped a cog in time, like poor Soames.

(*A* YOUNG GIRL *rushes down the aisle followed by the* USHER. *Awkwardly she crawls over* MAX, *the* PORTLY MAN, *and* HIS WIFE.)

YOUNG GIRL

I beg your pardon. I beg your pardon. I *do* beg your pardon. I beg your pardon——

MAX (*As if translating to the* PORTLY MAN.)

She begs your pardon.

(*There seems to be some confusion about seating, then an examination of all ticket stubs, so that the epicene* YOUNG MAN *is banished to seat number 5, and the* YOUNG GIRL *takes number 4. All of this takes place above* MAX's *silent and long-suffering head.*)

WIFE (*Breathlessly.*)

Mr. Beerbohm, may I ask an impertinent question?

MAX

Do.

WIFE

How is it that you're only Max Beerbohm, while your brother is Sir Herbert Beerbohm Tree? Did you drop the Tree? Or did he—uh—uh——

MAX

Herbert grafted it on. You see, when my brother was very young, he had delusions of becoming an illustrious actor. But can you imagine anyone up there in the gallery shouting down: "Bravo,

Beerbohm! Beerbohm! Beerbohm! Beerbohm!" No matter how loud they shout, it's faint praise.

(*The* YOUNG GIRL *makes a sudden discovery.*)

YOUNG GIRL (*A loud whisper.*)

That's Max Beerbohm!

MAX

I'm sorry to disappoint you, child; it's only Herbert Beerbohm Tree's brother.

WIFE

He's so witty. Isn't he witty, Eric?

(*The* PORTLY MAN *nods glumly.*)

MAX

Dear lady, I advise you to avoid, at any cost, the reputation of being a wit. Deserved or not. It's a sad and sorrowful condition. Can you imagine what a burden it is? Every time you part your lips, people expect something positively hilarious to emerge.

(*Simultaneously, all lean forward expecting a bon mot.* MAX *is a little pained.*)

Of course, I like to think that I *could* have said most of the amusing things that are being said these days—if I'd had a bit more time and a little less brandy.

(A FRENCHMAN *stalks down the aisle and stops beside* MAX.)

FRENCHMAN (*Erect.*)

Monsieur Beerbohm?

MAX (*Looking up.*)

Oui?

FRENCHMAN

Vous avez outragé notre Sarah immortelle! Vous avez souillé le nom de notre divine Sarah!

(*The* FRENCHMAN *slaps* MAX *across the face with his gloves, then stalks back up the aisle.*

Shocked pause.)

MAX (*As if nothing had happened.*)

I was saying something about brandy.

PORTLY MAN

You're not going to let that chap get away with that, are you?

MAX

What would you suggest?

PORTLY MAN

Well, we can't have these foreigners crashing across the Channel, throwing gloves in our critics' faces. It's not done.

WIFE

Whatever did he say to you?

MAX

Well, a jagged translation would be: "You have sullied and insulted the name of our immortal Sarah."

PORTLY MAN

Sarah who?

YOUNG MAN

Oh, God.

YOUNG GIRL (*Helpfully.*)

I think he meant Bernhardt.

MAX

You see, when Bernhardt played the role of Hamlet, through the entire performance I had an almost overwhelming desire to laugh. Now, there are many funny things in Hamlet. Not many, really— but some. However, those weren't the places I wanted to laugh. Oh, Miss Bernhardt's gifts are enormous. But the gloomy Dane doesn't really need to be gifted with such a copious bosom and so bountiful a bum.

YOUNG MAN

No wonder he slapped you.

MAX

Oh, I didn't *write* that; I only *thought* it. All I said was: "Bernhardt's Prince of Denmark was, from first to last, a very great Queen!" By the way, my brother has decided *against* playing Ophelia. His gifts are all in the wrong places.

YOUNG MAN

Mr. Beerbohm, have you no respect for actors?

MAX

A little. Not much.

YOUNG GIRL

But you loved Dusé.

(*Lyrically, with exaggerated Italian accent.*)

Eleanora Dusé!

MAX

She was terrible.

YOUNG GIRL

But when she was younger——

MAX

She was worse. She had more energy then.

YOUNG MAN

That's not very sporting of you.

WIFE

I try to like everything!

MAX

So do I. I just can't seem to pull it off. I suppose it's my satiric temperament: when I'm laughing at anyone I'm generally rather amusing, but when I try to praise somebody I'm always deadly dull.

YOUNG MAN

How do you endure your brother?

MAX

Quite simple: I think of him as a brother, not as an actor. Of course, I do have a constantly recurring nightmare: What if Herbert were Max and Max were Herbert?

(*He shudders.*)

What if I, God help me, had to display myself on stage . . .

(*He comes slowly to his feet as the lights concentrate on* MAX *and fall away from the others in the row.*)

. . . instead of sitting safely in the dark. What if I had to strut about with those poor devils, a hot light burning into me, my naked ego about to be knifed by some wretched reviewer like myself in the fifth row?

53

(*A hat rack slides on.* MAX *changes his tie, collar, and jacket, turning from a first-nighter to a country gentleman.*

The theater seats and the four patrons have vanished.)

How ghastly to be the slave of some idiot playwright. The actor has sold his birthright as a human being. He's paid to pretend that he *is* what he *isn't.* If he's simply himself, he's either a bad actor, or a mere personality—which is not acting at all. And his troubles are compounded by directors, managers, and technicians who make his task almost impossible by trying to help him. But the *true* actor seizes you by the lapels and tells you: "I am *not* an actor. This is not a lie, not a playwright's trick. This is *really* happening!"

(*The sound of sea and sea birds.*)

This is the Beach Hotel, Linmouth, Sussex. Proprietor: R. Garrow.

(*The lights come up on the corner of a lobby. A very, very old* HOTEL CLERK *hobbles across.*)

CLERK

Raining a bit, sir.

MAX

I noticed.

CLERK

We're having quite a spell of it this year.

MAX

Had quite a spell of it when I was here last year.

(*Motioning off.*)

May I ask why my luggage hasn't been taken up to my room?

CLERK

At once, sir. I'll tell the pageboy. He's my father.

(*The* CLERK *goes off.*

MAX *stares after him, then looks around.*)

MAX

I came here to do nothing. And that may be exactly what I'll be forced to do.

(*He walks up and down, shrugs, squints outside.*)

You can look out of one window, which is precisely as wet a view as you get when you look out of another window.

(*He wanders to a letter board on which a dozen or so envelopes have been stuck beneath crisscrossed tapes. A hotel notice is alongside.* MAX *reads it and laughs.*)

THERE WILL BE NO SUN-BATHING ON THE FRONT LAWN!

(*He points to the letter board.*)

Unclaimed letters, eating their hearts out. No, I don't suppose the envelopes give a damn. But the poor fools who wrote these letters think they've been received.

(*He glances around, making sure he's not being watched, then takes down several letters. He studies one.*)

"Rodney Smallwood, Esquire." You poor little letter. What's inside? A check? A bill? Tender words of love? How rude of Rodney never to come and claim you.

(*He glances with amusement at another envelope.*)

To "A. V. Laider, Esquire."

(*But suddenly he is no longer amused.*)

That's *my* handwriting! That's a shock. This is the first time I've ever seen a letter of mine—unclaimed—after a whole year. This is outrageous! Let me give you some advice. This is a lesson. Never, never go out of your way to write to a casual acquaintance.

(*Muttering.*)

Even if he *did* cause me nightmares.

(*He turns his back deliberately on the letter board.*)

It was a year ago. I had seen him several times in the hotel. I could tell that, like myself, he was recovering from influenza. I liked him for that. He seemed—how shall I put it?—impertinently mild, but somehow *sad*. We never spoke. Very like the British, I suppose. But the last evening of my stay I found him in the smoking room reading a copy of a magazine *I* had purchased.

(*The wagon comes in with a round library table and two rocking chairs. A Tiffany lamp descends from the flies just above the table.*)

And so conversation became imperative.

(A. V. LAIDER, *seated in one of the rocking chairs reading a British magazine, is a gentle-looking man, a total contrast to* ENOCH SOAMES. *Yet despite his look of a mild country gentleman, he does have flashes of sudden intensity.*

MAX *sits, rocks.* LAIDER *coughs, suddenly looks up from his reading.*)

LAIDER

Oh, I have your magazine.

MAX

Please keep it.

LAIDER

No, no.

MAX

I insist.

LAIDER

Well . . . thank you.

MAX

I'd *almost* finished reading it.

LAIDER

I've been reading this article on "Reason Is Faith, Faith Reason." What did you think of it?

MAX

Well—it's quite restful after influenza. To read something that means absolutely nothing whatsoever.

LAIDER

That's a coincidence. I've just recovered from influenza myself.

MAX

Congratulations.

LAIDER

However, I find this piece on "Faith Is Reason" quite good.

MAX

But faith and reason are two separate things.

LAIDER

Oh?

MAX

Sometimes I have faith in things that are absolutely *un*reasonable.

LAIDER

Really?

MAX

Take a simple matter like—well, this probably sounds ridiculous, but despite every rational impulse I have, I find myself drawn, unwillingly, to an almost primitive belief in—no, it's nonsense; I don't believe in it at all.

LAIDER

What don't you believe in?

MAX

Palmistry. Utterly unscientific.

LAIDER

Palmistry.

(*A little light goes on somewhere behind* LAIDER's *eyes.*

In the distance there is a slight striking of a vibraphone as if a little bell has gone off in LAIDER's *mind.*)

You don't believe in palmistry?

MAX (*Hesitating.*)

That's the trouble. Somehow I do. We all have our superstitions.

LAIDER (*A bit hard.*)

But is it still superstition when there's evidence?

MAX

Well, all I have is my own irrational belief. And that's no evidence.

LAIDER

Have you ever made a study of palmistry?

MAX (*Laughs.*)

Passively only. Oh, sometimes I've turned over my palm to some charlatan who offered to "read it."

LAIDER

What a lot of nonsense you must've heard. They're ruinous, those amateur palmists; they all say the same things. "You can be led, but not driven." Or: "You are likely to have a serious illness between forty and fifty." Or: "You are by nature lazy but can be energetic by fits and starts."

(*They laugh at the absurdity of the generalizations.*)

57

MAX

The one I always get is: "You are going to take a trip across water."

LAIDER

The trip! The trip!

MAX

Now, I ask you, what Englishman of substance doesn't regularly cross the Channel?

LAIDER

"A trip across water." That might include stepping across a blob of spittle.

(*They both laugh—rocking and laughing harder and harder.* LAIDER *suddenly stops.*)

But it's not all a joke.

MAX

I beg your pardon?

LAIDER

Did you ever find a palmist who *actually* predicted the future?

MAX (*Startled by* LAIDER's *intensity.*)

Yes—in a way. But I thought it was a fluke.

LAIDER (*Superiorly.*)

Oh, did you?

MAX

Naturally. I believe in free will.

(LAIDER *stares penetratingly, as if there were something wrong with* MAX's *mind.*)

LAIDER (*Tight-lipped.*)

You believe in free will?

MAX

Yes, of course. I'll be hanged if I'm an automaton.

LAIDER

And you believe in free will just as in palmistry—without any reason?

MAX

Damn it all. Every hour of the day I exercise my free will. I can hold my breath or *not* hold it—as I please.

LAIDER

Oh, can you?

MAX

No doubt a palmist would try to tell me it's "written in my hand" that I'm a believer in free will.

LAIDER

I've no doubt it is.

MAX

You believe in palmistry.

LAIDER

I have reason to.

MAX

All right. Suppose we *haven't* any free will whatsoever. Is it likely or conceivable that the power that fashioned us would take the trouble to jot down in cipher on our hands precisely what's in store for us?

(*Impetuously and suddenly,* MAX *thrusts his hands palms up toward* LAIDER.)

Look at my hands. What do you see there?

(*As if shocked by a high-voltage electric current,* LAIDER *leaps up, turning his back.*)

LAIDER (*Sharply—frightened, agitated.*)

No! Never again! I'll never read anyone's palm again.

(*He shakes his head as if he were trying to beat off some memory.*)

MAX (*Embarrassed.*)

I'm sorry.

(*There's a pause.*)

I suppose if *I* could read hands, I wouldn't—for fear of the awful things I might see there.

LAIDER (*With an awed whisper.*)

Awful things, yes.

MAX (*Defensively.*)

Not that there's anything very awful, so far as I know, to be read in *my* hands.

LAIDER (*Staring at the floor.*)

You aren't a murderer, for example?

MAX (*With a nervous laugh.*)

Oh, no.

(LAIDER *raises his head and the blood seems to go out of his face.*)

LAIDER

I am.

MAX

Good Lord.

LAIDER

I don't know why I said that. I'm usually a very reticent man. But sometimes . . .

(*He presses his fingers into his forehead.*)

What you must think of me! I assure you I'm not the sort of murderer who is "wanted" or ever was "wanted" by the police. I should be bowed out of any police station at which I gave myself up. I'm not a murderer in any convictable sense of the word, no.

MAX (*Relieved.*)

Ah.

LAIDER

But I'm a murderer all the same.

(*He moves toward* MAX, *who backs away in terror.*)

Here's your magazine.

(MAX *sighs with relief, taking the magazine.* LAIDER *starts to go.*)

Good night.

MAX (*Unwillingly fascinated.*)

Wait! Uh—wouldn't you care to give me a detail or two?

LAIDER

You're merely being polite.

MAX

Not at all. I'm fascinated. I've never shared a magazine with an "unconvictable murderer."

LAIDER

I warn you that what I tell you may stiffen your unwilling faith in palmistry—and shake your cherished faith in free will.

MAX

I'll freely take that chance.

LAIDER

Very well.

(*His eyes narrow.*)

Do you mind if I turn down the lights?

MAX (*Nervously.*)

Not at all.

(LAIDER *reaches up, dimming the lamp. Then he thrusts his hands toward* MAX, *palms up, so that the light burns down on them.*)

LAIDER (*Hushed.*)

Look. Look at my hands.

(MAX *leans forward, fascinated.*)

These are the hands of a very weak man. I dare say you know enough about palmistry to see that for yourself. Notice the elasticity of the thumbs and of the two little fingers? These are the marks of a weak and oversensitive creature—without confidence. A man who would certainly waiver in an emergency. Rather Hamlet-ish hands. Hamlet was luckier. He was a murderer by accident. But the murders I committed—not just one but many!—all of them were due to my own weakness.

(*The light fades slightly on the Tiffany lamp.*)

I suppose the entire thing began—the first time—I ever—went—to a—palmist!

(*There is a strain of mysterious music in the distance.*

A huge palm, with all the palmist's codes marked on it, appears on the back screen. The VOICE OF A GYPSY WOMAN *is heard.*)

VOICE OF GYPSY WOMAN

Young man . . . at about the age of twenty-nine, you will have a narrow escape from death—from a violent death. See, here in your hand? A clean break in the lifeline. And a square joining it— the protective square, we call it. Ahhh. Ahhh, yes. The markings are precisely the same in both hands. There is no doubt about it. It will be the narrowest escape possible. At the age of twenty-nine.

(*The palm on the screen fades, and the light builds back to full on the Tiffany lamp. Again* LAIDER's *hands are visible beneath the hot intensity of the burning light.*)

61

LAIDER

You can imagine how I felt as I approached my twenty-ninth birthday. I thought it might happen at any moment . . . some catastrophe, some terrible accident. And I tried to be careful—ridiculously careful. Crossing streets. Avoiding high places. I tried never to go into a train—or even near one. Like yours, my reason rebelled against the whole bondage of palmistry. So that's why I began to study it. And so I got an undeserved reputation for being rather good at it.

(*His voice lowers as if he were frightened and shaken.*)

But, my friend, it was like living at the knife edge of a precipice—never knowing when I might plunge to destruction!

(*He suddenly stiffens and pulls his hands abruptly from under the lamp.*)

Then my twenty-ninth birthday arrived.

(*Like a quick cut in a motion picture, like the fastest of jump cuts, the light beneath the Tiffany lamp goes out, and the light rises on the other side of stage.*

As the lights come up on the new area, UNCLE SYDNEY *leads in a group of guests as if they were leaving a dinner table.* SYDNEY, *the host, is followed by* COLONEL ELBOURNE, MRS. ELBOURNE—*a stately colonial couple—and two handsome British newlyweds,* MR. *and* MRS. BLAKE. *The scene continues without interruption. The wagon with the hotel table is drawn off to the wings; the Tiffany lamp flies.*

[*While he is offstage,* LAIDER *makes changes in his hair and collar to suggest a younger man.*]

They are all talking and laughing.)

MRS. BLAKE

Charles and I were married just before Christmas.

MRS. ELBOURNE

Married only six months! Why, child, you've hardly been introduced.

UNCLE SYDNEY (*Opening a humidor.*)

A cigar, Colonel?

62

COLONEL ELBOURNE

That's the true sweet after a good dinner.

(*The* COLONEL *takes a cigar.* MR. BLAKE *starts to, hesitates, turns to his young wife.*)

BLAKE

Do you mind, darling?

MRS. BLAKE (*Smiling.*)

Just so you don't banish us to the women's quarters.

MRS. ELBOURNE

Oh, that's a primitive ritual, my dear.

COLONEL ELBOURNE

When I got back from India, I decided to join the ladies—permanently.

(*They laugh.*)

MRS. ELBOURNE

What's happened to the birthday boy?

UNCLE SYDNEY (*Calling off.*)

Algernon? Have you found the port?

(*No answer.*)

Oh, I shouldn't have called him that; he despises his first name.

MR. BLAKE

Now I see why he calls himself by his initials. *I* would, too.

UNCLE SYDNEY

Dear boy?

LAIDER (*From off.*)

Yes, Uncle—I'm bringing it.

MRS. BLAKE

If the "A" is for Algernon, what's the "V" for?

UNCLE SYDNEY (*Quickly.*)

Oh, I couldn't possibly tell you—I'm sworn to secrecy.

(LAIDER *enters with a tray of glasses and a cut-glass decanter. He looks younger, but his face is grave.*)

Thank you, A.V.

(*Each accepts a glass of port—except* MRS. BLAKE.)

MRS. BLAKE

One will be enough for both of us.

(*The* BLAKES *affectionately share the same glass.*)

UNCLE SYDNEY

A toast. To my nephew! A long life—and a happy one!

ALL

Hear, hear!

(*They all drink, except* LAIDER. *His uncle looks at him curiously.*)

UNCLE SYDNEY

No port for you, A.V.?

LAIDER

Not tonight, Uncle Sydney.

UNCLE SYDNEY

On your birthday? Time to celebrate.

MRS. BLAKE

I think the birthday guest should display some of his rare talents.

LAIDER

Talents?

MRS. BLAKE

Yes, Mr. Laider. Everyone in London is talking about how skillful you are at it. Please read our palms.

LAIDER (*Quietly.*)

No, Mrs. Blake.

MRS. ELBOURNE

Oh, you must. I adore this gypsy business. Please do our hands. Please?

LAIDER

Ladies, I assure you, it's all nonsense. Besides, I've forgotten what little I ever knew about it. I—I——

COLONEL ELBOURNE (*Scoffing.*)

Palmistry! Dear me. Don't tell me people still believe in that sort of thing.

LAIDER

Nobody really does, Colonel. Ladies, I ask you as a favor, let's drop the subject.

UNCLE SYDNEY

Well, we wouldn't have time. I apologize. I didn't realize it was so late. You must catch the ten-forty for London—or you'll all be stranded out here in the country.

LAIDER (*Pale.*)

The ten-forty!

UNCLE SYDNEY

Don't mean to hurry you off, but it's the last train.

LAIDER

Train?

UNCLE SYDNEY

Reservations all booked. The five of you are traveling back to London in the same compartment.

LAIDER (*Stiffly.*)

Uncle . . . Why don't Mr. and Mrs. Blake and Colonel and Mrs. Elbourne go on ahead? I'll stay an extra day here.

UNCLE SYDNEY

But you can entertain them with some of that gypsy business.
(*A maid brings hats.*)

LAIDER (*In a small voice.*)

Uncle, may I beg off the journey? I——

UNCLE SYDNEY

What's wrong?

LAIDER

May I take a carriage—may I stay over a few days—may I——

UNCLE SYDNEY

My boy, I don't understand. Are you unwell?

LAIDER (*Hardly any voice, embarrassed the others are overhearing.*)

It's nothing, Uncle Sydney. I'm fine. We'd best—get ready—for the train.

(*There is a high-pitched, screeching British train whistle.*

The lighting crossfades from the area of UNCLE SYDNEY's veranda, and the wagon moves on with a simple British train compartment— the red overstuffed seats facing each other. COLONEL *and* MRS.

ELBOURNE, MR. *and* MRS. BLAKE *chat amiably as they move in and take their seats—followed by the silent and reluctant* LAIDER.

As the lights come up, the high-pitched train whistle pierces the air again. The compartment seems to shake into action, and the sound of a train in motion starts them on their perilous journey.

They all settle comfortably in their seats, smiling, except for LAIDER. *His eyes are closed and his breath is held.*

Flickering lights move quickly by outside, going faster as the train picks up motion.

The people jiggle slightly in their seats, and then the train seems to pick up a more regular rhythm, and they settle back, more relaxed.)

MRS. BLAKE (*Pleasantly.*)

Now, Mr. Laider, we have you trapped and you have no excuse. I insist you read our palms.

LAIDER

Mrs. Blake, you are relentless.

MRS. ELBOURNE

It would be a jolly way to pass the time.

(*She starts to peel off her gloves.*)

Gloves off, Mrs. Blake.

MRS. BLAKE

Oh, dear, yes. I suppose with kid gloves on you could only tell the future of a goat.

(MR. BLAKE *laughs at the joke, but none of the others do.*

MRS. BLAKE *thrusts both hands forward.*)

Which do you want first, my right hand or my left?

LAIDER

I—I——

(*Sighing.*)

It doesn't matter, really.

MRS. BLAKE

This sort of thing always excites me. Shall we see what the right hand says? I'm right-handed. Does that have anything to do with it?

LAIDER (*Numbly.*)

Very little.

(*Taking her hand.*)

The first thing we look at is the lifeline. Yours, Mrs. Blake, is . . .

(*In the distance there is a low hit on the vibes.*)

I would like to pass on to another hand at the moment . . .

MRS. BLAKE (*Scowling.*)

Is anything wrong?

LAIDER (*Lying.*)

No. I merely like to get a general picture of everyone's palm before I particularize.

(MRS. BLAKE *stares at her palm.*)

MRS. ELBOURNE

Oh, you'll probably uncover all sorts of wicked secrets in my hand.

(*Girlishly thrusting her hand forward.*)

There you are.

LAIDER

The lifeline . . .

(*There is another hit on the vibes, a note higher.*)

Colonel Elbourne, may I look at your palm, sir?

COLONEL ELBOURNE

Well, I thought this was to be an entertainment for the ladies.

(LAIDER *is looking away.*)

A bit of a grizzled hand at that. Too much sun in India. But, there you are. Left-handed, you know.

(*He thrusts his hand out.* LAIDER *forces himself to look at it. There is another distant hit of the vibes, a note higher yet.*)

COLONEL

Well, what does it say?

(LAIDER *doesn't answer.*)

Certainly not that I'm going to die in childhood.

(*He chuckles.*)

LAIDER (*Quickly dropping the* COLONEL'*s hand.*)

Now—*your* hand, Mr. Blake.

MR. BLAKE

Rather dull hand, I'm afraid. Not much excitement in my life.

MRS. BLAKE

Charles!

MR. BLAKE

Until lately.

(LAIDER *is almost certain of what he is going to see in* BLAKE's *palm.*

The vibes hit again, a note higher, and seem to ring.)

MR. BLAKE

Well, *what*, Mr. Laider? What does it say?

(*There is another screech of the train whistle, which seems to reverberate throughout the theater.*)

LAIDER

Excuse me. I need a breath of air.

(LAIDER *takes a step toward the audience as if he were continuing his story to* MAX. *Numbly.*)

What did it say? I knew only that the train whistle sounded like a woman screaming—that I was twenty-nine years old—that each of the palms I had read had a lifeline that *cut off* abruptly—and that all of us on that train were hurtling through the night toward certain catastrophe!

(*There is another high screech of the train whistle.* LAIDER *covers his eyes.*)

What would you have done, Mr. Beerbohm?

(*Guiltily, reaching his hand forward, then half pulling it back.*)

There *was* a thing for me to do. I wanted to do it. I wanted to spring into the corridor and pull the communication cord. Quite a simple thing. Nothing easier than to stop a train. You just give a sharp pull, and the train slows down and comes to a standstill, and the guard appears down the corridor. You explain to the guard. What? How do you explain? So I did nothing. Nothing.

(*A little panicky now.*)

I couldn't tamper with fate. It was prescribed—in their hands. How could *I* change it?

68

(*The sound of the moving train comes up slightly as* LAIDER *turns back into the carriage and sits—as if he had been temporarily somewhat train-sick. He leans his head against the overstuffed cushions.*)

MRS. ELBOURNE

Why, Mr. Laider, you seem quite pale.

LAIDER

It's nothing, Mrs. Elbourne. Nothing anyone can——

MRS. ELBOURNE (*Concerned.*)

Train-sickness, that's what it is. I get it myself now and then.

LAIDER

Possibly. But I'm quite better now.

COLONEL ELBOURNE

Go on with this palmistry business, Laider. You really haven't told us much of anything yet.

LAIDER

Yes, Colonel.

COLONEL ELBOURNE

Tell us, for example, how long will Mrs. Elbourne and I be separated? As you probably heard me tell your uncle, I'm off for India again in a few days.

MRS. ELBOURNE

And I'm remaining in England.

COLONEL ELBOURNE

And it would be interesting if we could know just how long the Foreign Office intends to keep us apart. Can you read that sort of thing in our palms, Laider?

(LAIDER *takes a deep breath.*)

LAIDER

Let me begin by telling you what your palms say about your pasts.

MRS. BLAKE

Oh, that would be very dull. We all know about our pasts. Tell us about our futures.

LAIDER (*Half to himself.*)

About—your—futures.

(*He looks from one to the other.*)

69

MR. BLAKE

Go ahead, Laider. Read away. We're all broad-minded here. If you uncover a few skeletons in our closets—or in our palms—we'll just keep it in this compartment.

(LAIDER *nervously takes the palms through the following.*)

LAIDER (*His voice rising in volume.*)

Mr. Blake, I find you of a—*generous* nature. Note the full Mound of Venus. I find that you can be—"led but not driven." I also see here—that "you are by nature lazy, but can be energetic by fits and starts."

MRS. BLAKE

You're remarkable. That's quite true of Charles; that's exactly the way he is.

LAIDER

Yes, Mrs. Blake.

MRS. BLAKE

Please, read mine. I'm dying for you to read mine.

LAIDER (*Hesitantly.*)

Mrs. Blake . . .

MRS. BLAKE (*Holding forth her hand.*)

It's even a clean hand—in this sooty old train. The miracle of gloves.

(*Hesitantly*, LAIDER *takes her young hand.*)

Well—what do you see?

LAIDER (*Tentatively.*)

Mrs. Blake—what is your age?

MRS. BLAKE

Why, what a strange question to ask a woman. Can't you read that in my hand?

LAIDER (*Glancing quickly at her hand again and just as quickly away.*)

I would say—twenty-four.

MRS. BLAKE

Exactly. However, Mr. Laider, when I pass thirty, forget that you know.

LAIDER

I'll try.

MRS. BLAKE

What else do you see?

LAIDER

I—it's the strangest thing. The four of you have amazingly similar palms.

MRS. ELBOURNE

Well, how jolly. We must see more of each other.

COLONEL ELBOURNE

In what particular way are we alike? After all, there can't be much of my stuffy character in this lovely young lady and her handsome husband.

MR. BLAKE

Yes, how are our palms similar?

LAIDER

Well—each of you——

(LAIDER *gasps as there is a sudden accelerated roar of the train, and the lights plunge into darkness.*

The women give out little frightened gasps.)

COLONEL ELBOURNE (*Calming them in the darkness.*)

Just the Bixby Tunnel, my dear. Means we're almost to the outskirts of London. We'll be out of it in a moment.

(*The lights snap on again, and the train changes pitch as it emerges from the tunnel.*

Again there is the screech of the whistle.

All sigh. The tone of all of their voices, other than LAIDER's, *is amazingly calm.*)

MR. BLAKE

I do detest these tunnels. Never trust them. Claustrophobia, or such, I suppose. You see a symptom of that in my hand, Laider?

LAIDER (*Shaken.*)

No.

(*Red and green signals flash on, deep on the stage.*)

MRS. ELBOURNE (*Looking out of the window.*)

Oh, there's fog too. Look how the air is thickening.

COLONEL ELBOURNE

It's not only fog, my dear. It's anthracite. Should be prevented. Could be easily, too, by a short act of Parliament.

MRS. BLAKE (*Trying unsuccessfully to see out.*)

It *is* rather thick out there. Tell me, how does the engine driver see up ahead. How fast do you think we're going?

COLONEL ELBOURNE

The legal limit is sixty-five. But on a downgrade like this——

MR. BLAKE (*Reassuringly.*)

There are signals, my dear. Those red and green lights cut right through the fog. Keep on with the palmistry business, Laider, and it'll take our minds off that muck outside.

COLONEL ELBOURNE

See more in here than you can out there.

MRS. BLAKE (*Suddenly trying to snap out of her mood with laughter.*)

Tell me something amusing. Do I have a repressed desire to throw things at my husband? Am I really a shrew?

LAIDER

No, Mrs. Blake.

MRS. BLAKE (*To her husband.*)

You see, dear, you married a woman with civilized hands.

MRS. ELBOURNE

This *is* a lark. I must admit I used to shy away from any fortune-telling. Rather frightened of it, I suppose. But, Mr. Laider, the way you go about the whole business is completely charming.

LAIDER (*Numbly.*)

Thank you, Mrs. Elbourne.

(MRS. ELBOURNE *stares fascinated at her own palm, as if seeing the lines in her hand for the first time.*)

MRS. ELBOURNE

These *are* strange lines in my palm. It's curious, isn't it, how you live with your hands for years and years and never really pay much attention to the lines on them?

LAIDER (*Sympathetically.*)

You have a very good palm, Mrs. Elbourne. You have given much of yourself in this life—warmth and kindness.

MRS. ELBOURNE (*To her husband.*)

I told you he was charming.

(*Turning back to* LAIDER.)

But what lies up ahead, Mr. Laider? Is there any *fun* left for us? Will we dance? Will there be laughter in our lives? Will we travel to sunny places—and hear the surf, taste the sea air?

(*An affectionate laugh.*)

And will my husband always love me?

COLONEL ELBOURNE (*A little embarrassed.*)

Really, Mildred, *what* a question!

MRS. BLAKE

I suppose you should look in the colonel's palm for the answer to *that* one.

MRS. ELBOURNE (*Self-consciously.*)

I've asked a lot of silly, girlish questions. I don't suppose all the answers are in this one old hand.

LAIDER (*Resigned.*)

All the answers are there, Mrs. Elbourne.

MRS. ELBOURNE

Then you mustn't keep me in suspense. Tell me, Mr. Laider.

LAIDER (*Almost to himself, like second sight, but softly.*)

You *will* travel to distant shores—and hear the surf—and laugh—and dance—

(*His voice even lower.*)

—and your husband will always love you.

COLONEL ELBOURNE

You see?

MRS. ELBOURNE (*Gently, smiling, but on the verge of happy tears.*)

How nice. How nice you are, Mr. Laider. And how quickly you've made the trip pass. I don't know when I've enjoyed a train journey so much. Now, please read the colonel's palm. I feel I'm really just beginning to know my husband. And after all these years!

(*They all laugh.*

Resolutely the COLONEL *crosses to* LAIDER, *puts out his hands.* LAIDER *takes one. He tries to bend back the thumb, but it doesn't bend.*)

LAIDER

You see, Colonel, how firm your thumb is? You, sir, have great will power.

COLONEL ELBOURNE (*Joking.*)

I didn't have the will power to resist your parlor entertainment, Mr. Laider. Read on.

LAIDER (*With increasing tempo.*)

Colonel, it is extremely difficult for me to tell you all the things I see in your hand. But it is apparent that you are brave, basically the bravest man I have ever met. It's there—all of it—in your palms. I salute a valiant man.

COLONEL ELBOURNE (*Distantly, a touch of tears in his eyes.*)
Valiant?

(*Quickly, impulsively, as if racing to finish,* LAIDER *grabs* MR. BLAKE's *hands. His tempo increases.*)

LAIDER

Mr. Blake. You bring to life—honor, strength, decency—a ringing sincerity that will make people remember you always.

MR. BLAKE

One *tries* to be these things. But it takes a whole lifetime. Meanwhile, one merely tries.

(LAIDER, *racing on, drops* MR. BLAKE's *hands and grasps* MRS. BLAKE's, *as if to tell her something vital, urgent, pressing, precious.*)

LAIDER

And you, Mrs. Blake—beauty—rare, fresh—like cool water when you are thirsty. Like gentle sleep when you are very tired. You have this gift of graciousness——

(MRS. BLAKE *takes out a handkerchief and is rather overcome by it all.*)

MR. BLAKE

Oh, my dear.

(*Turning to* LAIDER.)

Mr. Laider, you've made my wife cry.

MRS. BLAKE (*Softly.*)

Charles. When are you going to learn that most of the time women cry—simply because they're happy?

(*There is the sound of the high-pitched whistle, particularly penetrating and close.*)

COLONEL ELBOURNE

We're coming into London.

MRS. ELBOURNE (*Staring out front, as through the window, worried.*)

How black it is!

(*High on the stage, red signal lights flash urgently.*

The sound of the rushing train seems to be coming closer to the audience.

MR. BLAKE *puts his arm around his wife.*)

MRS. BLAKE (*Squirming away, pulling on her gloves.*)

I have to put my gloves on, silly.

(LAIDER *looks around white with panic. The train seems to be plunging.*

LAIDER *rises, stretching out his hands, as if to protect them all.*)

LAIDER (*Loudly.*)

My friends, there is something I must tell you. Something in your palms! IN YOUR PALMS!!!!

(*They all lunge forward in their seats. There is the screech of a whistle.*

The compartment plunges into darkness.

Simultaneously the headlight of a train glares straight into the audience. It irises out, expanding as if hurtling forward.

The sound of the rushing train becomes deafening.

The red signal lights flash frantically all over the stage. Screams.

75

The Incomparable Max

There is a tremendous crash from the speakers stereophonically throughout the theater.

The headlight dies.

In the ominous black, there is nothing but the hiss of escaping steam.

The hotel letter board descends. MAX *enters, wearing an Inverness rain-cape. He is troubled.*

MAX (*To audience.*)

And that's the story A. V. Laider told me—just a year ago in this sleepy hotel—making sleep after that often totally impossible. A horrifying wreck: the engine driver failed to see a signal because of the fog, and crashed into the back of a goods train. Everyone in that compartment dead except Laider—wishing he were too because he couldn't make himself pull that communication cord. That's why I wrote him that letter—

(*Pointing vaguely toward the letter board.*)

—so he would know there was a fellow human being who shared his agony. "I have been haunted as you are haunted, my dear Mr. Laider." That's what I wrote him—something like that. "Forget it!" I told him, "forget the whole thing!"

(*Sighs.*)

But I'm afraid I wasn't very convincing. I couldn't forget it myself.

(*Shrugs.*)

What a waste of time! He never got the letter, so I might as well destroy the damned thing.

(*He moves across stage to where the letter board has descended.* MAX *stands before it, puzzled, squinting at it.*)

Why, it's gone!

(LAIDER *comes on, wearing, for the first time, the distinctive cap and muffler of the Beerbohm caricature.*)

LAIDER

Yes—I picked it up . . . since it was addressed to me.

MAX

Mr. Laider. You're back.

LAIDER (*Nodding.*)

Yes.

76

(*Holding up the opened letter.*)

Mr. Beerbohm, I've just read your letter to me.

(*Glancing at the date.*)

Why, you wrote this almost a year ago. I can't tell you how touched I am.

MAX

I was simply tryir.g——

LAIDER

Oh, I can see that. And you make me feel very guilty indeed.

MAX

That's exactly what I've tried to make you *not* feel. Get rid of your guilt, dear fellow—what good is it? Does the Lord on High feel guilty when He sees the sparrow fall and doesn't reach out to catch it? It's the same with your train cord! And you're not God Almighty!

LAIDER

Well, Mr. Beerbohm—in a way—I *am!*

MAX

Laider, you are not a well man.

LAIDER (*Quickly.*)

Your advice in this letter is exactly what I'm going to do. I'm going to forget everything I told you a year ago. *You* forget it, too.

MAX

No, no! Tear up the letter. It's terrible advice; it won't work. Shoving a thing down into your subconscious—it's unhealthy! Like sowing dragons' teeth, it'll erupt with new terrors.

LAIDER

For God's sake, stop cheering me up!

MAX

You don't want to be cheered up?

LAIDER

No.

MAX

I don't understand that at all.

LAIDER (*Miserably.*)

I don't *want* you to understand——

77

MAX (*Erupting.*)

How many more sleepless nights do you plan to give me? I never hear a train whistle, I never look at the palms of my hands without my flesh creeping!

LAIDER (*Desperate.*)

I'm never coming back to this hotel again!

(*Calling.*)

Pack my portmanteau——

MAX

No, damn it all, you're not leaving. What the hell are you hiding from me?

LAIDER

Mr. Beerbohm, you're a dear, considerate man——

MAX

I'm a critic and I'm a bastard. And I simply want to know if——

LAIDER (*A smile wreathes his face.*)

You're *that* Max Beerbohm! The famous critic! The celebrated author! Oh, my!

MAX

What's that got to do with it?

LAIDER (*Raising his eyebrows.*)

And did you want to make what I told you into a story? Put me in a book?

MAX

Good God, no! I wouldn't think of it!

LAIDER (*His face falls.*)

Why not?

MAX

I couldn't do that to another human being. Trading on the pain of another man, tearing the scab off an old wound—it would be un-Christian.

(*Change.*)

I'm a liar. I did want to write it. I *do* want to write it. To purge *your* experience out of *my* system.

78

LAIDER

Oh? How do you propose to obtain the rights?

MAX (*Blankly.*)

I beg your pardon?

LAIDER

Well, if you'd read the whole thing in a newspaper, I expect you could write whatever you pleased. But you didn't, did you?

MAX

Well, I could dig through back issues of the *Times*——

LAIDER

I doubt if it would help.

(*Reluctantly.*)

You see, Mr. Beerbohm, after an illness—influenza usually— something happens to my mind. My brain gets to ticking . . . and . . . I suppose it's because *I* always wanted to be a writer and never was.

MAX

A writer?

LAIDER (*Quickly.*)

I told you, I haven't any will power. Wobbly thumbs. Both hands! (*He demonstrates.*)

I have a galloping imagination. Usually my will keeps it in check. But when influenza attacks, my will fails and my imagination stampedes. I tell myself the most preposterous fables and—the trouble is—I can't help telling them to my friends. And when you mentioned palmistry, well . . . a little chime went off in the back of my head somewhere—and——

MAX (*Level.*)

I even tried to locate your Uncle Sydney.

LAIDER

Did you? My dear fellow, I'm afraid—I'm afraid——

MAX

You don't *have* an Uncle Sydney.

LAIDER

I'm—uh—I'm afraid——

MAX

There was no train journey?

LAIDER (*Shrugs.*)

I—I——

MAX

You made the whole thing up!

LAIDER (*With a tentative little laugh.*)

I——

MAX

I've been having nightmares about your story for a whole year. Even during the day.

LAIDER (*Pleased.*)

Have you, really? Come to think of it, I did tell it rather well. Perhaps I *should* write.

MAX

Impossible! You could never be a writer; you're too convincing. An actor, yes. Oh, yes! Go seize people by the lapels and tell them lies. Then you'll get paid for it.

LAIDER

Imagine a famous critic saying that to me!

MAX

Mr. Laider, I'm trying to insult you and you won't let me.

LAIDER

But I have such respect for your opinion.

MAX

The hell you do! Now I suppose you want me to review your appalling performance.

(*Muttering.*)

I wish to God I could close you tomorrow night.

LAIDER (*Apologetically.*)

A man can't really be blamed for having an oversized imagination. It's rather like large feet, or a birthmark, or a tendency to baldness. And I'm so flattered that you'd want to take my poor imaginings, put them on paper, set them in type for posterity to read!

MAX

Oh, *you've* got a bug up your bum about posterity, too! Damn it all, I *will* write it.

LAIDER

But it's my life.

MAX

You just said it was fiction. Which is it?

(LAIDER *coughs.*)

Have you had influenza again?

LAIDER

Just a touch.

MAX

So sorry to hear that . . .

(*Suddenly his eyes narrow.*)

Wait a minute! If you were lying last year after influenza—how do I know that you're not lying *this* year? Even more convincingly!

LAIDER (*Bemusedly.*)

I could be, couldn't I?

(*Now* MAX *is totally frustrated.*)

MAX

Influenza be damned! Were you lying before, or are you lying now? Did it happen? Didn't it happen?

LAIDER

Do you know, I—I'm not really sure myself!

MAX (*A cry like Oedipus.*)

Is *this* happening?

(MAX *throws up his hands.* LAIDER *is meek.*)

LAIDER

I wouldn't blame you, Mr. Beerbohm, if you never talked to me again.

MAX

Well, I'm not that uncivilized. *I'll* talk. Don't *you* talk.

(*Moving away.*)

Now, if you'll excuse me, I need a bit of sea air to clear my head.

(MAX *moves downstage.*

The sound of sea gulls emerges from the balcony rail, and the wavy light of *the sea plays on his face.*

Silently, LAIDER *comes up beside him.*)

LAIDER

The sea!

(*He quickly covers his mouth with the letter.*)

MAX (*Looking up.*)

Clearing a bit. You can always tell the way the sea gulls line up along the shore—waiting to take off.

LAIDER (*That glint in his eyes.*)

Sea gulls?

(*The vibraphone strikes a note in the distance.*)

MAX

I don't think I ever realized how extraordinarily beautiful they are when their wings catch the light.

LAIDER

Beautiful? You think them beautiful?

MAX

Why, yes.

LAIDER

Well, perhaps they are. I suppose they are. But—I don't like seeing them.

(*Squinting, his hand up to his eyes.*)

They always remind me of something—rather a dreadful thing—that once happened to me . . . Those sea gulls suddenly swooped toward me——

(LAIDER *backs away.*)

MAX

Oh, no you don't. Not again! Not another story! I don't want to hear another word!!!

(*He waves the man away, as if wanting to blot out* LAIDER's *voice.* LAIDER *flaps his arms like a possessed sea gull and careens off.*

MAX *lowers his arms and turns to the audience.*)

It was inevitable. I finally heard his story about the sea gulls. It was

terrible. It was very terrible indeed. In fact, it was one of the worst stories I've ever heard in my entire life!
(*Confidentially.*)
I also found out what the "V" in his name stands for. And you can't be too hard on a man whose Christian names are "Algernon Vivien."
(MAX *shrugs.*)
And there you have it. Mr. Soames in hell. And Mr. Laider—if I have anything to say about it—*on his way!*
(*The original theater seat slides on again.*)
Why do we keep running into things that couldn't possibly happen—but do? Or grazing against things that haven't quite happened yet—but might! What if I'm guilty as the reprehensible Mr. Laider, and possibly concocted the outrageous Mr. Soames?
(*He thinks. Then he shakes his head positively.*)
No, no. That sort of thing only happens in theaters.
(*A dreadful thought crosses his mind.*)
Good Lord! What if *theaters* vanish by 1997, along with books? What if actors disappear—living, breathing actors, sharing the same zone of air with living, breathing audiences! What if they are all merely bottled and pickled and preserved in something resembling Soames's celluloid? A lot of jiggling photographs with gramophones in the wings to make them seem to talk?
(*He shudders at the idea.*)
Or what if nobody goes to the theater at all anymore? What if everybody just sits at home and presses buttons?
(*Laughs.*)
No, no, that's *too* preposterous. Could never happen. I'd best not write *that* in a story—nobody would believe me.
(*The hat rack appears again.* MAX *removes the rain-cape and is in evening dress again, as if ready for another play.*)
Still, it would be jolly if we *could* look ahead. Predict the——
(*Almost unwillingly, he lifts his palms and begins to study them, then glances at the audience, as if it had caught him at something naughty, and he quickly drops his hands behind his back.*)

Now, that is really absurd. The lines on your right hand are of no use whatsover except to *collide* against the lines of your left hand. Like this.

(*He smacks his hands together, applauding.*)

You do that, too.

(*Quickly.*)

Oh, not for me. For the *theater*. Not necessarily *this* one, but *some* theater. March down that aisle again soon. You don't have to take any marriage vows. Just have a two-hour affair with—

(*He makes a broad gesture at the whole stage.*)

—this seductive trollop.

(*Confidentially.*)

And if you're lucky, you may even get a peek into the future—without going to hell for it!

(*He moves to the aisle seat.*)

All right—this critic is ready.

(*He sits, facing upstage, settling back, waiting for a new play to begin.*)

Ring up the curtain!

(*At which, the curtain falls.*)

(*For curtain calls,* MAX *in his theater seat, facing upstage, waves his cane at the screen and the Beerbohm sketch of* LAIDER—*in cap—appears. Then* LAIDER *steps in front of it, matching it, taking his bow.*

While the rest of the cast takes its calls, LAIDER *changes into* SOAMES.

MAX *waves toward the screen again with his cane and his self-caricature appears. He rises, matching it. Then he turns, taking his bow.*

Again he waves magically upstage, and the SOAMES *sketch is projected on the screen, and a hell-weary* SOAMES *appears, shuffling into register with the caricature. There is an unearthly acknowledgment of earthly applause.*)